DISCRETION AND FOLLY

A NOVEL OF FACTUAL HISTORY CONCERNING
MURDER, METIS, SOLDIERS AND SITTING BULL

BY

J. HOOLIHAN CLAYTON

AUTHOR OF:

COMMENDABLE DISCRETION
WITH GREAT DISCRETION
SMALL LIGHT OF DESCRETION
DISCRETION IS VALOR

WITH ILLUSTRATIONS AND ENGRAVINGS
FROM HARPERS WEEKLY

DOG SOLDIER PRESS
TAOS

Published April 2026
Dog Soldier Press, PO Box 1782
Ranchos de Taos, NM 87557
dogsoldierpress.com

Graphic Design: book interior and cover
Ananda M. Sundari, Visionary Alchemy Arts
visionaryalchemyarts.com

Library of Congress Control Number: 2026937923
Printing: Ingram Sparks
Print ISBN: 979-8-9877380-7-8
ePub ISBN: 979-8-9877380-9-2

*"How modest in exception, and withal
How terrible in constant resolution,
And you shall find his vanities forespent...
Covering discretion with a coat of folly."*

Henry V, Act II, scene 4,
- William Shakespeare -

"To plainness honor's bound when majesty falls to folly."

King Lear, Act I, scene 1
- William Shakespeare -

"The first serious crime which was committed in the valley was the dual murder in December, 1880. Three men known respectively as Boulder Fritz, French Phil and Donnelly had been living together in a cabin on the Hell Gate River. On Sunday, December 26, 1880, some men were horrified to find Donnelly and French Phil both dead on the floor."

History of Montana 1739-1885
Warner, Beers & Company

"In 1870 the Manitoba half-breeds and metis (as those of British and French origins may be distinguished) were estimated at 10,000. Besides them, there was a population of uncertain number scattered through the territories, and a tribe of half-breed hunters which one early explorer deemed to be 6,000 strong."

Jamestown Weekly Alert, Jamestown D.T.
February 1887

*"In his warpaint and his beads,
Like a bison among the reeds,
In ambush the Sitting Bull
Lay with three thousand braves
Crouched in the clefts and caves,
Savage, unmerciful!"*

From "The Revenge of Rain-in-the-Face"
-Henry Wadsworth Longfellow-

"On first meeting Sitting Bull I naturally studied his appearance and character. He was a strong, hardy, sturdy looking man of about five feet eleven inches in height, with strongly-marked features, prominent nose, and strong under jaw, indicating determination and force. He was a man of few words and cautious in his expressions, evidently thinking twice before speaking. At first he was courteous, but evidently void of any genuine respect for the white race."

Personal Recollections and Observations of
General Nelson A. Miles

"Of one thing, however, it is our duty to inform you, that you cannot return to your country or your people with arms and ammunition in your possession, and should you attempt to do so you will be treated as enemies of the United States."

General A.H. Terry, Commander of Department
of Dakota, speaking to Sioux chiefs as part of
the Sitting Bull Commission, 17th October, 1877,
reported by James F. McLeod, Commissioner of
the North-West Mounted Police, to David Mills,
Minister of the Interior.

"We did not give you our country: you took it from us; look at these eyes and ears; you think me a fool but you are a greater fool than I am; you come to tell us stories and we do not want to hear them; I will not say any more; you can go back home; that is enough---say no more. That part of the country we came from belonged to us and you took it from us, now we live here."

> Sitting Bull, principal chief of the Sioux Nation, speaking to General A.H. Terry and the Sitting Bull Commission, 17th October, 1877, reported by James F. McLeod, Commissioner of the North-West Mounted Police, to David Mills, Minister of the Interior.

"Sitting Bull and his personal following is the only band remaining out of the control of the government. On the 19th, word was received at Ft. Keogh that Sitting Bull had retreated again across the border."

> The Yellowstone Journal, January 22, 1881

"Although Sitting Bull was not much of a warrior, and had no prestige among Indians on that account, still he was stubborn in his resistance to the government reservation system and naturally had many adherents among the disaffected."

> Lieutenant General Philip Sheridan, as quoted in The Yellowstone Journal, November 26, 1881

DRAMATIS PERSONÆ
PRINCIPAL AND SUBORDINATE HISTORICAL FIGURES
INCLUDED IN THIS BOOK

IGNATIUS LOYOLA DONNELLY Republican Congressman, lawyer, writer

THOMAS DONNELLY Miner, rancher

FRENCH PHIL Itinerate Frenchman

BOULDER FRITZ aka Fritz Schwack or Schwabe

WILLIAM STEELE Deputy sheriff, Helena, Montana Territory

FREDERICK WILEY, THOMAS SHELDON, MARION GAMBLE Road agents

JAMES S. MCANDREWS Sheriff, Deer Lodge County, Montana Territory

THOMAS MCTAGUE Deputy sheriff, Deer Lodge County, Montana Territory

CAPTAIN JAMES MILLS Publisher, editor of New North-west, Deer Lodge City

ARCHIBALD MCPHAIL Proprietor of New Chicago Hotel, New Chicago, M.T.

MATILDA MCPHAIL First wife of Archibald McPhail

JOHN O'NEILL Proprietor of several businesses, Deer Lodge City

ALEX RALSTON Proprietor of Farmer's Corral Livery, Butte City, M.T.

INEZ MAYBERT Known prostitute in Butte City

JENNY RIVERS Known prostitute in Butte City

GEORGE MARSH Telegrapher, Montana Central Telegraph Company

C. A. SMALL Deputy sheriff in Butte City

GEM KEE Proprietor of Kim Chung Lung & Co, Deer Lodge City

MR. OLIVER Retired sailor, Chinese language translator in Deer Lodge City

GONG SING Chinese procurer and slave owner in Butte City

GRANVILLE STUART AND BROTHERS Founders of Deer Lodge City

CONRAD KOHRS German immigrant, "Montana Cattle King"

JOHN BIELENBERG Conrad Kohrs' half-brother, cattle and horse breeder

GENERAL ALFRED TERRY Commander, Department of Dakota

GENERAL NELSON MILES U.S. Army commander during Indian Wars

CAPTAIN ADAMS Acting post adjutant, Fort Assiniboine, M.T.

LIEUTENANT HAYT Quartermaster, Fort Assiniboine, M.T.

WILLIS EUGENE EVERETTE Scout for the U.S. Army, polyglot, M.T.

CAPTAIN OGDEN READ Commanding officer, Camp Poplar River, M.T.

LIEUTENANT ORRIS HEISTAND Adjutant, Camp Poplar River

JOSEPH GOURNEAU Métis hunter

JEAN LOUIS LÉGARÉ French Canadian trader, rancher

ANDRÉ GAUDRY, NARCISEE LECERTE, JOHNNY CHARTRAND, AMBROISE DELORME, ANTOINE GOSSELIN and LOUIS PICHÉ Métis employees of Légaré

LEIGHTON AND JORDAN Post traders, Fort Buford, Wood Mountain

LOGAN Employee of Leighton and Jordan, Wood Mountain

NWMP Royal North-West Mounted Police

INSPECTOR A. R. MACDONELL Commander, Wood Mountain Post, NWMP

SUPERINTENDENT L. F. CROZIER (*Tȟaté Tȟáŋka*) Commander, NWMP

SUPERINTENDENT JAMES MORROW WALSH Founder of Fort Walsh, NWMP

LOUIS DANIELS Former policeman with NWMP

JERRY POTTS Métis interpreter for NWMP

CAPTAIN WALTER CLIFFORD Officer stationed at Fort Buford, D.T.

MAJOR DAVID HAMMETT BROTHERTON Commander, Fort Buford, D.T.

PHILIP F. WELLS Interpreter for Fort Buford, Dakota Territory

CAPTAIN JAMES BELL Officer with 7th Cavalry in Dakota Territory

LIEUTENANT F. W. KINGSBURY Officer, assigned to Fort Maginnis, M.T.

SCOUT ALLISON ("FISH") Interpreter, freebooter

JOSEPH CULBERTSON Government scout

JAMES BECKWOURTH Ex-slave, freebooter, trapper, abuser of women

AMERICAN INDIANS Sitting Bull *Tȟatȟáŋka Íyotake*, Gall *Phizí*, Crow Chief *Kȟaŋǧí Wičhášayatapi*, One Bull *Tȟatȟáŋka Waŋží*, Bone Club *Čhaŋȟpí Čhetúŋte*, Crow *Kȟaŋǧí*, Spotted Tail *Siŋté Gleška*, Little Thunder *Wakíŋyaŋ Čík'ala*, Conquering Bear *Matȟó Wayúhi*, High Forehead *Itúhu Haŋska*, Old Bull *Tȟatȟáŋka Eháŋni*, Low Dog *Šúŋka Khúčiyela*, Her Many Horses Woman *Tȟa Šúŋkawakȟáŋ Óta Wíŋ*, Flying By *Hiyáyakinyán*, Peppermint *Čheyaka*, Four Horns *Hétópa*, Red Thunder *Wakíŋyáŋ Lúta*, Rain in the Face *Itéomaǧážu*, Bear Face *Matȟó Ité*, Moving Robe Woman *Ptehahinšma Mani Wíŋyaŋ*, White Dog *Šúŋka Ská*

Foreword

After decades of defending their lands, customs and traditions, the Lakota (*Lakȟóta*) warriors, along with many of their allies among the Arapahoe (*Maȟpíya Tȟó*) and Cheyenne (*Šahíyela*), fought soldiers on the Little Big Horn River (the Greasy Grass or *Peji Sla Wakpa*) in June of the centennial year for the United States. White people across America were shocked and appalled that the Indians had been victorious and that over two hundred and fifty soldiers had been killed, including Lieutenant-Colonel George Armstrong Custer, who had built his reputation through violent and ill-considered assaults on Indian tribes across the western territories. For years, Custer had been a favorite of General Philip Sheridan, commander of the Division of the Missouri, and his death signaled a concerted effort on the part of the military to round up or wipe out all remaining hostile, non-reservation Indians in the West, taking advantage of the vitriolic public sentiment resulting from the Lakȟóta victory on the Little Big Horn.

A principal chief of the *Húŋkpapȟa*, Sitting Bull (*Tȟatȟáŋka Íyotake*) became the foremost brutal and fearsome savage in white America's imaginings, particularly among the settlements of Montana Territory, despite the many courageous and powerful warriors and leaders of the other *Thítȟuŋwaŋ* (Teton) bands, as well as the Cheyenne and Arapahoe warriors, who had triumphed on the Greasy Grass. In the autumn of 1876, Colonel Nelson

A. Miles, commander of the 5th U.S. Infantry Regiment, joined the offensive to punish the Indians and force them onto reservations. He chased Sitting Bull across the eastern plains of Montana Territory in a winter campaign through 1876 and '77, taking up the pursuit after General George Crook and General Alfred Terry had failed to capture the formidable chief and his people. Miles met with Tȟatȟáŋka Ìyotake twice, demanding his surrender, but to no avail. During the ensuing months, the Lakȟóta suffered from cold and hunger, while Miles destroyed their camps and supplies at every opportunity.

By April of 1877, several of the other principal men of the Húŋkpapȟa had already crossed the boundary (*Čaŋgú Wakȟáŋ*, Medicine Line) into the North-West Territories of Canada. Finally unable to find a way for his people to survive while being endlessly hunted by soldiers and while northern buffalo herds, the very epicenter of their lifeways, were being exterminated, Tȟatȟáŋka Ìyotake traversed the border into the British Possessions, known to the Lakȟóta as Grandmother's Land (*Uŋčíya-pi Makȟóčhe*). Eventually forging cordial relationships with Métis hunters and settlers, many of the men of the Royal North-West Mounted Police, especially Superintendent James Morrow Walsh, and Jean Louis Légaré, a French Canadian trader, the Lakȟóta pledged to abide by the Grandmother's (Queen Victoria's) laws in hopes of finding sanctuary within the vast northern prairies.

Prologue

"Nearly all the ammunition traded to hostile Indians across the border and even upon American soil was obtained from Canadian half-breeds. Now, it is a well established fact that these English half-breeds are in some respects a greater injury to this Northern country than even Sitting Bull's tribe of hostile Sioux, for they not only supply the latter with the means of warring against the whites, but encourage them to leave the Northwest Territory and infest the settlements on this side of the boundary line. A half-breed camp is nearly as great an attraction for hostile Indians as a herd of buffalo is to a pack of famishing wolves, and while the half-breeds are allowed to roam at will the hostiles will never want for ammunition or cease to prowl on the outskirts of civilization and rob the white settlers of life and property."

The Benton Weekly Record October 17, 1879

FEMALE REBEL

1

The rough planking of the tavern floor pressed splinters into his cheek. Opening his uppermost eye, the man scanned his surroundings and, after a minute or so, recalled events of the preceding evening. Wincing in palpable shame and chagrin, he strove to elevate from a supine to a kneeling posture. Reeling from the aftermath of bounteous spirits, the man finally achieved his feet.

"Back with us, then?" came a caustic inquiry from behind him.

Turning to survey the room and finding a robust and unkempt fellow ensconced on a chair beside a table and a whiskey bottle, the erstwhile and formerly reclining inebriate answered in a grumbled affirmative.

"You shore had a bugaboe up your ass 'bout something," his companion observed.

"Perhaps."

"Sit."

"I believe I require some air."

"Suit yourself," said the seated gentleman dismissively.

The man departed the three story brick building that housed "The Horse" saloon, perused the cobbles of Baltimore's Thames Street and pondered the state of himself. His heart was truly and comprehensively shattered, ergo the daily bouts of dipsomania. His youthful naivete had placed him irretrievably in the arms of a rebel spy, beautiful and beguiling. Now his nascent career as a detective for the federal forces had been called into question and his paramour Miss Boyd, recently dubbed "the Siren of the Shenandoah," had shot and killed a Union soldier. There was no longer any doubt as to her fidelities.

Ambling through the early dawn of August 1861, awash with mortification at his reckless distemperature, Charles Wolfe Collins swore off ardent spirits and all consequential relationships with women. He briefly contemplated throwing himself into the Patapsco River, but the thought of bloated human and animal carcasses, frequently drifting with the currents, deterred any such rash action. Instead, he determined to throw himself upon the mercy of Mr. Allan Pinkerton. And if he was killed in action, so be it.

"You are visiting a long ago somewhere," Wú Peng said.

Collins came to himself and realized his copy of *David Copperfield* had slipped from his lap to the floor. He reached down to retrieve it and smiled sheepishly at his Chinese companion. They were seated together reading by the light of a paraffin lamp, situated on a small table between them. Peng was cradling an ancient copy of the philosophy of Confucius.

"I was woolgathering."

"May I inquire as to the substance of your distraction?"

"Love, I suppose," C.W. told him. "I am saddened by Arbuckles' loss of her dear friend, Kinealy. My sympathy has led me down the path of best-forgotten memory."

"Ah yes," Peng said sagely. "It is a good friend who experiences pain at another's bereavement."

"I sincerely hope she will return to us soon."

"It is perhaps the superfluity of winter storms which has hindered her."

"Perhaps," Collins said, taking out his pipe and filling it slowly. "I, myself, will have to embark upon a new commission as soon as the weather clears," he added.

"We require fortified coffers."

"This is employment for the attorney from Minnesota? A Mr. Donnelly, as I recall?"

"Why yes," C.W. said, glancing at his companion in mild astonishment.

Wú Peng's immense capacity for retaining all manner of intelligence never ceased to confound him. "I mentioned the telegram to you in passing several days ago."

"And you will seek the brother's murderer?" the Chinaman asked.

"Yes...if he *was* murdered, as his brother maintains," he answered, lighting his pipe with a paper spill kindled above the lamp's chimney. "The trail is cold, but a man willing to brutally slay two men with a shotgun must be remarkable in some regard."

Peng came to his feet, fetched the tea pot from the stove and refilled their mugs.

"*Ta*," Collins said and laid aside his book to sip the steaming brew. He was becoming more accustomed to the types of tea favored by his Chinese friend, although he remained indifferent to green tea, despite its putative health benefits. "A man of this disposition would, perforce, be very treacherous."

"No doubt."

" 'The superior man, when resting in safety, does not forget that danger may come.' "

"Confucius?" Collins asked, nodding at Peng's battered volume resting upon the table.

"Yes Charles." The small dog at his feet began to yelp softly and twitch. The Chinese man smiled. "Perhaps our little Gal has an unfortunate premonition."

"Or perhaps she is chasing phantom deer."

Mutually retreating into their own thoughts, the two men became immersed in comfortable silence. Peng once more perused his Confucius and C.W. reminisced about his first meeting with Ignatius Donnelly, a fellow Irishman and former congressman from Minnesota. The Radical Republican had been investigating avenues through which the Freedman's Bureau could achieve education for emancipated slaves that would endure long after Reconstruction. Collins had been briefly posted to the Bureau by Grant and he found Donnelly to be a principled individual possessed of a shrewd legal acumen. Having become aware of Collins' sporadic employment as detective with the Pinkertons, Donnelly had forwarded a written request that he investigate the murder of his younger brother, along with another man, in a cabin on the Hell Gate River.

In truth, he was grateful for a lucrative commission. Excepting employment as payroll guard for various mining operations and the pursuit of road agents who had robbed a Gilmer and Salisbury coach in the Dog Creek hills the previous July, revenue had been elusive. Given his nearly fatal exchange with the scoundrels who had raided the stagecoach, Collins thought ruefully, trailing a murderer might be ill-advised, but necessary all the same. And Donnelly was offering substantial remuneration.

His thoughts were drawn back to his search for and capture of Wiley, Gamble and Sheldon, the road agents. Thaddeus Martin, owner of a prosperous livery stable and Chicago Joe, a former paramour and the notorious proprietor of a Helena bordello, had apprised Deputy Sheriff Steele of Collins' particular talents. Steele sought and obtained his assistance and together they had tracked the miscreants and discovered a deserted shack near Mullan Pass that displayed evidence of recent occupation. They had taken cover in a small grove of fir trees at a vantage point above the cabin and waited. After a tedious interval of several hours, three men on horseback had appeared, two of them with carcasses of whitetail deer slung before them.

Overeager and untried, Steele had busted out of the

trees inopportunely, instigating a prolonged exchange of gunfire. Collins could all too keenly recall the susurration of bullets passing his ears and the thudding of lead into tree trunks. The bandits took refuge in the shack and only after being provided with vivid descriptions of the consequences of fire upon the ramshackle structure, did they surrender. At the last instant, Frederick Wiley, the stoutest member of the gang, had charged Steele with a skinning knife. Swift response on Collins' part had dropped the outlaw with a blow from the butt of his Colt revolver and averted a dire wound. Upon their return to Helena with the prisoners, justice was expeditious. Several of the Gilmer and Salisbury passengers gave testimony and the bandits were found in possession of a large sum of money, a distinctive watch chain, finger rings and various other items belonging to their victims.

"Will you be tracking the assassin unaided?" Peng asked, breaching C.W.'s reverie.

"Yes."

The Chinaman raised his eyebrows inquiringly. "Would it not be decidedly more prudent to engage an ally?"

"Perhaps. I do not, however, choose to diminish any financial gains and, as you are aware, I prefer to work alone."

"What of the woman?"

"She will doubtlessly not return prior to my departure and it would not do to expose her to the environs I may have to frequent."

"Then it is best."

STAGECOACH

2

By the first week of January, the harsh winter weather slackened its bitter grasp. Preparing to commence upon his investigation for Mr. Ignatius Donnelly, Collins decided he would ride his buckskin gelding Ulysses and leave off taking a pack animal. There was a hotel near to his destination and he would be able to billet there. Donnelly's brother, Thomas, had been found dead in a cabin on the Hell Gate River, not far from the hamlet of New Chicago, alongside a fellow known by the sobriquet of French Phil. Donnelly had written that both men had been brutally slain by double-barreled shotgun, their heads blown away. The weapon had been left at the scene and the other occupant of the shack, one Boulder Fritz, had disappeared. According to Donnelly, the three associates had been prospecting to no good effect and were living hand-to-mouth as hapless ranchers.

As C.W. laid out his clothes on the bed, attempting to minimalize weight and bulk to be carried in his saddlebags, Gal, his dog, sat with her chin on the bedclothes, attentive to every motion.

"Will you take the dog?" Peng asked. He was sitting in a chair by the stove, sewing a patch on the knee of a pair of overalls.

"Do you think I should?"

"Yes Charles. She becomes enormously distraught when you are not in residence. This dog is immeasurably devoted to you," the Chinaman said, gesturing at the animal.

"I believe she has become very attached to you as well."

"Perhaps. But it is tremendously difficult to restrain her when you are absent."

Smiling to himself, Collins contemplated the fact that Wú Peng had now been with him on the ranch for many months. His friend had become as proficient in all manner of work and animal husbandry as could be desired and Collins never felt apprehensive about leaving for prolonged interludes in order to pursue profitable employment. Peng was a valued companion, a reliable hired man and trustworthy confidant.

"Very well. I will bring her along."

"This would be an auspicious determination."

The dog jogged at his heels as Collins carried his saddlebags and carbine out onto the porch. He set them on the floorboards and stepped down into slushy snow mixed with mud, the result of two days of milder weather.

Peng emerged from the dwelling. "Do you require my assistance?"

"No," answered C.W., making his way to the barn. "But if you choose to pack up some provisions, I would be grateful."

Ulysses and Mona, a stocky black mare, were standing together near the corral, dozing in the morning sun. Collins retrieved a bridle from a peg just inside the open barn door and walked over to the horses, speaking lowly as he drew near so as not to startle them. He laid the reins across the crest of his gelding's neck and eased the light grazing bit into his mouth, slipping the headstall over the ears. Leading the horse into the barn, he tethered him by slipping the reins through an iron ring, affixed to a wall for the purpose, and proceeded to brush the animal. Mona stood hard by, appearing to be somewhat forlorn, no doubt sensing that her pal was about to depart. The dog sat serenely in a band of sunlight that pierced the gloom of the building.

When Ulysses was saddled, he walked the gelding over to the porch with Gal and Mona trailing behind. He secured the saddlebags on the saddle. Wú Peng brought a package of brown paper and handed it to him.

Accepting the bundle, Collins said, "Thank you. *Xièxiè*."

"*Bú kè qì*."

As he stowed away the food and tightened the cinch, C.W. realized he did not look forward to his journey. The clouds were hanging low on the horizon, a damp chill suffused the air and he was probably about to track down a pitiless killer. He hoped the man could be found in some Missoula disorderly house and not on a solitary and bleak road. It was a short ride of around five hours to New Chicago and it would be there, at the scene of the crime, that he would have to decide how to proceed.

"Do you possess sufficient cartridges, Charles?" Peng asked, standing on the porch and watching him slide the Winchester repeater into its scabbard.

"Yes." Collins donned a thick woolen greatcoat and pulled his Stetson snug. "I may return very soon. Especially if I require a pack animal for a protracted quest." He climbed into the saddle and slapped his thigh. The dog leapt to her accustomed position behind the saddle swells, lodging herself upon his lap. "I will try to discover the bare facts of the case and see if I cannot rendezvous with Sheriff McAndrews somewhere in the vicinity."

"One would assume that he is persisting in an investigation of such an appalling occurrence."

Ulysses bowed his head to rub his nose on a foreleg.

"Sheriff McAndrews is a true Scot. Cautious and not overly eager to press forward. We will see." Collins caressed his dog's ear. "I must be off."

"Your absence will be a desolation."

Bending his horse away from the cabin, C.W. rode

down the mushy track that crossed his land and merged with the Mullan Road, following the Hell Gate River toward the west. The road was a course of deep snowdrifts, melting ice and muddy ruts. The gelding labored gamely along, occasionally catching his balance on slippery footing and jolting Collins sharply in the process. A few flakes of hesitant snow drifted down, a slight breeze nipped his face and it grew colder. He occupied his thoughts with the gruesome crime he was about to confront.

Not a stranger to violence and shattered human bodies, he knew the damage inflicted by a shotgun could be ghastly. It would take a specific type of fellow to use the weapon on anyone, let alone at close range on two men he had shared lodging with. And Mr. Donnelly had described his brother as quiet and decent. A long time resident of Deer Lodge county, the unfortunate man's luck had never been propitious and he had fallen on hard times. He had had no occasion to encounter the man, but it certainly seemed that Thomas Donnelly did not deserve such a gruesome end.

It was not uncommon in his experience, however, that men in mining or trapping camps in deep winter, confined for months within cramped quarters, could impetuously turn to brutality, especially if spiritous liquor was consumed. Perhaps the third man, with the incongruous moniker of Boulder Fritz, had slain the other men in a fit of inebriation. Or maybe he had succumbed to supreme aggravation at a repetitive and habitual gesture or word favored by one of his companions. More than once, C.W. had certainly endured circumstances wherein an associate drove him near barmy by monotonous and wearisome conversation and he had seriously considered manslaughter.

The dog rearranged her position and nearly slid from the saddle, precipitating a lunge by Collins to catch her. The horse balked, slipped on a patch of ice and almost went down. Barely maintaining his seat, Collins pulled in the horse, rallied himself in the saddle, caught the right stirrup again with his boot, settled the dog and swore loudly. A crippling accident as a result of inattention would certainly not suit his purposes. Pressing the gelding back into a walk, they continued down the road. Their path was auspiciously empty of fellow travelers and, mercifully, he had been spared witnesses to the incident.

"Mind yourself or you will be wading through the muck behind Ulysses," he told the dog and patted her head.

Snow flakes began to fall in earnest and the wind grew more keen. The hours dragged and Collins had difficulty shepherding his thoughts along a single corridor. A curtain of white descended, shrouding the terrain that already offered little to hold his interest. They came to a shallow ford across the river that marked the spur of stage road to New Chicago. It was all ice and rock and he urged the gelding forward, all the while holding him in to oblige a cautious progress. On the other side, they passed near a small herd of Angus cattle, hoary with snow and huddled beneath a copse of naked trees.

Leaving the stage road that curved southward toward the mining towns of Gold Creek and Pioneer, Collins rode along the banks of the river. The snow was deeper, but the footing was more sure, their route was more direct and the line of brush and trees was clearly evident in spite of increasing snowfall. C.W. moved the reins to his right hand and removed his left glove to blow on his fingers. He was chilled through, despite layers of warm clothing, and he regretted leaving his old bearskin coat behind. Gal was wet with melted snow, but he was grateful for her warmth.

At last, he felt the horse's gait quicken, signifying some knowledge that food and rest lay ahead, or at the very least, other equines. The animal's ears turned forward and he whinnied abruptly. An answering call hailed from a distance upriver and in a short while, Collins could just make out the shapes of buildings, like shadows through the thickening twilight of diaphanous obscurity.

3

A fire roared in the Great Western parlor stove at the back of the room. The hotel lobby was narrow with a built-in counter to the right and stairs to the second floor on the left. Collins stamped snow from his feet in the entryway and crossed a threadbare Turkish carpet to the front desk, behind which was seated a woman of middle age, her unremarkable visage frayed by care and ill temper. She looked up from a piece of embroidery she was stitching, held very closely beneath an oil lamp perched upon the desk.

"May I take a room?" Collins asked.

The woman laid aside her needlework and deliberated a long moment, as if perplexed by the question, then said, "We have a room. Four bits."

"That will do. I also require board for my horse. Will you direct me to the stable?"

"Across the way. We operate that as well and you can pay a dollar for the animal and you. Includes found for both."

"That will be acceptable." He handed over a Morgan dollar. "Will there be a stable hand to tend my horse?"

"Billy is there."

A man came bounding into the lobby from a door beside the stairs. He was all vitality in contrast with the woman. He stepped toward Collins with hand outstretched. "Good day, friend...and quite a day it is," he said in a booming and hearty manner. "I am Archibald

McPhail, proprietor. Has Matilda served you then?"

"Yes, thank you," C.W. said, shaking the man's hand. "I am Charles Collins. I was about to quarter my horse in your livery."

"Well then, let me accompany you," the man said, fetching a heavy coat. "Quite the squall now, eh?" He donned the garment and opened the door. "Come along... this way," he directed Collins, as if he were numbskull. "Only a minute, Mattie. Get some coffee and victuals sorted for when we get back."

They stepped into the heightening storm. The wind roared down the river from the west, assaulting them with icy pellets of snow. Ulysses was hunched against the driving gale, his head turned leeward. McPhail stood by as Collins unfastened his saddlebags and placed them near the door of the hotel. The dog appeared from under the porch planking. The four of them navigated hazardous purchase of frozen ruts and drifts to cross the main avenue of the town to the stables. The single story log barn was warm and ripe with the smell of hay and horse manure and a lone railroad lantern, suspended from a rafter, illuminated the interior. A ginger-haired boy of early adolescence, stooped on a wooden chair beside a kerosene heater, awoke from a nap at the sound of their arrival, yawning noisily. Gal slipped inside and lay in a far corner, chewing ice balls from her front feet.

"Guest, Billy," the hotelier bellowed, as if against the howl of the wind without.

"Yessir, Mr. McPhail. Here mister..." Billy said to C.W. and nodded at a roomy stall. "Put the pony here. There's a bucket of water and the bunk is already full."

The boy assisted Collins in unsaddling the horse and rubbing him down.

When Ulysses was comfortably billeted with his nose in the hay, McPhail ushered Collins back across to the hotel, its windows spilling a cheery radiance upon the deepening swathe of pallid ramparts.

"I would be grateful if my dog is allowed within," Collins said as he retrieved his saddlebags, brushing away the snow that had drifted onto the porch.

"Mattie may balk, but the animal is welcome...come in, come in now," McPhail said, opening the door and allowing Collins and Gal to precede him.

Removing their outer garments and hanging them on pegs by the door, they made for the stove and warmed their hands. The dog leaned shyly against Collins' leg.

"Come now," said McPhail. "Let us show you your room and you may situate your traps. Will your dog make a rumpus if we leave it there?"

"No, she should settle down without fuss."

"Excellent." The man turned and went springing up the stairwell two steps at a time, never once touching the banister, moving with the agility of a much leaner fellow.

Following behind, carrying his belongings and calling Gal, Collins climbing the stairs to the top. The corridor was pitch dark. He heard a door creak and his host reappeared, holding an oil lamp that emitted a bright glow.

"Here we go, then. This room should do nicely," McPhail said, motioning with the lamp to his right. "Mattie has it all done up."

Collins stepped into the narrow room and found it quite unpretentious, populated by a narrow iron bed draped with a slightly stained coverlet and ragged quilt at the foot. There was a ladder back chair and a washstand. The floor boards were bare and the wallpaper was a drab tan bedaubed with odd and inscrutable shapes; certain to preoccupy the unsettled mind in attempting to decipher them. He placed his saddlebags on the floor and told the dog to lie down, knowing she would inhabit the bed as soon as the door closed behind them.

McPhail left the lamp on the washstand and blew out the flame. "Now let us see what Mattie has done," he said, launching himself from the room and down the stairs, as if both were not engulfed in absolute shadow.

Closing the door and feeling his way through the corridor, Collins gained the top of the steps and descended into the hotel lobby, which he found deserted. He called out and a voice beckoned him beyond the door from which McPhail had first appeared. When he opened it, an agreeable aroma of cooked meat greeted him.

"Come in, Mr. Collins. Do come in," McPhail summoned, waving toward a chair at a table set in what appeared to be the family kitchen. Mrs. McPhail, or so C.W assumed her to be, poured a cup of coffee and scooted it toward him as he took a seat. The wood range, stationed in a corner of the room, was producing an extraordinary amount of heat and Collins removed his frock coat and draped it on the back of his chair. He accepted a heaping plate of food, that Mr. McPhail had dished up from various bowls and pots crowding the table top, and began to eat. The meal was predominantly bland, much like Mrs. McPhail herself, but more than welcome all the same. There was a dearth of conversation and McPhail's conduct seemed wholly contrary to his previously voluble nature, unmistakably absorbed by concentration on his repast. His wife poked at her plate as if not entirely sure of its contents.

When Collins had finished the entirety of his supper and refused seconds, he thought to broach the matter of his investigation. McPhail had given way to a prolonged and truly impressive belch and scooted his chair away from the table, crossing his legs. Mrs. McPhail began clearing dishes and placing them in basins upon a sideboard against a far wall.

"That was very enjoyable, Mrs. McPhail," C.W. said. "Thank you."

The woman did not respond, but carried on with tidying the remnants of the meal with abundant racket. Her husband did not appear to notice.

"May I inquire as to whether you have heard of the grisly crime committed late last December?" Collins asked, directing his question to Mr. McPhail.

"Oh my word, yes. We have all heard of it hereabouts."

"Did you know the men?"

"Not much. Thomas Donnelly more than the others." McPhail measured Collins with curiosity. "And what interests you about the bloody deed?"

Matilda McPhail ceased rattling dishes around and departed the room without ceremony or farewell.

"I will be frank," Collins told him. "I was hired by Donnelly's brother to inquire into the affair."

"Oh I see. Well, Sheriff McAndrews' deputy has already been and gone."

"Were you privy to his conclusions?"

"The townsfolk were all anxious to know if a murderer was on the loose. Deputy McTague merely concluded it were a double suicide and naught else. He returned to Deer Lodge City."

"And the bodies?"

"Still there I calculate, froze stiff. None of us knowed what to do with the corpses since the coroner never came. I heard that French Phil, Philip Heenal as was, bequeathed his property to one Mr. Berry, but there is none of us knows who the hell that is. And precious little property by any reckoning. Tom Donnelly owned the buildings, such as they are, and most of the land."

Collins brought out his pipe. "Do you believe it was suicide? That both men killed themselves?"

McPhail delivered a thunderous guffaw. "Aw hell no. That damned Boulder Fritz, or whichever his name actually is, has lit out for parts unknown. A trace suspicious, I would say. No one has laid eyes on the man for all these days. Had a reputation for sly dealing too."

"Murder?"

"Could be. Could well be."

"May I smoke?" Collins inquired.

McPhail nodded.

"Would you be able to provide me with directions to the cabin?" he asked, filling his briar methodically.

"Sure enough, Mr. Collins. Tom Donnelly was not unpopular in these parts. Others knew him better, but I have not a sorry word to say for the man despite his love of alcohol. There are those who will be pleased you are here to do him justice."

"I am glad to hear it."

The men sat in silence for a while, Mr. McPhail laboring at his teeth with a wooden pick. Collins smoked and pondered the abundance of 'macs' in the vicinity... McPhail, McAndrews, McTague. It was rather droll. Two Scots and one Irishman.

"I will accompany you," McPhail said, interrupting his thoughts.

"I beg your pardon?"

"I will ride with you tomorrow."

"Oh," Collins said, uneager for company. "It might be distasteful."

"No matter," McPhail said, coming to his feet. "Should be intriguing all the same."

"Intriguing" would not have been the word he would have chosen for the sight of a human head blown to bits, Collins thought as he fumbled his way up the unlit stairs to his room. Gruesome might be more apt. Or repugnant. He, himself, did not anticipate the loathsome spectacle with curiosity. He had seen enough of human tragedy.

4

He had his first real glimpse of the New Chicago hotel in the searing brightness of the morning, reflected off newly fallen snow. It was a narrow, two-story building constructed of rough hewn lumber and painted white, almost undistinguishable from its bleached background. Gal romped through massive drifts, burrowing and rolling and scampering madly in circles. A mild breeze made the frigid cold more insistent. They saddled their horses, the animals blowing clouds of steam in the freezing air, and set out downriver to the west.

The distance to the Donnelly shack was only a matter of four miles. McPhail rode a stocky black gelding that looked to be mostly Percheron. The little dog bounded behind Ulysses most of the way, then yipped insistently when she wanted to ride. McPhail cocked an eyebrow at the sight of her perched upon Collins' saddle.

"Extraordinary," he mumbled to himself.

The journey took over an hour, a consequence of their having to break trail through deep snow on the stage road from Missoula that tracked the Hell Gate River. The cabin squatted not far from the river bank and was half-buried in drifts. The door was tightly closed. It was a single room dwelling constructed of peeled logs and appeared to be poorly built, already listing to one side like a ship taking on water. The lone window displayed a broken pane repaired with a wad of newspaper shoved through. A rusted stove pipe poked out above the low roofline and gaps in the mud chinking between logs had been plugged with more newspaper. All in all, thought C.W., the shanty exhibited neglect, despair and ennui.

"Surely not prosperous," McPhail said, dismounting.

"Not a bit of it."

They tethered the horses to spindly cottonwood saplings that protruded from snow near the leeward side of the cabin and Collins told the dog to stay. There were no fresh tracks around, apart from a few coyote imprints. The scavengers had probably been seeking entry to an opportune meal.

"Guess we better take a look-see," McPhail said, almost eagerly, and led the way.

Together they worked the door free of an icy anchor and kicked away a snow bank that blockaded the entrance. Shoving past McPhail, Collins ducked through the low frame and paused a moment to allow his eyes to adjust to the shadowy interior. His companion squeezed in beside him. They stood silent for several minutes as the scene revealed itself.

The cabin was cheerless and sparsely furnished. Crudely fashioned bunk beds occupied one wall and an iron spring bed stood perpendicular. A makeshift table sat across from the beds, surrounded by two decrepit wooden chairs and one crate. A small Excelsior stove took up the rest of the limited space. A pan sat upon it, bearing the rancid remains of cooked meat. An assemblage of empty whiskey bottles lay upon the table and were scattered on the dirt floor. Some were broken. Collins found the room miserable in the extreme, eloquent with failed hopes and desperation, and it was faintly redolent with putrid rankness of corporeal excretions.

" 'Thou detestable maw, thou womb of death,' " he whispered to himself. He was deeply grateful that inexorable cold suppressed the pervading odors and turned his attention to the remnants of carnage.

One body was lying full length in a great pool of frozen blood. The sunken eyes were open and frost laced the lids and coated the blank orbs. Rime whitened the skin of the face, traced eye lashes and brows and etched the rim of a bullet hole above the left eye. The mouth was seized in a petrified grimace, the mangled tongue and hardened gobbets of blood, dispersed in proximity, testified to the cavity having received a hideous wound. The body was costumed in typical clothing common to men living rough in the western reaches. A Colt six shooter lay not far from the corpse. Clearly, this man had not perished by shotgun.

"Good god," McPhail muttered. "That is almighty wretched."

"Is that Donnelly?" Collins asked. "Do you know?"

"I...I...I guess so...yes," the man answered, visibly shaken. "I only ever see'd him once or twice."

C.W. glanced around for the other victim. French Phil was seated, back against the wall, just to the right of the door and partially concealed by it. He stepped over to pull the door away from the body. The entire left side of the head, from the mouth up, was blown off. Gelid lumps of gory brain ornamented the logs behind and the remaining portion of visage seemed to express surprise and alarm. In this instance, a shotgun was evidently the author of mutilation. Although quite practiced in encounters with plutonian mortality, Collins was made slightly ill by the macabre sight. McPhail pushed past out of the hovel and noisily relinquished his breakfast.

Bending closer, Collins inspected the position of the double-barreled shotgun. It was clasped between the feet, the barrel end wedged in the wound in a way that held it in position. The placement of the weapon implied artifice, unless one of the men who discovered the scene had jostled the gun. He left the cabin and looked for Mr. McPhail. The man was seated on a stump near the horses and appeared to be thoroughly nauseous. Gal lay curled nearby in a hollow she had made in the snow.

"Do you know the gentlemen who first found the bodies?" C.W. asked.

McPhail shook his head. "No. They were passing through on the way to Helena and stopped to warm up. I heard their names were Childs and Corcoran. They hot-footed it to Deer Lodge and that is when McTague came out."

"Did McTague speak of moving the weapons?"

"No. He left everything as was. He thought Sheriff McAndrews would want to see it. Then the weather turned fierce and no one came."

"What of the people in the vicinity?"

"Townsfolk were spooked. Nobody wanted to come around."

"You did," Collins said sardonically.

"Thought maybe...I guess I thought I could help."

"Quite."

"And do you think Phil murdered Donnelly and then suicided?"

"I do not."

"By harry." McPhail let out a whistle and seemed to regain a degree of steadiness. "That would mean there is a killer somewhere about."

"Perhaps."

"Will we be leaving now?"

"Not yet. I need to examine the bodies and their contexture once again and entrust all to memory. You may depart if you please."

"I do believe I should return and see if Matilda has need of me."

"Of course. Thank you for guiding me here."

"Will you be staying another night?" McPhail asked, using the saddle horn to clumsily drag his bulky frame onto his horse.

"Perhaps. It is early yet."

Turning the gelding toward New Chicago, McPhail gave him a wave. "Stop for coffee on the way by, then. I would hear of your conclusions."

"I may require a wagon," Collins said as the man rode away. McPhail did not, in fact, hear him in his haste to retreat.

Impressing upon the dog that she should stay put, he returned to the cabin and once more entered the company of unnatural death. Without distraction and conquering his instinctive abhorrence, he perused every detail, noting that both weapons were empty of loads. Powder marks around the hole in Donnelly's forehead told of close contact with the Colt, probably evidence that threats had preceded the fatal wound. The second shot into the mouth evinced disdain or calamitous rage. He moved to the other corpse and a further scrutiny of the shotgun, in regards to the ruination of French Phil's head, persuaded him the scene was arranged after death.

Using a three tined fork retrieved from the table, Collins excavated within the injury and found one of the .44 caliber slugs from the Colt revolver. This was testimony that Phil had been shot with the Colt prior to having his head blown apart by both barrels of the shotgun. Phil Heenal had been murdered then, he determined, just previous to or promptly following the slaying of Thomas Donnelly. It was probably a foregone conclusion that the truant Boulder Fritz had, indeed, committed the crime, for whatever reasons of his own. Now, C.W. would have to hunt the man and attempt to bring him to justice.

His pursuit would have to wait, however, as he had promised Ignatius Donnelly that he would see to his brother's remains. The nearest undertaker was in Deer Lodge City and this meant returning to New Chicago, obtaining a wagon from McPhail and retrieving the body for transport. Stepping out the door, Collins considered the difficulties that might arise from any attempt to move a corpse that was rigid and solid as a rock. He would, no doubt, require assistance. After deliberating upon all contingencies, he resolved to return home, enlist Wú Peng and make use of his own buckboard.

Not sorry to be shed of the despicable scene, C.W. secured the door to the cabin against carrion feeders and persons with a taste for the grotesque and was soon riding eastward, the dog trotting along behind. Ulysses moved out at a good pace, despite the snow, and Collins gratefully breathed the crisp air, filling his lungs to wholly unfetter himself of lingering malodorous vapors. There were many hours remaining of daylight and the moon was waxing. The sky was cloudless and he could easily make it back to the ranch as long as the weather held.

5

The two men stood looking down at their quarry. It remained deeply frigid in the early morning and Collins wondered how they were to pry Donnelly's corpse from its frozen lake of blood. If they built a fire to thaw him out, the stench would be unspeakable, especially given the ample brown stain that had oozed from French Phil upon his demise.

"What are your thoughts?" he asked Wú Peng

"I am certain that if we both extend our efforts upon the shoulders, we should be successful in prizing this entity free. His garments appear quite flimsy and will, no doubt, succumb."

A thought occurred to Collins. "You do not have moralistic restrictions regarding death, do you?"

"No Charles. A person does not have fear of death nor its derivations if one has lived a moral life. Confucius wrote, 'While you do not know life, how can you know death?' Therefore it evokes no anxiety."

Relieved, C.W. reached down and tentatively yanked on the shoulder of Donnelly's tattered woolen shirt. Peng knelt and pulled on the other shoulder and together they managed to wrest the body loose from congealed gore, the back of the moth-eaten blouse tearing away. C.W. rolled him onto a blanket, taken from one of the beds, and they dragged him out the door. It took them sustained exertion to load the stiffened and unwieldy body onto the buckboard while Joey, the mule, demonstrated a lack of cooperation, apparently able to smell blood.

"And the other?" Peng asked, when their burden was at last reposing in the wagon beneath the purloined blanket.

"The right honorable French Phil must be left to another's ministrations. He is no concern of ours."

"Perhaps we should close the door and spare him the ministrations of insalubrious nibbling?"

"It is the best we can do for the poor fellow," Collins said, grinning.

He prepared the mule and buckboard for travel while his companion secured the door to the cabin and barricaded it with blocks of firewood he found stacked against an outside wall. They climbed onto the seat and called the dog. Gal hurdled into the wagon and wedged herself between them. Collins slapped the lines lightly and Joey moved down the trail. A stagecoach had passed along the road sometime after he had departed the area on the preceding day, and the way was cleared through crusty snow, making their journey much facilitated.

About five hours later, Collins drove up alongside the establishment of John O'Neill. The sign above the clapboard edifice proclaimed him to be a "funeral director," which, it was to be supposed, was one step above an undertaker. He jumped down and entered the building while Peng held the lines and ensured that the dog stayed in the wagon.

The parlor was somber and dimly lit, surely appropriate to the purpose, and there were a few uncomfortable looking chairs spread about. Disturbingly, two small coffins were propped in a corner, displaying twin female toddlers costumed in starched white frocks. An offensive aroma seemed to emanate from them. In another corner, a grandfather clock marked the time, ticking raucously in the silent room. Collins coughed loudly in an effort to attract attention and was rewarded by a thin, somewhat unremarkable gentleman emerging from a rear chamber. He wore an obligatory black frock coat and high collar of an older style.

"Good afternoon, sir," the man said in a hushed voice, as if reluctant to wake the two dead girls. "How may I serve you?"

"I have a body in the wagon there," C.W. said, nodding toward the front of the room. "It is frozen solid and requires burial. The brother has requested interment in the New Chicago cemetery."

"I will require particulars of name, dates and so forth. What of preparation?"

Confused a moment by the question, he quickly remembered that embalming had grown in practice in recent years. "No preparation. Just a simple pine coffin and interment."

"And services?"

"No funeral. Do you have someone who can assist me with bringing in the corpse?"

"I will have my associate come to you. Just a moment, if you please."

Gratefully exiting the dismal atmosphere of the building, Collins immediately saw that there were three men studying Donnelly's body. The dog was growling from her place on the spring seat and beside her Peng was hunched over, making himself as small as possible. Collins strode to the back of the buckboard.

"What do you do here?" he asked in a commanding tone, startling the onlookers.

"This here is Tom," pronounced a shabby man in a blacksmith apron.

"Yes. Thomas Donnelly."

"How came you and a Chink to be totin' his stiff around?" another bystander demanded.

Regarding the men coolly, Collins said, "If you must know, I have been commissioned by his older brother to see to the burial." He pulled the blanket back over the corpse.

"He were a good man, was Tom," the blacksmith said. "Not much luck, but honest."

"Shame he done himself like that," someone said.

"Might be problematic to shoot yourself twice," Collins merely said, unwilling to engage in further conversation.

A stout man in work clothing came out of the building carrying a stretcher and together they conveyed Donnelly into the undertaker's establishment, the onlookers making editorial comments all the while. When he returned, the group had moved down the road and were speaking animatedly. Undoubtedly, thought C.W., the riff raff were exchanging theories about Donnelly's demise and most probably would be doing so for the rest of the day.

" 'O gull, o dolt, as ignorant as dirt,' " he quoted under his breath and climbed onto the wagon. "Did they pester you?" he asked Peng.

"Most assuredly they did not." The Chinaman stroked the dog's head. "She was ferocious in my defense."

Reclaiming the lines, Collins drove up the street and turned toward the courthouse and jail. Newly planted sapling trees, denuded in winter, encircled the two imposing structures, built of sturdy brick. He pulled up in front of the jailhouse on First Street, again placing Peng in charge of the mule and dog.

"I will see if Sheriff McAndrews is in residence," C.W. said, climbing down. "If anyone else happens along to annoy or threaten you, do come find me."

"Do not be apprehensive on my behalf."

"I am in earnest."

The building was generous with windows and the interior was bright, made more so by the white paint that coated the walls. Three desks, a safe, cupboards, bookcases and a variety of mismatched furniture filled the sheriff's office. Two unoccupied jail cells, secured by stout iron bars, lined one wall and a narrow staircase provided access to the second story. Oil lamps were mounted in various positions on the walls and a sizeable parlor stove provided heat, although Collins found the room to be chilly. Sheriff James McAndrews was seated behind the largest desk, set beneath a window, studiously writing in a notebook. He had short hair and full beard, neatly trimmed, and wore a fashionable suit of clothing. A bowler hat rested upon the desktop.

"Yes?" McAndrews inquired high-handedly, looking up from his work.

C.W. noticed a spaniel dog lying quietly at his feet. "Good afternoon, Sheriff. My name is Charles Collins. We have been formerly introduced."

Some months earlier, McAndrews had braced Collins in the street, mistaking him for a road agent from a federal handbill, and they nearly came to fisticuffs. No apology had been forthcoming when the Scotsman had, at last, become convinced of his error and Collins remained skeptical of the man's competence, not to mention civility.

"Mr. Collins," McAndrews said with the barest hint of a sneer. The Highlands brogue tumbled around inside his mouth like pebbles.

Discounting the lack of cordiality in the sheriff's mien, Collins said, "I would expect that Deputy McTague has fully apprised you of the bodies in a cabin west of New Chicago."

"Aye."

"I have just brought Thomas Donnelly to O'Neill, the undertaker, as per his brother's request."

The sheriff regarded him with steely grey eyes, deprived of expression, and offered no comment.

"I am here to inform you that Phil Heenal, otherwise known as French Phil, remains in situ. I also propose to offer my opinion that both men were murdered."

"Oh do you now?" McAndrews asked acerbically. "And

what proficiency do you bring to bear, then?"

"*Is dána gach madra i ndoras a thí féin.*"

"Are you insulting me in your bastard Irish?"

"Not a bit of it," Collins said evenly. "I am merely endeavoring to impress upon you that both Donnelly and Heenal were murdered. It is manifest."

Curious in spite of himself, the sheriff asked, "And how came you to this presumption?"

"The method by which Donnelly was shot and the Colt .44 slug in Heenal, no doubt lodged there prior to the shotgun blast that ravaged his head. What did McTague detect?"

"Deputy McTague has just been married. I do believe he is abstracted."

"Just so," Collins said. He did not inquire as to why the sheriff had not examined the scene for himself, once the weather eased, nor dispatched the coroner for an inquest. "Can you tell me aught of Boulder Fritz, the missing partner?"

McAndrews stood, waking the dog. The animal stretched, turned around twice and lay back down. Filling a cup from a coffeepot on the stove, the sheriff returned to his desk. He had very deliberately not offered any coffee to C.W. nor invited him to sit in one of the vacant chairs.

"And for what purpose would you want to know about Boulder Fritz?"

"I have been engaged by Mr. Ignatius Donnelly to investigate the circumstances of his younger brother's death." Collins steadfastly reminded himself that he required information and must not succumb to vexation at the man's thickheaded obfuscation.

"So you offer comprehensive service, I take it? Interment, investigation and deduction." McAndrews coughed. "Impressive." He sipped his coffee, then sat silently for several minutes as if deliberating whether to provide crucial particulars or withhold them.

His patience corroding, Collins gazed out the window over McAndrews' head. Clouds were building above the mountains to the west.

Seeing that his recalcitrance was not having the desired effect, the sheriff cocked an eyebrow and said, "Boulder Fritz is a German who moved into these parts a scant year ago and somehow managed to wheedle his way into Donnelly's good graces. Given his taste for whiskey, Tom never was a capable judge of character and this fella dug in. Neither French Phil nor Fritz were a friend to poor Tom. Heard he was about to sell out."

"Any clue where Fritz had come from?"

"Rumor had it that he hailed from Silver Bow. Failed miner or some such."

"Can you describe him?"

"Aye."

"And so?" Collins was now genuinely exasperated with the man.

McAndrews eyed him a long moment, then shrugged. "He was a slim, jack-a-dandy with eyes set too close together. Weasel looking sort of dude. His clothing had once been costly, but long since seen excessive wear. Heavy accent and cunning ways about him."

"I am obliged. Now I have a place to begin."

"We are all confidence that he is well-nigh captured. *Ní chaitheann an chaint an t-éadach.*"

There was a similar proverb in Collins' native Irish. The talk doesn't wear the clothes. It was an affront, but then he had implied the sheriff was a cowardly dog, after all.

"And now I will take my leave," he said, making for the door. "Much gratitude for your generous assistance," he added with abundant lacings of sarcasm.

"Kindly remember you are not an officer of the law," McAndrews bellowed as C.W. departed the building.

"That is as may be," he said to himself, walking away. "But at least I am not a bloody peeler."

After leaving Wú Peng in the Chinese quarter to shop and visit, Collins headed down Second Street to the office of *The New North-West*, Deer Lodge City's only newspaper. Captain James Hamilton Mills, proprietor and editor of the weekly journal, was an old acquaintance from the war. They had met during the aftermath of the dreadful Battle of the Wilderness, in which almost 18,000 Federal casualties were reported. The memory of those frightful days was not a pleasant one.

General Grant had requisitioned C.W. as an aide-de-camp at the beginning of the Overland Campaign of 1864 and he was present throughout three days of profligate death and devastation in the nearly impenetrable woods of Spotsylvania County, Virginia. Many of the wounded were consumed by fires that raged through the labyrinthian forest, while soldiers on both sides stumbled through dense smoke, blinded and terrified. Grant was deeply affected by mounting losses; the dead and dying haplessly incinerated and beyond succor. Collins stood by while the general lighted one cigar after another as they awaited reports from the field. Ultimately, the battle had been indecisive. General Grant, albeit bereft at the heavy fatalities, pushed south undeterred. He interrupted Confederate supply lines, laid siege to Petersburg and kept General Lee's forces extended, never allowing him to regroup and mount an offensive. His dogged determination eventually led to Lee's surrender a year later.

A soldier with the 40th Pennsylvania Infantry, Mills had received a series of promotions for heroic conduct during previous battles. He was given a field promotion to captain at the Wilderness by Grant himself and Collins had officiated. Mills and Collins were both abolitionist Republicans and they became friends, sporadically corresponding over the years. Not long after moving to the ranch, he had discovered that Captain Mills owned the local newspaper. The man was a font of regional gossip, history and intelligences and was always prepared to lend advice. Collins was confident his friend would know something about Boulder Fritz.

Taking the hitch weight from the wagon bed, Collins tethered Joey, scratched the mule's forehead and allowed him to snuffle his coat, searching for treats. "Nothing in my pockets, boyo," he told the animal. "Sorry."

The dog jumped down and followed him through the door of the newspaper office. A woman was standing at a slanted work bench, studiously picking type from assorted trays and arranging lines of text on a composing stick. A heating stove stood against the far wall, its pipe crooked an implausible three bends. The printing press, with its gears, cylinders and wheels, took up half of the room. James Mills was seated at a table shuffling through issues of various papers. He had a full moustache, wild grey hair and his clothing was demonstrably rumpled. The man had always tended toward the bedraggled when consumed by his labors.

"Charles!" he shouted and sprang to his feet to extend a hand smudged with newsprint. "I have not laid eyes on you for many a day." He knelt down to give Gal a playful rub and she wagged her stunted tail enthusiastically.

"To be sure," C.W. said, smiling. "We were mostly snowed in for weeks and the livestock needed tending."

Mills glanced out the front window. "Where's Peng?"

"Shopping."

"Of course. Come, sit down. Cora, could you pour us some coffee?"

They took chairs beside the table that was buried under newspapers. The woman brought mugs of coffee and they thanked her. She returned to her work. The dog lay down by Collins' feet.

"How is your new cylinder press?"

"A dream," Mills said enthusiastically. "My boy and I are able to turn out nearly a thousand impressions an hour."

"What is all this, then?" Collins asked, gesturing at the piles of broadsheets.

"I always plunder news from eastern papers." Mills raised his cup, as if in a toast. "This has been on the stove all day. Fairly thick I should guess."

Taking a sip, Collins grimaced. "Jesus, mary and joseph, Captain, this could strip paint."

"Just the way I prefer it." He took a great noisy swig and asked, "Now then, is this a social visit or are you in pursuit of some information?"

"Both, I suppose. I stopped by to see that damnable McAndrews and he was not instructive."

Mills grinned. "Not much of a lawman, I will warrant. More attentive to his feed and livery enterprise."

"Not much of a lawman, indeed. At any road, I brought Tom Donnelly's body to O'Neill today and wanted to inform the sheriff that it was a double killing, no question about it."

"Really?" Mills asked, exhibiting the keen interest of a news correspondent. "I heard Deputy McTague deemed it suicide and left it at that. He was supposed to send the coroner out to the cabin, but the storm moved in."

"The weather has broken," Collins said, frowning.

Mills shrugged expressively. "Tell me more."

"Yes well, the bodies were still there. Donnelly had been shot twice, once unnecessarily and callously in the mouth. And the same Colt revolver was used on French Phil. The slug had been disguised by a shotgun blast."

Mills eyed him curiously. "How, pray, did you discover that?"

"I burrowed around in the wound. The shotgun was jammed in the unsightly remains of his head in order to secure the barrel. The freezing cold did the rest."

"Suspicious, then?"

"Decidedly."

Rubbing his hands together gleefully, Mills said, "There is a story there. I printed an account last week based on McTague's suppositions. *The Press* in Benton had a piece about it, but likewise hinted at an alternative theory of the crime. Will you look into it further?"

"Not ordinarily, but Donnelly's brother has employed me to investigate. I am now obliged to pursue the murderer, whomever that may be."

"And you will keep me abreast of your progress, of course," Mills said, squinting at him craftily.

"If you now provide me with the information I was unable to garner from McAndrews."

"Fair deal."

"Was Thomas Donnelly fond of whiskey, as McAndrews and others have suggested?"

"Donnelly was addicted to drink, but not quarrelsome. His neighbors knew him as a quiet, inoffensive man."

"And Phil Heenal?" Collins hazarded another sip of coffee.

"A native of France, hence the nickname. He had been in the valley around four or five years and inclined to be troublesome, especially when in his cups. He and Tom would get stewed and Heenal tended to become truculent."

"And what do you know of Boulder Fritz?"

"I know he cannot be found and is doubtless beyond the reach of the law, if he is, in fact, guilty of this heinous deed. His real name is Fritz Schwack or Fritz Schwabe." Mills glanced at the woman, still hard at work setting type. "Go home, Cora."

"Yes sir."

Cora, a pale and prim looking lady, gathered her shawl, gloves and unadorned bonnet and departed.

"Widow...Diligent worker and a marvel for reading backwards, but not much for discourse," Mills said with a wry smile. "Now then, where was I? Ah yes, the German miscreant...he had an oddly reptilian deportment and one always had the sense he was not quite right."

Gal jumped up and ran to the door.

"Meaning what?"

Mills scowled. "Aberrant. Gave me the jimjams. I was only in his company on a few occasions and I kept my distance."

"And what could have been the instigation to murder, in your opinion? Drunken brawl?"

Leaning back in his chair and clasping his hands behind his head, Mills said, "As you know, I came to Montana Territory in 1866. I joined some other fellows in a mining claim at Emigrant Gulch. When we needed to resupply, we gave most of our cash to a packer to obtain provisions in Bozeman. The scoundrel swindled us out of all our wealth and we were forced to give up our claim. I was never able to track the bastard down, but could have easily murdered him. Perhaps, your man Fritz felt ill-used, foolish as that may have been."

The door opened and Wú Peng entered. "I have loaded our goods in the wagon. Should we not begin our journey home?" he asked.

"Good day to you Peng," Mills said.

"Very good health to you, Captain Mills."

Getting to his feet, Collins said, "We must take our leave, Captain. We will be traveling by moonlight, as it is. One more question?"

"Of course," Mills said, rising from his chair.

"Any astute conjecture as to where Fritz may have gone?"

"Butte City, perhaps? There is a fair population of Germans over there."

"A place to begin, I suppose."

"And I have one last question for you," Mills said.

"Yes?"

"What have you done with French Phil?"

Collins grinned roguishly. "He is biding his time, awaiting the thaw."

37

WHOLESALE MURDER.

——

Two Bodies Found in a Cabin Near New Chicago.

——

Information was received in this city last night of the perpetration, near New Chicago, several days ago, of a most horrible crime. From what particulars can be obtained it appears that up to last Sunday three men, known familiarly as Boulder Fritz, French Phil and Donnelly, together occupied a cabin on the Hellgate river about three miles above New Chicago. They had alternately followed the business of mining and ranching, and held a common interest in considerable property in the vicinity of New Chicago. On Sunday last the three men were seen alive and living in apparent peace together, though it was known to some of their friends that disputes had several times arisen between them in reference to their ground.

MURDER!

6

The gelding stood calmly as Collins set the saddle and slipped on the bridle. He wrapped the reins around a corral railing and tied his old valise behind the saddle and slid his Winchester into its off-side scabbard. Peng and Gal sat nearby, watching the proceedings. A few delicate flakes of snow floated about them like downy feathers in the bluish gray gloaming before dawn.

"You will journey to Butte City, as discussed?" Wú Peng asked.

"It is a place to begin."

"And you will be exceedingly cautious in your pursuit? The Master said, '*Yǐ yuē, shī zhī zhě xiān yǐ.*' With caution, those who err are few."

Collins smiled. "Thank you for your apprehension, my friend. I will be vigilant." He stepped over to Ulysses, pulled the reins loose from the fence and passed them around the gelding's neck. "I have encountered this breed of scoundrel before," he said, mounting up. "Finding him will be the trick."

"I am already looking for your safe homecoming."

"I need for you to keep our Gal here. It will not be safe for her."

"The netherworld of frail sisterhood is no place for this small person."

"Do please remember to keep her restrained until I have departed the vicinity," C.W. said.

Removing a small string from a pocket, Peng nodded

and made a loop around the dog's neck. "Yes Charles, I will hold her. She will be obstreperous."

"My gratitude, as always," Collins said, reining the horse away from the barn. "I will return as soon as I am able."

More snow had fallen in the night, but it packed well and the footing was sure. Brooding clouds darkened the sky and an increasingly stout breeze tugged at Collins' Stetson hat. He planned to stay in the Centennial Hotel and his intention was to make it all the way to Butte City without respite. As such, he was traveling light and was able to push Ulysses into a swift walk, maintaining the pace and covering the distance to Deer Lodge in good time. The snow had turned to driving sleet and the streets were empty but for a few men straggling from saloons and solitary children trudging hurriedly to school.

Riding straight through the town, Collins crossed over a sturdy little bridge at the end of Third Street and continued along the main road that led south, following the east bank of the Deer Lodge River. The long established route steered him through a wide flatland bounded by two mountain ranges. The tardy sun sporadically broke through clouds, sending misshapen shadows skating like eerie ghosts across the open valley. Cattle and horse herds punctuated the snowy landscape, leaving muddy patches here and there while prospecting for forage. Off to the west, a heavily loaded hay rack moved slowly behind two large draught horses. A man stood balanced on the heap of hay behind the team, pulling forkfuls of fodder down to a trailing bunch of hungry cows. Old feed trails made irregular rows in the pasture on either side of the wagon, like worm traces. Occasional buildings in the near and far distances issued forth smoke from chimneys and stovepipes into the chilly morning air.

There were infrequent travelers out in the blustery squalls that came whipping down from the western peaks in quick succession. C.W. pulled his neckerchief up across his face against stinging ice and the gelding tossed his head in protest. A canary yellow Gilmer and Salisbury coach almost ran them down near Warm Springs, its approach unheralded due to bellowing wind and a curtain of pelting sleet. Ulysses bolted off the track and crow hopped a couple of jumps to show his displeasure. Keeping his seat, Collins pulled him in and let him blow, speaking to him calmly. The animal's sides stopped heaving and he guided the horse back onto the road.

Periodically, he was forced to dismount and walk so as to keep his blood moving. The wintry gales knifed through his many layers of clothing and old bearskin coat, resurrected for the journey. Collins chewed on biscuits and slices of cold beef and halted once to offer Ulysses a few handfuls of oats from a small cache in one saddle bag. A rickety farm wagon rattled past them not far from the town of Stuart. An elderly couple were perched on the spring seat, both man and woman swathed in blankets. They made no sign they had seen C.W. and moved by without greeting.

The hour was late and the sun had set as he rode through the hamlet of Silver Bow and entered Butte City. The main road into the town became Park Street and he followed it to Main Street, riding to the Farmer's Corral Livery, Feed and Sale Stable on the southwest side of town. After making arrangements for the care of his horse, Collins tramped his way back up Main through a mixture of mud, sodden animal manure and dirty slush, occasionally dodging horses and carriages that threw up clods of muck. Each time he made for the planking that fronted the line of buildings along the street, clusters of men, most of them drunk, jostled him back into the viscid mire.

Upon arrival to the hotel, his boots were clad in at least three inches of sludge. C.W. made thoroughgoing use of the boot scraper mounted outside the door prior to entering. The Centennial, being one of the more modest hotels in Butte City, provided a lobby that was functional rather more than luxurious. In spite of this, a finely dressed and comely woman was descending the wide staircase from the second floor, making him keenly aware of his mud spattered clothing. He removed his hat and nodded, but she haughtily swept past him into the dining room. Stepping over to the front desk, he signed the register, handed the clerk two silver dollars and was given a key. Climbing the stairs, he passed by a couple of slovenly male patrons and felt less notable by comparison.

When he had cleaned up, shaved and donned more respectable attire, Collins went down to the dining room. Beyond the entrance to the spacious restaurant, raucous clamor issued from the barroom. Having visited Butte City in the past, he was accustomed to the local pursuit of consuming extraordinary amounts of liquors and wines. This was due in part, he supposed, to the large Irish population of miners and the fact there was no real law in town. He was promptly met by an aged waiter who skillfully negotiated his way through a warren of crowded tables with Collins in pursuit. Fleetingly, he espied the pretty woman he had noticed earlier and she was gazing directly at him. On this occasion, her perusal of him seemed vastly more favorable and he smiled to himself, succumbing to a minor bout of vanity.

The waiter, with perfunctory courtesy, seated him at an empty table in a back corner, which suited him perfectly, and C.W. ordered the evening's special, uncaring as to its particulars. The meal appeared with astonishing speed, consisting of roast pork, mashed potatoes drowned in inordinate dollops of gravy, with a side dish of stewed tomatoes and a platter of freshly baked rolls. Upon his request for coffee, Collins was promptly supplied with a china pot and cup.

While he ate, he surveyed the ample room and its inhabitants. They were a miscellaneous gathering of varied economic and social standing, some individuals elegantly dressed and others in grimy work clothes. Collins had found this to be the rule for most mining towns as places that attracted people from far and wide. At least two of the diners were unambiguously of the soiled dove flock, bedecked in noticeably garish costumes replete with velvet, feathers and lace. What they lacked in winsome physiognomies, they made up for with ostentatious finery. None of the other patrons seemed to be incommoded, even in the slightest manner, by their presence.

The food was good and Collins ate all of it, having been without much to eat for most of the day. Departing the dining room, he sat a while on an upholstered bench against one of the walls of the lobby, observing the entrance to the saloon and the men ambling back and forth, some of whom being distinctly unsteady. He had formed a mental picture of Boulder Fritz from the portrayals provided by Mills and Sheriff McAndrews, but he seriously doubted he would be fortunate enough to discover the man so early on in the chase. C.W. knew his quarry may not even be in Butte City, a detail he did not wish to contemplate at the moment.

He would send a telegram to Mr. Donnelly in the morning, informing him of the brother's burial and his own whereabouts. If he did, in fact, find Fritz, he planned to hand him over to the law, which would mean taking him back to Deer Lodge City and Sheriff McAndrews. There were forthcoming plans to form a separate county for Butte City and its vicinities, but for now, the nearest jail was back up north. However, if the fugitive German proved an obstinate character and Collins was finally confident of his guilt, then all bets were off.

The rest of his plan entailed visiting the more degraded districts of Butte. Certainly any male resident would be able to direct him to the streets that maintained disorderly houses. To his thinking, a man who desired to evade arrest for a brutal murder would do well to blend into the criminal element. Neighborhoods that bartered flesh and opium were prevalent throughout the mining towns of western territories and the iniquitous denizens thereof would always afford a population into which an individual might vanish. He had found this to be true during his years as an operative for the Pinkerton Detective Agency and his present search was bound to take him to less than respectable environs. Therefore, Collins had not only brought along his Colt revolver, but also a .41 caliber Remington derringer he had purchased years prior.

Weary from travel and anticipating an eventful morrow, Collins rose from his seat and ascended the stairway. A fellow was lying in the middle of the upstairs corridor, quite insensible, apparently too full of whisky to achieve his room. Stepping over the man, he continued down the hall and was reminded of a quote from Act II of *Othello*. "O God, that men should put an enemy in their mouths to steal away their brains!" He was certain to witness much of this debauchery during his sojourn in a city possessed of every sort of resident imaginable and where the imbibing of spirits was a cherished diversion. It was simply commonplace.

7

While eating an early breakfast, Collins read *The Daily Miner*, which contained an improbable item entitled "Impressment and Shooting" concerning an incident involving a press gang operating out of Charleston, North Carolina. Supposedly, a saloonkeeper had endeavored to kidnap four men and convey them to a British barkentine just off the coast. The men had resisted and the captain had opened fire on the rowboat, killing one man and injuring two others. On the west coast, he was aware that a practice called crimping continued to be prevalent, whereby drunkards were kidnapped or "shanghaied" and delivered to undermanned ships. "Shanghai Kelly," in San Francisco, had once kidnapped a hundred men in one evening. But he had thought impressment and press gangs delivering men to British ships had ended with the Napoleonic Wars.

There was a damning account regarding Tammany Hall in New York and an article about two ladies struck and killed by a train locomotive while they were riding in a sleigh near Cleveland, Ohio. There was even mention of former president Grant travelling to Mexico for the benefit of the Consolidated Company of Mexican Railroads, of which he was a member. It seemed evident that the *Miner* was pilfering news fragments from eastern papers, much the same as Mills at the *The New North-West*.

Interestingly, the front page also contained an excerpt from a telegram from the commanding officer of

Fort Buford in Dakota Territory. Major Brotherton had sent a message to General Alfred Terry that three Hunkpapa chiefs had been captured and brought in. These chiefs had been with Sitting Bull in Canada and Collins became anxious for his friend Arbuckles, who was presently either in the Lakota camps near Fort Walsh in the North-West Territories or on the way back to his ranch. He had difficulty believing the chiefs had actually been captured unless U.S. soldiers had stolen across the border and taken them prisoner in their sleep.

It was snowing again when he stepped out onto the hotel porch. As planned, his initial foray would be to visit the lair of gambling dens, brothels and dance-houses that, according to the scrubbed and cherubic desk clerk, were located at a distance on east Galena and Park streets. Unwilling to wade through depths of sullage on foot, Collins made his way along the boarded walkway to the stables, this time unmolested by carousing miners. The large sliding door to the spacious barn was open about halfway. Just inside, a dapper fellow in a worsted wool suit was mucking out a stall. His face was flushed and beads of perspiration made rivulets down his cheeks and collected on the ends of his luxuriant moustache, despite snow drifting in on wintry gusts of wind. The fellow seemed to be lamenting a grave malefaction committed by one of his employees, with ingeniously vulgar terms, to no one in particular.

Standing patiently, and mildly amused by the man's singular performance, Collins waited to attract notice. The fashionably-attired laborer caught sight of C.W., just as he was preparing to propel a full wheel-barrow out the door, and produced a flow of additional expletives that was no minor feat. Impressed by the man's virtuosity, Collins smiled and held his ground.

"I have come to fetch my horse," he said.

As if emerging from a stupor of aggravation, the man

said, "God, I am fucking...damned apologetic. My boy has not shown up this morning and this place is in a fucking...damned unholy muddle. Pardon me," he said and extended a hand. "I am Alex Ralston, one of the proprietors."

"Charles Collins." They shook hands.

"Which is your animal?" Ralston inquired.

"The buckskin down the way."

"Ah yes. Do you want me to bring him?"

"Not necessary," Collins said, shaking his head. "I will saddle him and take him out. It seems you have enough work at the moment."

Ulysses was munching hay in his pen. C.W. spoke easy words and the horse turned to come to him, blowing warm and fragrant breath in his face. Finding a worn curry-comb hung on a peg, he brushed the gelding briskly. His saddle was balanced upon a wooden rack protruding from a wall across from the stall, with the bridle suspended from the horn and the blankets folded neatly across the seat. Ralston's workers might be astray at present, but they had undoubtedly taken very good care of his horse and tack. He saddled the gelding and led him to the front of the barn. Instead of the owner, a young lad was now furiously shoveling a fetid concoction of manure and straw into the wheel-barrow, his face almost plum colored from apparent temper. Collins assumed the young man had received invective-ridden opprobrium from Ralston.

Securing Ulysses to a hitching ring just inside the barn, he stepped into the office. Ralston was seated behind a desk piled high with a disarray of papers and ledgers. He appeared to be considerably less agitated and he grinned shamefacedly.

"Once more I must tender a heartfelt apology for my previous outbursts. I am really quite accustomed to hard work, having begun as a stable hand. 'I cannot draw a cart, nor eat dried oats. If it be man's work, I'll do't.' "

"You know Shakespeare," Collins observed.

Ralston's features brightened perceptibly. "I do...I do indeed. You do as well, I surmise?"

"I carry him with me always."

"A sure means by which to find entertainment and erudition."

"No doubt." Collins wished to proceed upon his investigation without delay and abruptly altered course. "Might I reserve a place for my animal? I am intending to remain within city limits and will surely return before sunset. Shall I pay in advance?"

"Oh my goodness no," Ralston said strenuously. "I will vouchsafe the exact same stall for your excellent horse."

It seemed to C.W. that the man had miraculously banished all obscenities from his vocabulary in exchange for language entirely suitable for church. "Yes, well that is very kind of you," he said. "Until later, then."

"Until later," Ralston called as Collins departed the office.

Swinging into the saddle, Collins rode out into clearing skies and greater magnitudes of gelatinous mud. He headed over to Galena Street and east toward the district of dubious repute. Some of the dwellings along the upper part of the road were quite tidy, while farther down stood miserable shacks with peeling paint and boarded up windows. In spite of the early hour and the biting wind racing downslope from the north, partially clad prostitutes of various races could be seen lounging on the sagging front porches of their miserable cribs. Men were loafing here and there, mostly disreputable types either drugged by opium or in varying stages of drunkenness. He found the tableau to be a wretched scene of desolation. The finer brothels displayed none of their wares, but smoke rose from chimneys and lamps burned invitingly through curtained glass panes. C.W. thought he might have better luck in one of the parlor houses.

Dismounting and tethering Ulysses to a porch pillar in front of a two-story board and batten house painted bright yellow, he knocked on the door. It opened to frame an enormous woman with blonde curls piled high upon her head, dark circles under her eyes and bulges of pink flesh compressed into a burgundy satin gown trimmed with a profusion of silk flowers. Collins removed his Stetson and bade her good morning.

"Do come in, my dear," the lady said in a delicate voice that seemed at odds with her massive bulk. "My name is Jenny. Jenny Rivers."

Entering the lavishly decorated salon, resplendent with velvet upholstery, plush carpeting and floral draperies, he was ushered by his hostess to a spoon back chair, heavily padded and covered in forest green velour. Collins perched on the edge, not wanting to give the impression of repose, and watched as the woman arranged her vastness upon a mauve settee, half expecting it to collapse under her weight. A quantity of glasses and empty crystal decanters were distributed on various surfaces and the floor, testifying to a lively time the preceding night. The room reeked of cigar smoke and other odors he did not care to identify.

"It is rather early, darling," she said. "My girls have just now retired, but I can awaken one or two I suppose."

"That will not be required," he responded. "I am merely seeking your assistance with quite another matter."

The woman's languorous manner evaporated and she sat up and crossed her arms, accentuating the tremendous mounds of her bosom. "What sort of matter?" she asked briskly, in tones far less dulcet than previous.

"My name is Charles Collins. I am searching for a German man named Boulder Fritz, otherwise known as Fritz Schwack or Schwabe."

"Why?" Jenny asked bluntly.

"He murdered the brother of a friend of mine."

"Are you a law dog?"

"No ma'am, just a friend of the brother."

The woman appeared to become slightly less wary. "There are a good many Germans in Butte City."

"This man is a weasel-looking, flashy fellow and is capable of brutality beyond measure."

Jenny studied him with interest. "What did he do?"

"Killed two men he worked with." He paused a moment and decided to offer the grisly particulars he knew she craved. "Blew one man's head apart with a shotgun. His blood and brains were painted across the cabin wall."

She gave a long whistle in appreciation. "Must have been quite a sight."

"Indeed. And I have promised the dead man's brother I will bring the murderer to justice."

Giving the impression of someone who has arrived at a decision, Jenny came to her feet. Collins followed suit.

"I will put the word out, dearest. Give me one or two days and come back to me. If this fellow is around Butte City, I will know it."

Collins took her hand with the utmost of delicacy and kissed it. "My deepest gratitude, Jenny. And I will not fail to remunerate you for your kind assistance...most generously."

He meant to beguile the woman with feigned gentility and was rewarded by her sudden breathlessness. Long ago he had learned to wield his manly charms to good effect.

"I will anticipate your return with delight," Jenny said, making a visible effort to collect herself.

"As will I," he said. "For now I must say farewell."

When she had gently closed the door behind him, Collins stood a moment on the porch allowing his eyes to recover from the dimness of the interior and taking in great breaths of fresh air. He pondered his next move as he pulled the gelding's reins free and climbed into the saddle. When a begrimed tramp approached with his hand in a gesture of supplication, he turned the horse away and rode back toward Main Street.

DIORDERLY WOMEN

8

Reluctant to rely solely on Jenny's questionable good will and ambiguous promises, Collins rode around the demimonde of cribs, saloons and gambling houses and the higher class parlor houses on Park and Galena streets, familiarizing himself with the neighborhoods. He eventually discovered an alleyway between Colorado and Main that was entirely composed of Chinese establishments, including a row of squalid shacks, each with one narrow door and a tiny barred window. Behind the bars of one window he noticed a very young Chinese girl making gestures to him. He rode closer and heard her beckoning.

"China girl good. China girl make you happy." She bared her torso and pushed her pubescent breasts against the bars.

He sat his horse and watched her a moment, overcome by a sense of regret at this caged child offering her body to him. Standing in the shadows at the end of the line of cribs lounged a Chinese man, with shaved head and traditional clothing, watching him impassively. Abruptly, Collins shook his head and nudged Ulysses forward, anxious to be shed of the disturbing apparition. He knew of Chinese prostitution and the plight of slave girls sold into whoredom, but to have encountered it in such an intimate manner was disconcerting. Her face haunted him all the while he proceeded in exploration of the insalubrious enterprises of Butte City. Noon was approaching and derelict opium eaters, luridly attired women, sharpers and tosspots began to rouse themselves and roam the avenues in pursuit of gain or entertainment.

He searched the faces and listened for hints of German vernacular to no avail.

The sun crested through erratic clouds and Collins found he was famished. Returning to the livery stable, he was met by a wizened gentleman of advanced years who assisted in settling the gelding back in his stall. The lad he had seen earlier was not in evidence.

"No fear, mister, I will rub him down and provide water and provender," the gaffer reassured him in a German accent.

C.W. was instantly alert to this unforeseen happenstance. "Might I ask if you are Prussian?"

"Yes. Many years ago." The man stood still as if awaiting censure. He was slight in stature, but agile for his years and his clothes were newly laundered.

"I do not wish to offend, but are you acquainted with many Germans in this city?"

"Some."

"I am in search of a fellow who answers to the name of Boulder Fritz or perhaps Fritz Schwabe. By some peculiar coincidence, have you heard of him?"

The old man considered him for a bit. "Why would you want to know such a man?"

"You are acquainted with him then?"

"Perhaps." He narrowed his eyes in suspicion. "Again, I ask, why would you wish to know him?"

"He murdered two men. I have been commissioned to find and bring him to the law."

Lowering his guard, the stable hand nodded. "Fritz Schwabe enjoys the favors of a low woman named Inez Maybert. She has a small cottage on the northeast corner of Galena and Wyoming. Be warned, Fritz smokes opium, is a habitual drunkard and is never without a knife."

Ralston emerged from the office and walked over to them. "Ah, Mr. Collins, has Kaspar been attentive?"

"He has indeed. Would it be acceptable if I tendered a monetary expression of appreciation?"

Momentarily taken aback, Ralston hesitated, then said, "That would be acceptable, yes."

Removing four bits from a jacket pocket, C.W. offered the coins to Kaspar. "And may I request you give special care to my horse?"

"Of course," the German said deferentially, accepting the money and making a tight fist around it.

"I will return after partaking a midday meal," Collins told him. He headed for the front of the barn with Ralston joining him.

"It seems you have a good hostler there," he told the proprietor.

"Somewhat aged perhaps, but he is certainly more reliable than my younger employees. They are wild and footloose."

Upon leaving the livery stable, Collins ambled along the walkway toward the hotel. Most of the pedestrians and people on horseback or in wagons, now bustling about the town, were male. It seemed the preponderance of female residents was to be found in less exalted areas of Butte City. According to his experience, this state of affairs was another prevalent fact of mining communities. This particular town, however, could claim two churches and a school, which guaranteed a certain number of women not occupied by more ignominious endeavors.

Upon entering, Collins was immediately seated at a table in the hotel restaurant and ordered steak and eggs with coffee and apple pie. Once again, the food was prompt and satisfactory, but pity for the Chinese child would not leave him. He chided himself for sentimentality and finished his meal contemplating the very real possibility that he would be able to find Boulder Fritz. Rather than subject his horse to possible theft or vexation, and in the interest of appearing less conspicuous, he decided to proceed on foot. Armed with his Colt revolver and derringer, Collins felt he would be amply prepared for any eventuality.

He departed the dining room and headed back to the stable. Alex Ralston was no where to be seen, but Kaspar was harnessing a shiny black thoroughbred gelding. A stylish barouche sat waiting in front of the barn.

"You are here," Kaspar said. "Do you require your horse then?"

"I think not. I was curious whether you are able to offer any further information about Boulder Fritz?"

"No, no, no," the old man said with certitude. "I have told you he is dangerous and that is sufficient. He is a bad man...a very bad man."

"Very well. Then thank you."

Kaspar paused in his task and looked at C.W. "Will you go there now?" he asked.

"Yes."

"You must be watchful. He is cunning."

"I will, thank you."

By summarily returning to his labors, Kaspar signaled that his side of the discussion was at an end. Collins decided to postpone sending a telegram to Ignatius Donnelly until he had made an attempt at locating Fritz and made his way down Galena toward the very outskirts of town. Without benefit of a footpath, he was forced once more to endure copious mud, noxious slops thrown from windows and an unending supply of horse manure. He passed the northern access to the Chinese district and undertook to abnegate any further contemplation of the detestable cribs down the alley, reminding himself he needed to be in full possession of his shrewdest faculties.

The bungalow situated on the corner of Galena and Wyoming was once painted a light blue with darker trim, but the colors had faded and blistered and the structure exhibited doleful neglect. Collins stood in the shelter of a billiard hall across the street, unmindful of the customers coming and going, and examined the house looking for signs of occupation. He leaned against the side of the building for over an hour before a woman and man came out of the dwelling. They moved off down Wyoming Street in the direction of several saloons and gambling houses on Park. The couple entered Allen's saloon, a dilapidated clapboard edifice, and C.W. followed them a minute later.

Standing just inside the door, Collins surveyed the room. Aside from an ornately carved bar, much abused, the place was empty of furniture. Dingy wallpaper adorned the walls and two oil lamps were suspended from the ceiling. Several men, two young boys and three women stood at the bar and every one of them was gazing at him, including the barkeep. Easing aside his frock coat and resting his hand on the butt of his pistol, Collins strolled to the far side of where a fellow, who answered to Fritz Schwabe's description, stood with a blowzy, unappealing woman in a striped dress. The man did, in point of fact, resemble a weasel.

"You are Boulder Fritz," he said conversationally.

"*Leck mich am Arsch*," the man responded glibly.

C.W. was not certain of the meaning, but was confident his words were less than cordial. He moved in closer to the German, pulled his Colt and pressed the barrel end into the man's ribs.

"That there is Fritz Schwabe, sure as hell," one of the other men at the bar told him.

"You are Boulder Fritz, you murdering son of a bitch," Collins said in barely audible tones. "Come with me or I will open you up right here."

"Go to hell!" Fritz shouted and leapt aside, pulling a ten inch boning knife and brandishing it adroitly. "*Ja*, I murdered *deise Schweine*. Now you, *Arschloche*."

All the saloon's patrons withdrew down the bar except for the German's woman, who screamed and clutched at Collins' arm. He elbowed her hard in the breastbone and she went down. Dodging a backhanded slash of the knife, which narrowly missed lacerating his cheek, he shot Fritz in the knee. The man rolled around the floor, holding his leg, cursing in German and bleeding profusely. The woman crawled over to him and he punched her in the face.

"You takin' him outta here?" the barman asked Collins.

"That depends."

"On what?"

Fritz made another determined lunge at him with the deadly blade.

Collins lifted his revolver and blew a hole in his belly.

"On that," he said quietly.

Smoke from his Colt choked the room and the stench of perforated entrails seeped from Fritz's calamitous injury as he yowled in pain. The woman, in a heap on the grimy floorboards, wailed hysterically while blood streamed from her nose.

"Jesus, pal," said a man from the other side of the room. "You gonna clean that up?"

"No. His woman can do that," C.W. said, sliding the pistol back in its holster. "He will die soon and she can bury him."

"What the hell was it all about?" asked one of the saloon girls. Her manner was merely curious and she did not appear dismayed in any way.

"Fritz ruthlessly killed two men up on the Hell Gate River last December for no plausible reason. Unpacked one man's head with a double-barreled shotgun."

All and sundry seemed to accept this as sufficient and went back to their whisky and individual preoccupations. Collins caught a final glimpse of Boulder Fritz, now lying on his back and moaning faintly as his life ebbed away. His woman rested her head next to his, weeping less riotously. He left Allen's saloon and headed up Park Street toward Main. The telegraph office was over on West Broadway. A long walk would do him good.

BAR-ROOM BRAWL

9

Mr. George Marsh, telegrapher for the Montana Central Telegraph Company, announced his name and credentials with a hand-painted sign above his apparatus. The walls of the small office were cluttered with maps, chromolithographs, a giant clock and a calendar advertising tooth powder. Rows of cubbyholes lined the back wall and a long counter barricaded Marsh and his equipment from unnecessary contact with the public.

"Blanks are there in the box on the desk," the operator told Collins as he came in. The key tapped a steady rhythm as he engaged in transmitting a lengthy communication.

Removing his billfold from an inner pocket, C.W. found Donnelly's address in Minnesota and copied it onto the blank. The name of P. A. Largey, superintendent of the telegraph company, was conspicuously printed at the top of the paper. He penned a brief missive to Donnelly, informing him of his brother's interment and the fate of Boulder Fritz.

"How much?" he asked when Marsh finally stepped over to peruse the message, seemingly unaffected by its contents.

"That will be a dollar and two bits."

Counting out the exact amount on the countertop and picking up his billfold, Collins left the office without another word. His encounter with the German cutthroat had brought on a dour turn of mind and the officious telegrapher set his teeth on edge. Outside, heavy clouds darkened the afternoon sky, befitting his mood. He walked down Broadway, back toward the Centennial, mulling over the fact that he had given his name to Jenny as well as divulged to her he was searching for Boulder Fritz. The most prudent course of action would be to pack his belongings and decamp as soon as he was able.

Once again, C.W. scraped lumps of mud from his boots before entering the hotel lobby. Twilight was swiftly approaching and a young lad was busy lighting oil lamps. Striding purposefully to the front desk, Collins waited for the desk clerk to finish registering a foppish whisky drummer. Unremarkably, the man's occupation was manifestly advertised by a label on his traveling case. An iron grip suddenly took hold of C.W.'s right shoulder and he spun around, ready to do battle.

"Easy fella," a bulky, broad-shouldered man said and pulled his hand away. "Just want to talk a spell. My name is Small. Deputy Sheriff Curtis Small"

Suppressing his annoyance and regarding the man blandly, Collins said, "I have no objection."

Noticing that the clerk had finished with the drummer and was keenly interested in their exchange, the deputy beckoned Collins away from the desk with a gesture. They moved to a quiet corner of the lobby with an unoccupied bench seat. C.W. was cognizant that Sheriff McAndrews kept a full time deputy in Butte City as a matter of expedience, but had never heard his name. He sat down nonchalantly and waited for the deputy to explain himself, fully aware that the topic of discussion would be the premature demise of Boulder Fritz.

Small joined him on the seat. "Are you Charles Collins?"

"Yes."

"It has come to my attention that an altercation took place in Allen's saloon earlier today."

"Yes."

"A scoundrel going by the name of Boulder Fritz is lying dead over there."

"Yes."

"And a loose woman named Inez Maybert says you killed him. Says Jenny Rivers told her you were looking for him. It is how she learned your name."

"Yes."

Deputy Small appeared to be losing patience. "Now see here, fella, the tale is all over down on East Park. Did you murder this Boulder Fritz?"

"I killed him. I did not murder him." Collins was enjoying himself. He did not intend to make the peace officer's job easier.

"Do you mind telling me why you killed him?"

"Of course not," C.W. said, shrugging perfunctorily. "I was hired by a former senator of Minnesota to find his brother's murderer. I suspected Boulder Fritz was guilty of the deed and when I confronted him in the saloon, he verified my suspicions. I made an attempt to apprehend him with the purpose of bringing him back to Deer Lodge for incarceration and trial, but he came at me with a colossal knife and I shot him."

"It seems you shot him twice."

"He came at me twice."

There was a long pause during which it appeared to Collins that the youthful deputy was attempting to preserve his composure. "And what credentials do you possess which would give you the authority to apprehend Fritz and take him into custody?"

Collins ignored the question. "Out of curiosity, might I inquire as to the testimony of the other witnesses in the saloon?"

Noticeably flustered, Small said, "They told me Fritz tried to knife you and you shot him in self-defense."

"That is the long and the short of it. Upon my word."

The deputy eyed him dubiously. "And why is your word any good?"

Antagonized anew, Collins chose not to respond.

"Well? Nothing to say?" Small asked impertinently, as if he thought he had regained some measure of dominance over the parley.

Taking a grip on his rancor and gazing at the deputy with derision, Collins spoke slowly and calmly, as if to an imbecile. "Listen carefully, you sodden-witted pup...I informed the sheriff I was searching for Boulder Fritz. I endeavored to restrain and take him to Deer Lodge. The man would not be taken and assailed me with a great knife. I shot him in the knee, but he came off the floor and went at me again. I shot him in the gut. He was not dead when I went away."

"Did you strike Miss Maybert? She told me you assaulted her."

"Maybert tried to hold my arm so that her sweetheart could cut my throat. I knocked her down." C.W. stood up. "I am leaving now. You have already acknowledged that it was self-defense and I am certain you were previously conscious of the German's shifty character. Yet you are making accusations against me based upon the word of a strumpet. Perhaps Sheriff McAndrews is unaware you have too much time on your hands."

Coming swiftly to his feet, Deputy Small braced him with the intention of using his significant brawn to bullyrag Collins, a tactic that had, no doubt, been previously effective. Fully as tall and almost as broad, Collins stood dispassionately and awaited the deputy's next maneuver. There was a prolonged deadlock, during which Small must have come to the realization that nothing would be gained by squaring off, for he took a step backwards.

"Go on, then," he said pugnaciously. "But you had best report to the sheriff upon your return to Deer Lodge or there will be hell to pay."

"Allow me to make something very plain," Collins said agreeably, as if commenting on the weather. "You cause trouble for me and I will return here. If I do, my dealings with Fritz will seem like a sociable event."

"I am an officer of the law," Deputy Small protested.

Without a rejoinder, Collins strode over to the front desk and told the clerk he would not be staying another night.

"That deputy gets above himself," the clerk said, conspiratorially.

"Do you require additional remuneration?"

"What is that?"

"Do I owe you? I will fetch my belongings now."

Comprehension dawning on his insipid face, the clerk told him there were no other charges. "It is a slack time of year," he said.

Surfeited with idiocy, Collins turned on his heel and climbed the stairs to his room, not bothering to note whether Small remained in the lobby or not.

He surely had made an adversary of the man, but since Sheriff McAndrews already held him in disdain, it did not matter much. After packing his clothing and scanning the room for stray items, he buckled the strap on his carpetbag and left the chamber.

Back down in the lobby, he found that Deputy Small was no longer there. He side-stepped an intoxicated individual at the front entrance and walked into a bitterly glacial night, genuinely desirous of escaping the confines of the overcrowded town and its inhabitants. The old man, Kaspar, was still in attendance at the livery barn. Together they caught, brushed and saddled the gelding.

"You found Fritz." Kaspar said quietly, adjusting and fastening the breast collar.

"Yes."

"Any trouble about it?"

"Some. Not much."

Collins secured his valise on the back of the saddle and led his horse to the front of the barn. "What is the charge?"

"Seventy-five cents."

He handed the hostler six quarters. "I am grateful for your assistance and advice."

"Too much."

"Not enough."

Mounting up, Collins nodded to the elderly German and prodded Ulysses into the gummy quagmire of the street, grown thicker from deepening cold. He rode over to Park Street. Nightly revelers meandered along the thoroughfare, many headed toward the purlieu of brothels and saloons. Certainly, Jenny Rivers would have no scarcity of guests and he wondered idly how long it would take Inez Maybert to latch onto another villain. Several children of both sexes wandered among the throngs, remarkably dirty and clothed in tattered raiments. He knew these youngsters took any type of work, often sold their bodies and endured truncated and squalid lives. Thoughts of the degradation of the human spirit and the toll that poverty and abiding hunger took on men, women and children distressed him mightily.

Sighing, Collins resolutely threw off the persistent Celtic melancholia that had plagued him since the fight. The crowds thinned as he moved out of the business district and, except for the intermittent glow of lamps burning in house windows, the street was sporadically lit by a waxing gibbous moon shining through scuttling clouds. Suddenly, Ulysses reared and pitched to one side. Collins peered into the shadows and discerned a large heap of rags in the middle of the road. He thought he saw it stir a little.

Stepping down from the saddle, he approached the bundle. It scurried to the side until blocked by the wall of an outhouse. The horse snorted and balked at the un-known entity. He wrapped the reins around a fence post beside the shed. Advancing cautiously, C.W. squinted into the blackness and made out a figure, hands raised in supplication.

"I will not harm you," he said gently.

"No hurt, no hurt," came a muffled voice.

"No hurt."

He came closer and knelt down. Beneath a tangled, matted shroud of hair, he could just make out a pale as-pect, evidently Chinese.

"Can you understand me?" he asked.

"No hurt."

"No hurt," he repeated. "I want to help."

"No help. No help."

He edged a bit closer. "I will help. I want to help."

The person let loose a barrage of Chinese words, sob-bing throughout the soliloquy which then ceased abrupt-ly. Collins touched an arm lightly, allowing his hand to rest on the cloth covering. The creature shivered wildly and was reeking with unpleasant odors and was wet and chilled. He guessed it must have been crawling through the muck of the road for a while.

"Come," he said. "Come with me."

"No hurt. No good."

"No hurt."

Collins carefully placed a hand behind the figure and lifted. The person collapsed in a faint and he carried it to his disobliging horse. Calming the animal with soft speech, he managed to balance the frail body on the front of his saddle and swing up. Unsure of what this was or what difficulties may arise from the rescue, he was incapable of abandoning a destitute human being in the freezing filth of a pitiless town.

⎯⎯⎯⎯⎯◦✦◦⎯⎯⎯⎯⎯

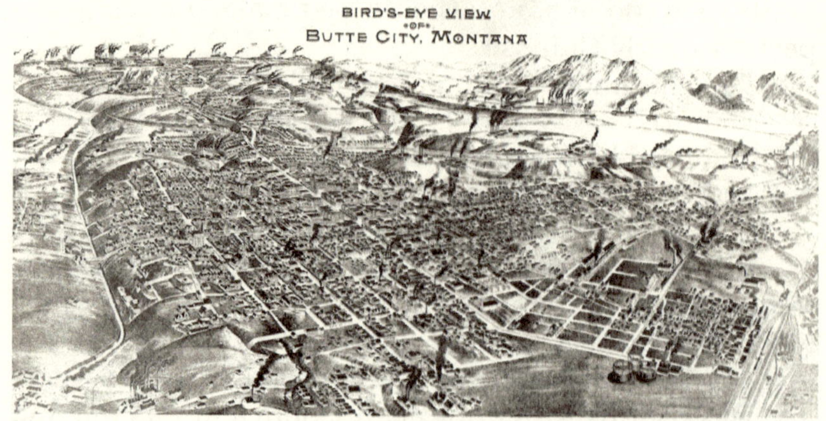

BUTTE CITY MT

10

Wú Peng contemplated the crouched and woebegone personage squatting upon the floorboards, the face obscured by snarls of knotted hair.

"Well Charles, it has a very disagreeable odor," he said.

Collins laughed. "Of this I am assured. I have ridden with the fragrance most of the night. Will you speak with it?"

"Does it speak?"

"It spoke quite a torrent when I first discovered it. Chinese, I am sure. Ascertain if it is female or male at the very least."

The dog hunkered beneath the table, growling persistently at the stooped figure. Collins sat down in a chair and waited patiently.

Speaking slowly and distinctly, Peng addressed their peculiar guest at length. When he had concluded, there was an extended pause. Finally, a timid and protracted response was given.

"Well?" asked C.W.

"This person is female. She was sold by her family in China and was transported here to work as a depraved woman. Her owner in Butte City threw her away over two weeks ago, after cruelly beating her for insolence. She has been hiding and eating from garbage whenever possible."

"How old is she?"

Peng asked the question and she gave a brief answer.

"She does not know for certain, but perhaps sixteen or seventeen years of age. It is not clear how long was her servitude."

"But she appears to be an old crone," Collins said, aghast.

"It is the way of things. These women receive indecorous abuse, are used up precipitously and fed inadequately. She is lucky her master did not kill her outright. When these women are no longer useful, they starve or thrash them to death."

"And her name?"

"The name her mother gave her was Min."

"Does she remember her family's name?"

"She seems to remember it was Li. But perhaps that was the name of her master." Peng shrugged.

"Well, we will call her Li Min. It will suit."

Looking at him askance, Peng said, "What will suit more is a bath. But this requires us to allow her privacy to perform her ablutions."

Finding his friend's propriety amusing, Collins laughed. "How many men do you suppose this girl has been with? Fetch the tub and heat some water and then you may absent yourself if you are delicate. I will assist with the bathing since I do not believe she is able to do a thorough job of it alone."

"Then I will stay as well. Sustenance can be prepared during the procedure and in this way, there will be mutual chaperones in a comportment that is more acceptable."

When the tub was steaming and a clean towel and new cake of soap were at hand, C.W. bent to where Min was huddled in a corner. He took hold of an elbow and lifted her to her feet. Peng spoke to her and she shook her head violently.

"No hurt. No hurt!"

"No hurt. No more," Collins said in soothing tones. "No more," he repeated.

As Peng explained what was intended, Collins slowly removed her soiled garments while the girl shuddered as if buffeted by high winds. When she was finally disrobed, the two men gasped simultaneously. Her ribs made furrows like corduroy under the skin of her torso, her chest was as featureless as that of a young boy and bruises and suppurating wounds overlay a multitude of scars across her back, arms and legs. There was negligible flesh between skin and bones. Unbidden thoughts of the row of cribs in Butte City, and the girl who displayed herself to him, intruded momentarily. Collins gestured toward the galvanized tub. With his assistance, Min lowered herself into the hot water and sat with her arms around her knees, still quaking irrepressibly. Wú Peng made a face and, using a stick of kindling, scooped up her rags and tossed them out the door. Gal, no longer growling, came to sit nearby and survey the proceedings.

Kneeling by the tub, C.W. gingerly washed the girl's back, legs and arms, vigilantly keeping clear of her nether regions and breasts, while Min bowed her head with closed eyes. The girl was categorically stoic about the cleansing of her many cuts and abrasions. Using a comb and scissors, he hewed his way through the wads of hair on her head and scrubbed what remained, bringing some semblance of tidiness, if not fashion. At last, he raised her to her feet, poured clean water over her from a pitcher and gestured for her to step out of the blackened, soapy broth of water that remained in the tub. Astonished by how small she was, he found her to be far too childlike to inspire even the slightest prurience and he wondered what sort of contemptible men could have found pleasure in the tiny body. Her face was, by contrast, starkly haggard, careworn and bereft of innocence. He patted her dry and Peng gave him ointment to dab on her injuries. Together they dressed the girl in one of Collins' cotton flannel undershirts and it fell below her knees.

A delicious aroma permeated the room and Peng led Min to the table and bade her sit. He ladled soup into a bowl and placed it before her along with a saucer of rice. Her large black eyes, heretofore benumbed and expressing no emotion aside from fear, gazed at the dishes, seemingly mesmerized by the food. Peng sat down beside her and laid a set of chopsticks on the table before her, motioning that she could eat. Collins sat across the table and observed.

Tentatively, Min picked up the chopsticks and lifted the dish of rice to beneath her chin. All at once, she began to shovel the rice into her mouth at an alarming rate.

"Slow her down," Collins said, concerned the girl would make herself sick.

Reaching over, Peng placed gentle fingers on her hands and lowered them. He said something in Chinese and pushed the bowl of soup closer, offering her the spoon. Refusing to take it, she picked up the bowl and drank its contents in entirety.

"She is a very stubborn creature," he said, shaking his head.

"Or merely a very hungry girl," Collins said. "I believe she would take more soup if you gave it to her."

When Peng went to the stove to get the pot, Min scooped the rest of the rice into her mouth and glanced at C.W., as if to see whether he was angry. He smiled at her and she managed to chew and swallow the bulges in her cheeks. Peng ladled more soup and when he saw the rice was gone, he gave the girl a disparaging squint. Collins thought he caught an impish spark in her eyes, but could not be certain. She ate the soup more slowly and used the spoon, so Peng gave her more rice and some tea, then fixed eggs and toasted bread for Collins' breakfast and egg and rice for his own. As C.W. finished his meal, he saw that Min was swaying to and fro in an effort to stay awake.

"She should sleep now, Charles." Peng said, between bites.

"How shall we arrange this?"

"I will prepare a pallet for myself down here and she may have my bed upstairs."

Peng arranged a corner by the stove, placing folded blankets and a quilt in a stack. Gal climbed onto the pile and curled up. While Peng was attempting to coax her off, Collins guided Min up the stairs and pointed at the bed.

"No good, no good," she said forcefully, plainly misunderstanding. Her body was rigid with arms crossed over her chest and she was scowling in apparent rage. The girl commenced a tirade in Chinese.

By shaking his head vigorously and mimicking sleep, he tried to make her comprehend his intentions. Peng ran up the stairs and spoke to her sharply, silencing her diatribe. Min climbed into bed and pulled the covers over her chin. Collins saw tears welling in her eyes as she looked from him to Peng and back. He reached out to stroke her raggedy hair.

"How do I say, 'you are safe?' in Chinese?"

"*Nǐ hěn ānquán.*"

"Nee hen anchan."

Placing a hand over his mouth, Peng suppressed his mirth. "That is acceptable," he finally said.

Collins looked at Min, whose face was now almost completely hidden beneath a blanket. Her dark eyes were trained on him. Slowly the lids closed and her breathing changed.

"She will sleep now," Peng said. "We must attend to the animals."

Outside, Collins saw that the sun had risen above the mountains. He caught Felix the mule and led him to the barn while Wú Peng headed for a fenced stack to fork hay down to the other horses and mules. As C.W. harnessed the giant draft mule, he caught himself thinking about Min with unaccustomed sentiment. Disconcerted, he paused and frowned, examining the animal's bristly mane as if elucidation could be found there. Not inclined toward paternal instincts, aside from those regarding his animals, Collins realized these impulses were now directed toward the diminutive Chinese girl.

Ever guarded when it came to females, he shook off these superfluous and maudlin inclinations and ground-drove the mule out of the barn and over to the hay wagon. They would have to find her a position with a family in town, he decided. James Mills was bound to know of an appropriate place.

Meanwhile, he mused, he would remain aloof and she would be able to regain her strength and equilibrium. As far as he was concerned, nothing could possibly be gained from forming an affectionate bond. *Mairg léigeas a rún le mnaoi.* Woe to him that gives his trust to a woman.

11

"Damn," said Captain James Mills, slapping his knee for emphasis. "I should have printed various theories of Heenal and Donnelly's demise. Why in hell did I trust the word of that chuckleheaded McTague?" He rubbed his forehead in frustration. "If only you had brought this news in time for yesterday's edition."

Tentatively sipping some of Mills' vile coffee, Collins grinned. "No worries. You now have occasion to amend your blunders with an exclusive account of Fritz' inopportune end...as long as you leave my name out of it, of course."

The woman, Cora, was busily sorting type and appeared to be completely oblivious to their discussion.

Mills gave him a sharp look. "Why would I keep your name out of it? You are the hero of the hour."

"I do not wish to court unwarranted attention nor the ire of Sheriff McAndrews." He paused and shook an imperious finger at Mills. "I mean it, James. You are not to publish my name in connection to Fritz or the crime. I value my privacy and do not care to invite scrutiny, especially in the interest of shielding Peng and the girl."

Pretending to be distracted with shuffling newsprint around on an adjacent table, Mills said, "Ah yes, the girl. What is it you intend for her?"

"Are you playing coy with me?" C.W. asked scornfully. "She is to be placed in a good home here in Deer Lodge."

The captain looked up. "She is a Butte City whore.

Even a Chinese family would not take her."

"I had not considered that," Collins said, feeling moderately doltish. "Surely it is not the girl's fault."

Looking to the heavens in exasperation, Mills said, "I never fully comprehended the extent of your naivete." He crossed his arms and examined his friend a long minute. "Every civilization values their virgin women. Do you suppose a Chinese wife, such as the 'little footed' woman whom Gem Kee recently married, would welcome a dissolute girl into her household? And besides, there are very few bona fide Chinese families in Deer Lodge, mostly just bachelor men."

Unwilling to concede that he was to be perpetually encumbered with a hapless waif, Collins said, "There must be one kind soul in the entirety of this town's Chinese population."

The dog, Gal, sat up and energetically scratched an ear with her hind foot.

"Sorry, my dear Charles, but you must realize that Celestials all over western territories are enduring belligerent hostility. Even if you could find someone to take her in, she would not necessarily enjoy abiding security." Mills gave him a cynical grin. "No doubt you could find a kind soul who would subject her to an existence similar to that from which she escaped. Otherwise, you are stuck with her."

Sighing theatrically, C.W. shook his head. "My good deed has become indentured servitude."

Mills stood to pour more coffee. "What are the difficulties?" he asked, sitting down again. "Peng could use the help. And perhaps a sympathetic fondness will grow. You are a confirmed bachelor, but is Wú Peng?"

"Can you not see the potential for disaster? The girl's true nature has yet to be revealed."

"Come now, Charles, she is a poor victim of terrible circumstance. I know you. You simply do not desire to have your life upended."

"Perhaps not. But neither did I intend to found an aid society for wayward Chinese."

Mills laughed. "You have benefited greatly from Peng's arrival."

"I can see I will receive no benevolent commiseration here," C.W. said, coming to his feet. "I must now subject myself to the calumniations of Sheriff McAndrews."

The captain stood up and patted his shoulder. "He may bellow and bluster, but the case for self-defense is plain. And I will blast him in my paper if he endeavors to vilify you."

An idea suddenly occurred to Collins. "What of you and your wife? You could take the girl in."

"Not a hell's chance. Ella May is a generous woman, but I am certain that would be a line in the sand. No, my friend, the girl is your cross to bear and yours alone."

"I am not your friend...for you are not mine," Collins said as he made his way to the door, the dog on his heels.

"Come by for supper, if you have conquered your sulk," Mills called after him.

Ulysses was tethered to a rail across the street, in front of E.L Bonner and Company. Leaving him where he was, Collins and Gal walked over to the jailhouse. Upon entering, he saw that the sheriff was not at his desk, but one of the cells was occupied by a young man in shirt-sleeves, seated on a solitary narrow bedstead.

"Ain't here."

"Pardon me?" Collins asked.

"Fucking sheriff ain't here. You a pal of his?"

"Not particularly."

"That your dog?"

This seemed a remarkably odd question. "Yes."

"I had a dog." The incarcerated fellow got off his bunk and came to the bars. "Good dog too. Brainy dog."

C.W. stood in the middle of the room looking at the

man.

"Goddamn neighbor killed that dog," the jail-bird continued. "Killed that dog deader'n shit."

Now convinced the orator was not quite *compos mentis*, Collins remained silent. Gal pressed against his leg, as if following the discourse.

"Don't seem like you give a shit 'bout my dog, mister."

The door opened and McAndrews came in, with his spaniel close behind. "Hope you are not disturbing my prisoner," he said, taking off his coat and flinging it on a chair. "He is not right in the head."

"I noticed."

The sheriff sat behind his desk and began sorting through the pile of mail he had brought with him. The canines engaged in a ritual of sniffing and posturing.

"He don't give a shit about my dog," the prisoner complained.

"Shut up, Edmond," McAndrews said. "No one gives two shits about your dog."

Edmond seemed to accept this rebuke and lay down on his bunk.

"Heard you caught up with Boulder Fritz," the sheriff said off-handedly, while continuing to examine the stack of letters and flyers.

"Yes. In Butte City."

"Deputy Small sent a telegram."

"I have no doubt that he did."

McAndrews looked up at him. "Said it was self-defense."

"Which it was."

"And you were certain Fritz had committed the crime?" the sheriff asked.

"He said as much."

Leaning back in his chair, McAndrews studied him. "You are not planning to embark on another bloody excursion any time soon, are you?" he asked after a while.

"No."

"Well then, I have nothing to reproach you with."

"You should know that Phil Heenal is still in residence, last I was aware. Frozen but pungent."

"O'Neill will fetch him before long," the sheriff said indifferently, returning to perusal of his mail.

Taking a curious last glance at Edmond, now reclining with his back to the room and talking to himself, Collins left the jail. The late morning had grown inclement. Pellets of ice were coming sideways from the northwest and he sheltered his face with an arm until he rounded the corner of Bonner's emporium. The gelding was protected on the leeside of the building and he was glad to find his saddle was not overly wet. He wiped the seat with a coat sleeve and mounted up.

He rode down Second Street and over to Third. In the past months, the Chinese quarter of Deer Lodge City had grown to occupy the entire patch of ground behind the McBurney Hotel. The Zheng Bai enterprise had been eclipsed by Kim Chung Lung & Company, a two-story dry goods and grocery establishment. Several other businesses, a joss house, cabins and modest frame houses crowded the alley that bisected the district. Collins was pleased that Wú Peng, albeit westernized, had opportunities for broadened contact with more of his countrymen. Unfortunately, there had also been an increase in the smoking of opium, by both Americans and Chinamen, affording yet another excuse for localized antagonism toward the tiny community.

Tying Ulysses to a post outside Kim Chung Lung & Company, Collins told his dog to stay with the horse and entered the building. It was amply lit by several windows and abundant with all manner of goods. Shelves, jam-packed with porcelain dishes and comestibles, lined every wall, while draperies, rugs, silks and various other items were suspended from the ceiling. In spite of the superfluity of merchandise, when he located a corner that displayed feminine attire, there was very little of it. A Chinese gentleman came out from behind a counter and joined him. His traditional clothing consisted of a three-quarter length quilted jacket worn over an ankle length skirt and his shaved head was covered by a brimless silk kepi. The costume was colorful and immaculate.

"May I give help?" he asked, bowing formally.

"I require practical clothing for a very small woman."

The Chinaman walked into a back room and returned with an aged white man. His beard and eyebrows were snowy and remarkably bushy, his skin was brown leather and he peered out from beneath a bulky knit cap favored by sailors. The two men conversed in Mandarin, then the old-timer turned to Collins.

"Name's Mr. Oliver. This here's Gem Kee. You yammer at me so's I can pass along your musts," he said in an accent that C.W. identified as a blend of Cockney and some other foreign tongue.

"Very well. I require clothing suitable for an adolescent girl. Nothing cumbersome or impractical."

"You be wantin' Chinee gear?"

"Yes, that was the idea."

Mr. Oliver spoke to Gem Kee. He slipped behind a curtain and returned in a couple of minutes, holding out a small collection of folded garments.

"Very nice," Gem Kee told him.

Collins accepted the bundle.

"Suit you?" Oliver asked, almost belligerently.

Since Collins had no idea what would suit him in regards to Chinese female fashions, he said, "Yes. Thank you. *Xièxiè.*"

Mr. Oliver told Collins what amount to tender, a noticeably dear sum, while Gem Kee wrapped the clothing in a tidy package. He thanked them once more and departed the store. The sky had cleared and he was pleased that his ride home would not be as unpleasant as he had anticipated. As he rode out of town, C.W. brooded over his new obligations. Somehow, he would have to weave Li Min into the fabric of the ranch or take her back to Butte City. He truly did not wish to do either.

CHINATOWN

12

When Collins awoke early in the morning, Li Min was already busy, almost noiselessly moving around the cabin. A fire crackled in the cookstove and she was carrying firewood in from the stack on the porch. Upon his return home the night before, Wú Peng had informed him the girl had scrubbed every inch of the house. When Collins sat up, he was promptly handed a mug of fresh coffee. He saw that she was still clothed in the undershirt, the waist now gathered by a piece of rope. Her feet were bare and he chided himself for a simpleton to have forgotten footwear.

Raising the mug, he nodded his thanks.

"Happy," she told him and bowed.

"Peng?" he asked.

Min pointed at the door.

While Collins dressed, the girl kept her back to him, occupying herself among pots and pans. Gal bounced around the room, getting in the way and whining, quite ready to begin the day. The door opened and Peng came in, stooped under the weight of two galvanized buckets, sloshing water. Even though it was still dark, C.W. felt a pang of guilt that he had slept later than his two roommates. He sat at the table with his coffee and watched Min preparing rice, tea and scrambled eggs. Peng joined him.

"She is working very diligently," he said. "I believe she is frightened you will wish to send her away."

Li Min brought a pot of tea and cup for Peng.

"Were you able to procure a position for her in Deer Lodge City?"

"No. Our friend, Captain Mills, made it patently clear that no respectable household would have her, Chinese or otherwise."

C.W. packed his pipe and Li Min hastily brought a match, striking it on the tabletop and holding it in readiness. He accepted the gesture, smiling at the girl. A fleeting bow and transitory quiver of her lips was his reward.

"Any suggestions?" Collins asked his companion.

"There are many unmarried Chinese miners. Perhaps we would be able to find a willing husband who does not entertain reluctance with regard to the girl's earlier vocation."

"But would such a man treat her well?"

"No Charles. I do not believe so."

Rubbing the back of his neck in consternation, C.W. knew he would be forced to accede to the inevitable. Having delivered the girl from starvation, abject ruination and quite probably death, he had acquiesced to personal responsibility for her welfare. He could no more cleave her to an arbitrary husband, nor consign her to a continuing life as a prostitute, than he could have abandoned Gal on the Kansas prairie when she had come to him for succor. He puffed hard on his briar and realized his friend was watching him closely.

"We are agreed then?" he asked the Chinaman.

Wú Peng nodded.

"I purchased some clothing. I am not certain it is appropriate or the correct size." He got up and removed the package from under his bed.

Li Min brought plates of food and he laid the parcel on the empty chair beside him. Peng spoke to her and Min brought a dish for herself, sitting next to him. They ate in silence. When the plates had been cleared, Collins beckoned the girl to his side and handed her the package. Her eyes became very large as she held the bundle before her, resting upon open palms. He nodded at her and she sat down, laying the parcel on the table and untying the string that bound it with utter attentiveness and deliberation. When the unprepossessing garments were finally revealed, Min inhaled sharply, holding up a simple jade green tunic and roomy trousers, decorated with embroidered yellow flowers down the sides of the legs. There were also some undergarments. She gazed at Collins and tears began to stream down her cheeks.

"Shall I now tell her she will not be sent away?" Peng asked.

"Yes," C.W. answered gruffly.

When Peng had finished speaking to her, Li Min flung herself at Collins' feet, laying her forehead on the toes of his boots and grasping his ankles. He stood and lifted her to her feet. Peng said something and she bowed. Gathering the clothing in her arms, she bounded up the stairs to her room.

"She will dress," Peng said.

"Since she is here for good and all, we must provide her a place of her own."

"Perhaps we may make a congenial arrangement in the contiguous shed. Many tools are able to reside in the barn."

"Excellent notion. Let us embark upon the task today."

They heard the girl coming downstairs. Li Min's hair remained a tousled disarray, the results of Collins' handiwork, but she had been transformed, by unmistakable joy and suitable attire, into a lovely young woman. Her saturnine countenance was metamorphosed into one more befitting her age.

Both men spontaneously applauded, propelling the dog into a fit of silliness. She began barking, dodging here and there and racing around the room. The girl sat on the bottom step and covered her face with her hands. Concerned, C.W. went to her and was dismayed to see her trembling. When he touched her lightly on the shoulder, she looked up and he could see she was silently laughing, even though her cheeks were once again wet with tears.

"Happy," she told him, once more hurling herself at his boots, kneeling before him.

"No, no, no" Collins said, thoroughly discomfited.

Wú Peng came to his rescue, speaking to her and gently pulling her away. He led her to the table, poured her a cup of tea and patted her head.

"I forgot shoes," Collins said.

"It is fortunate her feet were not bound before she was sold."

"If she was sold, would that not mean she came from a peasant family?"

"Sometimes even rustic persons bind the feet. Especially if they intend to sell the daughter."

"Barbarous."

"It is exceedingly barbarous, yet Chinese men swoon at the sight of tiny feet, such as Mr. Gem Kee in Deer Lodge City."

"And you?"

"As an educated modern person, I do not espouse such practices."

"Well, Li Min still requires shoes."

"Yes. I am able to manufacture a serviceable pair of slippers. There is a quantity of feed sacks in the barn loft."

The two men left the girl to adjust to her new clothing and went out to feed animals and check on the cattle. They each hurried through their separate chores, haste encouraged by a freezing wind and heavy snow. It was quite cold and the trodden places, where snow had melted the day before, had become frozen ridges and furrows of ankle twisting topography.

It was almost noon when they were finished. Peng and Collins warmed up by the stove and fortified themselves with hot drinks and a simple meal.

Min was entirely preoccupied with her new apparel, stroking the front of the tunic and closely examining the embroidered flowers.

"Jesus, Mary and Joseph...Peng, please tell her there will be more clothes...that this outfit is not her last."

Peng began an extended monologue in Chinese. At first Min did not appear to be listening, but eventually she began to pay attention. Her expression conveyed anguish and she asked a question in a very strident manner.

"What is she saying?" Collins asked with vexation "You truly need to teach her English."

"Li Min is not believing that she may receive gifts without providing the same...ministrations required previously."

"Oh for..." Collins stood up and paced around the room. "Would you be so kind as to inform her there will be none of that? Not ever or for any reason." He sat back down and drummed his fingers on the tabletop with exasperation.

"But Charles, she does not know any better. She *has* not known any better," Peng said mildly.

C.W. was compelled to acknowledge that Peng was doubtlessly correct in this. How could the girl trust that her circumstances would not suddenly degenerate into a more accustomed system of barter? Especially while rooming with two men.

"Yes of course. Please reassure her that she will earn her keep in other ways."

Li Min was standing motionless, watching Collins. The Chinaman talked to the girl in a measured tone. Slowly and palpably, her rigid stance relaxed. It appeared as if she were about to again propel herself at C.W.'s feet when Peng intercepted her.

"We have to break her of that." Collins said.

Peng spoke to the girl with a commanding air. She bowed her head and stared at the floor, then lifted her eyes and looked at Collins with a combination of beseeching and sorrow. It was all he could do to keep from enfolding her in a Platonic embrace, but he was vehemently opposed to becoming emotionally ensnared by this slip of a girl. If he could not be rid of her, then he would keep his distance.

"Let us get to fixing accommodations," he told Peng.

While Collins transported tools and equipment from the shed to the barn, with Gal in constant attendance, Peng measured Li Min's feet and set about making footwear. During one of his trips back and forth, making a trail through crusts of snow, the dog became occupied with poking her nose into one of the drifts along the side of the building. Out of curiosity, Collins went to see what she had discovered. He caught sight of ginger colored fur and reached past Gal to remove a limp feline body from the snowbank, recognizing one of his favorite barn cats. It was dead, but not quite frozen.

Cradling the small body, Collins waded through deep snow to a copse of trees in the horse pasture. The mules and horses wandered over to spectate as he placed the cat high up in the crook of a tree. The ground was rock hard and so he gave the little animal a burial of sorts, along the order of certain Indian tribes who placed their dead on scaffolds or in trees. Making his way back toward the house, the equines trailing behind, he pondered the brevity and fragility of life. He felt certain that Li Min would have gone the way of the cat, had he not found her. Despite the devout certainty of theologians and his Catholic mother, the random nature of fate seemed to him to be immutable.

When the shed had been cleared of excess clutter, Collins fashioned a sleeping platform from apple crates, which he padded with an old bedroll and covered with extra blankets and a thick quilt that had been stored in the shed. He determined to take a wagon to town when the roads cleared, so that he would be able to procure a bedstead and mattress, shoes and other articles for the Chinese girl. Funds were pending from Ignatius Donnelly and an abundance of other supplies were needed as well.

Wú Peng opened the door that led to the house and peered into the annex. "It is exceedingly frigid in there. And most unwholesome."

"The girl can scrub it out. Does she have shoes now?"

"Exceptional footwear. Li Min has made fresh coffee. Come in and you may admire my handiwork."

They sat at the table and the girl served them coffee and a plate of bean buns.

"These are delicious," Collins said to Peng, reaching for a second bun.

"Li Min made them."

"She can cook something other than eggs?"

"It is surprising, when considering where she has been."

The girl came over and lifted a foot so that Collins could see her new slippers. They were fashioned of what looked to be old bean sacks with deerskin soles.

"Very handsome," he told Peng, smiling.

"Very hannnsome," Li Min mimicked.

"She will learn English most quickly," Peng said.

"Tell her she may begin scouring out her new abode."

Peng addressed the girl, passing along Collins' wishes. She shook her head and pointed to her clothing. Peng spoke again and she ran upstairs.

"She says she will not work in her new beautiful clothing. I told her to open the trunk and find an old shirt and pants."

When Li Min returned, she wore a baggy shirt and pants rolled up several times. Her old length of rope held the ludicrous outfit together. She cheerfully fetched a broom and some rags and went into the shed, closing the door after her.

"Have you learned any of her history?"

"She is from a small rice farm near Huangdu village in Shandong Province. There occurred a drought a few years ago and then came a great famine. That is when her family sold her to the Hip Yee Tong and she was conveyed to San Francisco. From there she was purchased by a man named Ah Quong and transported to Butte City, where she was sold to a new master."

"But she has no notion of the number of her years in servitude?"

"Previous to her family's dereliction, Li Min remembers *chángshòu miàn*, longevity noodles, for a tenth birthday. Not long after came the famine and she was sent away. Consequently, if she is approximately sixteen years of age now, she was captive for many years."

The girl emerged from her new room and filled a pail with hot water from the reservoir on the cookstove. She bustled back through the door and the dog followed her. It seemed to Collins that Gal was becoming quite fond of the Chinese urchin.

"Longevity noodles?" he asked.

"Uncut noodles that signify long life. They are uncommonly fortunate and a very old tradition for Chinese people."

"For birthdays?"

"It is said this began with Emperor Wu of the Han Dynasty."

Finishing the last bun, Collins thought about birthdays and noodles. "So she would be ten years of age in addition to the years she was...the years she spent in captivity."

"We begin our first birthday on the day we are born, therefore in American estimation, Li Min would have been probably eleven years, if she is correct."

There was a great deal of commotion and barking and Gal trotted in with Li Min behind, carrying the bucket and broom.

"You come," she said firmly.

The two men obediently followed Li Min into her new domain. The back door and lone window were open and clean cold air purged all musty odors and dinginess. The makeshift bed was rearranged and the girl had unearthed a threadbare saddle blanket from somewhere and it now lay upon the floor.

"Good?" she asked eagerly.

"Good," Collins told her, smiling. He thought briefly of this child being wrenched from her mother's arms and sold into an unforeseeable and appalling destiny. Human cruelty knew no constraints.

Peng said, "*Fēicháng hǎo de gōngzuò*. Excellent work."

"Eggcellent werk," Li Min repeated and smiled her very first smile since coming to the ranch.

CHINESE QUESTION

13

"Confucius professed that people at birth are naturally good. It is reasonable to believe that Li Min remains so in spite of her lamentable past," Wú Peng said.

"Even so, we risk calamity by either leaving her behind or bringing her to town."

Joey stood beside them, already hitched to the buckboard. Gal was perched on the spring seat as if prepared to drive.

"She has been with us several days now and may be fully trustworthy. It is infinitely more prudent to leave her here than carry Min to a place where a man may recognize her from before."

"I suppose you are correct in this," Collins said. "But you must make it very plain that she is to stay in the house and answer the door for no one."

"I will make it exceedingly manifest that she is to attend to her duties, conceal her person from strangers and make no annoyance in any manner."

Peng walked back to the house to provide instructions to the Chinese girl while C.W. loaded empty crates and several grain sacks into the wagon bed.

The snow had moderated to a degree and the road had become passable. Relying on the prospect that Donnelly's remuneration had arrived in the mail, in response to the telegram sent from Butte City, he was planning on resupplying animal feed, flour, salt, sugar and other basic foodstuffs, as well as Peng's requirements for

Chinese recipes. He also intended to purchase various items for Li Min; especially warm clothing and a decent bed. He joined Gal in the buckboard and awaited the Chinaman's reappearance.

"There will be no tribulations on the occasion of our homecoming. Li Min has made a solemn vow," Peng said upon returning. He climbed onto the wagon seat.

"Get up there," Collins said, releasing the brake and slapping the lines lightly on Joey's rump. "Pray there is a home to come back to," he said wryly, as the mule leaned into the harness.

The wagon plowed through piles of dirty slush through the main gate and onto the road to Deer Lodge City. The sun had just appeared above the ridges of the mountains to the east. The sky was cloudless and barely a breeze stirred among the skeletal trees that bordered the river. Joey moved along at a lively gait and the journey was pleasant. Peng and Collins discussed strategies for improving the ranch, breeds of cattle, history and philosophy. They arrived in town by mid morning. After a visit to Gilmer, Salisbury and Company, where he found a letter and generous cheque from Ignatius Donnelly, Collins made straight for the bank. Now flush with capital, he drove Peng to the Chinese quarter then headed for Mr. Bien's furniture store.

It was nearing dusk by the time Collins and Wú Peng had loaded the buckboard with all their purchases and provisions, secured the load with a canvas tarp and headed out of Deer Lodge City. Sinister clouds were building over the Flint Creek range in the west and the breeze was growing in intensity.

Soon the setting sun was completely obscured. The skies grew murky and most of the remaining light of day was in retreat. With a sense of foreboding, C.W. urged the mule into a quicker pace, but only a few miles along the road they were engulfed by a broadside of snow driven by ferocious and unrelenting winds.

Pulling in the mule, Collins secured his Stetson with his neck scarf and handed the lines to Peng. He climbed down from the wagon and burrowed around under the seat for woolen blankets, which he handed up to the Chinaman. He stuffed Gal under the tarp in the wagon box, told her to stay and walked around to Joey's head. The animal was distraught, rearing and tugging at the lines and C.W. thought it best to navigate on foot, lest they lose their way. Trapped as they were in an unmitigated blizzard, he debated whether they should attempt to make it back to town, but thought better of it. The girl would be terrified, alone and unaided. It would not do to weaken.

Steadying himself by holding onto the mule's bridle, Collins fought to withstand the onslaught of the tempest. Becoming almost totally blinded by nightfall and impenetrable veils of white, he stumbled along the road, making use of frozen wagon ruts for his guide. Several times, he tripped and would have gone down were it not for his hold on Joey. Occasionally he would glance back at Peng, merely a hunched spectral figure upon the wagon seat, and wondered whether the two of them would survive the night.

An eternity of benumbed extremities, exhaustion, piercing cold and nauseating vertigo finally wore Collins down and he drew up the mule. His legs buckled and he collapsed into the snow beside Joey's front hooves, uncaring as to any eventual consequence. All of a sudden, fists were pummeling his back and a voice was shouting through the haze of incomprehension. Rousing himself to the insistence of the assault, he came to his senses and realized that the assailant was Peng, desperately working to revive him. The Chinaman wrapped one of the blankets around his shoulders and bent down to offer himself as a buttress. C.W. got to his knees and, making use of Joey's bridle and Peng's support, he was able to stand.

"Very nearly home," the Chinaman yelled in his ear. "Very nearly home."

Patting his friend on the arm, Collins nodded emphatically and waved for him to climb back up on the buckboard. When Peng was situated, he endeavored to haul the reluctant mule along, one step after another. He noticed a dark margin of shadow on his left that he thought might be brakes of cottonwood trees along the river. If this were so then they were, indeed, close to the ranch. His spirits emboldened, Collins labored obdurately through knee-deep drifts until he collided with a gate post. Almost undone with relief, he realized they had made it. The mule brayed loudly and was answered by Felix or Molly. With renewed strength, he opened the gate and led Joey and the wagon through.

Somehow, with stiffened and unresponsive fingers, Collins unhitched Joey from the buckboard and led him into the barn. Wú Peng fumbled around until he had lit a railroad lantern and its kindly and welcome radiance filled the building. Slender shafts of white made a pattern across the floor where the blizzard had thrust snow through gaps in the walls. The wind whistled eerily between the cracks, wanting to enter their sanctuary, as if distraught they had escaped its clutches. Gal jumped from her shelter in the wagon bed and sat quietly just inside, licking a paw and shivering. Together, Peng and C.W. clumsily unharnessed the mule and placed him in a stall, filling the hay bunk and brushing ice from his back and neck.

"This mule saved our lives," Wú Peng said gravely.

"He did indeed."

"You saved our lives as well," he added.

"I do believe you saved mine," Collins told him. "Thank you, my friend."

Peng shook his head. "Your courage and obstinacy were our deliverance." He fetched the lamp from where it was suspended on a hook. "Come, let us discover how Li Min has fared."

Peng carried the lantern and Collins carried the dog as they floundered their way across the ranch yard toward a faint glimmer of light coming from the house. Halfway there, a figure came hurdling out of the darkness, throwing itself upon them and causing the dog to fall from Collins' arms and begin barking furiously. The Chinese girl took C.W.'s arm and practically dragged him onto the porch. Peng and Gal came up behind them.

"Mr. Charles...oh Mr. Charles," the girl sobbed, then began wailing in Mandarin.

Peng opened the door and shoved them all through, the dog expeditiously making for her favorite corner. Inside, the exquisite warmth of the stove made Collins momentarily giddy. Casting off the quilt in which she had swaddled herself, Li Min took their coats, hats and gloves and placed them on a chair beside the stove to dry. Still weeping, her face glistening with tears, she motioned for them to sit at the table. Soon, bowls of soup and scalding cups of tea were before them. Collins saw that a great amount of firewood had been split and stacked behind the cookstove.

"Did you teach her to chop wood?" he asked Peng skeptically.

"Yes. She learns very quickly."

As the chill loosened its grip in his core and hot tea reinvigorated his mind, C.W. found that he was overwhelmed with gratitude at their salvation. It had been a near thing and now that his little clan was once more intact, he gave himself over to familial affection for his Chinese companions. Beckoning the girl and gesturing to the chair beside him, he bade her sit. Taking her petite hand in his, he smiled at her. Peng observed the proceedings with interest.

"Very good, Li Min," Collins told her, finally relinquishing all his objections to the child's presence. "Excellent work."

Sinking into another bout of tears, Li Min hid her face in her unencumbered hand. "*Guǐhún*," she said, through sobs. "*Guǐhún*," she said again.

Collins looked helplessly at the Chinaman, who shrugged.

"You were very good," he said again and squeezed Min's hand.

She wrenched it free and sprang out of the chair, running up the stairs and leaving both men staring after her.

"What did I do?" Collins asked, after a moment of astonished perplexity.

"One must ponder the vagaries of female behavior," Peng said and poured more tea.

14

Coming in from feeding the cattle, hoping that Min had prepared a hearty dinner, Collins found that the house had been thoroughly cleaned. The floor had been scoured and freshly laundered curtains and bed clothes were drying on ropes stretched across the ceiling above the stove. The windows sparkled and red paper designs were pasted on several of the panes. Two red paper lanterns were suspended above the table. Wú Peng came down the stairs carrying the dustpan and broom. He opened the firebox on the stove to throw in the rubbish from his sweeping.

"Just toss it out the door," C.W. said, annoyed that the girl was no where in sight nor was his noon meal.

"That would be a very unfortunate act," Peng told him, hanging the broom and pan on their respective nails behind the stove.

Collins poured himself a cup of coffee, grateful for that at least, and sat at the table with Gal at his feet. He took out his briar and pouch, hoping to curb his appetite with a smoke.

"And why would that be unfortunate?"

"*Chūnjié*. Chinese New Year. To throw the contents of that which is captured by the broom outside the house would ensure that there would be much parting with wealth in the year to come." Peng joined him at the table.

Thoroughly confused, C.W. smoked his pipe and brooded over the fact that his home had been invaded by Chinese food, traditions and oddities. The front door swung open and Min came in, dressed in the shapeless shirt and rolled up pants and wearing the canvas slippers Peng had made. She carried a bundle of washing, which she took to her room. When she returned, she ran over to Collins.

"Oh Mr. Charles, look...*Chuānghuā*." She pointed to the red paper cut outs on the windows.

"Where are your shoes?" he asked irritably. "*Xié?*" Peng said.

"Shooz," Min said. She looked at her feet. "No shooz for..." she looked at Peng and asked a question.

"*Gōngzuò*," he said. "Work."

"No shooz for werk."

Peng had gone over to the stove and was filling a plate from a large pot under the warming oven. He brought it to Collins. "Stew," he announced.

"Thank you. I thought I had been left to starve." He made a comical grimace at the girl.

Li Min covered her mouth, but her eyes showed humor. It seemed to Collins she smiled more now and had even laughed once or twice. Laying aside his pipe and beginning to eat, he found he was no longer displeased. Peng sat with him, drinking tea. The girl watched him expectantly.

"Very pretty," he said between bites and nodding at the windows. "What are their purpose?"

"*Chuānghuā*," Peng told him. "Traditional decorations for the new year."

Min pointed to the lanterns. "*Dēnglóng*."

"It is well past the new year," Collins said, again not grasping the caprices of his Chinese companions.

"It is the Chinese New Year. At the termination of January came the year of the snake. It was the first day."

Finishing his meal and pushing his chair back to cross his legs, Collins frowned at the Chinaman. "The first day?"

"Oh yes, the celebrations last many days, but only for a very small interlude will there be disturbance here."

Li Min brought the big graniteware pot over to pour C.W. more coffee. Her expression was full of inquiry as she looked from him to Peng.

"You must explain all this more fully," Collins said. "I do not know about such things and you are being mortifyingly abstruse."

Peng motioned for Li Min to sit with them at the table. He spoke to the girl and filled a cup of tea, which he placed in front of her. "I told her she must learn English as quickly as possible," he said. "So now, we may begin."

"Never mind about the English language lesson for now," Collins said, again losing patience. "Will you please enlighten me in regards to this new year's muddle?"

"Sorry Charles...yes I am certainly required to enlighten you as to the particulars of this most auspicious time in the Chinese calendar."

"Thank you."

"Our months begin with the new moon. Therefore, the new year begins on the first new moon between winter solstice and spring equinox. This year, according to the American calendar, it was last Sunday. Therefore, Li Min and I have cleaned the house and decorated with the lucky color red to bring good fortune and so that the beast, *Nian*, will not come to destroy the ranch and eat all the cows."

"*Nian!*" Min said. "No good...no good, Mr. Charles."

"I had understood you to have been well educated, my friend." Collins said to Peng. "You truly believe some mythical creature will come to eat our cattle?"

"Surely not. However, it is great amusement to pretend. And as our Li Min has not had a very happy life, I desired to offer her a traditional new year and the affiliated joy."

Collins considered a moment. "I think it is a grand idea."

"That is most providential...for all Chinese people in Deer Lodge City and the vicinity have been offered an invitation to a prodigious celebration in honor of the year of the snake."

"Who tendered the invitation?"

"Mr. Gem Kee, proprietor of Kim Chung Lung & Company, has provided the invitation. I would be most indebted if you were to allow me to escort Li Min to the festivities."

The girl was gazing at the two men, first one then the other, as if attempting to decipher their conversation. Her entire demeanor was resonant with anticipation.

Crossing his arms, Collins glowered at the Chinaman in displeasure. "How many times must I say that you do not require permission to engage in your own pursuits? Of course both of you should attend."

Misreading his countenance, the girl patted his arm. "Okay, okay, Mr. Charles."

Peng said something in Chinese. A smile lit up her face and she clapped her hands together in delight. "*Xièxiè, Xièxiè!*" She patted C.W.'s arm again several times.

"When is this new year soiree?" he asked.

"It is scheduled for tomorrow. There will be much food, music and a grand pyrotechnic display."

Li Min spoke to Peng, waving her hands with excitement. Collins heard her say "Mr. Charles" several times.

"This girl says you must come as well or she will not attend," Peng explained.

"Will I be welcome?"

"You shall indeed. There are many *gwáilóu* who cannot be allowed, for they cause trouble and maybe violence, but you are most welcome. Numerous residents of the Chinese district know of you and your generosity."

Slightly embarrassed, Collins nodded at Min and

smiled. She jumped up and threw her arms about his neck. He gave Peng an imploring look, but the Chinaman sat still, refusing to come to his rescue. Finally, Collins extricated himself, standing up and giving the girl a gentle cuff under the chin.

"I would enjoy seeing some of the revelries," he told Peng. "But I would prefer that neither of you be encumbered by my presence for long." He stretched his arms, stiff from pitching hay all morning. "We can take the buckboard and leave early. My only concern is the possibility of Min being recognized. I had thought this was a concern for you as well."

The girl now sat on the floor playing with the dog, scratching the animal's belly and fooling with her paws.

"Only among Americans. Li Min has told me that there were never any Chinese men, other than her master, who came to her hovel."

"There may be one who knows her all the same."

"Perhaps...perhaps not. Her deportment has been substantially altered and I sincerely doubt anyone could perceive familiarity now. I am of the opinion that, after several weeks, it is proper she should no longer be a prisoner here."

"I agree. She was prisoner enough and for long enough. We must take our chances. Homer said, 'A decent boldness ever meets with friends.' May this be so."

"Ah yes, Homer," Peng said in all seriousness. "He was almost as wise as the Master Confucius."

CHINESE NEW YEAR

15

Making his way through a throng of Chinese men and an extempore band creating an unruly din, Collins and his dog departed the bedlam and walked north toward the newspaper office. Peng and Li Min were happily occupied with eating and visiting with new acquaintances. Second Street was mostly deserted but the main section of town was bustling with Saturday traffic consisting of area miners and ranchers purchasing supplies. Some of them, Collins assumed, had come to watch the evening's fireworks and Celestial celebrations. He overheard the occasional complaint regarding the large gathering of Chinese from around the county, and its accompanying hullabaloo, and he hoped that no one would instigate a brawl.

When he entered the headquarters of *The New North-West*, C.W. found James Hamilton Mills fast asleep in a chair, his head resting upon a pillow of stacked newspapers atop a large workbench. He was snoring thunderously and his typesetter, Cora, was absent. Gal trotted over and reached up to lick Mills' face, causing him to sit bolt upright and curse imaginatively.

"Come, come now, Captain, what intrepid journalist sleeps in the middle of the day?" Collins chided him. "What if all hell broke loose in the streets?"

"It most certainly *has* broken loose," Mills said with ill humor. "Goddamn Chinamen. That unholy race, which Denis Kearney has declared must go, have been celebrating their New Year *Day* for several days past. They are having quite a time, which consists of the discharge of innumerable fireworks, accompanied by feasting and music by the band. The instruments are an old gong, a small drum head, triangle, and other noisy, diabolical and disagreeable instruments. The louder the noise the better and they have been eminently successful on two or three occasions during the week."

"I had the pleasure of their efforts." Collins helped himself to a cup of coffee and sat down in a chair beside Mills. "Wú Peng and Li Min are enjoying the revelries. My house has been duly decorated and I have partaken of some interesting cuisine."

"I do fancy your visage appears dimly Mongolian these days."

Collins gave him a sour look. "You must not succumb to prevailing prejudices, Captain. I know you are exceedingly fond of Peng."

Outwardly chastened, Mills said, "'Tis true, but you must admit he is a remarkable individual."

"Westernized, I believe you mean. More acceptable to your delicate sensibilities." Removing his pipe from a jacket pocket, Collins filled the bowl with tobacco. "But indeed Peng is quite a remarkable person and a dear-friend."

"And how is Li Min fitting into the scheme of things?" Mills asked slyly. "Have you fully acquiesced to her presence?"

"She is a cheerful, sharp-witted girl. I have no complaints."

"And Peng? Has he grown fond?"
Smoking contemplatively for a long interlude, Collins was not certain of the answer. "He does not seem overtly attentive, but he is kind and patient with her," he finally answered. "If he did become fond, I would have no objection. It would seem to be a serviceable outcome for the

two of them."

Mills burst into a guffaw. "What you mean is that it would be entirely expedient for you to have Peng settle down. You would be assured of his presence *ad infinitum.*"

"You are a contemptible old scout and no mistake," Collins said derisively. He stood up and poured them both more coffee.

"You find my sturdy brew more acceptable now?" the captain asked.

"No," C.W said, sitting back down. "It is abominable."

Shuffling through the stack of newsprint before him, Mills pulled out a sheet and struck it with the back of his hand. "Well, in another note, the carping has commenced. *The Weekly Miner* has been castigating me rigorously merely because I do not care to have over half the population of our county taken up by this new Silver Bow county nor do I wish to have the greater amount of taxable property removed. Those bastards Kessler and Brown, once friends and journalistic compatriots, have accused me of mercenary motives and have stated that my only interest is defending my portion of the county's public printing."

"I believe the new county will be created forthwith," Collins said, regarding Mills through a puff of tobacco smoke. "They are only asking to encompass a mere 792 square miles and even the residents of Philipsburg prefer to be placed in the new county."

"You are a Judas."

It was Collins' turn to laugh. "Perhaps your old chums have hit the nail on the head."

Captain Mills appeared about to offer a scathing retort when the door was thrown open and Wú Peng ran in.

"You must come. Come now," he shouted.

The dog was barking excitedly and both men stood up.

"What is it?" Collins asked, grasping the Chinaman by the shoulders in alarm.

"Li Min. There is a man who is chasing her. He is pursuing her with a hatchet."

Collins and Mills hurried out the door, locking the dog in the office to keep her safe. They trailed Peng, who was already sprinting back down the street. When they arrived at the Chinese quarter, the band and revelers seemed to be unhindered by any discernable confusion. Collins espied Peng hastening toward the decrepit hut that housed the opium den. When C.W. arrived, with Mills just behind, he found Li Min cowering against the east wall of the shack with a Chinaman shrieking at her and brandishing a small axe. She was plainly terrified.

From somewhere, Peng had found a shovel and began threatening the man with the handle. Without a word, Collins yanked it from him and swung the spade end against the assailant's head. The man went down on his knees. Pulling him up by his queue, he dragged the Chinaman several feet, then stood over the supine villain and punched him in the face, prompting a gush of blood.

He was about to deliver another blow when Captain Mills came over and pulled him away. "You have an audience," he said and nodded toward a large crowd of Chinese men.

Turning to face the mob headed in his direction, Collins placed a foot on his quarry before he had an opportunity to get up. Mr. Oliver, the old sailor, and Gem Kee, the host of the New Year's gala, were the first to confront him. Kee asked a question of the man, who was lying docilely beneath Collins' boot. He answered at length. Then Gem Kee spoke to Mr. Oliver.

"Mr. Kee wantin' to savvy why you be workin' this fella over at his doins," the old man told C.W. "What be the goppin' barney, mate?"

Li Min now stood with Peng and Mills a few feet away.

"He attacked that girl with an axe," he said, nodding toward Min.

After translating Collins' words and obtaining Kee's response, Oliver said, "That there is Gong Sing and the gal be his slave."

Taking his boot from Gong Sing, Collins hauled him to his feet and held onto his braid like a leash. "You can tell your boss that this man beat her almost to death then threw her away. She belongs to me now."

After Oliver had passed along his words, Gem Kee gazed coldly first at Collins then at Gong Sing. Then he made some sort of a pronouncement that everyone seemed to accept and the multitude of Chinese men returned to the tables of food and drink. The band renewed its cacophony and firecrackers were lit. Collins let go of Sing's queue and shoved him hard in the small of the back. Peng came over and belligerently harangued the man in Chinese until he scurried away, holding a hand to his bleeding nose.

Li Min timidly approached Collins. "Mr. Charles," she said softly.

"You are safe," he told her, taking her hand. "No hurt."

"Now *there* was a glimpse of your old Irish temper and I will state unequivocally that Gong Sing is damned lucky to be alive," Captain Mills said gleefully.

"Nothing in your paper, James," Collins said as they began to stroll away from the scene. He let go of Min's hand. "Thank you, Peng," he added.

"I am most certainly not the genuine hero such as you, Charles. That was an enormously noteworthy education for Mr. Gong Sing."

At the further mention of the man's name, Li Min commenced a longwinded and passionate speech, waving her arms expressively. Tears rolled down her cheeks. Wú Peng now took her hand and spoke to her evenly.

"Min says that Gong Sing is not her master," he told

the others. "He is the cousin of her master."

"She has no master," C.W. said.

"The matter of 'cousins' among Chinamen is a puzzler," Mills said. "Every Chinaman seems to have a hundred or more. It is supposed by some that those coming from the same town call themselves cousins."

"We Chinese have an exceptionally distinctive manner of recognizing relations," Peng told him. "It is not the same as with Americans. Where we share a common ancestor within a village in the distant past, all descendants are cousins, or more accurately, we are from the same clan."

"Still a puzzler," Mills insisted. "How can you keep track?"

Min had visibly calmed as the four of them made their way back to the newspaper office. A few pedestrians turned to glance at the unlikely little assembly, but made no remark. Collins thought that perhaps he would forego any future Chinese New Year celebrations and sincerely hoped Sheriff McAndrews would not hear of his latest altercation. And as far as "a decent boldness" was concerned, Homer be damned. As Shakespeare wrote in *As You Like It*, "The fool doth think he is wise, but the wiseman knows himself to be a fool."

16

Days, then weeks, passed and spring finally came to the valleys and mountain slopes. Collins' small family of Wú Peng, Li Min and Gal had all settled into a well ordered routine. Calving season had come and gone and his small herd of mother cows and calves were thriving. He had inherited a red shorthorn bull from the former owner of the ranch and the robust animal produced hardy offspring. His cows were mostly grade shorthorns, but he had culled the scrubby stock and now had a healthy and fine looking bunch. The previous October, he had sold his calves to the local markets in Deer Lodge and Butte City and planned to do so again.

Peng and Min were evolving a scheme for a summer garden of various plants, especially radishes, cabbages, carrots and ginger. Peng was already hard at work on a root-house that would provide storage for the harvest. For his part, Collins took Felix and the buckboard up to the hills and cut posts and poles for a garden fence, shooting a brace of fat snowshoe hares and a few prairie chickens on the trip home into the bargain. While Li Min labored at turning the soil and Peng exerted himself with a pick and spade, excavating his cellar, C.W constructed a quantity of pole jacks. An occasional spring storm forced them indoors, but they all endeavored to remain outside as much as possible, toiling at their miscellaneous tasks.

One mild forenoon in April, as Collins and Gal were

out on foot checking on the cow and calf pairs and mules and horses, he heard a blood-curdling scream from the direction of the house. He and the dog ran back and rounded the dwelling to find Li Min on the porch, brandishing a cleaver. Turning to discover whatever menace she was facing, he saw Wakalyapi sitting impassively on a blue roan horse. Behind her was a rawboned black pack animal loaded with what appeared to be bulging panniers topped with ribs and quarters of an elk.

"*Yěmán de!*" Min cried and made a chopping gesture with the cleaver at Arbuckles. When she saw Collins, Min shouted, "Get gun, Mr. Charles. Get gun!"

Peng arrived at a jog and slowed to a walk as soon as he saw Arbuckles. As he approached her horse, he said, "You must come down, my dear friend, so that I am able to survey your heaven-sent and anxiously longed for person."

Min stood staring at them and the cleaver fell from her hand, thumping upon the wooden planks of the porch floor. When the Indian woman had dismounted and stood beside her gelding, Peng took her hand in both of his and smiled broadly.

"You are very welcome," he told her. "We have been remarking your absence every single day."

Collins walked over to Wakalyapi. Their eyes met in corresponding affection and they stepped forward and gripped each other's shoulders. "I am glad you have come," C.W. said. "We were worried."

"It is good to see you, Charles." She took his hand and pressed it lightly, not shaking it as in the white man custom. Her scarred mouth pulled into a lopsided grin. "You have a new body-guard," she said blandly.

After unloading and hanging the meat and unsaddling the woman's horses, they all went inside the house. Min had disappeared into her room and closed the door. Peng made tea and coffee and served sweet rice cakes that the girl had made earlier.

"What is happening?" Collins asked Wakalyapi. "You have been gone several months."

"All is not well."

"Does Sitting Bull remain in Canada?"

"He does, but many have left to reservations at Poplar Creek and Buford."

"Will he finally be forced to surrender?"

"Perhaps, but *Tȟatȟáŋka Íyotake* still fears he will be hanged for the fight on the Greasy Grass if he returns. There was an attack on a village during the Hard Moon when the snow was deep and the cold was fierce. I will tell you of it at another time, but this has made him more reluctant to surrender."

Li Min's door creaked as the girl opened it a crack and peered through, her face a pale shard in the gap. Collins beckoned her with a wave of his hand. Slowly she emerged, all the while watching Arbuckles with wide and frightened eyes, as if prepared for an imminent assault.

"Li Min, this is our friend Arbuckles," C.W. said. "Come and sit beside me. There is nothing to fear."

Peng said something to the girl in Chinese. She crept closer, ever keeping her eyes directed upon Wakalyapi, and pulled a chair over right next to Collins, perching upon it and pressing against him. The Indian woman regarded the girl without expression.

"You are very alarming," Peng told her. "Perhaps she believes you will eat her up."

"Eat?" Min cried. She pressed closer to Collins. "No eat, no eat!"

"Quiet now," Collins said crossly. "There is no danger." He pushed her away from him with his shoulder, poured a cup of tea for the girl and placed it before her. "Enough now."

"Perhaps I am the only Indian she has seen," Arbuckles said.

"This must be true," Peng said. "But also this girl must welcome our dearest friend."

"How did she come to be here?"

Collins smiled drolly. "She was a cast off."

"Then you are living as a true warrior. It is your obligation to care for those who cannot make shift for themselves."

"How goes it with Kcanptepte?"

"The boy, not so much a boy now, and the dog will not return across the Medicine Line. They choose to stay among white men of the village who remain alive. They will be protected."

"None of the Irishmen are intending to surrender?"

"No. I do not believe it would go well for them."

"Neither do I."

Li Min had not taken a sip of her tea, but maintained a steady and wary scrutiny of Wakalyapi. Gal stealthily crept forward and placed her front feet on the Indian woman's lap. She rubbed the dog's ears then gently pushed her back down onto the floor. The girl watched attentively.

"Gal remembers you as always," Collins said.

"She is a cherished comrade."

Min stole from her chair and went over and knelt beside Gal at Arbuckles' feet. "Doggie likes you," she said, looking up at the woman.

"Yes."

"You not eat me?"

"I will not eat you." Arbuckles reached a hand to gently caress the girl's cheek.

Peng and Collins exchanged looks at their taciturn companion's anomalous gesture.

"Okay," Min said, getting to her feet. "Okay," she said again and smiled shyly.

Smiling back, Wakalapi said, "Perhaps the girl will not be so afraid now."

"I think not," Collins told her. "Now, what else have you to tell me of the situation in Canada?"

The girl went to the door and called the dog. "We will dig more garden," she announced.

"*Shì de*," Peng said and nodded.

After the door had closed, Wakalyapi's face became grave. "There is a man named Allison. He has been hanging around forts for many years, always wanting to make himself important and sometimes acting as interpreter. He speaks our language very badly, which, of course, the soldiers do not know."

"I have heard of him here and there. I believe they call him 'Fish.' "

"My people call him *Hosáŋ* after the fish that lives in river bottoms and subsists on the scraps that collect there. Allison is certain the name is a show of respect."

Collins laughed. "You mean a sucker fish. His comprehension of the Lakota language must be weak indeed."

"It is a foolish person who finds respect in an insult," Peng said.

" 'Against stupidity the very gods themselves contend in vain,' " C.W. added.

"Is that your Shakespeare?" Arbuckles asked.

"No, it is from a German playwright named Schiller."

"It is an appropriate sentiment," she said.

"But what of Allison?"

"He convinced the commander of Buford that he would be the one to persuade *Tȟatȟáŋka Íyotake* into surrendering. In truth, he talked Man Who Goes in the Middle, known by whites as Gall, into returning. The soldiers attacked his camp at Poplar Creek and he has lost his heart. He turned his back on those who remain in Grandmother's Land and is swiftly becoming a white man."

"Did Allison persuade Sitting Bull?"

"No, but people are leaving him. There are persons

with cunning words and devious and unwholesome intent...and those with ears to hear. Hosáŋ is responsible for much."

"There are always those who foment discord and those who are willing to follow," Peng said. "Confucius has written that 'To see and listen to the wicked is already the beginning of wickedness.' "

"I am certain," Wakalyapi said.

Collins pushed his chair back and crossed his legs. "Tell me of the attack on Gall's camp."

Wú Peng left the table and poured more coffee. "Please excuse me," he said, placing the coffeepot back on the stove. "I am going to continue excavations as they are nearly complete." He went out the door.

"Peng is working on a place to store vegetables and Li Min is preparing a garden," Collins told Wakalyapi.

"It is good to cache food for the winter." Arbuckles took out her pipe and Collins handed her his tobacco pouch.

"*Philámayaye*," she said and filled her pipe in a deliberate manner. "Now I will tell you of the assault on the camp at *Waȟčhíŋča Wakpá*.

Filling his own briar and sharing a match with Wakalyapi, Collins waited for his friend to begin. He could hear Peng calling to Li Min in the distance.

"By the end of the Moon of Starting Winter, *Hosáŋ* had talked *Phizí*, Man Who Goes in the Middle, into bringing twenty families down to the agency on the Poplar River to wait for *Tȟatȟáŋka Íyotake*. It seemed that the slithering whispers had done their work and many people wanted to give up. It is true that they were very poor and food was scarce, but *Tȟatȟáŋka Íyotake* desired to protect them. He brought over one hundred lodges across the Medicine Line and held his camp at the place of the river called Milk where it joins the *Mnišóše Wakpá*."

"The Missouri?"

"Yes. There they stopped to hunt buffalo for they had come across a large herd. Finally there was meat and their spirits became stronger. I was with them and soon there was talk about returning north. The Fish was still there and I saw he was afraid that his influence might be lost, so he made an argument that the chief should send three men to see that Fort Buford would make a good camp. He talked and talked and finally a head man, *Kȟaŋǧí Wičhášayatapi*, known as Crow Chief or Burns the Medicine Bag, said he would go there. With two other warriors and Allison, he went to Fort Buford. When they returned, *Phizí* and *Kȟaŋǧí Wičhášayatapi* persuaded some more of the people to go to the fort, but the weather was not good for travel and they stopped at the Poplar Agency. The head men did not want to continue to the fort just then because the women and children were suffering. The snow was very deep and the ponies were also weak."

"So the army did not attack Sitting Bull's camp?"

Wakalyapi drank some coffee and, noticing that it had burned out, placed her pipe on the table. "No. Only the camp near the agency among the trees in a bend of the river. I am sure you know the winter has been long and harsh with much snow and there were many other families there who had already come down from Grandmother's Land searching for a way to survive and willing to give up. There were *Húŋkpapȟa, Oglála, Mnikȟówožu* bands that had joined many of the *Dakhóta* people which already belonged to the agency."

Collins nodded. "Yes we had it tough enough down here."

"As I said, the chiefs, *Phizí* and *Kȟaŋǧí Wičhášayatapi*, I will now call them by their white names Crow Chief and Gall, had been influenced by the Fish and intended to surrender." Arbuckles continued. "But now they were only wanting to wait for better travelling and mixed with this other camp where some had relatives. By this time, in January, there were many more soldiers at the agency who had come from Fort Keogh, the place near the *Heȟaka Wakpá* where we had trouble before."

"That is where we were requisitioned by Miles and marched north. Another hard winter."

"Before we joined *Tȟatȟáŋka Ìyotake*." She smiled. "It is lucky Bear Coat Miles has been sent away by his bosses. It may be that he remains angry with you for running away."

"And you as well," Collins said and grinned. "I had read in the newspaper that Miles enraged the Dominion authorities when he attempted to cross the line back in '79."

"I think he wanted to hunt us all the way to our camps, but some of our chiefs and the man Walsh, who is a redcoat soldier of the Grandmother Country, met with Miles and told him the people would stay north of the line. I believe Bear Coat had been told he should not cross, but intended to go anyway. There was a newspaper writer there at the time and he went with Walsh to the lodges of *Tȟatȟáŋka Ìyotake*. That is also when a man was brought in who had been hunting to feed his family. Bear Coat's soldiers had shot him in the stomach and he died. After that, the newspaper writer left."

"I read that Sheridan pulled Miles back. Mostly I believe they did not want a repeat of the Greasy Grass."

"The warriors were angry enough and the soldiers were outnumbered. It did not help that Bear Coat Miles had been coming after any people who crossed the line to search for meat. And also the soldiers were building the new fort near the mountains where the *Pȟóǧe Ȟlóka* were killed and captured."

"Fort Assiniboine?"

"Yes."

Standing up, Collins added wood to the fire box on

the stove and moved the coffeepot to heat. "But we were speaking of the attack this last winter."

"New soldiers joined the ones already there to protect the agent and the agency people on the Poplar Creek. The other soldiers arrived from Fort Keogh when the snow was deep and what I heard was that they wanted to force those who had just surrendered to travel to the Fort Buford even if the children suffered. As a holy man, *Tȟatȟáŋka Íyotake* knew not to come too close to the agency."

"Were you at the agency or in Sitting Bull's camp?" C.W. asked, pouring hot coffee then returning to the table.

Wakalyapi nodded her thanks. "I had come to the agency to see what was going to happen. The fat soldier in charge who had come from Fort Keogh had warned Crow Chief that if his lodges were not ready to travel straightaway he would force them to move. The chief became angry. He went to talk to the two-tongue man named Culbertson who belongs to Bear Coat and is not straight. Then he spoke to the trader and warned of trouble."

"Did these men report what Crow Chief had said?"

"Yes. That is what made the fat soldier decide to attack." She paused and drank some coffee.

Collins again filled and lit his pipe. "Please continue."

"The soldiers attacked the camp along the river from two sides, firing a big gun into the lodges, then flanked the village and demanded the people's guns. Two warriors and a woman had already been killed. Some of the people hid in the woods along the river and refused to give up. Some other warriors made to run and the soldiers shot several. Then that man Culbertson ordered that everyone should come out. No one showed themselves and that is when the big gun and another one just like it were fired several times and there were screams and some of the lodges were knocked down."

"What was the fat soldier's name?"

"I heard it, but I do not remember. There was more fighting here and there with shooting around, but then someone put out a white flag. After that the fat soldier warned he would fire the big guns at any lodge that was not taken down so many people packed up and came out, offering their guns to the soldiers. Many many were made prisoners and later the soldiers burned any of the lodges left standing and destroyed all the remaining belongings, making more people to suffer from cold and hunger. All the ponies were taken. Eight people had been killed and maybe fifty escaped to *Tȟatȟáŋka Ìyotake*. I went back there that night."

"What happened to the prisoners?"

"They were forced to march east to Fort Buford. I heard later that there were frozen feet and hands and the children were very sick."

"And Sitting Bull?"

"Word reached us that the fat soldier was going to come after us, but *Tȟatȟáŋka Ìyotake* was already leading his camp back across the Medicine Line. There was food for a while and many robes from the *tȟatȟáŋka* after a successful hunt. Most importantly, we had learned that surrender would mean only betrayal and bondage."

17

The telegram was unexpected. Collins had taken the wagon into town to check the mail, pick up a few supplies and visit with James Mills. He had stopped in at the Montana Central Telegraph office on a whim and found there was a message awaiting him. Not surprisingly, the communication had been sent via the Pinkerton Detective Agency, as few people knew of his whereabouts. It seemed that Allan bore him no real ill will and continued to forward messages to him, in spite of C.W.'s estrangement from the agency.

The telegram was from General Terry and had been transmitted a few days before.

St. Paul Minn April 4 1881
Dept Dakota
To C.W. Collins c/o Pinkerton National Detective
Agency Chicago
Desire that you accept commission and
proceed to Fort Walsh, NW Terr. to meet with
Sitting Bull. Allison, interpreter, as well as others
have failed entirely in effecting Bull's surrender.
Request you make attempt. I am aware of your
attributes in such matters. Require prompt
response if amenable to the undertaking. All
discretion is mandatory and I will authorize
generous remuneration regardless of outcome.
Gen Terry, Department Commander

It had been quite some time since receiving payment for his services from Mr. Donnelly and funds were dwindling. C.W. sent an immediate response in the affirmative. His past unofficial employment with government officials had proven quite worthwhile. He communicated a stipulation for a considerable sum in his responding message and permission to resupply, at government expense, with all post traders as required. Leaving the building, Collins contemplated the improbable turn of events that had brought Arbuckles back to the ranch just two days before this request from General Terry. Or perhaps, he thought, it was not so improbable.

With no intention of waiting for a response or any caviling from Terry, he would embark upon the assignment forthwith, hoping he could convince Wakalyapi to accompany him. Collins drove Joey over to Wm. Coleman and Co. for a supply of ammunition, having recently replaced his Colt .45 with a .44 caliber Colt Frontier revolver so that he could use the same cartridges for both his pistol and his Winchester repeater. He also purchased tobacco, an extra pipe and a sack of lemon drops for Li Min. From there, he made for E.L. Bonner's establishment to stock up on provisions for the trail. He was occupied with piling goods on the counter when James Mills came in.

"Saw you from across the street. Looks as if you are intending to supply a small army."

"Good day to you, Captain," C.W. said, clapping the man on the back. "I am bound for an expedition north." He paused. "And no, I am not going to reveal my destination nor my purpose to an old news hound, such as yourself."

"Come now, Charles, that is ungracious of you. Finish up here and saunter across to the office for some of my excellent coffee."

"I will come over but without the promise of drinking

your swill."

"Ungracious," Mills said and left the emporium.

After having collected an ample stock of goods for the journey, C.W. paid the clerk and loaded the buckboard with heaping boxes. Leaving Joey in the afternoon shade provided by the building, with Gal curled up comfortably on the wagon seat, he crossed the street to the offices of the *New North-West*.

Cora was standing at her station, setting type, and Mills was at his desk, scribbling on a sheet of paper. He looked up when Collins entered.

"How long will you be away from us?" Mills asked, getting to his feet and pouring a mug of coffee. "Here," he said, shoving it toward Collins.

"Thank you for another hole in my gut," C.W. said and accepted the cup. He sat down on a chair near the desk and Mills joined him. "I will be gone for some time. I would greatly appreciate if you would go out to the ranch and make certain all is well. I do not want my friends coming to town on their own."

"Of course."

"What are you writing so studiously? Still arguing against the division bill separating Silver Bow and Deer Lodge counties?"

"Too right," the captain said ardently "It is my duty as a citizen."

"I have told you before, it is done. 'What cannot be eschewed must be embraced.' "

Waving a hand impatiently, Mills said, "Damn your Shakespeare. I am not yet beaten." He leaned back in his chair and observed Collins for a long moment. "Just what is this expedition? Does it have financial implications?"

"Most definitely. As well as personal." Collins took a sip from his mug and scowled, but made no comment.

"Washington?"

"Perhaps, but as I said, you will not be extracting details nor destinations from me."

Making a rude noise, the newspaperman toyed with a pencil and beat a rhythm on the edge of the desk pensively. "I could use a bit of hearsay or innuendo," he said furtively, without looking at Collins. "There is not much to report beyond Sitting Bull's perpetually pending surrender and the flooding on the Missouri and both are becoming tedious."

"I will give you a tidbit."

Mills' eyebrows raised and he gazed expectantly at his friend. "Yes?"

"A man named Allison failed in coaxing Sitting Bull back from Canada."

"Who is this Allison?"

"You will have to find out for yourself."

"That is all?"

"That is all."

Mills thought a minute. "Now I reflect on it, there was something about him in the Helena paper last February. They called him a scout."

"Perhaps. I have heard he is a rascal."

"And where would you have heard this?"

Collins had never apprised Mills of his friendship with Wakalyapi and he did not intend to do so now. "It is a rumor, nothing more."

The captain grinned. "You are guileful, but I discern that you must be bound for the British Possessions."

"I cannot say, but I must take your leave, in any case," C.W. said, standing up and stretching his arms. "I will report back to you upon my return. I may have some compelling intelligence for you then."

"If you return, that is. You are always taking chances."

"I must return, for otherwise you would not have anyone to reproach."

"True enough," Mills said, arising from his chair. "My

life would be hollow and meaningless." He put out a hand to shake. "Good luck, my friend. And do be careful."

"Always," Collins said, accepting his hand. "And you be wary of Butte politicians. They may choose to muzzle you permanently."

The captain laughed loudly, causing Cora to look up. "They can but try."

They walked to the door together and repeated their farewells. Collins untethered Joey from the hitch weight, stowed it in the wagon bed, scooted Gal over on the seat and gathered the lines. As he was driving out of town, he chanced to espy a lovely young woman walking down the road, wearing a stylish mauve suit and large hat topped with a bow. She was carrying a basket and a parasol and was strolling along at a jaunty pace heading toward Deer Lodge. He had not seen such a splendid female in many a day and he pulled in the mule just as she strode by on the other side of the lane.

"Might I offer you a ride?" C.W. called to her.

Pausing, she turned to examine him in an unmistakably imperious manner. "No, I really do not think I could do that. But thank you." The lady had a distinctly Prussian accent.

Wrapping the lines on the brake handle and jumping down, C.W. ambled leisurely over to where the woman stood. The dog leapt from the seat and followed.

"Oh!" the young woman cried. "Keep that animal away from me!" She collapsed her parasol and waved it at Gal.

The dog cowered behind Collins and growled. "Please stop. She is quite harmless," he told the girl, frowning. "I only meant to introduce myself," he added, removing his Stetson and running a hand through his hair.

She ceased wielding the parasol as a weapon and rested its tip upon the ground. "Well then," she said, her brown eyes narrowing. "Who are you and why do you accost ladies in the thoroughfare?"

"My name is Charles Collins. I thought to give you a ride into town if you desired it."

"I have already told you I do not desire it. I could have easily had transport if I had chosen to do so. I wanted to walk and that is what I am doing."

"I apologize then." He gave a shallow bow. "Will you not offer me your name in any event?" Collins gave her a charming smile that he hoped would have the desired effect. If this bewitching woman was not entangled with some other gentleman, he intended to seek her out upon his return from the north.

"My name is Augusta Bielenberg. I am Mr. John Bielenberg's cousin from Glückstadt."

Collins knew that John Bielenberg was the half-brother and partner of Grant Kohrs, owner of the largest ranch in the vicinity. The headquarters were located just north of Deer Lodge. The young lady was from a prominent family then, but he did not consider this a deterrent.

"Pleased to meet you, Miss...or is it Mrs. Bielenberg?" He tilted his head to the side and smiled again.

She opened her parasol and gave him an icy stare. The girl seemed mildly flustered and this was precisely the result he had been seeking. "It is Miss Bielenberg and I must be on my way. I do not, as a rule, converse with strangers in the road." With this statement, she turned and marched briskly away, her head held high.

Climbing back up onto the wagon seat and calling Gal, Collins turned to watch the retreating female form. Then he slapped the lines and continued on his way home. He sincerely hoped Miss Augusta Bielenberg would still be in residence when he returned, as she was the most delightful creature he had encountered since he had come to Deer Lodge. The mere recollection of her enchanting figure brightened the fading afternoon and occupied his thoughts as the landscape slipped by unheeded.

128

MOUNTAIN PASS

18

They camped in a glade amid the timber east of Mullan Pass, along a small creek above Helena, turning their stock loose to graze upon abundant grasses interspersed among lodgepole, aspen and spruce trees. Wakalyapi had her two horses and Collins rode Ulysses, his gelding, and had chosen Molly as his pack animal. The sun was near the western horizon when the fire was built and elk steaks were sizzling in a pan. Gal had curled up on Collins' bedroll, spread out beside a pile of saddles and panniers. C.W. noticed that Arbuckles' old McClellan saddle had lost some of its beading and decorative brass tacks and was far more scuffed than the last time he had seen it. And there were more streaks of white in her hair.

"Have you found it difficult these past months?" he asked, turning the meat.

The woman was grinding coffee beans. She paused and said, "We have all suffered greatly. The buffalo are few and always slaughtered by greedy *wašíču* on both sides of the Medicine Line. The Fort Walsh and Wood Mountain redcoat soldiers and White Grandmother cannot decide to give us a home and the other tribes do not want us there, because they too are hungry for meat. The new head man at Wood Mountain is like the *t̪haté t̪háŋka*, the powerful wind, and he is not friendly. He does not want us and says go back over and over, always pushing against us." She resumed her grinding.

Walking to the stream to fill the coffeepot, Collins pondered the dilemma faced by Sitting Bull and his followers. Stay in the Dominion and starve, but remain at liberty, or return to the United States and live on a confined reservation in perpetuity, forced to relinquish tradition, language and beliefs. He had been old enough to feel the weighty sorrow of leaving his home in Ireland when the famine, compounded by British avarice, had compelled his mother to bring him to America.

Back at the fire, Collins placed the pot near the flames to heat. He took a seat on a chunk of flat shale, dragged to the hearth to serve as a bench by a previous occupant of the clearing. Arbuckles poured the ground coffee into the pot and slid the steaks onto two tin platters with a stick, while C.W. cut thick slices of bread with his Green River knife and added them to the servings of meat.

"You have that knife," the woman said.

"Yes. It is similar to the one I found at the Greasy Grass."

They began to eat, each ensnared within the private council of their own thoughts. Collins recalled the early days in Wakalyapi's company and abiding affection flooded his recollections. He glanced up from his meal and found her observing him.

"I remember much," she said in her uncanny manner of knowing his mind.

He smiled at her. "It is good to be here with you. I am glad you decided to come back with me."

"Know this, Wolf. I will not lose my life in defense of yours," the woman said, covering her crooked grin with a hand.

Chuckling, Collins pulled the coffeepot from the fire and settled the grounds with a splash of cold water from his canteen. Pouring them each a cup, he said, "Truly, you were a very recalcitrant companion early on."

"What is that word?" Wakalyapi asked, her eyes still

showing humor.

"Recalcitrant. Contrary."

"Oh yes… and you were a witless white man."

"Witless? You have been reading your Shakespeare."

She took a sip of coffee, then sliced off a piece of elk meat and impaled it on the tip of her knife. "Yes."

" 'There is many a man has more hair than wit.' Now I believe it has all evened up."

"You have good hair. It would make a handsome trophy," Wakalyapi said and became engrossed in finishing her food.

Coyotes yipped in the foothills as the sun finally vanished beneath the horizon. Smiling to himself, Collins wiped his plate with the last hunk of bread, stuffed it in his mouth, then laid the dish aside to take out his pipe. He filled the bowl and tossed the tobacco pouch to Wakalyapi. They drank coffee and smoked in silence, listening to the horses move about and nighthawks swoop after insects.

"I plan to follow the Mullan Road to Fort Benton," Collins said at last. "It is the shortest route."

Wakalyapi nodded. "I would not take this white man road alone, but I will go with you."

"And we will have to resupply farther north at Fort Assiniboine before heading across the line. Once again, you will be my guide and interpreter."

"It is of no consequence." She knocked the ashes from her pipe on a rock, made a hollow in the dirt and buried them.

"Where were you before you came to the ranch?"

"I was at Buford."

"Tell me about it." Collins slid from his shale perch to the ground and used the slab for a back rest. He stuffed his jacket behind him as a cushion.

Sitting cross-legged in her usual manner, the woman reached for a limb of pine from a stack near the fire and laid it upon the coals. She added another, then gazed into the rising blaze for a prolonged interval. After a while, she began to speak.

"*Tȟatȟáŋka Ìyotake* does not trust that his people are being cared for at the soldier forts or the agencies and believes many of them are being kept in chains. He asked to see the big wind redcoat major at Wood Mountain and told him he wanted to send two warriors to see what was going on at Fort Buford. He also asked that a redcoat soldier go along to also report what was seen."

"When was this?" Collins asked. He had taken the little silver fish charm that Peng had given him from a vest pocket and was tinkering with it. He had taken to carrying the trinket with him whenever he left home.

"Many days ago... maybe twenty? Long enough for me to follow them down to where the *Mnišóśe Wakpá* meets the *Heȟaka Wakpá*."

"The Yellowstone and the Missouri."

"Yes. And then travel south from there to your house."

"You went to Fort Buford?"

"I followed the two warriors, *Tȟatȟáŋka Waŋží*, One Bull, and *Čhaŋȟpí Čhetúŋte*, Bone Club, with the redcoat soldier called Mac something. Like in *Macbeth*."

"But not Macbeth, I take it," C.W. said jokingly.

Wakalyapi gave him a withering glance. "Not Macbeth."

"Do continue."

"There were hundreds of lodges and soldier tents along the river there. The head soldier, another major called Brothertown..."

"Brotherton?" Collins interrupted. "Could it have been Brotherton?"

The woman studied him. "You know this major?"

"Perhaps. Perhaps from a long time ago."

She shrugged. "I do not trust him. He made a big parade of our relatives and all their food, pots and blankets and clothing, but all they had was new. Some of them had been there for a long time and everything they had was new."

"That does seem suspicious." The dog left her place on the bedroll and came over to lie beside Collins. He played with an ear. "What else did you see?"

"People were sick and many of them coughed. Some of them behaved like they were afraid of the soldiers. I talked to Bone Club about it and he also thought there was something amiss. I have never trusted One Bull and so I did not share my thoughts with him."

Running a hand across his mouth to hide an involuntary smile, Collins recalled that some of the woman's vocabulary, such as the word 'amiss,' came from reading Sir Walter Scott, an author she admired. "And so the men returned to report their observations to Sitting Bull and the commander at Wood Mountain?"

"I suppose. I spoke with a few people I knew and they told me they did not know what would happen to them and they missed their old ways. They did not want to sit around all day without purpose and said they felt worthless. Many of them wished they could go back to *Uŋčíyapi Makȟóčhe*, Grandmother's Country, even if they would die from hunger. They told me it was sad they had listened to that Fish person and head men who had lost their heart. Some of the other people were trying to believe in the white man gods and some wanted to send their children to white man schools. When I had heard enough, I slipped out at night and came south."

"What will Sitting Bull do now?"

"I have seen him to be tormented about the hunger and suffering and yet unwilling to become a prisoner of the white men who have taken so much from us. They are always taking land, possessions, dignity. They shame us, treat us as children, scorn our traditions, lie to us, make us sick with their diseases. Now his friends

and relatives and many honored members of warrior societies and foremost principal men are leaving him because of creeping words and fear. What will you say to
him when you meet with him? Will you be the mouth of
General Terry?"

"I will tell him the truth."

Wakalyapi laughed mockingly. "And what is the truth
now? That we must all die so that white people do not
have to feed us and clothe us and see our sun-baked
faces in their nightmares?"

Filled with sorrow, Collins shook his head. "No, my
friend. I would speak with Sitting Bull and tell him of
the dreadful choices he must make now and how none
of them will be just or satisfactory or even tolerable. But
we must make certain that your people are able to find a
way to live and safeguard the next generation."

Illuminated by the dying fire, the Indian woman's
weathered and indomitable face unconsciously bespoke
her long years of hardship, loss, grief and rage. "Yes,"
she said softly. "It must be so."

"I am sorry. I am so sorry that it must be so."

She looked up and met his eyes. "You are my friend,
Charles. It is enough."

19

It was a soft, sunny morning and birds were chirping merrily among the trees along the great upper Missouri River. They had traversed the Sun River crossing just east of Fort Shaw before the dawning so that they would not encounter either soldiers or civilians. Proximity to the military post prompted Collins to recall his friend Lieutenant Bradley and their final meeting at the fort over four years before. It was Bradley who had introduced him to Wakalyapi and recommended that she become his guide into Lakota territory. Tragically, the young man had been killed the following year in the campaign against the Nez Perce Indians when they made their desperate attempt to escape across the boundary with the British Possessions.

"You are thinking of young James," Arbuckles said.

"I was. You are unnatural in your ability to know my thoughts."

"I was thinking of him also."

Never one to dwell upon maudlin remembrances, mostly because this offered too great an opportunity for him to plunge into Celtic melancholy, Collins resumed their initial conversation. "You were telling me of General Terry and the others who came with him to Fort Walsh after Sitting Bull had absconded to the Dominion."

The Mullan Road began to turn away from the Missouri and skirt the many precipitous and narrow tributaries that branched out as jagged tendrils from the broad river. The land was flat and featureless, except for an occasional sandstone butte lying low upon the horizon. Unlike his last glacial outing through Montana Territory with Arbuckles, warm breezes caressed his face and toyed with the gelding's mane.

"General Terry does not open and close his eyes like most men. They stay open most of the time. It is strange. And have you seen that he looks like the *thathŏkala*, the goats who live high in the mountains?"

Collins laughed. "Yes, come to think on it."

"Terry came with another general who had no arm on one side, some other soldier boys, a man who wrote words in a book and another white man who was supposed to speak and understand our language, but he was a lunkhead..."

"Good word."

Wakalyapi smiled her fractured smile. "I heard it from you."

A flock of birds flew by just overhead, diving and swooping in unison. C.W paused to admire their antics, then caught up with the woman.

"The redcoats had their own interpreter and he was a little better," she continued. "Then there were some men from newspapers. It seemed that they wanted to mock us and make us appear silly and the women to be like those that hang around forts. One of them spoke with *Thathánka Ìyotake* after the redcoat Walsh influenced him to make it happen. I was against it. I did not think this man would tell the truth. And there is good reason to not trust these newspaper men."

"What is the reason?"

"A while ago we were shown a picture of Thathánka Ìyotake made by such a man. It was a picture of a buffalo bull sitting down with a ring in its nose and a chain held by the old man of America who is dressed in your flag."

"Uncle Sam."

"It was agreed that this is how it would be if Ťhatȟáŋka Ìyotake were to surrender."

"I do not believe this. It was probably a ridiculous drawing meant to be amusing. I do not, however, find it amusing."

"Then it was a lie."

"Yes. Newspapermen search for a story and often lie to make it more interesting."

"*Kapémni*! It seems to me that white men lie more than tell the truth."

"Perhaps."

"There are some who are straight," Wakalyapi said, giving Collins an oblique grin. "Maybe men like you."

Removing his hat and giving a slight bow from the waist, Collins said, "Well that is kind of you. Now do go on."

"There was a council the day after these men came to Fort Walsh. They met in the house of Walsh who had been treating us as friends since we had crossed the line. I also came to the place so I could tell Ťhatȟáŋka Ìyotake the truth of what was spoken there. They did not see that I was not another man and nobody of our people told because they wanted to hear the truth and knew I would tell it."

"What did Terry demand?"

"He wanted us to swear we would no longer be hostile toward Americans and then we would be forgiven for all crimes committed in the past. What crimes? What of *their* crimes?"

It was apparent to Collins that his friend had become even more resentful of American turpitude in recent months.

"What else did he want?"

"We would be forced to give up our guns and horses. That we would have to give up all guns and ammunition at the line. We were told the horses would be sold to buy us cows and then we could live like white people and abandon everything that makes us *Húŋkpapȟa*. That we would be supplied with food and clothing and would not have to worry about feeding our children. Of what use are these things if we no longer own ourselves and our horses and the guns to hunt? They want for us to have our hands out all the time and call the white men our great benefactors."

"There must have been a threat behind all his demands."

"Terry told us that if we did not do these things and instead came across the line with our weapons, the soldiers would attack us. This was the one true thing that was said."

"How did Sitting Bull respond?"

"He shook hands with the redcoats to show pleasantness and told Terry and the other men that he was not the fool they thought he was. That Terry was the greater fool. He said the Americans came to tell lies in a place of honor, a place of council, where only honesty should live."

Collins espied a game trail that headed down to a small stream. He dismounted. "We should water the stock here," he said. "The road is taking us farther from the river."

They led their animals down the steep attenuated track to a small opening in the dense willows that lined the creek. Deer and elk droppings were scattered about in profusion and the grass on the bank had been eaten down. While Molly and Ulysses drank their fill, Arbuckles waited with her horses, then they swapped places and Collins took his gelding and mule back up to the road. Gal stayed behind to explore the myriad aromas and savor tempting piles of dung.

When he topped the hill, C.W. could swear he heard bells and turned to look down the way. Coming toward him was an enormous band of sheep following two old ewes with clanking bells fastened about their necks. Three dogs worked the edges of the flock, keeping the animals gathered along the thoroughfare. He turned and put up a hand as a signal to prevent Wakalyapi from showing herself and she held in her horses below the rim of the embankment.

Standing beside Ulysses and Molly, Collins watched as the wooly beasts came abreast. The gelding's ears were perked far forward as he scrutinized the sheep for signs of menace and snorted at one of the dogs as it trotted by in complete devotion to duty, wholly unconcerned with equine spectators. When Gal came bounding up to inspect this new scent that had caught her attention, the sheepdog suddenly roused itself and came at her snarling and barking. Giving a high-pitched yip, Gal dove behind Collins and pressed against the back of his legs. He twirled the ends of his reins at the canine's nose and stamped a foot and the sheepdog returned to its other responsibilities.

Chafing at the delay and attempting to guess at the number of animals that were flowing like an undulating, wooly billow along the roadway, Collins leaned back against his horse and contemplated the consequences of increased settlement in the western territories. The air was filled with the bleating of ewes calling for errant lambs, everywhere darting amongst the older sheep. Just when he became convinced there was no end in sight, he noticed a wagon coming up behind the band, pulled by a team of chestnut horses. As it drew nearer, Collins could see the driver was an elderly man accompanied by a young boy. A roan saddle horse was tied to the back of the wagon. After the last of the flock trotted past, the wagon, mantled with a tight canvas covering, followed in its wake. The man gave him a nod but did not hesitate and soon the entire procession was moving toward the skyline of unbroken land.

"That is a distasteful odor," Arbuckles said as she led her horses up onto the road.

"The Navajo greatly value mutton."

"I am not Navajo," she said and leapt into the saddle. "Those animals stink."

Grateful to finally be on their way, C.W. mounted up and they rode along in companionable silence. He hummed a tune and tipped his hat back to feel the warmth of the sun on his face.

"Terry was angry and asked whether he should tell the president that we refused all his offers," Wakalyapi said abruptly after quite some time. "A warrior called *Kȟaŋǧí* told him to go back where he came from and stay there. That is when Terry told us he had nothing else to say. All the Americans left the next morning."

"That was all?"

"The head man of the redcoat soldiers, another 'Mac,' came to talk to us. I believe Terry had asked him to do this. He told us that when all the buffalo are gone, we would have to find a new way of living. He said his white mother the queen would not feed us. Then Tȟatȟáŋka Íyotake spoke of American treachery and how the English were the ones who had taught his people how to use guns to kill meat for the women and children. He spoke of how the Americans kill many of us every day. How they have robbed, cheated and laughed at us. He told the head man Mac that he only met with Terry and the other men because the redcoats had asked him to."

"What was the response?"

"That we could go where we liked as long as we obeyed the laws."

"Were any of the Irish warriors at the council?" Collins asked.

"Two, maybe three. They would not have been recognized as white men in their clothing. Perhaps they were thought to be people sometimes called the Metis.

Half-breeds that have French names who began with the trading of furs many years ago."

"These are the people you used to call...let us see, what was the word? *Slotas*?"

"I am ashamed. We did not want them in our land because they killed buffalo for trading. But now these people have been good to us and have sometimes fed our children when they were hungry. *Slota* is a bad word."

The sky was beginning to fill with clouds. The landscape rolled on and on in open plains, now entirely monotonous. Gal whined and C.W. reined in to allow her to jump onto the horse.

"But now I am coming to Sitting Bull as a mouthpiece for Terry," he said as he urged Ulysses forward again and came up alongside the woman. "I hope you still trust me."

She turned to look at him. "You have said you will speak with your own mouth."

"Yes."

"There is no future in Grandmother's Land and none south of the Medicine Line," Arbuckles said, giving an expressive shrug of the shoulders. "There is a saying about frying pans?"

He laughed. "You know that saying. I remember. It is 'out of the frying pan into the fire.' "

"That is where the *Lakȟóta* are nowadays," Arbuckles said. "Jumping from a burning pan into the flames."

TERRY COMMISSION

20

After a brief night of a cold supper and rudimentary bivouac north of Fort Benton, they crossed the Marias River and climbed out of the floodplain of the mighty Missouri. The waterway was still running high and spreading wide after calamitous flooding from the spring breakup. Piles of debris and numerous putrefying animal carcasses were strewn along its borders. It was evident that all steamboat traffic to and from Fort Benton had ceased, no doubt due to the prodigious tangles of logs and indistinct wreckage that sporadically floated past upon swift currents. Disagreeable odors arose from the detritus and Collins was not sorry to be away from the stench and clouds of blue-bottle flies that ascended as the morning sun warmed the assemblage of carrion upon the river banks.

Soon, the terrain leveled into another stretch of uninspired topography. In the distance to the southeast was an insignificant stretch of mountains, barely discernable and grey-blue on the horizon. Wakalyapi and Collins kept up a steady pace, hoping to reach Fort Assiniboine before nightfall. North of the lofty mountain ranges, they were now well beyond gold-producing regions and the road they followed was unoccupied by fellow travelers. Collins figured that his companion would be less conspicuous the nearer they came to the great Indian reservation that traversed most of the boundary between Montana Territory and the British Possessions.

President Grant had established the reservation, for the Piegan, Blood, Blackfeet and other tribes, by executive order in 1873. This safeguarded tract of land, encompassing nearly three thousand square miles, had not deterred Miles and his soldiers from attacking any Indians that were deemed hostile.

"Tell me about the scout Culbertson," C.W. asked. "Is he related to the Culbertson who established Fort Benton for the American Fur Company?"

"He is the son of that man and *Natoyist-siksina*, a Blood woman. She has left Culbertson and does not want to know the son and lives with the Red Crow band across the line."

"When we were at the Tongue River Cantonment, Miles told me Culbertson is a drunk."

"He is a person that wanted to please Bear Coat all the time and lick his boots. This younger Culbertson, like the Fish, seeks to be somebody big by bringing in Thatháŋka Ìyotake. I do not know if he is a drunk."

" 'How does thy honour? Let me lick thy shoe. I'll not serve him, he is not valiant.' "

"Shakespeare?"

"*The Tempest.*"

"I have not read that one. Tell me the story"

"There is a magician on a remote island."

"Magician?"

"Like a holy man, but not...not..." Collins struggled with an adequate explanation.

"Not holy?" Wakalyapi asked, grinning.

"Not holy. More like someone who has power and plays tricks."

"We have *Iktómi* who can make things happen that are good and bad."

"He would be similar then. The magician, Prospero, is angry because his brother betrayed him and he was forced to escape with his little daughter to the island.

Twelve years later, his brother and some friends are shipwrecked...their boat is broken on the rocks...near the island. The magician wants revenge and makes a plan."

The time passed pleasantly enough as Collins recounted the story of the play and described the characters to the best of his ability. Arbuckles asked a question once in a while and they discussed certain details and insights. The sun reached its apex and began its descent toward the west. They forded several streams that were running high, but were not impassable, and skirted a sizeable butte to the south. Collins noticed the mountains on the skyline remained elusively remote. Wakalyapi interrupted his narration to explain that it was near those mountains that the *Pȟóǧe Ȟlóka* had been captured.

"They are the people the *wašíču* call the 'Nez Perces.' That is what I have heard them called by soldier boys."

"I believe it is French, is it not?"

"*Mais oui*. It is really *Nez Percé*."

Collins recollected that Wakalyapi had been taught to read and write by a French priest.

"Many of the *Pȟóǧe Ȟlóka* arrived in our camp later, wounded and hungry, seeking refuge," she continued. "Some of them returned across the line, but most have stayed, scattering across the land so they will not be sent back."

"What are those mountains called?"

"*Matȟó Sí Ȟé*. In English, the Bear Paw mountains. We will be coming to the fort soon," she told him. "I do not think we should stay there."

"We will resupply, send a telegram to General Terry informing him of our whereabouts and then depart. The Milk River is beyond the fort and we should be able to make camp there."

"How do you know where the river is? Have you been

to this place before?"

"No. I acquired a map of Montana Territory a while ago. It is fairly accurate." C.W. glanced at his companion. "And, of course, I have an excellent scout."

"Perhaps. Perhaps you own something I covet."

"Oh no. You still have my last rifle and will have to accept another form of payment."

Wakalyapi covered her mouth with a hand.

It was late afternoon when the extensive stockade of Fort Assiniboine appeared in the distance. Beyond, toward the southeast, lay unremarkable hills and the blue mounds of the Bear Paw highlands. Figures could be seen moving about and smoke rose from chimneys. The horse herd was grazing on the northeast side, under the watchful eyes of several mounted sentries. Small trees lined the creek that ran along the southern perimeter of the military post and several lodges were pitched nearby. Collins was struck by the thoroughgoing size of the fort. He thought it was remarkable, given the swiftness with which it had been erected.

Riding though an open gate, he headed for the guardhouse to announce his reason for being there. Dismounting and handing the reins to Arbuckles and telling the dog to stay on the saddle, C.W. entered the cool interior. An extraordinarily emaciated and freckled corporal directed him to the headquarters building. It was a small distance down a lane running along the enlisted men's row of barracks.

"I must go to the adjutant's office," he told Wakalyapi, who was now standing beside her horse with the dog at her feet and the other horses and mule gathered around. "Would you prefer to wait outside the walls?"

"You will find me just beyond the gate."

"Very well."

As he made his way toward the headquarters, Collins observed that most of the buildings were constructed of red brick, which was, in his experience, unusual for western posts. Most forts were collections of wood, adobe and log structures, many of them poorly built. The office was housed in a two-story square brick edifice fronted by a generous porch. Inside, he spoke with a Captain Adams, who was the post adjutant. The man was jovial and accommodating and remarkably lacking in curiosity. It seemed that General Terry had sent instructions to assist his civilian agent, C. W. Collins, with any reasonable request. The captain wrote out orders to the signal officer, who also happened to be the assistant acting quartermaster, that Collins should have access to necessary supplies as well as telegraphic communication.

He found one Lieutenant Hayt at the quartermaster storehouse across from the headquarters. After handing him the note from Captain Adams, he was provided with extra ammunition, blankets and a length of rope. The building also housed the telegraph apparatus, so C.W. composed a brief message for Terry, informing him of his location and proposed route. After his dispatch was reviewed by the officer and transmitted by a sullen and taciturn sergeant, the lieutenant strolled along with Collins back toward the commissary building near the front gate.

"Do I take it you are bound for the Dominion?" the lieutenant asked. "I inferred as much from your telegram."

"Eventually." He did not elaborate.

The officer seemed to be around thirty years of age and of even temperament. Unaffected by Collins' terse response, he chatted about the flooding on the Missouri and recent Indian activity until arriving at their destination. Inside, he directed the private on subsistence duty to bestow upon Collins whatever provisions he requested.

"Good luck to you, Mr. Collins," Lieutenant Hayt said

as he left the building. "Keep your powder dry."

"Thank you, Lieutenant. You have been most accommodating."

Loaded down with his acquisitions, C.W. passed through the front gates, grateful he had accomplished so much in such a brief amount of time. There remained plenty of daylight to reach the Milk River and arrange a comfortable camp. The animals needed a rest and he had managed to procure some beef steaks and potatoes that would make for a hearty meal. Beyond the stockade, he searched for Wakalyapi and found her sitting on her heels under a lone tree in conversation with a white man, who was seated upon the ground beside her. The fellow was almost distinguished looking, in spite of a long, unkempt mane of brown hair and unruly moustaches. He was costumed in civilian attire that was a collection of Indian and American garments.

Arbuckles was speaking in her native tongue. Looking up at C.W.'s approach, she said, "This Everette. Scout for army. He talk long Sitting Bull. Come north in Moon of Falling Leaves. No good."

Having not heard Wakalyapi descend into pidgin English in many years, he almost yielded to merriment, but restrained himself. "I am Charles Collins," he told the scout. "You encouraged Sitting Bull to surrender?"

"My name is Willis Everette," the scout said. "Last October, I was sent up to Wood Mountain to negotiate with the chief. Allison had been there, but with no success and he possessed no official authorization. At least not then. I received orders from the post commander at the Cantonment on Poplar Creek, who had received instructions from General Terry."

Conscious he was standing over the man, Collins put down his parcels and sat beside him. The dog trotted over from somewhere and lay down by his knee. "You did not achieve your purpose, I take it." He looked around for their stock and saw they were grazing out a little way to the west.

"He will not give a decided answer until he hears from Major Walsh, a superintendent with the North-West Mounted Police who was transferred east last year. Walsh has been a friend to the renegade Sioux. The Indians were bold and independent and I was kept a prisoner two days in their camp."

"No trust white men," Arbuckles said. "Too much lies."

C.W. thought she might be overdoing the parody of illiterate Indian. He gave her a look and thought he saw the trace of a smile. "Did they harm you?"

"Oh no. I was treated well and found many of them to be very cordial. A division existed in the camp. A part wanted to go back with me. The greater portion, under Sitting Bull, did not. But I found I comprehended their predicament. Later, this past March, I went to see Sitting Bull, when he had come over the border to hunt, and encouraged his followers to remain with their chief and only surrender when he does. I also warned Sitting Bull of approaching troops that were intending to cut him off from escape across the line."

"And you still work for the army?"

Everette laughed. "There was some suspicion, but nothing was proven. However, Captain Read *did* request I be reassigned to Fort Assiniboine." He spoke to Wakalyapi in her language and she answered him.

"You speak Lakota?" C.W. asked.

"And several other Indian dialects. I learn languages very quickly."

The three of them got to their feet. Wakalyapi went to gather the horses.

Deciding to be candid, Collins said, "Terry has requested I make an attempt to bring in Sitting Bull."

Everette evinced surprise. "Why you?"

"For several years I have been employed by men in Washington to reconnoiter delicate situations. And I have met the chief previously."

"And you are still with us."

"As are you."

Digging the toe of a boot in the dirt pensively, the scout said, "I would not care to be an Indian in this point of time."

"Nor I," Collins agreed.

"I have been learning metallurgy and will soon leave the army to become an assayer. I have no stomach for killing Indians."

Taken aback, Collins studied the man. "That makes you rather heretical as an army employee. It is certain that countless Indians would be pleased to kill you and me." He bent to gather up his supplies.

"Perhaps. Probably with good reason, but you have nothing to trouble you. I am convinced that your guide there is reliable," Everette told him, nodding toward Wakalyapi. "She aided me in Sitting Bull's camp and should keep you in good health."

They walked together toward where the Indian woman waited with the animals. "I think I can trust her," Collins said when within ear shot. He secured his bundles of goods on Molly's packs.

"No trust white men," Arbuckles said, squinting her eyes and swinging onto her horse.

The scout said something to the woman in her language. "I let her know she could trust you," he told Collins.

"My gratitude, Mr. Everette," he said and stepped over to tighten the cinches on Ulysses and Molly.

As they rode away, Collins asked Wakalyapi, "Did he tell you to trust me?"

"No. He told me to take your scalp at the first chance."
"That makes him a very sensible fellow."
"I agree."

GRATTAN'S MASSACRE

21

"It was an old cow that had wandered away and was almost dead. There was almost nothing left of it except a little life, laying there without food or water and would soon die. It was too lame to walk with feet worn through to the flesh and was shot by some boys who wanted a piece of skin, but a *Sičháŋǧu* warrior called High Forehead was blamed."

"And this was back in the fifties?" Collins asked, stirring the fire and adding wood.

They were camped near Little Porcupine Creek just east of the confluence of the Milk and Missouri rivers. Wakalyapi was guiding him along a road, traveled by both soldiers, civilians and Indians, that was bound for Fort Buford. The day before they had encountered a small troop of mounted 11th Infantry soldiers en route to Fort Assiniboine from Camp Poplar River. While Arbuckles faded out of sight into a coulee, C.W. had spoken with the soldiers and learned they were ordered to Assiniboine for material and supplies. The men were decidedly apathetic and had expressed their eagerness for a rousing battle with Indians. Most of them looked to Collins to be fresh recruits from the east and several of them could barely manage their horses.

"In summer. Perhaps '54 or '55. I do not remember which. It was the same summer the Snakes attacked and killed people on the big trail going west. The Snakes were angry because wagons were always coming and coming and the animals and grass and trees were taken. Many Indians were killed for no reason or treated like thieves."

"But what happened with the cow?"

"The *wašíču* with the cow were on the way to Fort Laramie and came there and complained to the soldiers. By then, according to the *Lakȟóta* way, a head man named Conquering Bear brought an excellent horse as payment for the worthless cow, but the white people only wanted money."

"Why were the Indians there at Fort Laramie? Why not stay away?"

The woman's hands were occupied with repairing beadwork on her rifle scabbard. "It was the time of treaty goods and there was a gathering of around six hundred lodges. There were people of the *Mnikȟówožu, Oglála,* some *Šahíyela,* Cheyenne, there and the *Sičháŋǧu* that had camped near the trading post of *Matȟó,* James Bordeaux. Everyone was weary with hanging around and knew the goods were stored at the big trading post up the river, but the agent did not come. Grass was almost gone for the ponies and we had very little food to eat."

"You were there?"

"Yes. I had left the *Kȟaŋǧí Wičháša* by then and was hunting mostly for the people. Sometimes I hunted for the soldier boys in the fort and this way I could have ammunition and some other goods. Sometimes I traded. I was a ruined woman and could not have a man."

"Beckwourth?"

She nodded but did not look up from her work. "There was a soldier boy there at the fort, a lieutenant called Grattan," she continued. "I did not come around him because he hated Indian people and walked around like a *maǧá tȟáŋka,* a big goose, with his head up and talking about his own bravery and great worth. He had a strong voice and the head soldier at the fort was weak and so let Grattan go with a handful of around twenty soldiers to arrest High Forehead. He started for the camp and I followed and saw. There was a Frenchman with him, drunk and foolish, who spoke some of the language. He told Grattan that the *Lakȟóta* are all women, then he rode his horse up and down by the big trading post near the fort and shouted insulting words at the Indians there. Some of the soldiers were drunk then too, but some of them were not and said they would be killed."

Pouring himself another cup of coffee and waiting for Wakalyapi to resume her narration, Collins thought about all the mishaps, born of arrogance, that had led to disasters throughout history. He did not believe the incident, as related by his companion, would end well.

Arbuckles went to her packs to retrieve more sinew, then returned to her place and began speaking again. "Grattan took his soldiers past the Oglála hoop and warned the head men to stay where they were or he would open fire on them. Next the troop came to the Bordeaux trading post and the drunk interpreter once again made rude talk to the Indians there and told them he would eat their hearts before sundown. Grattan told Bordeaux he wanted to talk to Conquering Bear and the trader sent a boy for him. In a short while, the chief came with some other principal men, including Men Afraid of His Horses. Grattan said he had come there to take High Forehead back to the fort. The chiefs explained to Grattan that High Forehead was a guest in the *Sičháŋǧu* village and it was for them to decide, but promised they would send more ponies to the cow people. They also wanted Grattan to wait for the Indian agent to come."

"Did Bordeaux try to talk sense to Lieutenant Grattan?" Collins asked as he packed his pipe for a smoke.

"The trader told him that he was going into a very bad place and that he had better prepare himself well. Grattan said he had two revolvers with twelve shots and Bordeaux told him to take them out of his holsters and be ready."

"But he did not attempt to stop him?"

"How could he? Grattan wanted to fight."

Looking out across the flat land to the north, C.W. watched fluctuating curtains of ethereal viridescent illumination. "What do the Lakota call the northern lights? I have forgotten." he asked.

"*Hóhe-tȟamáȟpiya*. Drifting cloud lights."

"Lovely." He tamped his pipe with a finger meditatively. "Please go on."

Having finished her task of mending the scabbard, Wakalyapi set about adding some decorative beading to her arrow quiver. "When he came to a hill over the camp, he told his men that once he gave the command, they were to fire as much as they damn pleased. I heard him say so. Then he came into the *Sičháŋǧu* camp with two big guns on wheels, the ones called howitzers, and aimed them at Conquering Bear's lodge. High Forehead's lodge was a little way over and he stood there and told Grattan he was willing to die. The head men tried again to ask Grattan to wait for the agent, but the drunk interpreter was confusing everyone by getting the words wrong. Then many Oglála and Sičháŋǧu warriors began to prepare for a fight."

"Could Grattan see this?"

"No and I believe the interpreter had convinced him the Indians were afraid. Grattan gave a command I could not hear from where I was and a couple of shots were fired and a young man was wounded in the camp. Then all of a sudden, the soldiers began shooting and Conquering Bear went down. Grattan fired one of the big guns that hit nothing, but then he was knocked down with arrows. The drunk Frenchman ran away and all the soldiers scattered like mice when the nest is opened. Even though most of the Indians had few guns at that time, they rode all the soldier boys down and killed them."

"Even the Frenchman?"

"Yes and then he was badly cut up and scalped. Soon many of the lodges were struck and people began to leave. Some of the warriors stayed until morning and took treaty goods from the big trading post. Then everyone went away and the bands separated. Conquering Bear died later. I stayed around with some of the Cheyenne that had several lodges there and were known to be peaceful. We were not bothered by the soldiers from the fort."

"What of reprisals by the military?"

"Reprisals?"

"Vengeance."

"There was vengeance. It was a year later the army came after the Lakȟóta, partly because of Grattan and partly because of raids on a stagecoach and other white people upon the big trail along the *Paŋkéska Wakpá*, what you call the Platte River. The soldiers found the Sičháŋǧu village of Conquering Bear, but the head man was now Little Thunder since Conquering Bear had died. The camp was near the river about halfway between Fort Laramie and Fort Kearny not far from the road. I was not there but was told later that horse soldiers came in from the north and foot soldiers came from the south. They had new guns that could shoot long and they opened fire on the camp, the foot soldiers driving the people into the other soldiers on the north. The horse soldiers chased everyone. Some of the women and children tried to hide in holes in the hills above but were shot dead. Many many women and children were killed or died later from wounds."

Collins stared into the dying embers of the fire and was made ill by yet another tale of carnage and malfeasance perpetrated by the U.S. Army. "Did Little Thunder live?"

"He was wounded but lived. *Siŋté Gleška* was also there

and fought bravely and got away. The soldiers stole goods and sacred items and lodge skins and burned what was left. Then they made prisoners of women, children and the old ones who could not get away and forced them to walk to Fort Laramie even if badly wounded. Some died on the trail." Wakalyapi laid aside her quiver and deftly packed away her beads, needle and sinew in a small pouch. "Some of the women were made to live with the soldiers in a way they did not want."

"Too often, justice does not seem to abide in the hearts of men."

"There was no justice on that day," Wakalyapi said, her face betraying resolute contempt. "The attack on the camp near *Paŋkéska Wakpá* was the place where mighty hatred between my people and the Americans really began."

"*Is fada siar a théann iarsma an drochbhirt.* The road of a bad deed goes a long way."

22

Camp Poplar River reminded Collins of the Cantonment on the Tongue River before it became Fort Keogh. Situated on the east bank of the river, north of the agency buildings by about a half mile, the tiny garrison consisted of a few shacks made of logs and crude lumber, surrounded by rows of tents. The camp occupied an elevated tract of land barren of every type of vegetation. Its unprotected site left it vulnerable to unbridled winds that swept in from the west, shaking and thrashing tent coverings. A few nearly denuded trees lined the Poplar River and small groups of lodges were dispersed across the expanse between the agency and cantonment. Far in the distance, spread out upon the skyline, he could see larger gatherings of lodges and assumed these belonged to some of the apostate Indians who had recently given themselves up.

Evidence of flooding along the Missouri and Poplar rivers was still visible. Remnants of blankets, clothing and broken lodgepoles were distributed in places upon the river bottoms. Indian families sat huddled together near their shelters or by the embankments, wrapped in threadbare blankets and staring with blank and spiritless eyes. Indian ponies, gaunt and spavined, stood here and there with heads down, seldom bothering to swish their tails at persistent flies. All in all, Collins found the entire scene to be grim and inhospitable.

They rode into the camp and he asked a passing soldier to direct him to the post commander. The fellow scrutinized Wakalyapi before answering.

"That is his tent over yonder," the private told him, pointing at a large wall tent on the lee side of one of the huts. He jerked a thumb at Molly's brand. "How come you got a damn army mule?"

"*Deineann ceann ciallmhar béal iadhta.*"

"What?" the private asked indignantly. "What? What the hell kinda palaver is that?"

Numerous mules and horses wandered the immediate area and several of them began to gather around. Ignoring the soldier, C.W turned to the woman. "We should get our horses away from this bunch, otherwise we may have a wreck."

"We will take them away."

They quit the congregation of equines, befuddled private and jumbled dwellings and made their way toward the river. Dismounting, he handed Arbuckles the gelding's reins and Molly's lead rope.

"What did you say back there?" she asked.

"A wise head makes a closed mouth."

She laughed softly, kneeling down and restraining the dog. "I will be here. Do not be long."

"No. The day is waning."

Collins walked back to the cantonment and found the post commander's tent. The door flap was closed and he heard voices within. He coughed loudly, waiting for a response. Perusing the camp and its inhabitants, he surmised that the officers were quartered in wall tents and most of the enlisted men were housed in the conical Sibley tents that were positioned in rows. As he waited, he noted that one side of the tent had been patched with a lighter colored section of canvas. All at once the flap was thrown back and a young second lieutenant stood in the opening.

"Yes?" he asked gruffly.

"I am here to see the post commander. My name is Charles Collins and I am acting for General Alfred Terry."

"Let him come, Orris," said a voice from within.

The lieutenant stepped to the side and desultorily motioned for C.W. to enter. The day was sunny and therefore the interior was lighted sufficiently for him to see. There was an officer seated behind a table, writing feverishly on a sheet of paper while periodically and energetically making use of an ink well, spattering droplets over other documents spread before him. Collins removed his hat, found a camp chair and sat down.

"See here," the lieutenant said, coming into the tent. "You should stand until recognized."

"I was once in the army, but no more," Collins said quietly. "I am not required to stand before an officer nor salute, for that matter."

"He is quite correct, Lieutenant," the superior officer chided, looking up from his endeavors. "I am Captain Read and this is Lieutenant Heistand, my adjutant. How may we assist you, and thereupon, General Terry?"

"I am required to seek out Sitting Bull. Do you happen to know his whereabouts?"

The captain considered this a brief while. He was pleasant of appearance and C.W. judged him to be no more than forty years of age.

"Seek out the Bull, you say?" the officer finally asked. "To what end?"

The lieutenant gave out a loud horse-laugh. "Yet another civilian scout commissioned by the general. Let me guess...you are to prod the old reprobate into surrendering."

"Now Orris," Captain Read said gently.

"Oh come along, sir. The rascal should be done away with, not wooed by every Tom, Dick or Harry."

The degree of familiarity shared between the two, thought Collins, bespoke a long acquaintanceship. He was also aware that this custom of casual exchange between superior and junior officers could be found only in the western territories.

"My apologies, Mr. Collins," the captain said. "Most of us in the northern reaches of Montana are sorely fatigued with the topic of Sitting Bull's imminent surrender."

Collins merely nodded, crossing his legs and examining the lighter patch of fabric behind the captain's back. It covered a considerable rupture in the cloth, now evident within the interior of the tent. Piled at the base of the opposite canvas wall was an accumulation of exquisite Indian costumes, clubs, coup sticks, ceremonial objects, headdresses and various other articles. It looked as if the captain was a collector of artifacts, no doubt plundered from villages such as the one that had been destroyed the previous January.

Sitting straighter and assuming a more professional comportment, Captain Read shuffled through a stack of documents as if engaged in searching for some vital information. Lieutenant Heistand simply glared at C.W., silently expressing his disapproval. There was a prolonged period of inexplicable silence wherein the dearth of conversation created a strange atmosphere.

"Well then," Collins said, coming to his feet. "I will not distract you from your duties any longer."

"Just a moment, Mr. Collins," the captain said, raising a hand placatingly. "Last we heard, Sitting Bull was camped at Jean Louis Légaré's trading post at Willow Bunch. There is a trail that follows the eastern branch of the Poplar River. It will take you there."

"Thank you."

"And I should warn you there is a white renegade named Thompson in the Bull's camp. He was formerly a member of the Mounted Police, but now lives among the Indians and dresses the part. He has talked against surrender and his influence is very bad."

"Thompson is a scoundrel," Heistand interjected with vehemence. "He is a worthless fellow who, by adopting the Indian mode of life, has abandoned his own race and relinquished his honor. It is shameful. Shameful."

"I will certainly look out for him," C.W. said, wondering how they had come to know of such a person. He donned his Stetson and searched for a tolerable pretext for an immediate departure. Both men gave the impression of being mildly peculiar.

"It was a mule," the captain said, seemingly as a non sequitur.

"I beg your pardon?"

"You were studying the rend in my tent. A mule kicked all the way through."

"The captain clouted it on the hindquarters with a chair," the lieutenant told him. "Had its rump leaning into the wall, about to sit down."

Assuming that whisky may have played a part, Collins said, "The mule won the battle, I take it."

"He did indeed, Mr. Collins. He did indeed," Read said jovially.

Anxious to be on his way, C.W. said, "I must take my leave, Captain. My gratitude for your assistance."

"You are welcome to camp here for the night," the captain offered. "There are hostile Indians roaming the border."

"I am well equipped and eager to proceed, but you have my thanks for the invitation."

"Your scalp is your scalp," Lieutenant Heistand said with acrimony. "Likely we will find it later on a lance shaft."

"Your kindly concern is touching, Lieutenant," Collins said and departed unceremoniously. Captain Read appeared to have small influence over his adjutant.

"Mr. Collins," the captain called, stepping out of the tent and coming after him. "We have few supplies here, but do you require provisions or ammunition?"

"No. I resupplied at Assiniboine."

"You must forgive us," Read said contritely. "With only two companies of men and such isolation, we have become erratic and not a little ill-disposed. We much preferred our assignment at Fort Custer."

"I quite understand. 'Men are as the time is,' Collins said, quoting from *King Lear.* "I thank you again, Captain."

Turning away with celerity, he made his way toward where Wakalyapi was waiting. They had adequate daylight left to make a solitary camp farther north along the trail that tracked the Poplar River. As he passed a small assembly of lodges, dilapidated and fraying, Collins was struck by the poverty and wretchedness that pervaded the scene. A wave of despondency swept through him. The threat of an entire multitude of hostile Indians could not have induced him to remain in the locality one minute more.

23

Smoke rose in fitful swirls from a fire to the northwest. Arbuckles held up a hand and they reined in, vigilant. Fiddle music and lively voices drifted to them upon the tenacious breezes that rustled the slough grass spreading out on either side of the trail.

"I see the tracks of carts," Wakalyapi said, pointing with her lower lip. "These are the carts that are used by the Red River Metis."

"What do you mean by Red River Metis?"

"They are half-breeds that came from a place to the east where there is such a river. This is how they are known."

Slapping his thigh so that Gal jumped onto the saddle, Collins asked, "Should we go around? Darkness is falling and we should make camp soon."

"They are trading folk and not usually treacherous. Perhaps they have news."

Kicking up her roan, the woman led the way off the road and down along the river. Beside a wide pool in the stream below an embankment, Collins could see several men and women and a few children gathered around a campfire. Just beyond, three two-wheeled carts sat piled with buffalo hides and other goods. Four horses grazed farther down the stream and a cow stood off by itself. A dog barked as they drew closer and two of the men reached for their rifles. They stood waiting, standing apart and clearly on the alert against any sign of threat.

The fiddle music stopped when a third man put down his instrument and the women and children moved back toward the carts. C.W. thought them to be handsome people, with a singular blending of Indian and Caucasian characteristics.

"*Taanishi*," called Arbuckles. "*Nous passons seulement.*"

"I talk English," one of the men holding a gun told her. "Who be you?"

Moving his horse up beside Wakalyapi, Collins said, "We are on our way to Willow Bunch and are hoping to find buffalo. Do you know of any in the area? This is my guide, Wakalyapi. My name is Charles Wolfe Collins."

"Joseph Gourneau *dishinihkaashoon*."

The women, costumed in dark dresses with scarves tied on their heads, began to move closer, outwardly curious. The children stayed by the carts, the oldest boy holding onto a big rangy brown dog.

"Buffalo? No," the fellow continued sullenly. "Do not know. No good here for *aen itraanzhii. Shipwaytay*. Go away." Mr. Gourneau made a dismissive gesture with his rifle. "*Shipwaytay*," he repeated and the other man raised the barrel of his rifle toward them.

"We will go now," Wakalyapi said and wheeled her horse to ride out of the camp the way they had come in.

Collins waited for her to move past, then turned Ulysses in behind her pack horse.

"Are those people always that unsociable?" he asked when they had traveled down the road a short distance.

"Not always. I have heard that Bear Coat and some of the settlers have accused them of selling whisky to the reservation bands and stealing livestock. Many of them were pushed south from their village on Milk River by soldier boys or back up across the line."

Having put a couple of miles between them and the Metis camp, Arbuckles chose a place to bivouac below a slight gradient alongside the river. The wind had been an incessant companion all day with nothing to thwart its progress on the great treeless expanses of the northern prairie. Even minimal shelter was welcome. After unsaddling and hobbling the stock and turning them loose to graze, Collins gathered dried buffalo dung for fuel while Wakalyapi took her bow to search for game. He had a small fire burning and the coffeepot heating when she returned with several grouse.

Swarms of mosquitoes found them, raising blotches on their hands, necks and faces resembling smallpox pustules. Molly and the horses stomped and twitched in misery and Gal whined persistently until C.W. tossed a saddle blanket over her. Wakalyapi left camp and returned with moistened handfuls of a long dense grass, placing them on the fire to produce clouds of smoke.

When they had eaten, they both took out their pipes.

"What is that grass?" Collins asked, puffing vigorously on his old briar. "The aroma is pleasing."

"It is *wačháŋǧa*. It is sacred and useful as medicine."

"And for warding off venomous insects."

"For the *čhapȟúŋka* also."

A delicate waxing moon was low in the western sky as dusk became night. The air grew cooler and the hordes of pestiferous intruders finally departed, much to everyone's relief. The dog crept from her refuge and Collins fed her the shreds of grouse meat he had kept back for her supper.

"That dog is pampered," the woman said.

"Perhaps. And why not?"

She shrugged and tossed a piece of bread to the dog. "Why not?"

Smiling, Collins stirred the modest blaze and added a few more buffalo chips. "Tell me about One Bull. You mentioned before that you did not trust him."

"I do not."

"Was he in Sitting Bull's camp when I was there?"

"He was the warrior who wanted to take your scalp."

A solitary wolf serenaded them from far off to the east. Its mournful song touched C.W.'s unalloyed marrow, calling forth ancient and elemental longing. He sighed deeply.

"It is your brother."

"Who is my brother?"

"*Šuŋgmánitu tȟáŋka*. The wolf."

"Yes indeed," said C.W., giving her a scowl. "I thought we dispensed with that nonsense a long time ago. Now do go on about One Bull."

The woman's eyes revealed a twinkling of humor then became thoughtful. "Tȟatȟáŋka Ìyotake is a strong leader. Stronger because he is tolerant of the weakness of others. *Tȟatȟáŋka Waŋží* has counted on this many times and because he is his nephew."

"One Bull is Sitting Bull's nephew?"

"Son of Good Feather Woman, his older sister."

"And why do you not trust him?"

"Even though he is an *akičhita*, he behaves dishonorably and makes his uncle ashamed. On a certain occurrence, there was a *Mnikȟówožu* woman who was promised to an honorable warrior. One Bull told her pretty words and sneaked around with her and gave her a child. When she could not hide the swelling, she caused the baby to go away and when her man found out about this, he killed her. Several Mnikȟówožu warriors wanted vengeance, but Tȟatȟáŋka Ìyotake convinced them of their mistake."

"Did he know One Bull was guilty?"

"Yes. It was why he was ashamed."

Standing up, Collins fetched his Winchester and revolver, then returned to the fire. "But why would that make you not trust him? Did he behave disgracefully toward you?" He removed the cartridges, broke down his firearms and proceeded to clean them, using soap and boiling water from a pot on the fire.

"No, he did not. But a man who is given a principal duty among the people and behaves dishonorably is not a man to be trusted."

"If you give me your rifle, I will clean it for you."

"Wait until you have completed the task with your own guns. We should not go unarmed."

"Of course." Collins felt utterly foolish for not thinking of this. "Were there other incidents with One Bull?"

"Some small happenings. Then there was the horse."

She was smoking her pipe again and Collins reminded himself they would have to purchase more tobacco at the next favorable opportunity. Arbuckles seemed to be enjoying an American blend more these days and seldom smoked the aromatic mixture she used to prefer.

"A horse?" he prompted.

"He stole a horse from Légaré, the trader at Wood Mountain. To do this was very wrong of a warrior in the *Čhaŋté't'inza Okȟólakičhiye*. In any warrior society."

Now that his guns were clean and dry, C.W. went to their packs and cut a small piece of fat from some side meat. He sat down again and, after warming it in his hands, he used the fat to grease all the moving parts. He reloaded the rifle and revolver.

"All finished," he said. "Now your rifle?"

Pulling her Winchester from its scabbard, Wakalyapi handed it over to him. "This has been an admirable gun," she told him.

"You do not miss your old Hawken?"

"I gave it to a friend."

After unloading the rifle, Collins set about cleaning it thoroughly as he had done with his own. "What happened about the horse?"

"The trader was an important man there and chose two half-breeds to capture One Bull. He would not go back with them. Then Walsh sent two redcoats to bring him in, but T̈haẗháŋka Ìyotake told them his nephew would not come. That is when Walsh sent five more soldiers and One Bull was arrested and taken back to the redcoat headquarters and several warriors followed, including his uncle. When Walsh told a redcoat to ride to get Légaré, One Bull grabbed the reins to hold him back. Walsh shoved One Bull aside and his men took him into the fort. T̈haẗháŋka Ìyotake became angry when he saw his nephew taken away. By this time, many of the Húŋkpap̈ha warriors had gathered around. Once One Bull was in the fort, they threatened the redcoats, but Walsh lined up his men and they held their rifles ready to shoot."

"You saw all this?"

"Kinealy and a couple of the other white warriors were there and I was there also. We stood back and watched. When Walsh said he would order his men to shoot if the warriors did not leave, they left. That night there was a council and there was reckless talk of attacking the fort. The head men all wanted to stay on Grandmother Land and anger was changed to wisdom. The trader Légaré had his horse back and he allowed One Bull to be freed. As a true Lakȟóta shirt wearer with traditional virtue, T̈haẗháŋka Ìyotake returned to the redcoat fort and made an apology."

Handing a cleaned and oiled rifle back to Wakalyapi, Collins said, "I understand now why you see One Bull as untrustworthy."

"*Blihéuŋkič'iyapi kte, na óuŋkičhiyapi kta waŋ héčha*. We should be strong and help each other. The men such as One Bull are weak and only looking to make themselves bigger."

24

Late the next morning, they came upon a rudimentary heap of stones, with a small trench dug around it. Other piles of rock, similar in appearance, were visible on a direct line east and west.

"This is the boundary to *Uŋčíyapi Makȟóčhe*," Arbuckles told Collins.

"The countryside ahead looks as insufferably dull as that which we are leaving."

"Once it was covered with *tȟatȟáŋka*," she said forlornly. "It was not dull then."

"The grasses are certainly luxuriant."

Rain clouds were gathering in the southwest and C.W. ardently hoped that they would not be caught in a storm without even a minor geographical barrier for protection. He had brought his sturdy tent and an adequate number of poles and this would have to suffice if necessary. The thought of lightning gave him pause, however.

To engage his mind and because Wakalyapi was being decidedly laconic, Collins deliberated upon the recent election of James Garfield as U.S. president and his subsequent appointment of Samuel J. Kirkwood as the Secretary of the Interior. Kirkwood had been a militant abolitionist in his day and, while governor of Iowa, had facilitated the escape of one of John Brown's Harper's Ferry raiders. He had also firmly supported President Lincoln's Emancipation Proclamation.

Although he had never encountered the man, Collins

knew of Kirkwood from President Lincoln himself. He had met President-elect Lincoln while newly employed as an operative for Allan Pinkerton's North West Police Agency. After Pinkerton had exposed a plot to assassinate Abraham Lincoln at a railroad station in Baltimore, precautions were taken. The president-elect was placed on a sleeper car in Pennsylvania and disguised in a nondescript hat and overcoat, arriving in Baltimore in the dead of night. From there, he was conveyed through the streets to a connecting train on the other side of the city and thereby safely transported into Washington D.C. for his inauguration.

Lincoln's personal bodyguard, Ward Lamon, as well as Pinkerton, Collins and Kate Warne, the agency's only woman operative, accompanied Mr. Lincoln throughout the entire journey. Impressed by Mr. Lincoln and his politics, Collins had taken the opportunity to talk with the president-elect. Abolition being the general concern of the day, as well as apprehension regarding secessionist sentiments, their conversations naturally turned to these principal topics. Despite Pinkerton's attempts to dissuade the youthful Collins from speaking with Lincoln, the president-elect had steadfastly engaged him in animated discussions, during which Lincoln had praised Samuel Kirkwood and his anti-slavery views.

Given Kirkwood's laudable perspectives concerning slavery, Collins hoped he would apply a similar magnanimity to his dealings with Indian matters. The Department of War was persisting in its attempts to convince Congress that control of the Indian Bureau should be transferred to its tender mercies. Carl Schurz had vigorously resisted such a transfer in the past and, ostensibly, Kirkwood would follow suit. Although C.W. was not in favor of the bureau's policies intended to forcibly civilize Indians, they were preferable to military aggression and sanctimonious barbarity.

"Someone is coming," Wakalyapi said, encroaching upon his ruminations.

Scanning the far reaching vista before them, Collins descried a caravan of horses, wagons and people approaching. A haze of dust obscured its particulars.

"There is no place for you to conceal yourself," he told the woman. "Shall we wait by the side of the road and beard the lion?"

"Lion?"

"Confront bravely whatever is to come."

"Is that Shakespeare? Beard the lion?" she asked.

"I do not believe so. Although he did write of a hare plucking dead lions by the beard. I am not absolutely certain what was meant by this."

"I have not seen any lion with a beard, only white men."

The indistinct convoy was drawing nearer and Collins was tolerably confident it was not of a military inclination. He could now distinguish what looked to be women and children riding in carts similar to the ones he had seen in the half-breed camp.

"Lions found in far away lands have beards," he told Arbuckles. The absurdity of their discussion was not lost upon him.

"It is of no consequence," she said, rubbing her mouth tellingly. "We will pluck this beard together."

C.W. observed that a man riding a dark horse, in front of the line of carts, had a long and generous beard. " 'He that hath a beard is more than a youth, and he that hath no beard is less than a man,' " he quoted.

"You have no beard."

"Too true. Make of that what you will," Collins said, laughing.

They sat their horses and watched as the bearded fellow rode up to them. A middle-aged Indian warrior rode beside him. The train of twelve carts, some of them drawn by horses and some by oxen, were mostly empty, except for four of them that were occupied by Indian women, elderly men and children. They were all driven by half-breeds who looked to be much the same as those they had encountered the day before. Some of the men wore brightly colored sashes girded around their coats or blouses. The wheels on the wooden carts made high-pitched shrieks that Collins figured would preclude any conceivable stealth, if so required.

"*Bonjour, Monsieur* Légaré," Wakalyapi said to the bearded man. She nodded to the warrior beside him and he gave a curt nod in response, while intently examining Collins.

"*Bonjour mon amie!*" the man shouted with pleasure.

"This is Jean Louis Légaré, post trader at Willow Bunch and lately at Wood Mountain," she told Collins. "Jean Louis, this is Charles Collins. He has come to speak with Tȟatȟáŋka Ìyotake."

"*Je suis désolé*. The Bull has gone to Qu'Appelle to seek his Major Walsh."

Strong winds had been steadily building and suddenly struck them with gusts of such force that Collins nearly lost his Stetson and a couple of the teamsters did, indeed, have their hats launched into flight. They leapt from the carts and chased their head gear while their comrades laughed heartily. Then driving rain and hail precipitously smashed into them and Légaré began to shout orders. The carts were summarily driven into a loose circle and people scrambled beneath them, while some of the women threw buffalo robes over the children. Légaré's men hastily unhitched the horses and oxen and tethered them on the leeward sides of the wagons.

Wakalyapi and Collins dismounted and held tightly to the reins and lead ropes as their animals swung frantically around to place their rumps against the lashing assault. One of the half-breeds gestured for them to come into the enclosure and they hurried into the make-shift corral. Together they unloaded their packs beside an un-occupied cart and secured the horses and mule to the spokes of its wheels. Collins worriedly searched for his dog among the cluster of huddled people, wagons and livestock and could not find her. Arbuckles dragged him down to the ground when a greater onslaught of hail battered into them. Hauling the canvas tent from their pile of belongings, Collins unfolded it over their trap-pings and them and they hunkered down against the storm's ferocity.

When at last the hail finally relented, peals of thunder began to roll across the firmament and bolts of lightning flashed around them, vivid beyond description. Sheets of rain arrived one after another like unyielding walls of water, beating against every solid object with seem-ing malevolence. A shivering and water-logged creature crept under their shelter and C.W. wrapped his arms around his sodden dog with an abundance of relief. After a while, he slumped down and fell asleep, despite the ca-cophony of howling wind, rain and thunderous reverber-ations. When Wakalyapi shook him awake, the gale had finally been spent. They flung back the canvas to find the sun was setting through an array of remnant clouds, sending gossamer rays into a darkening sky. There was industrious commotion among the carts and, against all logic, several fires had been lit.

While Collins began to unsaddle their animals, Wakalyapi spread the tent canvas on the cart to dry. Gal lay upon the damp grass and licked her paws.

"So you have survived *la tempête aussi*," Légaré said, walking over to them. "There are many *comme ça* along this road."

"Where are you bound for?" Collins asked, kneeling down to hobble Molly and the horses in turn.

"I make periodic journeys to Fort Buford for *march-*

andise...merchandise. I am taking these Indians there so they may remain if they choose." He waved a hand at the warrior who C.W. had seen earlier. "*Thathą́ŋka Ehą́ŋni,* Old Bull, is Sitting Bull's *beau-frère*, brother-in-law. He is coming to see whether there is good or bad treatment at the hands of the soldiers."

Freeing the stock to graze, C.W. saw that Wakalyapi was gone. "How were you able to light fires?"

"*Bois de vache* and quantities of kerosene oil. Come, there is no need of your own hearth. You may share mine."

They strolled toward one of the campfires. Three folding chairs were set about the unassuming blaze and one of the men was using a large wooden campaign trunk as a table on which to knead dough. A hunk of red meat was suspended over the fire on an iron skewer and a coffeepot rested on the edge of the flames. A stack of buffalo chips steamed nearby, drying in the heat. Night was swiftly descending and Collins could hear the distinctive sounds of nocturnal birds calling far away. There were fewer mosquitoes after the tremendous deluge and for that he was grateful.

"*Tire-toi une bû,*" his host told him, gesturing at one of the chairs.

"I see you make a comfortable bivouac," Collins said, taking a seat at Légaré's invitation. Gal curled up under him.

"Only with the most simple of indulgences." He stroked his ample beard pensively. "*Maintenant* tell me, if I am not too inquisitive, why do you chase the Bull?"

"I have been requested to meet with him to discuss surrender."

"*Tu me prends pour un poisson?* This has been tried many times. That fellow Allison made himself a grand pest." Légaré turned and spoke to his man. "Louis, *li koffii, sil voo play,*"

The fellow brought tin cups and poured coffee for them, then placed the pot back by the fire and set a greased cast iron skillet on some coals. He fetched the dough and dropped clods of it into the pan.

"What is the language you just used?"

"I employ many of the Metis, the half-breeds. It is their tongue."

Wakalyapi walked quietly into the halo of firelight and sat in the vacant chair. "I could find no game," she said.

"*Ce n'est rien*," the Frenchman said. "You will eat here."

The cook Louis left his pan of bread to fetch her a cup and some coffee.

She said, "*Maarsii*," and he smiled at her.

The meal was soon served to them and they ate from dishes balanced upon their laps. The venison meat was tender and Collins found the bread to be quite good, at once crispy and dense.

He motioned to Louis for his attention and pointed at the bread. "Good."

"*Miiyaashin*," Légaré said.

Collins repeated the word and the man nodded to him, saying, "*Maarsii*."

When they had eaten and were each smoking their pipes, Légaré gave C.W. a penetrating look. "And now, *Monsieur* Charles, will you not tell me of your true aim in seeking out the Bull?"

"I am certain you have heard of General Terry."

"*Mets-en.*"

"I have been commissioned by him to persuade Sitting Bull to surrender. That is all."

"But why would the general think you are *compétent* for this? And that the Sioux will not kill you *immédiatement.*"

"He has fought beside Thatȟáŋka Ìyotake," Wakalyapi told him. "He has hunted with him."

Légaré regarded Collins thoughtfully, then said, "You

confound me, *mon ami. Mais* how *exactement*, after the *l'idiot* Allison and many others have failed most miserably, can you achieve the Bull's *capitulation*? Not even Terry, *chef de l'armée*, could bring him in."

Knocking the ashes from his pipe and blowing the stem clear, C.W. refilled it slowly, searching for an answer. "I do not know," he said at last. " 'I stand in pause where I shall first begin.' I genuinely do not know."

"You have said that Thatȟáŋka Ìyotake has now gone away?" Arbuckles asked.

"He has taken *beaucoup* lodges with him to Qu'Appelle. They came to Willow Bunch *avec la langue à Terre* and said they had been sent away from Wood Mountain by the *connard* who was swapped for Major Walsh. I told them *la Grand-mère blanche* would not give them land and if they wanted *les enfants* to live, they should go back across the line to America." The Frenchman shook his head with obvious dismay. "*Calisse!* The Bull said he knew my word was good, *mais* the chiefs could not trust Americans."

"Major Walsh was generous to the Lakȟóta," Wakalyapi told Collins. "But they sent him away last year. I think he was too kind and they blame him for the people not wanting to go back across the line." She turned to Légaré. "Does Walsh remain in Qu'Appelle?"

"*Je ne sais pas.* The Bull has been waiting for Walsh to return to Wood Mountain, but he has not. So he is going *pour le trouver.*"

The dog raised her head and growled. Old Bull came to the fire and sat on the ground between Légaré and Wakalyapi. He looked at the woman and asked, *"Tókhiya lá hwo?"*

"Slolwáye šni kštó."

Old Bull shrugged and sat staring into the smoldering ashes of the fire. Collins glanced at Arbuckles inquisitively.

"He asked where we were going. I told him I did not

know."

"When will Sitting Bull return?" Collins asked the Frenchman.

"*Peut-être* after a month. Maybe more. It is a long way and they are traveling *lentement* with hungry children. And is Walsh at Qu'Appelle? *Qui sait*?"

"We will go to Willow Bunch and talk to the people," the woman said. "Then we can decide if we should go to Qu'Appelle."

"Wait at Willow Bunch," Old Bull said unexpectedly. "I will come back and tell you of Buford." He grinned broadly at Collins and took out a stumpy red stone pipe with a wooden stem. "Do you have tobacco?"

RAIN STORM

25

The morning broke gloomily. Collins had propped his small mirror on the wheel of the cart that had sheltered them from the storm and was shaving three days' worth of beard.

"You do not want to grow that and be a man?" Arbuckles asked. She was seated on the folded tent, drinking coffee and smoking. Old Bull was sitting on the ground beside her.

"You are a foolish woman," he told her. "No man of importance has a beard."

"You do not know Shakespeare," she said.

"No. Who is he?"

"Nobody. Just another *wašíču*."

Swinging around, C.W. glared at her. "Nobody?"

Wakalyapi gazed back at him without expression. "Maybe somebody."

"You are both foolish," Old Bull said, taking out his pipe. "Tobacco?"

When they had caught the animals and were about to begin packing up, Légaré invited them for breakfast. There was more bread, coffee, some side meat, oatmeal and molasses. Old Bull ate some of the bread, but Collins noticed he did not eat the pork. The meal was a hurried affair because everyone was eager to be on their way. The small host of Indians did not bother with a fire and swiftly prepared to depart, loading their meager possessions in the carts and climbing aboard to wait.

Old Bull helped Wakalyapi and Collins with saddling and loading their stock. "You will be at Willow Bunch?" he asked as they were about to mount up and head north.

"We will wait," the woman told him.

"*À plus tard!*" called Légaré, as he rode out in front of the waiting line of wagons. The warrior leapt onto his pony and took his place beside the Frenchman.

With the general impression that the Indian faces, peering from carts as they rolled by, were wholly bereft of either joy or a flickering of hope, C.W.'s heart fairly ached at the thought of the children entering a world of obligatory compliance with governmental edicts. The old life of a nomadic subsistence, rich and ancient traditions and boundless independence was ending. He sighed deeply and prodded Ulysses into a walk, looking around for his dog and signaling for her to jump onto the saddle.

The day wore on, cloudy and grey, with nothing to cheer the eye upon the endless prairie. Collins and Arbuckles spoke of this and that. After a while, the woman embarked upon an impassioned diatribe regarding illegal whisky traders and the devastation wrought by them on Indian families. These men crossed back and forth from America into the British Possessions, plying their wares to great effect among all the tribes on either side of the boundary.

"Many of the whites on the border are hard cases and do not scruple to sell whisky to our people if they think they can escape the vigilance of the law," she told Collins. "The Lakȟóta have little money or trade items, so most cannot buy whisky, but a few have traded guns, ponies and even women. It is shameful. The chiefs have punished those who have done this and the redcoats chase the bad men, but they are always coming back."

"Do the American soldiers try to stop these outlaws?"

"I have never seen this. The soldier boys only want to

hunt Indians and blame them for every murder or lost cow."

"The crusade against the Indians should be replaced with one upon whisky traders," C.W. said. "Indeed, it has been my experience that where the Indian is simply the victim of the whisky trader's avarice, and is led to commit crimes when drunk that he would not commit when sober, the trader is far more deserving of punishment."

Wakalyapi made a disparaging rumble. "But they are white men all the same and will never be punished in the same way as Indians."

"Too true. I fear that generals such as Terry and his bosses, Sherman and Sheridan, are incapable of learning that justice belongs to everyone. *Ní glic nach gabhann teagasg*. He who is not wise cannot be taught."

Not long after midday, Collins noticed what appeared to be a small group of people on the road, far off in the distance.

"Do you see that?" he asked Arbuckles.

"Yes."

As the travelers drew closer, he could make out that they were Indians. Most of them were on foot, but some rode gaunt ponies and there were children squatting upon lodgepole drags. When they met and everyone had stopped to look one another over, he could count three old men, six women and eight youngsters, none over the age of six or seven years. Wakalyapi spoke to one of the women. She was a fierce looking Indian who sat one of the horses with ease and bore an air of authority.

"This is *Matóha*," Wakalyapi told Collins, pointing her lower lip at the woman. "These are some people from Wood Mountain. They belong to the band of *Šúŋka Khúči-yela*, Low Dog, who has left for Buford some days ago."

"Why did they not go before?" he asked.

"They did not want to live as captives, but now they are starving. We should give them food."

"Certainly."

Swinging down off his horse, Collins lifted Gal to the ground and handed his reins to Arbuckles. He dug in Molly's packs and pulled out a sack of flour, potatoes, some jerked meat, a box of crackers and a parcel of dried apples and raisins. Gathering the items in a spare blanket, he carried them over to Matóha. She got down from her pony, accepted the bundle without a word and carried it back to the drag behind another horse. Shifting two children to one side, the woman secured the goods and walked back to where C.W. was standing beside Ulysses. She met his eyes and held them for a lingering moment.

"Philámayaye," she finally said and turned to vault nimbly onto her horse. She spoke briefly to Arbuckles, then the small procession moved south along the trail.

"Why did they not eat the food right away?" Collins asked, climbing into the saddle and calling the dog. "You said they were starving."

"It would not be courteous, for then they would have to invite us to join them."

"I wish we could have given more. We need to resupply."

"There will be more hungry people at Willow Bunch. I can hunt and Légaré will be back soon with more provisions."

The terrain was becoming less perfectly flat, with frequents swells breaking up its uniformity. Collins noticed a darker emerald boundary of trees ahead, contrasted against the brilliant green of prairie grasses.

"We are coming to the Big Muddy River," Wakalyapi told him.

The trail began to descend off the tableland toward a riverine flood plain thick with dense vegetation. Ahead, he could make out some structures and one large building perched upon a side-hill just above the valley. Collins could see there was not actually a river, but boggy ground interspersed with stagnant ponds. One rivulet of clear running water wound its way between squat single-room cabins. To the north, there were lodges grouped together on open ground.

As they rode through the hamlet of dwellings, C.W. saw half-breed men and women splitting wood, hauling water, hanging out clothes to dry and tending steaming pots suspended over smoky fires, while children and dogs ran and played among the cabins and adults. Some of the dogs began to gather around Ulysses, attracted by Gal who was seated in her usual place on the saddle. The gelding hunched up and side-stepped when an enormous mongrel ran up and put its paws on his flank. Arbuckles reached over and smacked it with the ends of her reins and Molly lunged forward to bite the canine on the haunches. It yelped and tucked its tail, cowering as the mule reared up to strike with her hooves. The dog dodged the blow then began barking furiously.

One of the older men trotted toward them and shouted, "*Pishkaayhta! Vatawn outa ouhchi!*"

A couple of boys ran up and grabbed the dog, dragging it away. The man walked closer, saying to Wakalyapi, "*Li shaagrayn dayaan.* I am sorry. I not see you there *mii naamii.*"

"*Taanishi,* Antoine," the woman said, smiling. "This is Charles. He has come to speak with Tȟatȟáŋka Ìyotake."

"*Maaka,* he is not here no more." Antoine looked up at C.W. "*Ni miiyeuyhtayn aen nakishkaataan,* Charles. Please to meet you."

"Pleased to meet you also."

"We have come to talk with some people, then we will go to Wood Mountain and wait," Arbuckles said.

"*Li koffii?*"

"*Maarsii.* But we will go to the camp now," Wakalyapi said. "Perhaps we may return later. It would be good to see your family again."

"*Wii!* They would be very much happy. *Miina*

kaawaapamitin."

"*Bonn apray miiji,*" she said, urging her horse forward.

Giving an off-handed salute in farewell, Collins followed Wakalyapi as she rode toward the cluster of lodges ahead. When he moved up beside her, he said, "You speak their language."

"I have learned some. It is a joining of French with *Šahíya* words. Antoine can speak some of my language and it is merely courtesy to know some of his."

"*Fearr béasa ná breághthacht.* Better good manners than good looks."

She gave him a scornful frown. "Then you are saying I do not have good looks? You who have no beard and are less than a man?"

"Foolish woman, no man of importance has a beard."

26

Sitting in the lodge, C.W. looked around the dim interior and was saddened by the obvious deprivation written on all the faces gathered there. Wakalyapi had gone off to hunt soon after they had established a camp of their own against some minimal hills to the west, where a few stunted trees offered some protection from persistent breezes. He had passed out the last of the jerked meat, crackers and dried apples and the people handed it around, sharing most of it with the children, but it was insufficient to assuage their abiding hunger. Having provided some coffee and sugar, Collins watched as the adults passed around gourd and turtle shell vessels, sipping the hot drink almost reverently.

Before leaving, Arbuckles had introduced him to a young man whose father had been a fur trader out of Fort Laramie. As a boy, he had been sent to St. Louis for three years of schooling. C.W. had heard it was a practice common to this class of men, who married Indian women, to send their progeny to white schools. During the child's absence, the mother had returned to her own people and she was killed by soldiers on the Tongue River. The youth had subsequently turned his back on his father and gone to live with relatives among his mother's people. Originally called Joseph Pourier, Arbuckles had explained, he was now known as *Hínyaŋka* or Wait Now. He could speak excellent English and was pleased to interpret for Collins.

"I do not believe Sitting Bull will go back," Wait Now told him. "It is always possible he will be killed or placed in prison."

"But these people are starving and the buffalo are almost all gone. Does he still think the British will give him a reservation here?"

"That is what he has gone to find out. The redcoat Walsh has always been honest with us."

An attractive girl brought Collins a gourd containing a last sip of coffee. He smiled at her and drank. She moved away, back toward where most of the women were seated.

"That is *Tȟa Šúŋkawakȟáŋ Óta Wíŋ*, Her Many Horses Woman, Sitting Bull's daughter."

"She is very pretty."

Grinning, *Híŋyaŋka* said, "She is not for you. *Hiyáyakinyán*, wants her."

"Oh no...I did not mean..."

The boy laughed. "Sitting Bull will not let her go even though Hiyáyakinyán, Flying By, has offered ten horses. The chief's family is his strength and he will not part with any of his daughters. Also, Fly is from a band of the *Sihásapa*."

"Is that an impediment?"

"No. It is an excuse for Many Horses Woman to not marry him." Wait Now got to his feet and stretched. "Let us go out."

Collins stood and followed Wait Now out of the lodge, moving sunwise behind the others gathered within and finally out of the door flap. The wind had intensified, but the air was pure and invigorating. Gal arrived with her muzzle pink from the gore of some small creature. They strolled in the direction of an incline to the north.

"Does Many Horses Woman wish to marry that fellow?" C.W. asked idly.

"She sneaks around with him when she can avoid her

father's vigilance. Now Sitting Bull is gone to Qu'Appelle, they are often together."

They heard a horse loping toward them and turned to see Wakalyapi on her roan. Blood oozed down the horse's shoulders from a large buck antelope slung across its withers. She reined in when she came up to them.

"You had success," Collins said. "Very fine."

"It will not go far," she said.

"Far enough," Híŋyaŋka said, stroking the animal with appreciation.

The two of them helped Arbuckles unload the carcass and carry it over to a group of women who were watching from among the lodges. They promptly began to butcher the antelope and one woman tossed a bit of viscera to Gal. A few of them built fires with buffalo chips while others went to gather more fuel. Soon the aroma of roasting meat brought everyone gathering around and the children watched with forbearance and expectation. Some of the little ones had distended bellies caused by extreme malnutrition. Collins had seen the condition before, during the Great Famine in Ireland, and it taxed him sorely.

"Come," Wakalyapi said, tugging on his sleeve. "Let us go to visit with Antoine and his family."

"Should we bring food?"

"No, they would be insulted."

Leaving Híŋyaŋka behind, eager for his share of fresh meat, they took the woman's horse to a small spring near their camp and washed it clean of blood. Then they hobbled it and turned it loose with the others and ambled back toward the half-breed settlement with the dog at their heels.

"Will she have trouble with the other dogs?" Wakalyapi asked, pointing a lower lip at Gal.

"I hope not. If I left her at camp she would only find a way to follow anyway."

They wandered past several cabins where men and women called greetings. It seemed to Collins that most of them knew his companion and all of them were more friendly than the people they had encountered on the Poplar River. When they came to Antoine's house, he was sitting on a stump out front, holding a multitude of colored threads in his hands that he was crisscrossing back and forth with his fingers. With one end of his handiwork secured to a horizontal rod suspended with rope from the top of a short post, Antoine was holding the strands taut and weaving an intricate design by nimbly manipulating the strands so swiftly that Collins could not follow the pattern of his movements. His efforts were producing a distinctive sash similar to those he had previously seen worn by some of the half-breed men with Légaré.

"*Taanishi!*" Antoine said, looping his work up on the rod and coming to shake their hands with enthusiasm. "Marie will have *li koffii, la soup pi li paen. Si li taan poor zhinii!*" He beckoned with a hand. "Come. Time to eat!"

Gal hovered behind C.W. while three dogs, including the large one from earlier, trotted over. Antoine tossed a rock in their direction, yelling "*Awas!*" The canines ran off around a shed beside the cabin.

"Come," he said again and pointed at Gal. "*Li shyayn* also come."

They followed Antoine into the cabin and were met with an appetizing fragrance of freshly baked bread and meaty broth. His woman, wearing a dark broadcloth dress made colorful with a variety of ribbons sewn across the skirt, was filling bowls and placing them on a long table set between two benches already occupied by two young girls and two adolescent boys. The single room was tidy in spite of being packed tightly with three beds, a stove, cupboards and a spinning wheel.

"*Awa kaa wiikimuk*, Marie," Antoine said, patting the woman on the shoulder. "Come. Sit," he added, waving toward the table.

Scooting in beside the two girls, Arbuckles and Collins sat at the table and Marie gave them each a bowl of soup and a hunk of bread, smiling at them in turn. Gal slipped unnoticed beneath the table. Antoine sat across from them and began to speak to Wakalyapi in her own language. After Marie had taken her place beside Antoine, everyone began to eat and all conversation ceased. Collins found the bread to be similar to the bannock his mother used to make and the soup was flavored with some type of wild herb. When the meal was over, the children climbed from their places and ran out of doors, while Marie poured cups of coffee.

"Do you farm here?" Collins asked Antoine, curious as to how the small community managed to survive.

"Hunt. *Mayshkoutoona*. Trade *lii pwel daanimaal*, trade fur. Trade hides *di bufloo. Mawka, lii bufloo,* buffalo, going away. Unlucky."

"In the autumn before the last, there was a large fire that ruined all the grazing around Wood Mountain and the Lakȟóta camps," Wakalyapi told Collins. "It is why Légaré moved his trading post here. It is also one reason why the tȟatȟáŋka has become scarce."

"What is the other reason?"

"White hunters on both sides of the line take the buffalo for robes and leave the meat. You have seen it before."

"I remember." C.W. recalled the terrible scene when he had encountered a field of slaughtered buffalo, the beasts stripped of hides and tongues, the carcasses laced with strychnine for the purpose of killing both wolves and starving Indians.

"The people must go back," the Indian woman said. "If the White Grandmother refuses to give land and food, they must go back or they will all die."

Marie poured more coffee and they sat in silence a

moment. Wind rattled the glass panes in the windows.

"*Li Mootawyn di Bwaw* burn bad," Marie said after a while. "*La tayr awn fwaen* was all burn bad. No more buffalo."

"How will you live now?" Collins asked her.

"*Lii vaash*, cows, maybe? *Namooya ni kishkayimow*. Pick the bones, maybe?"

"Many of these people are collecting buffalo bones to sell," Arbuckles said.

"I saw much of that in Kansas, now that the buffalo there are mostly gone. There is an excellent market for bones."

Her maimed lips curved into a cynical smile. "Perhaps the Lakȟóta can pick the bones of their dead relatives so they do not starve," she said irascibly. "Perhaps there is an excellent market for that."

" 'Then would I hide my bones, not rest them here. Ah! who hath any cause to mourn but I?' "

"Which play?" Wakalyapi asked, momentarily distracted from her perturbation.

"Richard the Third."

" 'Bid them achieve me and then sell my bones.' "

"Ah!" exclaimed Collins. "Henry the Fifth."

Antoine and Marie were observing their guests with interest.

"Shakespeare," Collins said by way of an explanation.

"*Awaana ana*? Who?" Antoine asked.

"A writer," C.W. said and made a movement with his hand to mimic writing.

"*Ay-ooshipayhikayt*," Antoine told his wife.

Nodding in comprehension, Marie said, "Shakespeare. "*Awn wii*, Shakespeare." She spoke to Antoine at length, then said, "I see Shakespeare *Li For* Benton. I see *disseu batoo*."

"On a riverboat at Fort Benton," Arbuckles explained to Collins.

"Shakespeare on a riverboat," he said ironically.

"*Wii*," Marie exclaimed, nodding with enthusiasm. "Shakespeare."

METIS

27

They spent the next few days hunting. Due to the scarcity of game, Wakalyapi and Collins were forced to search farther and farther afield and mostly northeast since the western areas of the region called *La Montagne de Bois* had been depleted of any fauna larger than a vole.

"How do you know so many of the half-breeds at Willow Bunch?" C.W. asked one morning as they rode along companionably.

"I told you there was a great fire around Wood Mountain and that is why there is difficulty finding meat. It burned up the grass and trees so that many of the Metis who had settled there moved east to the Big Muddy River. I knew these people from my time at Wood Mountain. Later Légaré moved to *Talle-de-Saules*...Willow Bunch."

"Do these Metis, the half-breeds, trade whisky?"

"Never. I have never seen them trade in whisky."

The dog began to squirm restlessly on the saddle. Collins reined in his gelding and lowered Gal to the ground. She took off and flushed a covey of sage hens that flew off a few yards. When Collins called the dog back, Wakalyapi slipped effortlessly from her horse and knelt to aim her Winchester. In short order, she had shot six out of eight grouse. Collins walked over and gathered up the birds and put them in a gunny sack he had brought along for the purpose.

"You managed to shoot them all without ruining the meat," he said, tying the bag to his saddle horn.

"Perhaps," the woman said, scowling with vexation. "But I missed two."

"The day is young," C.W. said, swinging into the saddle.

They rode on while Gal sniffed the ground and dashed here and there. The wind was blessedly in repose, the sun shone upon a sea of viridescence and shadows of clouds skated lazily across the landscape. Collins was content in his friend's company, grateful for their time together.

"Do your people still resent the half-breeds for hunting buffalo for trade?" he asked after a while.

Arbuckles shook her head. "Not so much. They have been generous to our children. And I have discovered in my time up here that the Metis, the Red River half-breeds, have very strict laws governing the hunting of thathánka."

"Truly?"

"Truly."

"Do you know these laws?"

"Most of them."

After a prolonged silence, C.W. realized she was not about to recite the laws without prompting. He smiled to himself, thinking about her innate and literal reticence.

"Are you able to tell me what the laws are in actuality?" he asked.

"If you would like."

"I would like."

She thought a moment, then said, "There is a law that they cannot hunt on their holy day."

"And? Please tell me all you are able to recall."

"No one may go off on their own to hunt without permission and no one may chase the thathánka before the order is given. If someone breaks these laws, their saddle is cut up or they are flogged. If any part of the animal is stolen, the thief is made to stand in the middle of camp and they are shamed."

"Do the Metis waste the meat and only take the robes?"

"No. They trade the hides, but also make clothing, feed themselves and make *wakápapi wasná*, powdered meat with lard and dried berries. Only white men leave carcasses behind to rot."

Gal began to bark, leaping about stiff-legged with hackles bristling. Collins looked ahead to see an approaching plume of brown dust through which he could perceive glimpses of scarlet red. He pulled in his horse, calling the dog to him. Arbuckles reined in beside him and they waited. Before long, three riders drew abreast of them and halted. Their red serge jackets were traced by powdered soil, their slouched felt hats shaded their faces and Winchester carbines were slung across their backs, each resting in a small leather open shoe attached to the saddles. This was C.W.'s first encounter with the Royal North-West Mounted Police and he examined the troopers with interest.

"Good day, Corporal," Wakalyapi said.

"Arbuckles!" exclaimed one of the redcoats in a notable Irish accent. "Why, where on earth did you spring from?"

"Willow Bunch. This is my friend, Charles Collins. We are hunting."

"A pleasure to know you, Mr. Collins. I am Corporal O'Neill and these are constables Labelle and McDunn."

"My pleasure as well, gentlemen," Collins said.

"Do you search for someone?" the woman asked.

"Whisky traders up from Benton. They have been trading for pelts and robes throughout the Montagne de Bois among half-breeds and Indians alike."

"I saw none in the camp at Willow Bunch."

"You know that Légaré would not abide it. And so do they." The corporal turned to Collins. "What brings you to our fair land?"

"Not the whisky trade, to be sure."

"Oh now, I did not believe it for a moment," O'Neill said, grimacing with mortification.

"I am up here merely to hunt and see the country-side," Collins said.

"Not much to hunt or see, for all that," one of the constables contended.

"Come now, McDunn, that is impolitic," the corporal told the trooper.

"He is correct," Wakalyapi said. "But there are hungry children in the camp and we must try to feed them."

"Too true...too true," O'Neill agreed.

"If they are hungry, then the Sioux should go back to America where they can have food," the other constable said unpleasantly, glaring at Wakalyapi.

"*Ní thuigeann an sáthach an seang, nuair bhionn a bholg féin teann,*" Collins said to him, wondering whether Corporal O'Neill knew the language.

"My apologies, Mr. Collins," the corporal said quickly. "Constable Labelle has come from Montreal not many months ago and does not have proper respect for our Indian brethren." He gave the young man a hard look. "Mr. Collins has fittingly said that the man with a full belly has little sympathy with the wants of the hungry."

The constable blushed a deep burgundy and dropped his gaze.

"Right," O'Neill said decisively. "We must pursue our quarry with alacrity, my friends. Grand to see you again, Arbuckles. May you have luck with the hunt, Mr. Collins. *An té is luaithe lámh, bíodh aige an gadhar bán 's a fiadh.*"

The corporal kicked up his horse and, with the two constables following close behind, loped away toward the west.

"What did he say to you?" the woman asked.

"He said, 'May he that has the quickest hand, catch

the deer.' Or near enough."

"Or *she* that has the quickest hand," Arbuckles amended, and rode off in the direction of some distant trees.

In less than an hour, they came to a chain of small lakes. Leaving their horses tethered on the periphery of the littoral stretch, they trod almost noiselessly toward the sandbar of the largest body of water. The dog was restrained with a short length of rope as they hunkered down into a sheltered refuge among some dense willow brush. The woman had brought only her bow and quiver of arrows, while C.W. cradled his Winchester in readiness. They waited patiently and Gal napped, silently paddling her legs in the pursuit of some illusory prey. When the sun began to descend from its apex, a few white tail deer moved cautiously out of a thicket of chokecherry to their right. Collins could see that some were heavy with gestation.

The dog awoke and he muzzled her with a hand, having trained her to be quiet when he did this. Slowly raising his rifle, he aimed at the largest animal, but before he could fire, Wakalyapi had dropped two deer with arrows and she rested a hand on his arm and shook her head. The other creatures sprang back into a dense copse of dogwood and chokecherry and soon there was no sound to betray their passing.

"I killed two young bucks that were still with their mothers," she said. "I did not want to kill the females in this time of year."

They crawled from their hiding place and Gal ran to sniff the nearest carcass.

"I did not notice the bucks," Collins said, now able to see embryonic antlers on both deer. He was glad the woman had stopped him from shooting the big doe.

"I have the quickest hand," Wakalyapi said, bending over to gut one of the yearlings.

"You always have," C.W. said and pulled out his Green

River knife to open up the other animal. "But Shakespeare wrote, 'Your hand, your tongue: look like the innocent flower, but be the serpent under't.' "

"It is white men who have the tongues of serpents. 'All wound with adders, who with cloven tongues; do hiss me into madness.' "

"Nicely done. 'Beshrew me, but you have a quick wit.' As well as the quickest hand."

"Yes," she agreed, pulling the innards free and putting them off to the side.

Gal nosed into the pile, but Wakalyapi pushed her away.

"You want to save most of this?" C.W. asked, nodding toward the viscera he had taken from the other buck.

"The liver, heart, lungs and kidneys. They make rich soup."

Deftly skinning the deer, she heaped organs from both animals onto the hide and secured it with the length of rope he had used to hold the dog.

Together, they carried the carcasses to where they had left the horses and then Collins returned to fetch the skin full of organ meat. After securing the load, they walked back toward Willow Bunch, leading their animals. Gal was dragging a chunk of offal, pausing periodically to gnaw upon it, then hurrying to catch up. Collins noticed the days were becoming markedly longer and that the sun was still well above the horizon.

"How came you to know so much of Shakespeare?" he asked after a while.

"*Itȟúŋkasaŋ*, Kinealy, read to me many nights from the book you gave him. Then, when he was taken sick, I read to him."

"I am very sorry to not have seen him again and sad you have lost your friend."

Arbuckles did not speak for several minutes, then said almost inaudibly, "We were not...not as man and woman…but we had much affection between us."

"I am very sorry," he said again.

"It is of no consequence," she said, straightening her posture visibly and taking longer strides.

He knew she would say no more.

EES & SAUTEAUX IND.
Mounted Police Hd. Quarters
CACTUS MTS.
More or Less Barren
ION OF CANAD
SITTING BULL'S
TRADERS ROAD
ENCAMPMENT
INTERNATIONAL
BLOOD, BLACKFEET
& RIVER CROW INDIANS.
Porcupine
West Fk.
Milk Cr.
MTS.
S. Fk.
BUFFALO BLUFF
N T A N
FT. PECK
MISSOURI R.
GENERAL DIRECTION OF SITTING BULL'S RETREAT
FT. HAWLEY
YELLOW
Greenwich 109

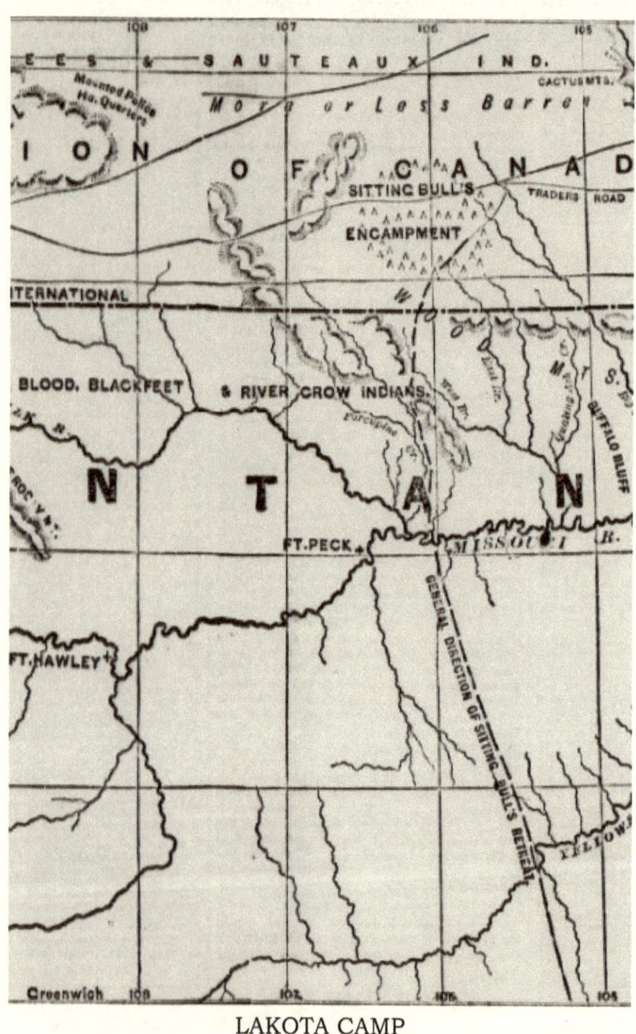

LAKOTA CAMP

28

When Légaré returned, Old Bull was with him, as promised. There was much commotion in the Indian camp and the Metis village at the sight of the burdened Red River carts when they descended into the river bottom and pulled up in a line in front of the large building overlooking the valley. Collins had learned this was Légaré's trading post, so he walked with Híŋyaŋka from the camp to where the half-breed workers were unloading and carrying goods into the storeroom, while their boss directed them in their labor. He recognized Antoine among them.

Old Bull was squatting on his heels in the shade of a tree, watching the proceedings. His bony horse grazed nearby.

"I came back," the Indian said when they walked over to him.

"What did you think of Fort Buford?" C.W. asked.

"There is food and the soldiers stay away. But the horses and guns are taken. Many of the people have been taken to Fort Yates."

Wait Now asked a question in their language and the warrior answered him.

"*Tȟatȟáŋka Eháŋni* says the people are not happy, but the women are pleased to have their children fed and some of them are going to school," the young man told Collins.

"They will be little *wašícu*," Old Bull added, taking out

his pipe.

"So you are not going back there?" Collins asked, handing the Indian his tobacco pouch.

"Maybe I will talk with Tȟatȟáŋka Íyotake first."

A group of Indian women came to observe the activity, along with Many Horses Woman and her sweetheart, Fly. The girl spoke to Old Bull and he answered her comprehensively.

"She wants to go to Fort Buford," Wait Now explained. "She wants to go with Hiyáyakinyán before her father returns."

"How will she get there?"

"Légaré told Old Bull he is going back for more supplies. He thinks Šúŋkawakȟaŋpi Óta Wíŋyaŋ can travel with him."

"If she goes with Fly, will there be hell to pay?"

The boy laughed. "Yes hell to pay," he said.

"What does he say?" asked Old Bull.

"Trouble. Hell to pay is trouble," Collins told him.

"If that girl goes, there will be hell to pay," the warrior agreed.

Some of the Metis people had joined the others and the crowd of onlookers was increasing.

Apparently satisfied that the unloading of provisions was proceeding agreeably, the French trader came over. "*Monsieur* Collins, you are yet here," he said, putting out a hand to shake.

"Yes. We have been waiting for you."

"*Trés bien*. That is good. And where is Arbuckles *aujourd'hui*?"

"I am not sure. She was gone before daybreak."

Légaré shrugged. "She will return, *sans doute*."

"Any word of Sitting Bull?" Collins asked.

"*Simonaque!* It is the talk at the fort...*seulement* the talk at the fort. But there is no word of him."

"We plan to go to Wood Mountain and wait for him."

"*Mais* he might not come there."

"We have friends there. Then we will see."

"Many Horses Woman wants to go to the fort," Híŋyaŋka told the Frenchman.

"*D'accord. Je suis retourner*, I am going back, *toute suite.* There is more to bring."

"There will be hell to pay," Old Bull said.

"*Oui. Peut-être.* But I have promised *le commandant* at Fort Buford to take all *les Indiens* who want to come," the trader said, gazing fixedly at his employees toting bundles from the carts into his trading post. "*Pardonnez-moi.* I must watch those *hivernants. Autrement*, they will unload *le stock* in places I cannot find." He walked back up to where his men were still hard at work.

Hearing voices behind him, Collins turned to see Wakalyapi squatting beside Old Bull, her horse's reins trailing in the grass beside her. They were speaking in their own dialect. He stepped over and sat nearby and Wait Now joined him.

"How is it Charles?" she asked when they had finished their discussion.

"You were gone."

"Yes. I was hunting. Later it became a different kind of hunt."

"Different?"

"I will tell you."

He knew better than to press her. "When shall we leave for Wood Mountain?"

"Tomorrow. We can see our friends there and ask the redcoats about Ťhaťháŋka Ìyotake."

"Does Sitting Bull remember me, do you think?"

"He has the bearskin you gave him."

"There will be a council with *Čheží Wašté* later," Old Bull said.

"He speaks of Légaré," Arbuckles said in answer to C.W.'s look of inquiry. "Some of the people call him Good

Tongue. He is sometimes harsh, but he speaks the truth always."

"The Frenchman can be brusque," Wait Now agreed. "But he has been generous with food and supplies. Very generous."

"Many want to go to Buford but want to wait for those with Tȟatȟáŋka Ìyotake," Old Bull continued. "I want to go back."

"Why do you wish to go back to the fort?" Collins asked him.

"There is little hope here. The new redcoat at Wood Mountain does not want us. *Uŋčíyapi Makȟóčhe* does not want us. The other Indians up here do not want us. I miss my *thiyóšpaye*. Many of them have gone there to Yates."

"Do you want to go?" he asked Wait Now.

The young man shook his head. "No. I want to stay up here in the Dominion. I plan to go north when work begins on the railroad there."

The carts were now almost empty and the assembly of Metis and Indians was dispersing. Everyone got to their feet and stretched. Wakalyapi's horse had wandered away and she went to look for it.

"You will come to the council?" Old Bull asked.

"Yes. I would like to hear what is decided."

"The Frenchman cannot delay," Hiŋyaŋka said. "His other goods have already arrived at Fort Buford, now the riverboats have resumed operation. He cannot afford to leave them lying about while we wait for Sitting Bull."

Wakalyapi returned with her gelding. "Where is the dog?" she asked.

"Over there," Collins told her, nodding toward some undergrowth where Gal had made a bed.

"*Bon, nous allons parler* with *les Indiens*," Légaré said, coming over to join them. "We must go to their camp."

They all walked together toward the Indian village and

Old Bull and Arbuckles followed, leading their horses. One of the Frenchman's Metis drove a cart behind them, bringing gifts of food and other items. They entered the council lodge, already filling with people. A little while later, the three elderly head men, who had journeyed to Fort Buford with Légaré and Old Bull, came in and sat in the honorary position of the lodge. When everyone had settled into their places, the Frenchman began to speak. One of the Metis men, who had been introduced to Collins by Wakalyapi as André Gaudry, translated.

It soon became evident to C.W. that, despite the wishes of most of the Lakota people, the trader did not propose to wait for Sitting Bull before returning to Fort Buford, as Híŋyaŋka had predicted. He explained about the supplies awaiting him and offered to take anyone who wanted to go. After the Frenchman had declared his plan to make the journey right away, the head men spoke in glowing terms of the circumstances at Buford and the satisfaction of their relatives there. All the while, Collins noticed, Old Bull made rude noises in his throat so faint only the nearest to him could hear. A lengthy debate followed among those present and finally they expressed their intent to hold another council amongst themselves before deciding.

After the council, Légaré and his Metis companions distributed food, first to the children and women, then to the few remaining men in the camp. Next, bolts of cloth, needles, knives and cooking pots were given out, but Collins noticed the trader's beneficence did not include ammunition or guns. He wandered through the village, looking for Gal, and finally found her eating a family of pocket gophers she had excavated from a ground nest.

When he got back to where he had left Arbuckles, Collins saw she was speaking earnestly with an Indian woman while holding what appeared to be a small animal pelt in her hand. He hung back and watched the people sharing food, despite their obvious hunger. Mothers fed their children methodically, sometimes chewing bits for the youngest. Suddenly, he was startled by profound wailing and turned to see Wakalyapi kneeling beside the woman with whom she had been conversing. The woman squatted upon the ground and was digging in the soil, rubbing handfuls on her face and pulling at her hair, all the while lamenting with strident grief. Abruptly, she sprang to her feet and snatched a knife from the hand of one of the men and began hacking at her arms. Collins made to hinder her self-immolation, but Wakalyapi held him back.

"It is her way," she told him and led him away toward their camp site.

29

Evidence of an enormous prairie fire was written across the land, even though traces of new grass were unmistakable. It seemed to Collins that it would take quite some time before the countryside could support any of the larger meat animals so essential to the Indians' survival. A lone hawk soared overhead, searching in rounds for a morsel of prey. He found himself saddened by the thought of the boundless populations of buffalo, elk and deer that would never return to the empty spaces of this great prairie. At best, a few herds of deer and antelope would move in when the vegetation had rebounded sufficiently.

"How did the fire begin?" he asked Arbuckles.

"White men."

"On purpose?"

She nodded.

His companion had been in a reticent mood all morning. He decided to draw her out. The landscape was unbearably dull and he was weary of his own thoughts.

"Will some of the Lakota go with Légaré this time?"

"I heard more than thirty people say they would go."

"Including Many Horses and her beau?"

"Yes."

"What was the woman weeping over?" he asked.

"Her son."

They rode in silence for a while, then Collins said, "You were going to tell me about your hunt."

"My hunt?"

"You told me it was a different sort of hunt."

Her face darkened. "Yes...a different sort of hunt."

"You did not have success?"

"In a way." Arbuckles reached to touch a long hank of light hair woven into her horse's mane.

"What is that?" Collins fancied he saw a flap of crusted blood at its base.

An unsettling smile passed across her crooked lips. "I will tell you of my...hunt."

Another long period passed wherein the woman did not speak. C.W. waited, knowing from past experience to let her come to the tale without prodding. The terrain was becoming less flat as it rose and fell in mild undulations. The dog bounded here and there, full of vigor in the enchanting spring morning, graced by abundant sunshine and gentle breezes.

"I went out early to hunt," Wakalyapi finally said. "I thought perhaps I would return to where we found deer by the little lakes."

He did not interrupt to say he would have gone along if only she had woken him. In truth, Collins was slightly vexed that she had gone out on her own, but reasoned that his friend was ever compelled by enigmatic forces.

"A young boy named Split Ears had left the village at dawn two days ago to hunt for game. His mother and small sisters were hungry and the father had been killed by soldiers when he crossed the line to look for buffalo. This boy was caught by whisky traders. Maybe the ones from Benton the redcoats were seeking, maybe some others. I think he had fallen asleep, because the white men caught him."

"Oh no," Collins said involuntarily.

"I found the boy. He had been murdered and scalped. I followed the trail and overtook the two men. They had mules loaded down with pelts and robes and one had a fresh scalp dangling from his bridle. They did not see me, but I saw them. I shot them both and took the hair of the blonde one with a long mane. Then I returned to wrap the boy in one of the robes and took him to the lakes and gave him a tree burial. I gave the horses and saddles to Antoine's family and the mules and pelts I gave to Johnny Chartrand, a half-breed who is a good friend to the people. He will sell the furs and help the mother and sisters of Split Ears. And the mother now has her boy's scalp to take to his body."

Stunned and mute, Collins glanced over at his companion. It was not that he found her actions reprehensible, but was, instead, rather daunted by her implacable resolve and daring. She had tracked down two dangerous men without hesitation and imposed bloody redress for a dreadful crime. He thought about his friend Jackrabbit, down in New Mexico Territory. If only he had been able to find the boy's murderers, he asked himself, what would he have *not* been willing to do?

"You do not approve," Wakalyapi said phlegmatically.

"On the contrary. I heartily approve. I only regret my absence."

The plains upon which they rode had now become distinctly more broken. Abundant hills and occasional lines of hardy trees interrupted the parched grasslands. C.W. also perceived that they were gaining in elevation. When they finally came to a tentative little stream, they dismounted and watered their horses.

"How much farther?" Collins asked.

"We will be there about dusk."

"Did the fire reach all the way to Wood Mountain?"

"Not quite."

"Are all the half-breeds gone from there?" he asked, checking his cinch and swinging into the saddle. As he reached for Molly's lead rope, the dog surprised him by jumping up in front of him.

"Some day that dog will make you walk while she rides," Arbuckles said, covering her grin with a hand.

"Perhaps. Or perhaps I should get her a horse of her own."

As they regained the trail and continued on their way, the woman said, "There are a few Metis families remaining at Wood Mountain. Also, around sixty lodges of Lakȟóta and a few of the Irish warriors."

"Now that Kinealy is gone, how many Irish?" Collins asked and then regretted his question. "I am sorry."

"It is of no consequence." She paused, then said, "Since Itȟúŋkasaŋ has walked on, there are only three of the Irish at La Montagne de Bois. You have met them all before."

"Is Aidan Mulhaire among them?"

"Yes."

"Where did the rest of them go?"

"When the redcoats became too curious, some of them traveled north to join *Wápaha Ská* of the *Dakȟóta*. Others have died."

"Who remains with Aidan?"

"When I left, there was the one named Duffy. The other is Connor, who married a half-breed woman and has a small farm where the fire did not go."

"I shall be glad to see them."

"We have spoken of you. I told them that you have never revealed their presence."

Feeling somewhat contrite, C.W. said, "Well, that may not be unreservedly true."

Wakalyapi glanced at him inquiringly. "What do you mean?"

"When I met with President Grant, I was forced to report the truth."

"Yet the soldiers never came for them and Terry never asked about them when he came with his commission."

"No. President Grant listened to me when I said the

Irish were no longer a threat and it would be best to never speak of them."

She seemed to ponder his words for a long moment. "It is remarkable."

"What is?"

"That a great man would listen to you."

He laughed. "Was that an insult?"

Appearing dismayed, Arbuckles said, "Oh no. That was not an insult. I meant that it is proof of your honor and truthful words."

" 'Act well your part. There all honor lies.' "

"Is that Shakespeare?" she asked.

"No. Alexander Pope. He was an English poet many years ago."

" 'Act well your part.' We must all do this."

"Sadly, many do not."

"No. Many do not. It is why I killed those men."

Collins looked at her. "I meant to ask...what did you do with the bodies?"

"I left them for the carrion crows and beetles."

He smiled. "A fitting end for corrupted flesh."

214

SETTLEMENT

30

"I would never have believed we would meet again," Aidan Mulhaire said, shaking Collins' hand with enthusiasm. "'*Fág an Bealach*'."

"*A dhuine mo chroí*. My friend. It is very good to see you."

Standing aside in the small room, Wakalyapi smiled at Mulhaire's delight in seeing C.W. once again. "There was a time," she said, "when you were not so eager to see this man."

"'Tis true...'tis true enough," the Irishman said, grinning. "But now you must sit here and allow me to ask you questions." He gestured at a rough hewn table surrounded by four maltreated ladderback chairs.

They sat down while Mulhaire brought tin cups and a queensware coffee pot that was out of place in the crude log and daub cabin. He joined them at the table and filled their cups.

"I purchased this fine bit of earthenware for my wife, *Čhaŋtéwašte Wíŋyaŋ*, many years ago. She loved the creamy shine of it and it cost me many pelts, but she was my darling. The cholera took her before the *Peji Sla Wakpá*."

"And you have kept it all these years?" Collins asked.

The man looked at him with tears in his eyes. "I have kept it and her memory safe and beloved."

Arbuckles brought out her tobacco pouch and Collins noticed it was the one Sitting Bull had given her. It was worn and some of the quillwork was damaged, but it remained a lovely keepsake. They all filled their pipes and smoked companionably in silence for several minutes.

"Wakalyapi tells me that Connor lives near here," C.W. said, breaking the lull.

"Wakalyapi?" Mulhaire asked, perplexed. "Coffee?"

"He is speaking of me," the woman told him. "It is an old joke." She turned to look at C.W. "Among some of the *Húŋkpapȟa* up here I am known as *ApsíčA Wíŋyaŋ*. Jump Over Woman."

"I seem to remember another name."

"Yes, but that was an old name. One that carried sadness."

"But what does this other name signify?"

Mulhaire laughed. "She jumps here and there. In the soldier forts, hunting for the people, a warrior or a woman."

"*Múineann gá seift.*"

"True. True enough."

"What is the meaning of your words?" Wakalyapi asked.

"Necessity teaches resourcefulness," Collins told her.

The woman gave him a crooked grin. "I am also known as Arbuckles."

Mulhaire nodded. "Oh I think I see...both names are coffee. I have heard some people call you by Arbuckles."

"An old joke," Wakalyapi said again.

"Anyway, Lorcan and Duffy Ryan both have taken half-breed wives and do what they can to survive," Mulhaire told Collins. "Many of the Metis moved to Willow Bunch after the great fire, but there are some families that stayed and then there are Lakȟóta women that have married the red-coated peelers."

"How many Indian lodges are near here?"

"Almost sixty. We are all struggling for life with no more tȟatȟáŋka and little enough other game."

"We must go to the camp and visit our friends, especially Kcanptepte," Collins said to Wakalyapi.

"Surely you remember Lorcan Connor? He took him in. The boy was not flourishing on his own and the warrior that was caring for him disappeared."

"*Thezi ŠíčA* is no longer here in the camp?" Wakalyapi asked with apparent concern.

"No," Mulhaire said, shaking his head. "He went to hunt not long after you left and never returned. Muse has been starving and the dog died."

"Muse?" Collins asked.

"It is our name for the boy. It is a near interpretation of his Lakota name."

"And the dog...his yellow dog...died?"

"Food has been shared, which is appropriate when there is very little, but the dog was old and there was not enough."

His heart fell as Collins thought about the yellow dog that had come to him in the frozen camp so long ago. "Where is Connor?"

"He changed his name to Charles Thompson and was a corporal for a while with the redcoats, but after he was discharged, he took back his old name and married *Khéya Wíŋyaŋ*, the half-breed daughter of *Wašícu Wakte*. They have a small ranch where they raise horses and have several children. When they saw that Muse was abandoned, Connor offered a home."

"The captain at the cantonment on Poplar River was convinced that there is a known scoundrel around here named Thompson."

"*Tá sé fá chác.* Shit. No one here believes it. The peelers buy many of their horses from him."

"What is a peeler?" Arbuckles asked. "I have heard this many times about the redcoats."

"Robert Peel was an English boss a long time ago," Collins told her. "He sent ex-soldiers to Ireland so they could oppress the Catholics. Later they became a regular police force to impose the queen's laws on our people. Therefore, they became known as 'peelers.' "

"Therefore the redcoats also work for the queen and are also peelers."

Collins laughed. "At least to the Irish."

"Come," Mulhaire said, standing. "Let us go to visit Connor. You will see he is not a scoundrel. Then we can go to call on Duffy Ryan."

They stepped into the warm, clear day and the dog woke from her nap in the sun by the cabin door, stretched and followed them to where the horses and mule were tethered to a rudimentary hitching rail built of piles of rocks and one lone narrow log. It seemed to C.W. that the limited amount of timber in the area gave rise to ingenious construction. Many of the buildings he had seen were amalgamations of log, stone and mud, much like many of the dwellings in New Mexico Territory. Even the Wood Mountain post of the North-West Mounted Police was built in a manner that reflected the scarce materials available for erecting durable structures.

"I will go catch my horse," Mulhaire said. "He should not have wandered far."

The woman sat on the ground, took out her pipe and prepared a smoke. Collins strolled over to a vantage point where he could peruse the small half-breed settlement where Mulhaire resided. The hamlet resembled its counterpart at Willow Bunch, with boisterous children, ubiquitous dogs and energetic men and women occupied by all sorts of pursuits. The houses were all similarly built and plastered with mud and all had an entry way with a main door that jutted from the middle of one wall. Some of the dwellings had grass and shrubs growing on earthen rooftops.

As he was surveying the scene, a solitary puppy cautiously approached Gal and in a short while, the canines were romping madly, feverishly engaged in a circuitous chase. He chuckled to himself watching their antics.

"*Ma shyayn*," said a faint voice beside him.

He looked down to see a small girl in a blue dress trimmed with red ribbons. After searching his memory for the right word, he said, "*Taanishi.*"

The child looked up at him, but said nothing. Then she clapped her hands and the puppy left off its game and came running to her. The two of them walked toward one of the cabins and disappeared from sight.

"The children can be very shy," Mulhaire said, coming over. He was leading a stocky grey gelding. "Except the ones what hang around the red coats. They tend to be more convivial."

They walked over to where Arbuckles was waiting. Leaving Molly and Wakalyapi's pack horse behind, they mounted up and rode to the other side of the N.W.M.P. post, with the dog trotting along behind. A short distance to the north and across a shallow creek stood a long, narrow log house. A two-story barn was situated a few yards away and Collins suspected that it must have been quite a feat to haul such a great quantity of logs to build it. Just to the side of the house was a good-sized buffalo hide lodge.

"We can secure our animals over here," the Irishman said, riding around to the other side of the barn and swinging down from his gelding by a split rail pen.

Collins and Wakalyapi alighted and tethered their horses a little way from Mulhaire's. A burly man met them as they approached the house. He was bare-headed with a thick shock of auburn hair and friendly brown eyes above a broad nose and thick moustache. He wore a breech clout over a pair of trousers and a buckskin shirt with intricate beading and quillwork across the shoulders. Collins found he did, indeed, remember the fellow from Sitting Bull's camp five years before.

"Good to see you, Aidan," Connor said.

"Lorcan, this is Charles Collins. He came seeking us after the Greasy Grass."

"You are back among us then, Mr. Collins. Hello Arbuckles. Muse is out back playing with the baby. Come this way."

At the sound of her old appellation, Collins gave Wakalyapi a glance. She shrugged and gave a skewed grin. They followed Connor to a clearing behind the cabin. C.W. beheld Kcanptepte on his belly in the grass teasing a young toddler with a scruffy-looking jumping jack. The child was giggling and making attempts at grabbing the toy. When the baby saw Gal, it let out a squeal of delight and began to crawl toward her at an alarming rate. The dog retreated behind Collins' legs and Connor scooped his progeny from the ground.

"My dog is unused to children," C.W. said, reaching down to stroke Gal's head.

Connor laughed, tossing the little girl over his shoulder like a sack of beans, inspiring more ecstatic hilarity. "Baby Bridget can be frightening in her determination. Sometimes she frightens me."

The young Indian man whom Collins had not seen for several years had gotten to his feet and was standing shyly a few feet away, his disfigured ankle bent in an abnormal twist. He walked over to the boy and gripped both his shoulders and said, "My friend, Kcanptepte."

"He speaks some English now," Wakalyapi told him. "And he is partial to the name Muse."

"I can speak well," the boy said. He had tears in his eyes as he looked at Collins.

"I am very pleased to see you, Muse. Very pleased indeed."

"Very pleased I am also."

A comely woman came from the lodge and snatched up baby Bridget, still slung across her father's shoulder, but quiet now and half-asleep. "We have coffee," she said. "Come inside the house."

THE QUEEN AND THE UNCLE

31

In the early hours, an insistent cry of a coyote woke Collins from an all encompassing and dreamless sleep. The camp was illuminated by a gravid moon and he saw that Wakalyapi was not in her usual place on the other side of the hearth ring. After pulling on his boots, he stood and looked around the vicinity for his friend. She was nowhere in sight so he strolled over to check on the stock, hobbled and left to graze. Walking west toward the Wood Mountain post from their bivouac at the base of some rambling hills, with Gal following along, C.W. heard what he thought was singing and aimed himself in that direction. He came upon the woman standing among their animals whilst she sang in a soft and melodious voice. He had never actually heard her sing before and was spellbound.

When he approached to hear better, she stopped singing and turned toward him. "You are not quiet," she said.

"I was not stalking you." Collins reached to caress the forehead of his mule. "You were singing to your horses."

"It is a song I made for them and they ask for me to sing it to them sometimes."

"Do they have names? I never asked."

"The roan is *Ȟeyúŋka* and the black is *Sápa*."

"And the song? Does it have meaning?"

She stood in the bright moonlight and stared off at the horizon.

"Am I being too curious?" Collins asked.

"No, you are not too curious," Arbuckles told him with humor. "I am trying to find the words in English." She paused then said, "The words of my song are much like this. 'My horses do you see me? My horses do you see me? You are my *thiwáhe*, my family. *Ókičhiya po*. Help one another. My horses do you see me?' "

"It is a good song. Did Molly and Ulysses enjoy it?"

"Yes. They listened."

A thin radiance of light had begun to show above the ridge line to the east and the gibbous moon was growing more pale. They left their animals and walked back to camp together. Wakalyapi built a fire while C.W. filled the coffeepot from a small spring that trickled out of a vein of rocks in a small grove of aspen trees nearby. Then he put the pot beside the flames and quarried the coffee grinder from their jumbled pile of belongings.

"Our camp is in need of tidying," he said as he worked the handle of the grinder. "We have been here too long."

"It has been many days," the woman said, accepting the little drawer full of grounds he handed to her. She lifted the lid of the coffeepot and tipped the grounds into the water. "Shall we travel to find Thatháŋka Ìyotake?"

"We could. But then we might miss him. How many days do you think?"

"We have been here for the remainder of *Čhaŋwápe Thó Wí*, what you call May, and many days of June."

"I heard the trading post has brought in more supplies. I should see if I am able to buy food for some of the families that are suffering most. Unfortunately the quantity will not be prodigious as I am unable to send another telegram to Terry for credit. I have learned that the telegraph line runs far to the north."

"We must hunt again."

"Hunt what? We will have to ride clear down into Montana Territory to find more game."

Wakalyapi thought about this. "Are we able to purchase a cow from someone?"

"Perhaps. I intend to ask Superintendent Crozier if he will use his influence on that fellow, Logan, at Leighton and Jordon's trading post. I heard they brought a few hundred head of beef up from Montana a while ago, but the man will not acknowledge the fact."

The coffee was ready and Collins poured them both a cup, then retrieved a nearly empty tin of biscuits. "This is the last of them. We require more supplies as well."

"The half-breed Lamarche still has potatoes and I may be able to find rabbits."

"If I manage to purchase a beef with my dwindling funds, I will certainly reserve a portion for our use."

When they had finished their coffee, Collins called his dog and went to check on the stock, then he walked over to the post. The detachment office was a long log and mud structure similar to every building he had seen in the region. It was situated at the head of and between a few smaller buildings. Another elongated edifice to the north served as barracks for the thirty odd men stationed there. Behind the post ran a procession of larger trees following the banks of a considerable stream. Men lounged here and there while others appeared to be dutifully employed.

The day was growing warm and the door of the headquarters stood ajar. C.W. could hear voices within. He entered the building and found Superintendent Crozier arguing with George Kennedy, the post surgeon. The superintendent was predominantly bald, possessed small, beady eyes and sported an absurdly grandiose moustache.

"Listen George," Crozier was saying in a voice too loud for their surroundings. "There can be no reason for so many headaches among the men."

Remembering Wakalyapi's description of the man as

a big wind, Collins stood back and waited, smiling to himself.

"I have told you before, several of the men should never have been taken on, for they were utterly unfit for the force in every way. Of the nine enlisted last year, at least three of them had diseases which should have prevented their being passed by the examining surgeon."

"Yes, yes, I have heard all this already," Crozier said, banging a fist on a tabletop unnecessarily.

"And I will say again," the surgeon persisted, "that there have been multiple cases of syphilis both here and at Fort Walsh. If the men persevere in fraternizing with Indian girls and, depending on the man and my own observations this may not necessarily be a choice for the women, then the disease will continue to play great havoc."

The superintendent made an impolite noise with his lips, puffing out his moustaches comically. "Those damn redskins are bringing their diseases from across the line."

"I do not believe this is so. One man, if he be not honorable, is able to spread the disease to a vast degree."

Waving a dismissive hand, Crozier said, "Very well, George, you have had your say. I still insist the headaches are symptoms of laziness and sloth. But to my profound delight, this will not be my concern much longer."

Demonstrably aggravated, Kennedy rolled his eyes, gave a brief nod to Collins and strode from the office. They had met on three previous occasions when the surgeon had visited the Indian camp to treat various diseases and an accidental gunshot wound. The man was a large, strapping Irishman from Ottawa, who truly seemed to take an interest in all his patients.

The superintendent sat down behind a table covered in stacks of paper and fixed his cold, marble-like eyes on C.W. "Well, Mr. Collins, what do you require?"

"The Indians are again starving. I have heard rumors that the Leighton and Jordan man is in charge of a small herd of cattle and I was hoping you would intervene on my behalf so that I am able to purchase one or two of the animals."

"God's teeth...I have explained to the savages at length how much their women and children would benefit from accepting American terms of surrender...that it is cruel to their families if they persevere in rejecting the offer. I am the reason that man Logan simply will not sell you beef and refuses to supply any to the Indian camps. Feeding those people is only prolonging their suffering."

Restraining his vexation with difficulty, Collins crossed his legs and altered his tack. "What did you mean when you said the condition of your men would not be your concern much longer?"

The man smiled with satisfaction. "You noted that, did you? I am departing this pest-hole for Fort Walsh in two days. Inspector Alexander Macdonell will be replacing me here. I shall no longer be in residence should that reprehensible scoundrel ever return here from his foray to Qu'Appelle."

"You mean Sitting Bull?"

Crozier gave Collins a scathing glance that plainly stated he thought him a dunce. "Of course I mean Sitting Bull. And do not be fooled into thinking you may possibly work your wiles upon Macdonell. He is a canny Scotsman."

Deciding he had had quite enough of Crozier, C.W. came to his feet. "Good luck to you, Superintendent. I feel certain we will not meet again."

The man did not respond and Collins departed abruptly, leaving the immediate environs of the redcoat post and striding back toward camp. He would have to purchase whatever rations he could with the remaining currency in his possession, ask Wakalyapi to go to the half-breed settlements to trade for what they could spare, and the two of them would have to hunt farther afield. He failed to hear the horse coming up behind him and spun around in surprise when he heard Gal bark and someone call his name.

"Sorry to startle you, Charles," said Connor, reining in his lathered gelding and dismounting. "I have just now returned from Fort Walsh and stumbled upon a small herd of buffalo not five miles to the west of here. Let us fetch Arbuckles and gather some of the warriors."

"What of the Metis?"

"Yes, of course, but please do not alert the redcoats."

"No fear. I will catch my horse, find Wakalyapi and clandestinely alert Mulhaire and the half-breed men around here. On the way west we can gather more at Hunter's Settlement."

"I must change horses. Then I can ride to the community at Légaré's Coulee and the Indian camp at Peppermint's Hill and meet you along Frenchman's Creek. Bring what ammunition you can spare."

They parted ways and Collins sprinted to where he had last seen the horses. He found Ulysses and used a piece of rope to secure the gelding. Hurrying back to camp, he looked around for Arbuckles but she was nowhere in sight. He saddled his horse, filled his saddlebags with surplus ammunition and the last of the jerked meat and hard tack and filled a canteen from the spring. When he was about to mount up, Wakalyapi came walking over the rise behind their camp carrying a single grouse.

"This is all I could find," she said, then noticed his horse was saddled. "Where are you going?"

"Connor sighted buffalo to the west. We must alert the Metis near the fort while he goes to bring back the Indians."

Tossing the bird carcass to the dog, Wakalyapi grabbed

her saddle and ran for her horse. Collins checked his Winchester, slipped it into its scabbard and swung onto Ulysses, making the dog drop her feathered trophy and jump up with him. Arbuckles returned, riding her blue roan, and they made their way toward the half-breed settlement, circumnavigating the Wood Mountain post.

BUFFALO HUNT

32

The hunt was a grand success and provided plenty of meat for every Indian lodge, Irish family and half-breed household. Collins found it tragic that the entire buffalo herd was almost wiped out, but customary respect for the animal among the Metis and Indian hunters allowed a few cows and calves to escape. Sadly, he knew that other northern tribes were starving as well and the beasts would probably not last long. The avarice of unscrupulous white men had driven the buffalo to near extinction and the indigenous inhabitants of the plains were paying the piper.

The days passed as Wakalyapi and Collins strove to establish a good rapport with Inspector Macdonell, the new officer in charge of the Wood Mountain detachment. As it turned out, Macdonell was the "Mac" who had gone to Fort Buford with One Bull and Bone Club the previous April. Although he was insistent that the remaining Lakota and Nez Perce Indians return to America, the middle-aged Scotsman was not without sympathy for their plight. The surgeon and some of the redcoats, who had been doing what they could to help, were now ably assisted by Macdonell. When food supplies were once more depleted, he coerced the Leighton and Jordan man into supplying a few cows and some essential provisions. Légaré brought carts loaded with what he could mete out and the half-breed farms were beginning to produce. Even so, some of the people from the Wood Mountain Indian camp rejoined their friends and relatives at Willow Bunch.

Beginning to run out of patience and resources and

abundantly worried about Wú Peng, Li Min and his ranch, Collins was about to make the decision to return to Deer Lodge. General Terry had stated that he would remunerate him for his efforts regardless of outcome and he intended to hold him to it. According to the calendar in Macdonell's office, it was almost July, which meant he had been gone for over two months.

One early morning, as C.W. and Wakalyapi drank coffee and smoked by the fire, he sat ruminating over the necessity of an overdue departure.

"What is within you now?" the woman asked.

Looking up, he said, "I know you will probably wish to stay on, but I must return south. There is much to be done this time of year and I have left my friends alone for far too long."

"*Táku wakȟáŋ škaŋ škaŋ.*"

"And what is that supposed to mean?" he asked, made irascible by worry and fretfulness.

"It means that the spirits are moving. Híŋyaŋka was in the camp at *Tȟa Pahá Čheyaka* yesterday and told me Tȟatȟáŋka Íyotake has come to Willow Bunch."

"When exactly were you going to inform me of this?"

She rubbed her mouth tellingly. "You were playing cards with the redcoats last night when I returned."

Feeling idiotic for his excess of ill-temper, Collins said, "Please forgive me."

"It is of no consequence."

"We should pack up camp and go to Willow Bunch."

"Tȟatȟáŋka Íyotake is coming here to see the redcoat officer, Macdonell."

"When?"

"He is coming today, but the families are traveling slowly with a redcoat escort."

Knocking out his pipe on one of the hearth stones, Collins laid it aside.

"Escort?"

"It was told that two redcoats have brought rations from Qu'Appelle and have been handing them out along the trail. Even so, the food is almost exhausted and the people are hungry."

"What of Légaré? Can he help?"

"Hínyaŋka said the Frenchman is coming along and bringing what he can."

Gratified that he would not have to abandon his commission, Collins asked, "Is Inspector Macdonell aware that Sitting Bull is en route?"

"Connor was also in the Lakȟóta camp yesterday. He may have told the officer."

Gal began to bark and they saw Mulhaire and Duffy Ryan walking up. Both impressive in size and breadth, the men blocked out the rising sun as they came into the camp.

Collins stood to shake hands with the men. "Have some coffee," he said and found extra tin cups in one of the panniers.

The visitors sat on the ground near the fire, there being a chill in the air from rain the night before. Arbuckles added more wood.

"Sitting Bull is coming," Ryan announced, accepting the cup that Wakalyapi handed to him.

"So I have heard," C.W. said, looking askance at the woman.

"And so you will do what you came for?" Mulhaire asked dejectedly. "You will convince him to surrender to the soldiers?"

"I will speak with him about it. Is there truly any hope for his people here? Did the chief receive news that the queen will give them land in the Dominion?"

"We have not heard," Ryan told him.

"Will you go back if Sitting Bull surrenders?"

They both shook their heads.

"No matter the aftermath," Mulhaire said, "we will blend into the half-breed settlements and conjoin our fates with theirs."

"We remain deserters from the army and I cannot believe the fact would remain unnoticed," Ryan added.

"Lorcan Connor successfully changed his name and

joined the North-West Mounted Police," Collins pointed out.

"True enough," Ryan said, "but they do not share records with America. In fact, there has been political tension between the governments since Tȟatȟáŋka Íyotake took refuge here, or so Superintendent Walsh has told me. Especially following the lamentable debacle of General Terry's commission in '77."

"But now the police commissioner wants to starve the Lakota down so they will want to return south...in order to appease the American president," Mulhaire said. "It is why poor Walsh was spirited away from the fort what bears his name."

"That man, Tȟaté Tȟáŋka Crozier, did his best to make the people starve," Wakalyapi said disdainfully.

"Well," Collins said, "I cannot believe that the two countries will go to war over whether Sitting Bull is allowed to remain in the North-West Territories. But given the desperate plight of all the Indians and half-breeds up here and the scarcity of buffalo, I must convince the chief that his people will not survive if he does not return to Montana Territory."

There was a momentary silence. Mulhaire reached for a stick of wood and poked at the fire.

Arbuckles set aside her cup, stood and stretched. "Tȟatȟáŋka Íyotake believes he will be hanged," she said quietly. "Miles is still angry about Custer."

"I cannot believe they will hang him," C.W. told her. "There are numerous Americans in the east who take an interest in his fate."

"And what of prison?" Ryan asked. "If they do not kill him, they will surely put him in prison."

"*Fearr súil le glas ná súil le huaigh*," Collins said.

"Better chance of release from prison than release from the grave," Mulhaire translated for Arbuckles.

"Perhaps," she said. "But 'modest doubt is call'd the beacon of the wise.' I do not trust white men and I do not trust soldier boys. It is better to be cautious."

Mulhaire and Ryan both came to their feet.

"I agree," Mulhaire said. "We must discover whether

Tȟatȟáŋka Ìyotake was able to meet with Walsh at Qu'Appelle."

Mildly aggravated by the reticence of his companions, Collins also stood up. "Meanwhile, the children are dying of hunger."

"When you were with us before, I learned you were honorable," Ryan told him. "But you are now a tool of General Terry. Am I mistaken or are you not receiving your fifty pieces of silver to carry out his wishes?"

Staring at the man in anger, C.W. held his tongue. Nothing would be gained from thrashing the Irishman for his insolence and the fellow's robust stature did not portend an absolute victory on the side of virtue and rectitude. Mulhaire stood off to the side as if in anticipation of a brawl.

Wakalyapi moved around the fire ring and stood beside Collins. "*Héčhetu šni kštó*," she said to Ryan emphatically. "*Lakȟóta s'e ophíič'iya ye!*"

The man looked at the ground with a countenance of a scolded child. After a minute, he raised his eyes to Collins. "I ask your pardon."

"Your question was not unfounded," Collins replied. "But I must always attempt to be practical, no matter who has retained my services. If you have a strategy whereby the Lakota may remain in the north, I suggest you disclose it to Sitting Bull at the first opportunity."

"There is no such strategy," Mulhaire said sadly. "Or hope, for that matter."

"Shakespeare wrote, 'The miserable have no other medicine, but only hope,' " Collins told him. "There is always hope."

"Not if the entire U.S. army desires you dead," Ryan said.

I MUST GO

33

Having learned that Macdonell could be impulsive and arbitrary, despite his fair-mindedness, Collins stood back and observed the altercation with dismay. Sitting Bull, too, seemed to be less calm and self-possessed than he remembered. Wakalyapi was watching alongside C.W. while Jerry Potts, the half-breed interpreter, attempted to render the tirade of indignant words between the two men into comprehensible articulation.

"He is not correct," Arbuckles whispered to Collins.

"Who is not correct?"

"That half-breed. He is getting the words wrong. It will cause trouble."

"Can you assist?"

"If I am asked. Not before."

From what he could understand, Collins surmised that Sitting Bull was requesting rations for his people. They had travelled far and the provisions supplied by the redcoat escort had run out. The chief appeared to have lost at least three stones of weight and all the people and the few remaining dogs and horses he had seen were severely emaciated.

"If you make a move to take any food by force, I will be obliged to ration you with bullets," Macdonell told Sitting Bull.

"The half-breed has made the redcoat to think that Ťhatȟáŋka Ìyotake was making threats," Wakalyapi said angrily. "It is not true."

"I can no longer see the way," Sitting Bull said in English. "The old life is gone. The game has been killed and driven away by the *wašíču*. Some of the bravest men have turned their faces toward the white man ways."

"You must leave here," Macdonell said, forcefully. "I am speaking for your own good and the good of your people and giving you good advice. You have been promised pardon and food and land if you return to your own reservation in the United States. You and your people should accept the terms that have been offered you."

"This is what I have heard since I came here," Sitting Bull replied. "You must leave here...you must leave here. My *thuŋkášila* fought for the England many years past."

"Is this true?" Collins asked Wakalyapi.

"Yes. His grandfather's father fought for the English side against the French because he hated their allies, the *Ḣaḣáthuŋwaŋ*...the people called Ojibway by the whites."

"That may be," Inspector Macdonell was saying to the chief. "But I have heard that the Indian commissioner, Dewdney, told you there would be no reserve for you. Nor food."

"I must see Walsh."

"He is gone. He will not be back."

"What have the *Óglepi Lúta* done with my friend?"

"Enough of this!" Macdonell exclaimed, his face becoming positively rubicund with exasperation. "I am certain you asked Commissioner Dewdney the same question at Qu'Appelle. Walsh is gone. He will not return."

The two men had been confronting one another not far from the detachment office and Macdonell strode resolutely back into the building. Potts, the interpreter, walked away toward the half-breed village and Sitting Bull came over to where Wakalyapi, Collins and Mulhaire were standing.

"We will do no good here, *Wazi S'e*," he said to Collins. "I am woeful."

Mulhaire spoke to the chief in the Lakota language. Sitting Bull shook his head and walked to his horse, grazing a few yards away. He mounted up and turned the animal to lope away in the direction of the Indian camp. The small group of Indian onlookers followed in his wake.

"I asked him to come to my house, but he refused," Mulhaire explained. "Now his people will be forced to eat more of their horses."

"But what of the food brought by Légaré?" Collins asked.

"There are many more lodges in the camp now," Arbuckles told him. "The food is gone."

"Then I must appeal to Macdonell," C.W. said, moving toward the N.W.M.P office.

The woman seized his arm and held him back. "The man is angry. Perhaps you will make it worse?"

" 'Tis true that damn Scot is in a fine temper," Mulhaire said. "Come with me to my house. I will make some coffee and then we may conspire."

They made their way to Aidan Mulhaire's tidy cabin and he built up the fire in the cookstove, leaving the door open to let out the heat. The days had been growing warmer and this made Collins even more anxious to return home. He thought about his Chinese companions and worried about local ruffians becoming dangerously meddlesome.

"They are safe and sound," Wakalyapi said.

He squinted at her quizzically. "What?"

"Your friends."

Before he could respond further, Mulhaire brought cups of coffee and a tin of biscuits. "I have a proposal," he said, joining them at the table.

"And?" C.W. asked, still scrutinizing the indecipherable Indian woman.

"Let us combine our monetary wherewithall and purchase what food supplies we may."

"We have nothing left," Arbuckles told him.

"It has already been spent on just such a scheme," Collins added. "I have access to credit from General Terry, but alas, the telegraph line runs a great distance away."

"I possess exactly two twenty-five cent shinplasters," Mulhaire said.

"Shinplasters?" Wakalyapi asked, raising an eyebrow.

"Bank notes. They are the sum total of my current wealth."

"Well then," said Collins, "we will not be purchasing sufficient provisions to feed a village of starving Indians."

"What of the half-breeds?" asked Wakalyapi. "Their farms have been producing potatoes and suchlike."

"The Metis have been in dire need of food as well. I think they have given everything possible," Mulhaire said.

Taking out his pipe, Collins filled it from his dwindling supply of tobacco and handed the pouch to Arbuckles. "I suppose we could fall back on stealing cattle."

"I will not smoke just now," the woman told him, handing back his pouch. "No, we cannot steal cattle. My people would be blamed."

Collins struck a match and lit his old briar. He smoked in silence, while the other two gazed at the scratched and banged up surface of the table.

Mulhaire finally stood up to refill their cups, then went to the door and leaned against the jamb, looking out.

"What was your meaning before?" Collins asked after a while.

Wakalyapi smiled. "Your friends down south are enjoying good health."

"Just how do you know this?"

"*Apsíč̣A Wíŋyaŋ* often knows things," Mulhaire said,

turning back from the door.

"Well then, perhaps she may know how to find food for the Indian camp. And for us as well."

"She may know things, but I doubt she is able to conjure sustenance."

Coming to his feet, Collins put away his pipe, finished his cup of coffee and put on his hat. The dog awoke from her nap under the table and sat expectantly, watching him. "It is early. We can at least hunt." He looked down at Arbuckles. "What do you think, Jumping Woman?"

"I think we can hunt," she said, standing.

"Someone is coming," Mulhaire said. "It looks like Híŋyaŋka."

The young man appeared in the doorway as Mulhaire stood back to allow him entry. "I come from Tȟatȟáŋka Ìyotake," he said. "The chief wishes to see *Wazi S'e*...Collins."

"We were going hunting. The children require food."

"*Čheží Wašté*, the Frenchman, has brought flour and the women are digging *thíŋpsila*. There will be food for a day or two."

"Then we will come," C.W. told the boy. "Will you accompany us?" he asked Mulhaire.

"Yes. I have a sack of beans. I can bring it."

"Excellent," Híŋyaŋka said. "This will ensure that more of the people might not go hungry."

"Perhaps for a day," Wakalyapi told him. "Tomorrow? *Uŋmáspe šni kštó*. I do not know how."

"They 'suffer us to famish,' " said Collins, quoting from *Coriolanus*. "It is a fine strategy for banishing a group of people."

"It worked on the Irish," Mulhaire said.

CAMP

34

The interior of the tipi was cool and pleasingly ornamented with a lining of bleached deerskins covered in painted depictions of horses and buffalo. Above their heads was suspended an array of leggings, parfleche packets, buckskin clothing and an immaculate head-dress adorned with ermine tassels and a stunningly beaded brow band. Collins was seated on a buffalo robe between Mulhaire and Wakalyapi. He noted the agreeable and earthy fragrance of the grass that Wakalyapi had burned to ward off mosquitoes in their camp on the Poplar River. It seemed to permeate the lodge along with the scents of sage and other herbage he could not identify.

The discussion around him was taking place in the Lakota language and he, therefore, was at liberty to peruse his environs. A very small boy and an infant were asleep on a blanket between two mounds of household goods, Sitting Bull's mother sat quietly in the dim hindmost of the lodge, smiling in his direction, and a young woman sat beside her, engrossed in repairing an article of clothing. Gazing out the opening, made by some of the lodge skins having been drawn back, Collins could see a few horses, their ribs delineated like ridges on a washboard. Smoke from the cooking fire in front of the tipi rose at an angle, propelled by a persistent westerly breeze. A woman tended the fire while minding an iron pot hanging from a tripod above the flames.

"It is good to see you, Wazi S'e," a voice said in English. "My mother is also happy."

Mulhaire elbowed C.W. He glanced over and saw that Sitting Bull was addressing him. The head man wore a single upright feather. His hair lay in wrapped braids down the breast of his shirt and he sat leaning against a willow back rest, his face care-worn and lean.

"I am pleased to be your guest once more," Collins said.

"You have come from Terry."

"Yes."

"Why?"

"To speak to you about surrender."

"I will be killed."

"Certainly not. I came to see how it is with you. I find that the children are hungry, that the buffalo are gone, that the White Mother will not give your people a home."

Sitting Bull said something to Wakalyapi in their tongue.

She spoke to him then told Collins, "I have interpreted your words so there would be no misunderstanding."

"Is he angry?"

"I am not angry," the chief answered. "You give the truth and I cannot be angry."

"It is difficult for me to say."

"I spoke with *Tȟatȟáŋka Eháŋni*. At the fort, people are not glad, but they eat."

"Yes, he told me."

"My daughter has gone there. I wish to see her, but I do not wish to be killed or give up my horses and guns. I am a warrior. *Miglúonihaŋ yeló*."

Mulhaire conversed with Sitting Bull for quite a while in the Lakota language. Throughout the interlude, Collins thought about the Irish during the Great Hunger. He remembered how his mother was broken-hearted at having to leave their coastal village and his father's grave. Yet English tyranny and the landed proprietors were heedless of suffering and famine and thusly forced people to emigrate or perish. The circumstances in which the chief and his remaining followers now found themselves were even more dire, given that their very freedom, traditions and right to retain ownership of their horses and guns, pivotal to their lifeway, were being threatened. He did not find this to be much of an alternative to starvation.

Having finished his discussion with Mulhaire, Sitting Bull passed around a tobacco pouch. When it came to him, Collins found it contained a mix of tobacco and aromatic herbs. They all filled their pipes, including Her Holy Door, the chief's mother, and Wakalyapi produced her match safe and offered a light to everyone. Soon, despite the front of the lodge being agape, the space became suffused with fragrant haze from their collective bowls.

"I am caught, Wazi S'e," Sitting Bull said presently. "I am curious...what would you do? Many other principal men have gone to the forts. I do not think they will remember who they are."

After contemplating the question judiciously, Collins said, "I have to say that I would not want to go back. I would not want to give up my horses and guns. I would not want to take a chance that Miles would not kill me." He paused a moment so Wakalyapi could interpret his words, then continued. "But you have grave responsibilities. You are looked to by your people and there is fading hope here. I understand that the decision to surrender to the very men who have committed crimes against you is not easy, but I can see no other choice. The children must survive."

When Arbuckles had finished translating his response, Sitting Bull was silent for a long time. "For sixty-four years the Americans treated my people bad," he finally said. "We did not give them our country, they took it from us. The soldiers never think of anything good for us, always bad. The Americans killed my children for nothing. They never tell us the truth. Everything that was bad always began with them."

"I have no words to defend the Americans or what has been done," Collins said.

"Up above us is *Tȟa Pahá Čheyaka*," Sitting Bull told him. "A while ago *Čheyaka* was a young warrior who went up there to make his *haŋbléčheya*." The chief glanced pointedly at Wakalyapi.

"The *haŋbléčheya* is a fasting and praying to seek blessing or aid," she explained.

"Yes," Sitting Bull said. "This boy was given a dream. When he told me, I knew it was telling me we would have to go back…At some time we would have to go back. Not long after, *Čheyaka* died."

"Then perhaps it is time."

"Perhaps. I miss my daughter. I miss my *Hohé* son, *Tȟatȟáŋka PsíčA*, who I hear is in irons at the fort."

There was a disturbance outside the lodge. Dogs were barking and Gal came running in to cower beside Collins. Everyone came to their feet and departed the shelter and saw there were two loaded half-breed carts coming into camp. Behind them rode Légaré alongside a young red-coated policeman. A small pack of hungry camp dogs ran at their heels.

"*Mes amis!*" he cried when he saw Wakalyapi and Collins. "*Comment allez-vous?*"

Collins knew enough French to answer, "*Bonjour, Légaré. Comment ça-va?*"

They walked over to the Frenchman who dismounted and handed the reins to one of the teamsters. The red-coat also swung down and stood back, waiting.

"*Oh la*," Légaré said and raised his shoulders and eyebrows skyward in a Gallic shrug. "I am an *imbécile*. This is Louis Daniels." He pointed his lower lip at the policeman. "The corporal has a *trés* important message for the Bull."

"And what of Old Bull?" C.W. asked. "Is he with you?"

"The Old Bull has left for Buford with *quelques* others. Come let us *baiser le cul du diable quand il est frette!*" the Frenchman said, then headed toward where Sitting Bull stood beside Mulhaire in front of the lodge. Daniels followed behind.

"What did he say?" Collins asked Wakalyapi.

She frowned. "I think he said something about kissing the devil's ass while it is cold."

"That makes no sense."

"No. I am an *imbécile*." Wakalyapi imitated the Frenchman's earlier gesture.

Laughing, they wandered over to the tipi.

"*Monsieur Taureau*," Légaré said to the chief. "I have brought the food, *comme promis*. And also several sacks of flour and some tobacco. *Mais mon ami*, much as I would like to feed you more, I am without *plus d'argent* to do so."

"*Philámayaye.*"

"You must go back. *Ça vient de s'éteindre.*"

Wakalyapi talked to Sitting Bull in a respectful manner. He listened courteously and nodded.

"I have explained to him what Čheží Wašté has said," she told Collins.

Légaré grabbed the young redcoat's arm and yanked him forward. "*Dis-lui*...Tell him."

Looking slightly ill at ease, the corporal cleared his throat. "I was asked by Superintendent Walsh to give you a message," he said to Sitting Bull.

"Walsh?"

"Yes. He asked me to say that you can with safety return to the United States. That the same treatment will be extended to you as that given to Spotted Eagle, Gall and the others."

The chief looked over at Mulhaire who proceeded to interpret the message.

"But you told me that Gall was attacked at Poplar

River," C.W. whispered to Arbuckles.

"Yes but Tȟatȟáŋka Ìyotake will believe Walsh's message. And Gall is still alive, nonetheless."

"*Et alors*, we may eat and then prepare," the Frenchman said. "I will send an *hivernant* ahead to *Commandeur* Brotherton and tell him we are coming."

"I must speak to my cousin, *Hétópa* and also *Wakíŋyáŋ Lúta*," said Sitting Bull. "I will have to think on this."

"*Calice de Crisse!*" yelled Légaré. "*It is pas possible!* You will not be hanged now. Walsh has said. *Je voyagerai* in seven days to Fort Buford. You must come to *Talle-de-Saules*. If you come, I will feed you *pour* the *voyage*. *Mais pas?* There will be no more food."

The Frenchman strode back to the carts and directed his men to unload them. He kicked at a dog that came too close, then turned to see children gathered close at hand, watching the bundles and sacks of provisions as they were carried over to Sitting Bull's lodge. The trader went to his horse and took a paper packet from his saddlebags. Kneeling before the group of youngsters, he handed out lemon drops.

" 'He is as full of valor as of kindness. Princely in both,' " Collins said, observing the change in Légaré's deportment.

Wakalyapi smiled. "*Henry the Fifth*. My favorite."

"Will Sitting Bull finally decide to surrender, do you think?"

"Maybe," said the man himself, walking up between them. "But you must remain with me, *Wazi S'e. Kȟolá, taŋyáŋ yahí yeló*. It is good you came."

35

There seemed to Collins to be a mingling of excitement and trepidation in the Indian camp assembled about a quarter of a mile from Légaré's store at Willow Bunch. A reliable supply of comestibles probably gave rise to much of the liveliness, he mused. Even though an unknown future lay ahead, hunger had been a constant companion of late and food was reassuring. Many of the half-breeds from the neighboring settlement kept their distance, disconcerted by the noise and tumult.

Prior to his visit with Sitting Bull at Peppermint's Hill, Légaré had divested himself of all his negotiable property, hides and furs and had impoverished himself by purchasing all foodstuffs available from the Leighton and Jordan storehouse in Buford. It was a noteworthy gamble, contingent on Major Brotherton's promises that the French trader would be reimbursed upon the chief's surrender. As the half-breed carts began to be loaded, more and more of the Lakota families gathered around, bringing their belongings. Légaré's Metis employees, of which their friend Antoine was one, exhibited generous forbearance in placing their treasured cargo among the other goods and supplies.

The Frenchman came over to where Arbuckles and Collins stood beneath a tree.

"I wished to thank you for the food you sent to us," Arbuckles told him.

"*Ce n'est rien*. It was my pleasure," Légaré said, smiling through his thick beard. "*Mais* there is another matter. "*S'il vous plaît*, Charles, would you *une fois encore* talk to the Bull? He is now telling me that he has *plus de familles*...more families... back at Montagne de Bois."

"I thought they had all come here."

"*Oui*. I think that he makes a delay. *C'est tout*."

Glancing at Wakalyapi, Collins said, "We will speak to him."

"Ah, *merci, merci. Trés bien*. Very good."

When Légaré went back to his preparations, the two of them walked toward the Lakota encampment where only a very few lodges remained intact. Many of the women were dismantling their tipis for the journey, while children, dogs and horses wandered among the skeletal lodgepoles and piles of hides, buffalo robes and other signs of imminent departure. Gal ran off to frolic with a camp dog of previous acquaintance. When they came to Sitting Bull's lodge, C.W. and Arbuckles found him playing with his little son, Crowfoot. They were on their hands and knees stalking a giant stag beetle. The chief saw them and came to his feet.

"You have come from Čheží Wašté," he said. "He is in a hurry."

"The food will not last," Wakalyapi said. "If there are people left behind, it is because they wished to be left behind."

"Do you want to stay?" Collins asked.

"*Wamátukȟa yeló*. I am tired. It is like the *maȟpíyohaŋzizi*. Sometimes there is light, sometimes not. It is difficult to know what is best for my children." He pointed his lower lip toward Crowfoot who now held the beetle and was speaking to it.

"When I was a child, we were always hungry," Collins told him. "There was no hope and there were soldiers. We had to leave."

"There are soldiers ahead of us, not behind," Sitting

Bull said.

"True, but there are redcoats here."

"When do my friends wish to leave?"

"In two days," Wakalyapi said. "We were going to ride to *Tȟa Pahá Čheyaka* and *Ȟečhaŋ* to say farewell to the white warriors. If we find people there who want to come, we can bring them."

The head man seemed to accept the plan and returned his attention to his son. Collins and Wakalyapi strolled back toward the trading post where the half-breed men were arranging what seemed to be a considerable number of carts into a jumbled column.

Skirting the chaos, Arbuckles said, "Let us ride over to Ȟečhaŋ, Wood Mountain. If no one comes back with us, perhaps Tȟatȟáŋka Ìyotake will then decide to go."

They made their way to where they had established a small camp. Their stock were hobbled and had not wandered far.

"Where is Wait Now? Has he left?" C.W. asked. "I have not seen him."

"Híŋyaŋka has gone to visit with Mulhaire and the others. He will stay with them for a while."

Walking over to where the animals were grazing, Collins looped a rope around his gelding's neck and scratched his forehead. The horse snugged his head against his shoulder while Molly came over to request some affection. Leaving the mule and Wakalyapi's pack horse to graze on the thick grasses remaining around their camp, he led Ulysses to where the woman waited with her horse and hurriedly saddled up. Gal came bounding over and sprang uninvited onto Collins' lap as they headed away from the mayhem near Légaré's store in the direction of Wood Mountain.

It was nearly nightfall by the time they rode into the Metis settlement near the redcoat post. They had gone by the camp at Peppermint's Hill, but the place had been abandoned except for a few coyotes scavenging abandoned debris. As they drew near, Mulhaire heard them and came out of his cabin.

"*Fáilte*," he said, greeting them in the Irish. "You have not yet left us."

"As you see," Collins said. " 'Tis sure we could not depart without we bid ye farewell," Collins said in his best brogue, dismounting.

"Has Ťhatȟáŋka Ìyotake gone with the Frenchman?"

Wakalyapi slid down from her horse and allowed the reins to drag. "No one has gone south. And Ťhatȟáŋka Ìyotake is worried."

Mulhaire laughed bitterly. "And why not? What have American promises been worth?"

"I believe he thinks there are some of his people still here," C.W. told him, easing the cinch on his saddle.

"There is no one left here that wishes to leave. A few have melted into the half-breed villages. Several people and all the *Pȟóǧe Ȟlóka* have scattered to hide from Macdonell and his peelers. And that bastard at Leighton and Jordan's accused Connor of passing a bad check, so he has gone to Battleford. Hiŋyaŋka went with him."

"*Kapémni!*" exclaimed Wakalyapi crossly. "I have heard that those who follow Ťhatȟáŋka Ìyotake were accused of robbing the same store last spring."

" 'Tis true," said Mulhaire. "And that was after the chief had already departed for Qu'Appelle." He motioned toward the door. "*Wakȟálapi etáŋ yačhíŋ hwo*? Coffee?"

A voice called from the gathering darkness. Gal began barking and shortly afterward Inspector Macdonell came striding into view. Collins reached down to hush the dog.

"Louis saw you ride in," Macdonell said.

Having earlier learned that Louis Léveillé was a half-breed scout for the North-West Mounted Police, Collins asked, "Why would that be a matter of concern to him?"

Ignoring his surly tone of voice, Macdonell said,

"Commissioner Irvine has just arrived here from head-quarters. I have been instructed to proceed to Fort Buford to notify the American authorities on Sitting Bull's surrender. I am also to telegraph Sir John Macdonald, Minister of the Interior."

"Sitting Bull remains in Willow Bunch," C.W. told him.

The man looked nonplussed. "But I had understood he was prepared to surrender."

"That is possible," said Arbuckles.

"But I must leave promptly in the morning."

"Well, Inspector," Collins said. "I believe Sitting Bull will go. I suggest you ride ahead to alert the Americans, then return to find us en route if you wish it."

Macdonell nodded. "That is a sound suggestion."

"If you are willing, I would like to make a request."

"Within reason," the inspector said, "I would be pleased to accede."

"Might I compose a brief message for transmission by telegraph to General Terry?"

The policeman frowned. "I am willing…but what could you, perchance, have to say to General Terry? Certainly Major Brotherton will inform him of all eventualities after I have brought the news."

"I am currently employed by General Terry."

"You never told me of this."

"The matter never arose."

Apparently unable to formulate an adequate rebuke, the inspector reluctantly said, "Then yes. Of course. Have you paper and pencil?"

"I have," Mulhaire said and went into his cabin. He returned with a small leather bound journal and pencil.

Collins flipped to a blank page and wrote:

Wood Mountain Post
North-West Territories
British Dominion
July 1881

Headquarters Department of Dakota
Brigadier-General A. H. Terry
St. Paul, Minn.

Sir:

In compliance with the request made by you, I have met with Sitting Bull and shaped an argument regarding prudence of returning to the United States for purposes of surrender.

I anticipate surrender to Fort Buford in Montana Territory no later than the 30th instant, whereupon I will compose and submit final record and accounting for settlement at that time.

Your Obedient Servant,
Charles Wolfe Collins

Collins handed the paper to Macdonell who accepted and perused the missive. "Ah, now I see. You intend to gain full credit for the surrender, I take it?" His manner was stand-offish.

Wakalyapi said something under her breath in her own tongue. Collins did not think it sounded friendly.

"I do not intend to take credit for the actions of others," he said quietly. "What has been decided by the principal men of the Sioux has been decided for the benefit of their people. If authorities within the police and government of your country refuse them land and rations, there is little choice left to them. How may anyone take credit for this? Unless you take pride in starving a group of people near to death."

"Aye and 'tis been done by you peelers before," Mulhaire said indignantly.

"Well then…well…I find I must apologize, Mr. Collins," said Macdonell, squinting uneasily at Mulhaire.

"See the signal officer at the fort," C.W. said. "There should be no problems with either telegram."

"Very well." The inspector hesitated and gave the impression of wanting to say something else but seemed to change his mind.

"If you wish to find us, search along the road you have travelled before," Wakalyapi told him.

"Very well," the man said again. "Until then." He walked away into the deepening night.

"Bastard," said Mulhaire.

"I fear that from now on," Collins said, "there will be many who wish to make a feast of Sitting Bull."

"Eat him?" the woman asked.

"Devour him as a prize. Claim him as a trophy."

"The moment he sets foot on American soil, Ťhatháŋka Ìyotake will be regarded as a source of curiosity. They will be blind to his virtues." Mulhaire told her.

Collins said, "Alexander Pope wrote, 'All human virtue to its latest breath, finds envy never conquered but by death.' "

"There are those among his own people who are fools and slaves to the whites at the fort," added Wakalyapi. "Perhaps they will want to eat him also."

PONY DRAGS

36

Great clouds of dust were raised by lodgepole drags and the train of carts and horses. Collins and Wakalyapi rode behind the lengthy and chaotic procession, following the few warriors who protected the rear. Several families had decided to stay behind at the last moment, but C.W. estimated that around two hundred Lakota people were now on the move. He doubted that food supplies would last for the nearly hundred and fifty mile journey to Fort Buford. The head men decided to make camp after only ten miles, having been delayed until the early afternoon. Sitting Bull had hesitated to the very last, even debating whether or not to make his way to Milk River instead.

While the lodges were being raised, two of the half-breed workers distributed flour, bacon, beans, sugar, coffee and tea. Légaré oversaw the rationing and when all the provisions had been apportioned, he walked around making certain there was no trouble. Collins joined him as the sun was sinking beyond the western skyline.

"Will there be enough?" he asked the Frenchman.

"*Sacrement!* Already it is *évident* the food will not last."

One of the Metis men, Louison Piché, came over. "*Li shavaezh son kakwy-akishihk,*" he said, shaking his head expressively.

"The Indians are *pas trés content*, not very happy," Légaré explained to C.W.

"Johnny must *vaw aan* Bufford," Piché said. "*Weehta*

Brodertown *kiyanawn bizwaen pleu di mawnzhee*."

"*Oui, chu troov* Johnny," the trader told him.

Piché trotted away in the direction of the carts and the half-breed bivouac.

"I must send Johnny Chartrand to Brotherton," the Frenchman said to Collins. "*Je lui dirai* that he needs to bring *plus de* supplies."

"But if Brotherton sends soldiers back, I think the Indians will become more agitated."

"*Sans doute*. I must tell him *peu de soldats*. Few soldiers."

They walked together to Légaré's camp. Collins smoked his pipe while the Frenchman wrote his message to Brotherton. Johnny Chartrand arrived. He was a wiry and sprightly young man with a chiseled face and C.W. could plainly see Indian lineage written upon his features.

"Take *cette lettre* to Brotherton at Buford," Légaré told Chartrand, handing him the communiqué.

"*Yaynk* Brotherton. *Nishtoohtamihk*?"

"*Wii*," said Johnny. "I give it to him only."

"Take Ambroise. *Ootina* Ambroise."

Another Metis man walked into camp. "Are you sending Johnny to Buford?" he asked.

"*Oui*," said Légaré, nodding toward the younger man who was standing nearby awaiting further instructions. "I have Ambroise going *aussi*." He looked over at C.W. "Narcisse, *souviens-tu* Charles Collins?"

"Yes. I remember. *Taanishi, Misyeu* Charles."

"Taanishi, Narcisse."

"Johnny," said Narcisse. "*Ootina deu lii zhwaal*. Ambroise *miina*. Go fast. Go *shaymaak*. *Tayhtapi toot la nwit*."

Chartrand sprinted into the mounting darkness and a few minutes later, Collins could hear pounding hooves pass by not far away.

"I told him to take two horses each and ride all night," Lecerte said to Collins. "I *paansi* that food needs to come soon."

"I agree."

Légaré invited Collins to eat with him and sent Lecerte to find Wakalyapi. Piché, the fellow who seemed to function alternately as teamster, cook and manservant, lit a lantern and made a fire with wood from a supply stacked in one of the Red River carts. The wagon's sole purpose was to transport fuel across the barren country where not even a stick of wood or buffalo chip remained. They sat upon camp chairs and smoked, talking of this and that, until Arbuckles walked into the glow of firelight with the dog following behind.

"I have been to see Tȟatȟáŋka Ìyotake," she said. "His spirit is very low."

"*Cha bhiann imirce gan chaill*," said Collins. "There is no removal without loss."

"*J'aime cette langue*. I like it. What is *la langue*?" asked the Frenchman.

"The Irish. It is my native tongue."

"I like it."

"It is quiet among the people," the woman said. "It is hard to know they will soon have white bosses to say you may go here, you may go there, you may not go over there. And they will say this is our land and do not cross it. You cannot hunt upon it. You cannot *wačhékiyA*...pray here."

"*Mais*, there is food and *les écoles* and *la paix*," said Légaré.

She snorted rudely. "Of what use is food and schools and peace when there is no *liberté*."

Collins noticed she had used the French word. He recalled the motto that was being carved on public buildings in France. *Liberté, égalité, fraternité*. There had been an article in a Butte newspaper the year before. Certainly, none of these fine sentiments would be applied to the Indians.

Lecerte walked into the camp and fetched chairs for Wakalyapi and himself. Piché brought cups of coffee for everyone. Collins put away his pipe and studied his friend intently. She seemed to be brooding over some further ominous notion.

"*Et alors, mon amie,*" Légaré said to Wakalyapi. "*Qu'est-ce que tu fais? Resteras-tu* at Fort Buford?"

Knowing enough to understand the trader was asking whether she would stay at Fort Buford, C.W. waited for her answer with much interest. The woman stared into her mug and said nothing.

"There is always a home with me," he finally told her softly.

She lifted her eyes and said, "*Philámayaye*...but we both know that very soon any Indian who is not on a reservation would be target practice for soldier boys and civilians alike."

"And also in the territory here," said Lecerte. "Even for the Metis on either side of the line it is becoming more difficult."

Heaping plates of beans, salt pork and hunks of bread were handed around by the cook. No one spoke for a while. Collins saw that Arbuckles remained preoccupied.

"Do you plan to go back to Wood Mountain?" he asked her.

She shrugged. "Remember many years ago I told you I was like the *gnugnúška*? I have lived too many lives and there is no place for me. We will go to Buford, then I must decide."

As he was finishing his meal, Collins tried to think of a solution. Always prey to sudden pangs of despondency, the impossible circumstances within which his companion and all the Lakota were ensnared suddenly overwhelmed him with indignation. The totality of his experiences investigating political machinations, avarice, corruption and malfeasance in regard to Indian tribes was enough to drive him to bold and wanton acts of violence. His own Irish history, however, was sufficient to dispel such inclinations.

Resting a hand on his arm, Wakalyapi said, "It is of no consequence, Charles. Let us see to our horses and walk together. There is moonlight to see by."

They thanked their host and departed Légaré's camp. C.W. found that sitting beside the fire had distracted him from the brilliant radiance cast by the rising moon. He called for Gal and then they ambled toward the place where they had left their saddles and packs. A gentle breeze and the simple beauty of the night did much to assuage his earlier tribulations. Along the way, the spectral form of a solitary lodge caught their attention and Collins saw there was no evidence of a fire within or without.

"Should we discover if all is well?" he asked.

"Perhaps."

As they drew near, Collins could hear mumbling and see the shapes of a man and a horse against the horizon.

"It is *Wakíŋyáŋ Lúta*," Wakalyapi said.

"How do you know?"

She went closer and said something. The man turned and called a greeting, then said, "*Yuphíyakel haŋwíyaŋpa yeló.*"

"*Háŋ*," Wakalyapi answered. "Will you speak English now? My friend does not speak our language."

"I said it was nice in the moonlight."

Finding the voice resonant and somewhat musical, C.W. said, "It is very nice. My name is Charles Wolfe Collins."

"Wolfe with an 'e' and not *šuŋgmánitu tȟáŋka*," the woman added.

"I know of you, Wolfe. *ApsíčA Wíŋyaŋ* has spoken of you

and I know you have brought meat for the children."

"It was an honor to do so."

"My name is Red Thunder in English. I was just now talking to my horse. I call him *Mniskúya* because he likes salt."

Gal wandered over and Red Thunder bent down to pat her on the head. "This is a nice dog. We used to have many nice dogs and horses but the people had to eat them. We are having a bad time."

"I know. I am sorry."

The Indian peered at Collins in the moonlight. "Do you want us to have a bad time?"

"No. Certainly not."

"Then you do not have to be sorry." He reached up to smooth back his horse's forelock. "I was telling *Mniskúya* that when we get to Buford, the *wašíču* soldiers will take him away from me. We have been together for a long time. He does not understand. Do you?"

"No," said Collins truthfully.

"I think it is because we can be less dangerous without our friends," Red Thunder said. "Perhaps if we are full of sadness and are lonesome for our friends and have to walk everywhere, they do not have to be afraid of us."

"Perhaps."

"Still, it makes me sad."

"I would be very sad if I had my horses taken. I would also be angry."

"I am angry."

"You have no fire," Wakalyapi said. "*Chežί Wašté* has wood to cook with."

"I am not hungry. I am thinking about my horse."

"Will you come to our camp and have coffee?" Collins asked.

"Coffee would be good. With sugar. Do you have sugar?"

"We have sugar."

"Then I will come to drink coffee with you."

GENERAL TERRY

37

Buffalo skeletons were scattered upon the uniformly even and bleak prairie. The wayward cavalcade straggled across the expanse with an eerie and uncanny shrieking of the wooden cart axles. Each of the Metis drove six carts in sequence, secured one to the other by leather bands and pulled by a team of horses. Légaré had told Collins he did not dare follow the old military road along the Poplar River for fear of running into a detachment of soldiers and thereby spooking the Indians. Instead they were travelling in a southeasterly direction, making for Big Muddy Creek and henceforth to the fort. The country was nothing more than dry and dreary monotony and the people and animals seemed mute with desolation as they made their laborious way across the weary land.

The day was becoming very warm and Collins found himself muddle-headed with ennui. The dog lay draped across the saddle swells like a limp carcass and as his gelding plodded along through the endless morning, he had nothing to do but resign himself to rumination. Once or twice he had attempted to engage Wakalyapi in conversation, but she manifestly wished to avoid idle discourse.

He began to think about Brigadier-General Alfred Terry. Although Arbuckles had been correct in that the man did not seem to blink his eyes, Terry was a gentlemanly soldier of impressive stature. Six and a half feet tall, well-proportioned and with a gracious manner, the general had bravely captured the pivotal Fort Fisher in the War of the Rebellion and had maintained law and order as Commander of the South during reconstruction. He had ably handled the barbarous agency known as the Ku Klux Klan, various other Southern white leagues, yellow fever epidemics and all manner of violence, murder and fraud committed by those who would not accept defeat. Collins was only slightly acquainted with Terry, but the fact that Miles did not care for him made it even easier to respect the man.

"You asked me about *Wakíŋyáŋ Lúta*," Wakalyapi said unexpectedly, rousing him from his musing.

"Who?"

"Red Thunder."

"Oh yes." He reckoned it had been a full two hours since he had asked about the old warrior.

"He is the brother of *Itéomaǧážu*."

"And who is he when he is at home?" C.W. asked sarcastically. He was uncomfortably warm, thirsty and irritable.

"The principal man Rain in the Face."

Interest replaced petulance and he said, "I read in a newspaper last spring that, having surrendered at Fort Keogh, he confessed to killing Custer. He told a correspondent that he ate his liver."

The woman scowled at him ferociously. " 'You speak an infinite deal of nothing,' " she said, quoting from Shakespeare. "There is no one who has claimed this. *Itéomaǧážu* would not claim this."

"Newspapermen are certainly known to prevaricate," he admitted. "Especially if their story garners much attention."

"He was a bold warrior, but he surrendered to Miles. He shot his own leg in a hunt after the Greasy Grass and was crippled. There were six brothers of the *Čhéoȟkpa* band...sons of *Matȟó Ité*. Bear Face."

"And what about Red Thunder?"

"He is the oldest and has been very courageous, but does not put himself forward as the others have done."

The screeching of the carts ahead had stopped and they saw that the wagons and pony drags were gathering together. Collins supposed it was finally time for the midday respite and he would be able to water his animals and fill his canteens. Gal leapt down and he dismounted and Arbuckles followed suit. The Frenchmen and his crew were pouring water from barrels into whatever vessels were proffered by thirsty women and children while the men stood back and waited.

When all the Indians had gotten their share of water, Wakalyapi and Collins filled two collapsible canvas buckets and their canteens and water skins.

"*Crisse!*" exclaimed Légaré. "We must come to water soon. *Les barils*, the barrels are *presque* empty."

"But you must know this route well," C.W. said.

"*Un peu, mais* I prefer the road on *la grande rivière*, Missouri, when I am not with *les Indiens*…The Indians who are *indécis* and wanting to leave *tout le temps*."

After watering their stock, they turned them loose to pick at sparse grasses, mostly brown from summer heat and inadequate rains. The sky was a sallow cloudless blue and a tenacious breeze had begun to blow. While Wakalyapi smoked her pipe, Collins gave the dog a good drink and quenched his own thirst, then lay down, placed his hat over his face and took a nap.

When the men began to rouse everyone and the carts were heard moving, they caught their horses, tightened their cinches and mounted up.

"Did Red Thunder fight at the Greasy Grass?" Collins asked, as they again rode across the lifeless terrain, where not even a solitary animal track was evident. It occurred to him that not long ago there must have been thousands of buffalo, deer and antelope roaming these open plains in every direction.

"Yes, he fought. He killed many soldiers."

"Did you?" he asked, finally posing the question he had wanted the answer to for several years.

The woman was silent for a very long time. He waited patiently, knowing her well enough to be assured that she would either answer him or remain taciturn if she chose not to. A lone raven soared overhead, riding air currents and no doubt seeking some dead creature upon which to feed.

"I was there," she said at last.

"And yet I found you at Fort Shaw not long after."

"I knew there would be a great vengeance and wanted to be close to the soldier boys to see what would come."

"Did *you* kill Custer and eat his liver?" he asked.

He heard Wakalyapi chuckling behind the hand she held over her mouth.

"Were you the only woman who fought?" he asked after a while.

"No. There were others. One of them is with us here."

"Truly?"

"Truly. Her name is *Ptehahinšma Mani Wíŋyaŋ*. Moving Robe Woman. She was among those who charged into the soldiers after her brother was killed."

"Is it true that Sitting Bull did not fight that day?"

"No. You should not read newspapers," she said and made a contemptuous gesture. "Tȟatȟáŋka Ìyotake went against the soldiers that attacked the bottom of the camp. The ones who went up on the hill and lived. Later, I heard he came back and killed some of the last soldier boys, but did not take scalps because it was almost over and there was no fight left in them."

The afternoon crept along and finally some low-lying ridges could be seen to the south. Collins thought maybe they were drawing near the Big Muddy Creek when he descried a dark margin of trees in the distance. Within an hour they had come to the confluence of two streams, shaded by intermittent cottonwoods. Signs of old stone tipi rings, cooking fires and discarded wooden stakes disclosed the fact that the location had been a popular camp-ground for a great many years. The half-breed carts formed into the customary circle while the Indian women began raising the lodges. The men took the horses to drink and the dogs and children explored their surroundings. Wakalyapi and Collins chose a place a little upstream under the shade of an ancient tree, its creaking limbs spreading wide over the creek bank.

Légaré's workers handed out the last of the provisions and they were solemnly accepted. Soon the aroma of cooking drifted over the encampment. As Collins was shaking out his bedroll and Wakalyapi was gathering wood, Lecerte walked up and invited them to eat with his boss. They followed him to where Légaré was seated by a fire. Piché gave them cups of coffee.

"Maarsii," said C.W., sitting in one of the extra chairs.

"Wii."

"*Alors*," said Légaré, "*C'est grave*. The food supply is all eaten."

Arbuckles sat beside Lecerte. "Have you heard from Johnny?" she asked him.

"*Namaakaykway*...nothing."

"What will the Indians do if there is no food?" asked Collins.

"*Ils quitteront*," answered the Frenchman. "They will leave."

"But where can they go?"

"Some of them have said they want to go to the Tongue River country or maybe to hide along the Milk River as before," Lecerte told him.

Collins shook his head. "That would never do. The military would chase them to hell and back again while they were starving to death in the meantime."

"Perhaps that would be better," said Wakalyapi sadly.

Piché served a modest meal of bread and side meat. Afterward, everyone smoked their pipes. Someone in the Indian camp was beating a hand drum and it sounded to Collins that two or more women were singing. An owl hooted from down the creek and he could hear night-hawks diving after insects. For the first time since leaving Willow Bunch, he was being pestered by mosquitoes. He was refilling his pipe when Gal began barking and growling at the sound of horses approaching. Two men dismounted and came into the firelight.

"Johnny! Ambroise!" exclaimed Lecerte, coming to his feet. "What is this?"

"The food is coming from Buford," Johnny told him. "*Maaka* we came in from *li norr*, the north, so *lii* Indians did not see."

Just then, a clattering of trace chains and wagon wheels could be heard coming from the south.

"*Vite*, Narcisse," commanded Légaré, "Bring the wagons here."

Lecerte ran in the direction of the noise and they all walked into the moonlit clearing near the Indian village. Soon, a four mule team advanced upon them, hauling two wagons which were joined together one behind the other. The civilian teamster, a big burly fellow in grimy clothing, pulled in the animals and leapt down as groups of Indian women and children congregated around. Without a word, the man climbed into one of the wagons and began tossing out bags of flour, potatoes and beans and crates of bacon, tea, sugar and coffee. Sitting Bull, Red Thunder, Four Horns and another head man walked over and watched as the women took charge of the provisions, dividing them out evenly so that all would receive a share.

"There will be a feast now," Wakalyapi told Collins.

"While 'chewing the food of sweet and bitter fancy,' " he said, quoting from *As You Like It*.

"Food is always sweet when you are hungry," she said. "It can also be a bribe."

SHERIDAN'S SOLUTION

38

The next day, the caravan advanced ponderously along the riparian bottoms, ever moving closer to the fort. The general spirit of the people seemed much improved by readily available water and a surplus of provisions. The civilian who had brought the supplies was one of twenty teamsters at Fort Buford and he told Légaré he had been ordered to stay and transport whatever people and baggage necessary to accomplishing the surrender. Some of the women with small children, and no remaining horses, chose to ride in the army wagons. Their belongings were stowed away in the Red River carts, but there had not been enough room for all the people. Collins imagined that ordinarily the Lakota women were capable of walking indefinitely, all the while carrying their offspring, but malnutrition and despair had weakened them.

Around noon, Légaré called a halt. All the stock was watered and turned out. Meadows along the creek offered lush grasses that had not recently been over-grazed. Some of the Indian women took their digging sticks to search for wild turnips out on the prairie to the east. Collins wandered off to relieve himself and when he returned, Wakalyapi had unsaddled the horses. Together they unloaded Molly and allowed her to join her equine companions. The animals rolled then made their way to the stream.

"We are now about two days' travel north of the fort," Wakalyapi told C.W. after they found a shady resting place and had eaten some jerked meat.

"What will you do when we get there?" he asked, worried that the soldiers might force her to stay with the other Lakota women and end with sending her to a reservation. "Major Brotherton may not let you go."

"I have not decided. Perhaps I will stay along the *Heȟáka Wakpá* and wait for you to tell me if I am safe to come visit my friends there."

"I am pleased," Collins said.

The woman smiled briefly, then leaned back against a tree and closed her eyes. Gal came over and rested her chin on one thigh. Collins thought about the possibility of never seeing his companion again after the ending of their present journey. He found the possibility unendurable. They had experienced many perils and predicaments together over the past six years and her friendship had been one of the most cherished associations of his life.

"We will not lose each other," Arbuckles said gently, her eyes still closed. "*Tókša akhé waŋčhíyaŋkiŋ kte ló.*"

Just then, the clank and clatter of wagons could be heard from a distance downstream. The two of them jumped to their feet, caught their animals and swiftly saddled them. They were arranging Molly's packs when three army escort wagons and eight mounted soldiers came abreast of where Légaré and his men were resting. After picketing the horses and mule, Wakalyapi and Collins walked over. Sitting Bull, the other head men and all the warriors were standing a few yards away, clearly agitated at the sight of soldiers. The only officer dismounted and ordered his men to move back down the creek so as not to alarm the Indians.

"*Capitaine* Clifford," Légaré said, walking up to the man. "*Qu'est-ce que c'est?* What is this?"

"*Bonjour* Jean Louis," the captain said pleasantly. "I was sent by Major Brotherton to ensure that no unexpected encounters will dissuade the Indians from surrendering. We have also brought more supplies, tobacco and some blankets for the chiefs."

"*Viens*, we must speak with the Bull."

The Frenchman called for Lecerte, his trusted interpreter, and waved Collins and Wakalyapi over to him. Then he warily guided Clifford to where the principal men stood, their faces unyielding and impossible to read.

"This man is from Buford," Légaré told Sitting Bull. "He brings more food and *les cadeaux*, presents, for you and the other chiefs."

"What does he want?"

"To make you safe."

"Safe?" The chief sneered. He spoke to Wakalyapi in their language, ignoring Lecerte.

"Ťhatháŋka Ìyotake has decided not to go to Fort Buford. He has been told his daughter is in irons at Fort Yates," she explained. "He says that if they punish his daughter, who has done nothing, what would they not do to him?"

"I have no conception of what scoundrel told you this or why, but your daughter is at Standing Rock and is free as a little bird," Captain Clifford said.

Sitting Bull understood him and tears came into his eyes.

"This is true?" he asked.

"Absolutely true." Captain Clifford said with unqualified sincerity.

Softening in his demeanor, the chief thanked him. "We will go with you," he said and all the men turned and walked back to their horses.

After the usual chaos of hitching and loading horses and rounding up children and dogs, the enlarged procession continued on its way southward beside the Big Muddy Creek. Collins rode up alongside Captain Clifford and introduced himself.

"I have heard of you," the captain said, glancing with curiosity at Gal, comfortable in her place on C.W.'s saddle.

Not particularly interested in any rumors concerning his activities, Collins said, "I was wondering about news from the wider world. I have been quite isolated of late."

The captain studied him a moment. "Then you will not have heard of the assassination attempt."

"What?"

"President Garfield has been shot in the back by a would-be assassin."

Completely dumbfounded, Collins asked, "So the president is not dead?"

"No. The last newspaper I read stated that his condition is favorable."

"Are you willing to relate all the details?"

"Of course. It occurred on the morning of July 2nd at the Baltimore and Potomac depot. The president and Secretary Blaine were about to board the limited express when two shots rang out. Blaine turned to find the president prostrated. He was taken to the White House and there he remains, attended by four physicians. They report that President Garfield has been making humorous speeches and quoting Shakespeare."

Thinking it was ironical that he had once protected President-elect Lincoln in the very same city, Collins asked, "And the assassin?"

"A foreigner. Charles Guitteau, by name. He seems to think he, alone, elected President Garfield and expected the United States Consulship to Marseilles, France. According to Secretary Blaine, the man is crazy and regards himself of very superior ability, although he was branded by the Hotel Association as a dead beat. A letter written by him and printed in the newspapers had him insisting that President Garfield's death was a political necessity."

"That indeed sounds crazy."

"Doubtlessly."

Changing tack, Collins asked, "Why did Major Brotherton send you?"

Hesitating a moment, the captain seemed to decide on frankness. "I was ordered to intercept Légaré's party and bring them into Buford. My orders were to allow nothing or any person to interfere with me to prevent my success."

"Any person?"

"In case I meet with other troops, I am to assume command, by virtue of my commission."

"The major is taking no chances."

"No," Clifford said sardonically.

The captain and Collins passed the time speaking of Montana Territory and several pivotal events in its recent history. Collins nimbly evaded any disclosure of his previous association with Sitting Bull, but he soon discovered that Clifford had served in the Montana Column under Colonel Gibbon as a captain with the 7th Infantry. The captain had known C.W.'s friend, Lieutenant Bradley, and had been grievously saddened by his death at the Big Hole fight with the Nez Perce Indians. Without prompting, Clifford unreservedly vilified Custer and his supercilious failure to follow orders, giving Collins a more promising impression of the officer.

In due course, the conversation lagged and Collins excused himself in order to find Wakalyapi. She was riding slightly to the east of the lean and raw-boned Indian ponies, patiently slogging along with their lodgepole drags and heavy loads of people and baggage.

"Captain Clifford knew James Bradley," he said, reining Ulysses to come up beside her. Molly lined out behind the gelding in her customary way. "He was with Gibbon before the Greasy Grass."

"So he did not fight there?"

"No."

They rode together in silence for a while. Gal jumped down and went to investigate a decaying deer carcass.

"I think the soldiers came to make certain that Tȟatȟáŋka Íyotake will truly surrender," Arbuckles said, interrupting their reverie.

"I agree."

"Do you trust that Clifford?"

"He seems like a good enough fellow. I believe he is just following Major Brotherton's orders."

"You have said you know Brotherton."

"I may have met him briefly many years ago down in New Mexico Territory. He was leading a detachment that was scouting for hostile Apache warriors."

"Then he is against the Indians."

Collins nodded. "I would expect so."

"Then perhaps it is unwise to go to Buford."

"Perhaps. 'Until I know this sure uncertainty, I'll entertain the offered fallacy.' "

"What play is that? It makes no sense."

"*The Comedy of Errors.*"

"That is where we are now."

He grinned at Wakalyapi. "Very amusing."

She gave him a scornful look. "It is of no consequence."

39

The Lakota chose a clearing beside a deep bend in the creek to camp. Collins thought it was probably so they could keep their distance from the soldiers. Légaré and the Metis circled the carts a little to the north and Captain Clifford and his men bivouacked with the escort wagons on a small rise to the east, overlooking the stream banks and Indian encampment. Unwilling to be ensnared in the edgy tension between all parties, Collins and Wakalyapi settled down in a meadow to the south of everyone.

Once again, the Frenchman sent Lecerte to invite them to dine with him. After hobbling their animals, they walked to the Metis camp. Captain Clifford was seated beside the fire between Légaré and Lecerte. Sitting down across from them, C.W. and Wakalyapi took note of their conversation.

"I have made up my mind," Clifford was saying. "The Bull will never again cross the line until he has come to Fort Buford. If he will not come alive, then he must come dead."

"*L'enterrement de Crapaud*! You must not say this!" Légaré exclaimed. "You have only eleven men and I have eight *seulement*."

"How many warriors are at Sitting Bull's disposal?" the captain asked, seemingly undeterred.

"Forty-three," Arbuckles told him. "And I will fight also."

"Captain," said Collins, "you should be more circum-spect and leave off making threats. These people you speak of are faltering because they are forfeiting every vestige of their previous life, their liberty and even the buffalo and horses that define their customs and tradi-tions."

Duly chastened, the officer sighed and stared at the fire. Piché provided coffee and food and no one spoke for a long time. When finished with his meal, Collins fed a few morsels of meat and bread to the dog and took out his briar for a smoke. When he was done filling his pipe, he handed the tobacco pouch to Wakalyapi.

"How came you to be here?" Clifford asked Collins, again finding his voice.

"I was invited."

"Invited? By whom?"

"Your boss," Arbuckles told him.

The captain laughed. "My boss?" he asked incredu-lously. "You mean Major Brotherton invited you?"

"*Mais non, Monsieur*," Légaré said. "*Le général* Terry."

Thunderstruck, the officer was about to make a re-mark, when they heard singing coming from the Lakota camp. They all paused to listen, then Clifford took out a small note book and pencil.

"Will you interpret for me?" he asked Lecerte.

"*Si kwaarek*. If you wish it. She is saying, 'Be brave my friends, the white men have brought us food. They will not hurt us. Their hearts are full of pity for us.' "

Clifford scribbled furiously in his little book. "And?"

" 'Mother, father, do not be afraid. Our hunger has been stopped. My brother, my sister, paint your faces and prepare. *Wakȟáŋ Tȟáŋka* has softened the hearts of our enemies.' Shall I go on? Mostly it repeats the same sentiments."

The woman's song continued, ebbing and flowing plaintively.

"That will suffice, I think. I am heartened by her words."

"There is no cause to be heartened," Wakalyapi said. "When the people are starving, you white men bring food so we will do what you ask."

Looking at her as if for the first time, the captain said, "Or we bring food as a gesture of friendship." He paused and studied her. "Who are you, exactly?"

"This woman's name is Wakalyapi," Collins told him. "She is my friend and interpreter."

"And *mon amie* also," Légaré said.

The singing had trailed off and the night was still, broken only by the whining of mosquitoes.

"Well," Clifford said deprecatingly, "a squaw should not meddle in the affairs of men."

"Captain," said Collins mildly, "you must mind your manners. Wakalyapi and all the women in the Indian camp have endured much and have certainly earned the right to formulate an opinion of events as they affect their lives."

"*Cette femme* has the admiration of *tout les guerriers*, all the Indian warriors," the Frenchman said. "She *mérite le même*, the same, from you."

Coming to his feet, Clifford stood a moment by the fire. They all watched him curiously. He turned to face Arbuckles and Collins placed his hand on the butt end of his revolver. Bending at the waist, the officer suddenly bowed.

"My humble apologies, ma'am."

Wakalyapi shrugged, stood up and stalked away into the encroaching darkness.

The captain sat down again. "I should not have offended her."

"No," said Collins.

Someone coughed politely just beyond Légaré's camp. Then Sitting Bull, Red Thunder, Bone Club and Four

Horns walked into the firelight.

"We want to hear of our friends," Sitting Bull told Captain Clifford. He nodded at Narcisse Lecerte. "Will you make my words known?"

"*Háŋ.*"

Collins sat quietly smoking as the head men enquired about the welfare of one person then another and Clifford did his best to tell them of the people who had surrendered at Buford or had passed through the fort to be transported by steamboat to Fort Yates and Standing Rock Agency. The officer had been appointed acting Indian agent for the post in January and expressed a certain amount of sympathy for the prisoners. Collins was unsure whether this was simply for the consolation of the chiefs or he was actually sincere. The man's earlier discourtesy toward Arbuckles had not engendered confidence.

After listening for a while, he unobtrusively slipped away. The night was lit by a half moon and he could see quite well. Gal heard a rustling in the brush by the creek bank and, with hackles raised, she padded almost noiselessly into the thick vegetation. When C.W. walked into their camp, a cheerful fire was blazing in a stone ring and Wakalyapi was seated on the ground beside it. She was punching holes in a piece of hide with a bone awl.

"There is coffee," she said, jutting out her lower lip at the pot.

"*Philámayaye,*" he said, using the one Lakota word with which he had grown comfortable.

Pouring himself a cup, he sat on his bedroll and watched his companion handle the sliver of bone, deftly puncturing tough leather seemingly without effort.

"What is that?" he asked.

"An old lodge skin."

"Why are you poking holes in it? Or do you not want to tell me?"

"I will show you later."

Collins dug out his whetstone and began sharpening his knife. "The chiefs came in to speak with Captain Clifford," he said. "They were asking about friends."

"Lecerte is the interpreter?"

"Yes."

"That is good. He gets the words right most of the time."

"I believe Clifford was truly mortified by his incivility to you."

"*Tókȟa šni.* It does not matter."

The dog wandered into the firelight and lay down beside Collins. Her mouth was crimson with blood, so he surmised she had augmented her supper with the flesh of some hapless varmint.

"I am going to Standing Rock Agency," Wakalyapi said almost peevishly.

Temporarily stunned, he stared at her.

Looking up from her work, she added, "There is no other place."

Overcome by a feeling of pessimism, Collins put aside his knife and stone. "You will be a prisoner," he said gently.

"Perhaps. But I may be of use to my people. There is no other place," she said again.

"What about the Dominion? What about Connor and Mulhaire and Muse?"

"They can make a home in the half-breed settlements. And yes, it is true that a few Lakȟóta people have stayed behind, but there is no hunting. There is no way for me to live."

Taking out his pipe, he packed the bowl absent-mindedly. The veracity of her words struck home. "Then you will surrender with the others?"

"It is the only road.'"

Arbuckles struck a match and, leaning forward, held it for him. Collins drew on the briar until the tobacco glowed, casting a ruddy flush over his dejected expression.

"It is not hopeless," she told him, smiling encouragingly. Her scarred mouth pulled to the side.

"I cannot bear it. I cannot bear the thought of you being told how and where you must go."

"I will not be alone in this."

He thought a moment, rubbing his dog's ears. "Then you must give me your guns and horses," he said resolutely. "Before we get to Buford, you must give them all to me. And somehow, some way, I will be able to return them to you."

"But the soldier captain has seen my weapons and horses."

"Leave that to me."

"You are my friend, Charles. I thank you."

"It is not enough by far. It will never be enough."

40

Two days later, when the lodges were thrown down and prepared for travel, the carts and wagons were loaded with baggage and people, and the soldier camp was struck, Collins found Captain Clifford. He was holding his horse at a standstill to the rear of the disorganized multitude, no doubt ensuring that nobody absconded.

"I must request a favor," C.W. told the officer.

Clifford raised an eyebrow. "Yes?"

"My interpreter will be coming into the fort with you and I am taking charge of her horses and guns. I must ask that you allow me to do this."

The officer glowered at him. "That is very irregular. I am not certain I can allow it."

"If my friend chooses to make me gifts prior to surrender, I cannot see any impediment."

Gazing ahead at the pony drags, carts and wagons lining out and beginning to move, Clifford sighed and shrugged his shoulders. "I suppose I cannot object if you portray the transaction thusly," he said archly. "But you had best attend to it soon. We will be coming to the post before midday."

"I agree. Thank you, Captain."

Wheeling his gelding, Collins loped back to where Wakalyapi waited with his dog and the stock. "It is settled," he told her, dismounting. "Come, let us secure your guns and saddle on Molly's packs under the tent and my bedroll, so nothing is visible. Then we will walk together into the fort, leading our horses."

When they had successfully secreted her Winchester, Webley revolver and saddle on the mule, Arbuckles asked, "What of my quiver and bow?"

"Keep them on you. If they object, I will claim them."

They tied her horses together in a train behind Molly and Collins wrapped the mule's lead rope around his gelding's saddle horn. Then, leading his horse with the dog astride, C.W. joined Wakalyapi and they merged with the straggling caravan as it wended its way toward the Missouri River. Collins thought the morning was appropriately dreary. The sky was heavy with low clouds and an unsympathetic wind drove intermittent rain showers against their backs.

Before long, the procession gradually made its way down some sandstone bluffs to the river's floodplain and onto a well-traveled road headed east. The land grew flat once more and the course was smooth and even. As the Missouri River curved and the road tracked its passage, Wakalyapi paused to point out the site of the old Fort Union trading post.

"It had red roofs and white palisades and always there were countless lodges from different tribes in encampments all around. The American Fur traders brought many fine goods, beads, guns and also sickness," she said bitterly. "I was here...with Beckwith."

"What happened to the structures?"

"I heard the soldiers took the wood and stone to build Fort Buford."

The trail straightened and aimed almost due east, leaving the river after it looped south. When the road bowed slightly to the north and he caught a glimpse of the head of the column, Collins saw that one of Clifford's troopers was departing at a gallop. He deduced that the soldier had been sent to notify the post commander in advance of their arrival. Then the entire rank and file abruptly halted.

Handing the Molly's lead to Wakalyapi, he said, "I will go see."

Swinging onto his horse and leaving the dog behind, Collins rode at a trot along the southern edge of the procession. Coming even with the group of Lakota men, he observed that they were donning their full regalia of warrior society insignia and painting their faces and bodies in accordance with tradition and dictates. Five of Captain Clifford's soldiers waited nearby, nervously standing at the ready with their Springfield carbines unslung, while the officer sat his horse behind them. The Indians presented a proud and undefeated display and Collins felt his heart swell at this final act of defiance, despite the ragged condition of some of the adornments and the emaciated state of their physique.

When, at last, the head men and warriors were prepared, they took the lead. The soldiers mounted their horses to ride just to the rear and Clifford moved to a flanking position. Not long after, Légaré joined him. Galloping back to Wakalyapi, Collins dismounted.

"The Lakota warriors have arrayed themselves in their finest ceremonial costumes," he told her.

"It is fitting," she said phlegmatically.

He once again took charge of Molly's lead rope and the string of horses and they picked up their pace so as to move past the Red River carts. The shrieking wheels seemed to be lamenting their final passage to the fort.

"I think we are very close now," C.W. said, when they came up just behind the soldiers, Indian warriors and their principal men.

"Yes."

Soon, the first structures came into view. Civilians and soldiers could be seen sitting and standing on rooftops of several buildings and on the porches of the officers' quarters. Just to the northeast, a tall flagstaff

displayed an American flag, snapping briskly in the unyielding breeze. Captain Clifford now moved to the head
of the column and said something to Sitting Bull. Collins
was surprised to see that they rode past the commanding officer's quarters, in front of which Major Brotherton,
a few of his officers and Inspector Macdonell conspicuously stood. Instead, after a hasty salute to his commanding officer, Clifford led the Indians toward the river
floodplain and an open expanse between the fort and the
Missouri.

The carts, escort wagons and pony drags converged
and soon families assembled and began to raise lodges, collect their belongings from Légaré's employees and
gather their children. A couple of the men herded the
Indian horses together and held them on the banks of
the river. Choosing a location near the post cemetery, at
some remove from the main encampment, Collins quickly pitched the tent and unloaded the mule and Wakalyapi's pack horse. They placed her saddle, guns and belongings out of sight within the shelter. They made a pile
of the pack saddles and panniers and other baggage in
front.

"I am taking all the animals to the stable," Collins
said. "Are you still determined to stay?"

"Yes."

"Then sidestep any soldiers and I will return forthwith."

He left Gal with Arbuckles and swung up on Ulysses,
leading Molly and the other two horses. He searched for
Captain Clifford and found him standing hard by the riv-
erbank, observing the melee of people and activity while
the Lakota camp began to take tangible shape.

"You have your horses, Mr. Collins," he said when
C.W. rode up to him.

"As you see. I would like to take them to the stables,
if you would authorize it."

"Very well." The officer took out his note book and pencil and wrote a brief message. "Take this to the private on duty. He will see to your animals." Clifford gave Collins a sardonic look. "All of them."

"You have my gratitude, Captain."

After settling the stock under the care of a genial and efficient young man, Collins walked back to the encampment just as Major Brotherton strode over to Sitting Bull's lodge with his portly adjutant, Captain Clifford and a couple of other soldiers. Some curious civilians were making their way among the lodges and the major ordered them out of the area and sent Clifford to arrange for guards to be posted. Collins shadowed Brotherton as he made his way toward Sitting Bull, who was standing in front of his lodge with Crowfoot, his son. His wives were tending a fire and the blackened kettle suspended from a tripod above it.

"Your people may rest and eat. I will send more food. But I now must collect your guns and horses," the major told the chief. "We can meet tomorrow to make your surrender."

"Your boss Terry made this law, I know. But I wish to give you my gun later."

"When?"

"At the time of surrender."

Brotherton thought about this then said, "I agree. But for now you must tell your people to give us their arms and ponies."

Sitting Bull called out in his language and the people came to hear him. He made a laconic speech then said, "*Waná ečhúŋ wo,*" in a forceful manner. The warriors and some of the women wandered over to the pony herd to find their own animals and began turning them over to the adjutant and his men. Red Thunder went up to Brotherton, spoke a minute and pointed at Collins with his lower lip. The major squinted in his direction, then nodded. Red Thunder led his horse to where Collins was standing.

"I am giving you my horse, *Mniskúya*. It means salt."

"I remember."

"You must take him and be good to him. He is a nice horse." He held out the lead rope.

"I will be very good to him." C.W. blinked hard as water welled up in his eyes.

The Indian smiled at Collins through tears of his own. "I too am sad. We are having a bad time."

"I am glad to know you and if I am able, I will bring your horse to you at Standing Rock."

"It would be nice to see you both again."

Red Thunder took his hand in a diffident grasp, whispered a few words to the pony and walked away. Collins endeavored to regain his composure as he leaned against Salt, running his palm down the horse's neck and scratching his jaw. He watched the lieutenant and two privates lay hold of the few guns the Indians still possessed and take away the small herd of scraggy horses, wormy and sore-footed. They were sorry looking specimens, but boon companions all the same, and their confiscation signified the end to a manner of living that was literally passing away before his very eyes. Quite paralyzed with malice and pity, he stood feebly by as the wind howled more tenaciously and slantwise rain lent further pathos to the scene.

41

"I had friends and classmates among the fallen in Custer's command," Major David Brotherton told Collins. "I am weary of Indians, their sullen natures, their treachery, their superstitions. I wish to depart this hellhole and am requesting to be relieved from duty."

A number of chairs had been arranged in a semi-circle within the parlor of the commanding officer's quarters in preparation for the surrender council. Already present were Captain Clifford, Major Brotherton, Post Adjutant George Young, Captain James Bell, N.W.M.P. Inspector Macdonell, the fort's interpreter Philip Wells, Jean Louis Légaré, two newspaper correspondents and Wakalyapi. Collins had been expressly invited by Brotherton after learning of his identity and current connection with General Terry. They had all been made known to each other and were patiently awaiting the delegation of Indians.

"I must remind you, Major, that my friend here is an Indian," Collins said, gesturing toward Wakalyapi. "I find her to possess none of those traits."

"Yes, General Miles has told me of your peculiar guide and interpreter. I have also heard how you deserted his command during the winter campaign of '76," the major said disagreeably.

"One cannot desert if one is not enlisted. Not to mention the fact that I was directly answerable to President Grant at the time."

The newspapermen displayed inordinate interest in his last statement, but a commotion arose beyond the door, announcing the arrival of Sitting Bull, Crowfoot, Four Horns, Red Thunder and five other warriors. Collins was grateful for the interruption. Everyone stood while the Indians took their seats. Sitting Bull had brought his Winchester rifle and, after taking a chair to the left of Brotherton, held the weapon between his legs. He motioned for Crowfoot to sit on his right. Collins thought the handsome little boy conducted himself with great dignity, despite his somewhat tattered clothing.

Having put aside their ceremonial regalia, the Indian men were attired in simple garments. Sitting Bull wore a calico shirt, breech-clout and leggings with a blanket wound around his waist. His braids were neatly wrapped, a single feather adorned his hair and he cradled a long and beautifully ornate calumet in the crook of one arm. When everyone was seated, Major Brotherton stood and spoke.

"The president has waited a long time for you to come in." he began. "But now that you are willing to make peace, you will be treated with kindness, just as those other chiefs who surrendered last winter are treated. And this can always be the way it is as long as you behave properly. In a few days, the steamboat will transport you to Fort Yates, where your daughter, Many Horses, is waiting."

The major sat down again while the interpreter imparted his speech to the Indians in their language. A long silence ensued during which the pens of the correspondents could be heard scratching vigorously. Finally Sitting Bull stood, said something to the interpreter and, holding the rifle in his right hand and the pipe in the bend of the other arm, addressed his people. Wells did not translate his words.

Under her breath, Wakalyapi interpreted for Collins.

"It is cruel, being without guns or ponies. We cannot hunt and have no choice but to sit in our lodges and think over all the stories that have been told to us...stories that turned us back many times when on our way to surrender. That we will be kept as prisoners and starved. Now we must protect the children. We must have compassion for the children so they may continue. Now we must live like prisoners for the sake of the children."

When he finished speaking, Sitting Bull turned to his son and handed him the rifle. Crowfoot carried the Winchester solemnly to Major Brotherton and presented it to him. The officer came to his feet and accepted the gun.

Nodding to the interpreter, the chief stood before Brotherton and said, "I surrender this rifle to you through my young son, whom I now desire to teach in this manner that he has become a friend of the Americans. I wish him to learn the habits of the whites and to be educated as their sons are educated. I wish it to be remembered that I was the last man of my tribe to surrender my rifle. This boy has given it to you and he now wants to know how he is going to make a living."

Sitting Bull looked down at his boy and smiled tenderly before continuing. "Whatever you have to give or whatever you have to say I would like to receive or hear now, for I do not wish to be kept in darkness longer. This is my country, and I do not wish to be compelled to give it up. I want my children to grow up in our native country. I wish to have all my people live together upon one reservation of our own on the little Missouri."

He proceeded to make known some other of his wishes and Collins could see expressions of derision on the faces of the military men and newspaper correspondents. As a powerful leader of his people, the head man manifestly believed he was negotiating as an equal, but it was also evident that his status would soon be diminished by U.S. governmental renegation and civilian chicanery.

Pausing a minute to survey the room and all its occupants, Sitting Bull finished by saying, "You may think that my people have many of them been bad. So all are good now that their arms and ponies have been taken from them. But you own this ground with me and we must try and help each other."

Remaining on his feet, the chief waited for Major Brotherton to respond. The officer shook hands with him and made some reassuring and vague remarks about the government dealing with the Indians in the best manner for their interests, but C.W. noted that he made no specific promises. He also noted that, although he still carried the pipe, Sitting Bull never offered to smoke it in the council room and this seemed to Collins to mean he did not trust Brotherton or his words. The major dismissed the assembly and the Indians silently vacated the building. Unwilling to engage in further discourse with Brotherton or the other men, Wakalyapi and Collins followed. The dog woke from her nap beneath the porch and sauntered after them.

"How was the interpreter?" he asked when they had moved a few yards away from the officer's quarters.

"I know him. He can be trusted even though his language is not precise."

They heard footsteps behind them and turned to see Légaré. "*C'est de valeur!*" he virtually bellowed at Wakalyapi, gesticulating with his arms. "Are you giving yourself to *l'armée*?"

"I am going with my people, Čheží Wašté."

"And you allow this, Charles?"

"It is not my decision."

"*Ça me rend triste*," said the Frenchman, his demeanor becoming infinitely more subdued. "It makes me sad, *mon amie*."

"*Merci*, Jean Louis," Wakalyapi said, placing a hand on his arm. "*Adieu*."

"Then *adieu* and *bonne chance*...good luck," Légaré said dejectedly and ambled away.

They stood a moment watching him. "You could go back with the Metis, you know," C.W. said. "Légaré could help you."

"No. I have decided."

Sighing and shaking his head, he said, "I must send a final telegram to General Terry if I wish to receive payment for my services."

"I will be at our camp."

The telegraph office was a small wooden structure situated just to the north of the post adjutant's headquarters. Like many of the newer buildings in the fort, it gave the impression of hasty and slipshod construction. He entered and found Inspector Macdonell bent over a telegram blank. He turned and smiled rather sheepishly.

"Mr. Collins, I regret not having spoken to you earlier."

"Quite all right."

"I am composing a message of Sitting Bull's surrender to Sir John Macdonald, as instructed."

"I am here to send a telegram to General Terry."

"Excellent. I should mention, however, that when I sent your last message, I found that the headquarters for the Department of Dakota has moved from St. Paul to Fort Snelling just this last June."

The fellow returned to his writing and the corporal, who also served as telegrapher, gave Collins a blank and a pencil. The operator had narrow, pinched features and did not seem to be pleased with his duties. Leaning on the counter beside Macdonell, Collins wrote out a brief missive.

Fort Buford July 20 1881
  To Brig General A. H. Terry Comding Dept Dakota
  Fort Snelling Minn
  Surrender of Sitting Bull has been achieved as you know Have completed commission Require immediate authorization for supplies Buford and remuneration to Donnell Clark and Larabie in Deer Lodge
  C. W. Collins

He then composed a message to send to Captain Mills in Deer Lodge, informing him of his general welfare and present location.

"That should do it," Macdonell said and gave his completed blank to the corporal. "I am returning north today," he told Collins. "Légaré and his half-breeds are preparing to depart and I shall travel with them."

They shook hands. "Well then," said Collins, "I bid you farewell."

The inspector went out the door. While waiting for the malcontent corporal to finish transmitting Macdonell's communiqué, C.W. thought about the formal surrender and Brotherton's smoldering resentment toward the Indians. It was bound to be shared by countless military personnel as well as civilians and did not bode well for the principal men and their people. He had found Crowfoot's presence in the council to be somehow poignant and wondered what the child would become in the shadow of fecund injustice. For decades, his father had been fiercely battling against the encroachment of white settlers and uncompromising military onslaughts. *Céard a dhéanfadh mac an chait ach luch a mharú?* What would a cat's offspring do except kill a mouse?

42

The cloudless sky was an azure dome overhead while relentless gusts of wind kicked dust in his face. Collins had followed the Yellowstone River from Fort Buford to Montague's old wayside dugout. From there he headed west toward Porcupine Creek and the plainly visible road created by Colonel Stanley's Yellowstone Expedition back in '73. His map showed that the trail would eventually come to the Musselshell River and he could then follow the north fork to Martinsdale and on to the Copperopolis stage stop. He wanted to stay north of Fort Keogh and thereby avoid detachments of troops and most settlements.

The land stretched out before him in open prairie, bleak and timberless. Collins found he overwhelmingly longed for a glimpse of mountain strongholds and crags of granite. He was certain he must have crossed some of the same country during his journey north from the Cantonment on the Tongue River with Miles' "walk-a-heaps" in the winter campaign after Custer's demise, but nothing was familiar. Molly, Wakalyapi's horses and Salt, Red Thunder's pony, made a train of four pack animals and he had loaded them with provisions at Buford, so he did not have to resupply. All the equines were amiable and mannerly and made pleasant companions. Gal had learned she could safely dodge between and around their hooves when not riding on Ulysses.

Although he heartily endeavored to shake off his

dismal melancholy, the parting with Wakalyapi at the steamboat landing, four days prior, abstracted him still. She had reassured him they would see each other again and soon, but even so the notion of his friend being detained under the hegemony of U.S. authorities, whether military or civil, was intolerable. All the same, Collins reasoned, Wakalyapi was her own woman if anyone was and he must accept her resolve. No matter how much he would have taken pleasure in her presence at the ranch, he knew it to be impossible.

In truth, just as Arbuckles had pointed out to him, any Indian off of a reservation would no longer be endured by his neighbors, no more than his Chinese companions were entirely acceptable. He was able to protect his Celestial friends by claiming them as domestic servants, but there was a consuming determination among men such as Sheridan, Miles and Sherman to permanently confine all Indians to reservations and transmute them into agriculturalists. Furthermore, this was largely in keeping with the strident contentions of white settlers that the Indian Bureau spoiled the Indians, furnished them with guns and allowed them to prey upon poor hard-working farmers.

Recalling the scene at the steamboat, Collins could yet envisage the Indians escorted onto the gangplank by twenty soldiers of the 7th Infantry under the command of Captain Clifford. They carried bundles and infants and held the hands of their frightened children. That morning, the Indians had built fires and burned lodge poles and hides, robes and all possessions they were not allowed to take to prevent the white men from getting them. The warriors and principal men, including Four Horns, Bone Club, Red Thunder and White Dog, brought up the rear, some of them turning to gaze back north, past the crowd of onlookers, as if yearning for their former wild and sovereign lives. He had made his final farewell to Sitting Bull, disturbed to observe the chief had an eye infection and seemed to be in great distress from it. Despite this, the remarkable leader and holy man maintained his dignity and made his way aboard the boat that, paradoxically, had been named "General Sherman."

Delaying Wakalyapi to the last, C.W. had lingered beside her on the banks of the Missouri River, unable to speak his mind. She had been allowed to keep her quiver and bow while some of the newer recruits loudly voiced their amusement at seeing a "squaw" with her toys. He gave her Peng's silver fish and some tobacco and she gave him a pair of moccasins.

"This is what you were doing with old lodge skins," he said, admiring the precise blue and white beading.

"Yes."

"Thank you." In spite of Wakalyapi's customary discomfort with being touched, he had embraced her for a long time.

"You must let me go," she had said uneasily. "I must go."

Just then, the steamboat whistle blew and someone yelled. The woman lifted the trussed blanket that held all her worldly possessions and strode up the wooden walkway that was leading her to a nugatory and circumscribed existence. On board, she had not looked back and the memory of her departure had seemed final, in spite of her assurances.

Coming back to himself and surveying the horizon, Collins thought he could see trees ahead, which would indicate he was nearing the Musselshell. He came to the river just at early twilight and began searching for a place to camp. Too late, he heard voices. A small troop of soldiers precipitously rode out of the river bottoms and encircled him before he could react. Gal jumped from the saddle and began barking frantically. Ulysses snorted and Molly brayed in protest while the other horses pranced about nervously.

"What in the hell is this?" Collins asked belligerently. He patted the gelding's neck to calm him and told the dog to be quiet. She slunk away growling and crawled beneath some shrubbery.

A young lieutenant raised his hand imperiously. "Silence. I demand to know where you got those horses."

C.W. counted eight soldiers and the officer. "They are my animals and who are you to inquire?"

"I am Lieutenant Kingsbury from Fort Maginnis and I am leading this detachment. We are searching for horses stolen from a homestead just north of Sanders. We have reports that a party of Crow thieves have been raiding off the reservation."

"As you can clearly see, I am not a Crow Indian and these horses belong to me."

"Why do you need so many pack animals?"

"That, Lieutenant, is none of your affair." Collins reined Ulysses to the left and prodded him toward the river.

"Sir," called one of the troopers. "The mule has an army brand."

The officer spurred his horse and grabbed for the gelding. Collins yanked his Colt free and aimed it at him.

"Do not make a mistake here, Kingsley," he said softly, purposely getting the man's name wrong. "I will not be hindered and you will not lay a hand upon my horse."

"If you look behind, you can see my men have their weapons aimed at your back."

"That may be, but I will certainly drop you from your saddle before they have the opportunity to save your life," Collins said conversationally, still aiming his revolver at the officer. "I have recently come from Fort Buford on a commission from General Alfred Terry, of whom you have no doubt heard. I own a ranch near Deer Lodge, am known to Deputy Sheriff Steele of Helena, Deputy Small of Butte and Sheriff McAndrews of Deer Lodge, although I must admit the man does not care for me much. I acquired the mule five years ago from General Miles at the Cantonment on the Tongue River and these horses were recently procured from those surrendered at Fort Buford by the Sioux Indians."

One of the soldiers behind him laughed scathingly. "Commission from General Terry? You must take us for fools."

"I do, indeed, take you for a fool," he said. "But I possess the telegram from Terry petitioning my services sequestered in my billfold," he told Kingsbury. "If you are amenable, I will holster my gun and produce it forthwith. Providing your men come around where I can see them and sling their carbines."

The lieutenant ordered the soldiers to assemble to his right, but they held their rifles at the ready. "They are all here within view," he said. "Hand it over."

Slipping his Colt home, Collins reached inside his frock coat and took out the billfold. He removed the telegram and held it out to the officer, who took hold of the paper, unfolded it and read. Incredulity crept over his features.

"At ease men and sling arms," the lieutenant ordered sotto voce. "This fellow is in earnest."

"He called us fools," one of the troopers said pugnaciously.

"I believe he called *you* a fool, Private Parmlee," Lieutenant Kingsbury said without humor. He leaned forward in the saddle to give the telegram back to Collins. "We grow weary of chasing Indians around the countryside every time they choose to abscond from their reservations. If an Indian thinks he can steal a horse and get off, he will do so and the Crows are the worst of them." The lieutenant's horse robustly shook itself and he paused.

"We have numerous settlements springing up, from the Yellowstone to the Musselshell. It is impossible that permanent white settlers and roving bands of thieving Indians can get along on the same lands."

It was evident to Collins that the officer was warming to a cherished subject. "I have seen the Indians cajoled and browbeaten out of their lands and am aware that more than half the pittance allowed them on reservations is stolen by agents and traders," he said.

"They are offered Christianity, civilization and education."

"A starving Indian cares but little for Christianity or education. Besides, if he could read he would find out that large bank and corporation robbers are generally church officials and that nearly every week we read of one or more Christian shepherds making free with the ewe lambs of their flock."

"That, sir, is a preposterous and sacrilegious line of reasoning," the officer said vehemently.

The soldiers were muttering amongst themselves and giving Collins indignant and hostile glares. Unaffected by their animosity, he said, "It would indeed behoove the Indians to assimilate our Christian civilization. I have heard reports that there are no fewer than eleven saloons in the new mining camp in Maiden Gulch, just five miles from Fort Maginnis. And along the ten miles from the post to Wilder's Landing there are five whiskey shops, one of which keeps prostitutes."

"And yet," said Kingsbury, gesturing with a forefinger as if schooling a pupil, "Montana has been retarded in her progress by continuous outbreaks and depredations upon her people. Women have been vilely outraged, families most hideously tortured, property destroyed and laid waste. These same Indians then return to their reservations and are received with outstretched arms and fed and pampered by the government."

The sun was sinking and Collins was surfeited with gasconade and the odium of contempt. " 'Here is such patchery, such juggling and such knavery. All the argument is a whore and a cuckhold, a good quarrel to draw emulous factions and to bleed upon,' " he said, quoting from *Troilus and Cressida.* "If I am at liberty to continue my journey, I will now depart."

Without waiting for a response, he wheeled his horse, slapped his thigh for the dog to jump up and cantered southwest along the river's course, with the mule and horses trailing behind. He found a gap in the vegetation and trees and promptly made his way into the redoubt, obscuring himself from surveillance or pursuit. He rode along the banks for a mile or so and then chose a secluded clearing for his bivouac, finding himself yet again disheartened by the rampant and misguided prejudices of his fellow citizens.

UNVANQUISHED

43

A lamp burned brightly on the table. The aromas of cooking, tea and pipe tobacco agreeably filled the room. Gal was at his feet and Collins leaned back in his chair, contented and gratified that his home was intact and all was well. Wakalyapi had been correct in her perceptions and he wondered if she knew he was thinking of her at that very moment. Li Min had providentially stopped weeping and sat nearby, gazing disconcertingly at him through tear-stained eyes, while Wú Peng busied himself at the stove.

"It is exceedingly gratifying to have you home once more, Charles," the Chinaman said.

"That is the third time you have announced this."

"I am compelled to reiterate my words of sheer delight."

"I also have delight," said Li Min.

"You have been improving the girl's English."

"Min is a most excellent and enthusiastic scholar," Peng said, setting bowls of soup on the table. He went back to the stove and returned with dishes of steamed buns. "I have made sustenance that is especially satisfying to your palate."

Smiling at his friend's stilted eloquence, Collins thanked him, laid aside his pipe and appreciatively began to eat his soup. Noticing that Li Min was not paying attention to her meal, but only him, he said, "You must stop staring at me, Min. I am not going anywhere."

Peng poured more tea, then joined them at the table. "Min thought you were dead. In point of fact, she was so enormously bereaved she proposed *zìshā*...to destroy herself."

"But you stopped her."

"I persuaded her that if you were not deceased, your torment upon discovering her martyrdom would be extraordinarily severe."

Swallowing a mouthful of bun, C.W. reached for Li Min's hand. "You must eat now and promise to never kill yourself," he told her.

"Oh Mr. Charles," she said, bursting into renewed tears. "I have delight you are not deceased."

"As am I," he said, pulling his hand with difficulty from Min's death grip. "Eat your supper now and stop crying."

The girl sat up and stuffed an entire steamed bun in her mouth. As its torrid contents burst upon her tongue, Min's eyes grew very large and she spit the doughy mass into her hand. Then, abjectly mortified, she stuffed it back in her mouth and chewed and swallowed as rapidly as practicably possible.

Collins and Peng were laughing irrepressibly and Gal woke up and began barking.

"It is not humorous," Li Min said solemnly.

Striving valiantly to suppress his mirth, Collins said, "No. I am sorry."

"I, too, beg forgiveness," Peng told her.

Min loftily nodded her acceptance of their apologies. Collins told the dog to lie down and they turned their attention back to their repast.

After a while, C.W. asked, "Were you able to sustain yourselves on the wherewithal I left to you? I did not anticipate such an extended absence."

"We were quite able," Peng told him.

"And food? How were you able to procure supplies?"

"Captain Mills did as you had requested. He very kindly appeared at four dispersed intervals and purchased such items as we required."

"Well," Collins said pensively, "I shall certainly have to offer him my undying gratitude."

After they had finished their meal, Collins, Li Min, Peng and Gal went out into the evening, the landscape washed with light from a nearly full moon, suspended high in the eastern sky. They strolled together into the horse pasture and stood watching the animals. After the preliminary squealing and biting and kicking, the mules and horses had settled down, grouping themselves according to their own inscrutable preferences.

"How is my friend, Arbuckles?" Wú Peng asked. "Why did she not return with you?"

Surprised he had not inquired about her whereabouts sooner, Collins said, "She has gone to an Indian agency on the Missouri River. She desired to stay with her own people."

"But we are also her people," the Chinaman said faintly.

"That is undeniably true. But tragically, as you have learned from experience, our neighbors scarcely tolerate Li Min's and your presence in this community. If Arbuckles attempted to reside here with us, what would be the ultimate outcome?"

"Then she will remain unscathed and secure in the agency?"

"That is my overwhelming aspiration."

Walking through the pasture and glancing up at the moon engulfing their environs in pale luminosity and playing hide-and-seek behind scattered clouds gliding across the Stygian sky, Collins thought about Wakalyapi and speculated about her future. President Garfield had proven himself to be no friend to the Indian. As a member of Congress, he had stated that it was mockery, "for the representatives of the great Government of the United States to sit down in a wigwam and make treaties with a lot of painted and half naked savages." And if Garfield succumbed to his wounds, his vice-president, Chester Arthur, would not improve the Indians' predicament. A great believer in the ascendancy of the white man, not only had he been advocating for restrictions on immigration, especially of Chinese laborers, Arthur was unambiguously of the opinion that Indians should be "civilized" through an enforced educational system, thereby removing any threat they may pose to the incursion of white settlers.

Collins had heard that around three thousand Lakota people were imprisoned at the Standing Rock Agency and he wondered, given the incompetency and corruption of the Indian Bureau and its agents, how it would be possible to keep them fed, clothed and housed. General Miles remained steadfast in his belief that the Indians should be placed under the control of the War Department, even though the question no longer received serious debate in the U.S. Congress. Regardless, Fort Yates was strongly garrisoned by several companies of troops and many of them doubtlessly shared Brotherton's intense antipathy towards the Indians

A pack of coyotes began calling from the creek bottoms. Li Min ran back to the house despite Peng's efforts to convince her they would not attack. A warm breeze brought the scent of conifers down from the mountains and the subtle fragrance of wildflowers from adjacent meadows. Although moved by the beauty of his surroundings, Collins could not shake a sense of gloomy foreboding in regard to Wakalyapi.

"You are worried," Peng said. "You are apprehensive about Arbuckles."

Sighing, Collins said, "Yes. She is capable and fierce, but they made her give up her guns and horses. Now she will be seen as a woman without a man and a prisoner and I do not know how she will be treated."

"Our friend will defend herself."

"Agreed. But will they give her shelter and rations? To them she is just a 'squaw.' My only solace is that she has her bow."

"Squaw?" asked Peng.

"It is a very ill-mannered word for an Indian woman."

Molly and Felix wandered over to greet them. Wú Peng had stale almond cookies in a pocket. He held one out for Felix, then gave another to Molly.

"I venerate my home here," he said gravely. "All persons should have a home such as this."

"I am very glad you are here."

They began to walk back toward the house, the warm glow from its windows cheerful in the gloaming.

"You must journey to assess the condition of her circumstances," Peng said.

"What?" Sometimes the Chinaman's obtuse and elaborate manner of expression bewildered Collins.

"Our friend Arbuckles. You must find her."

"When it is feasible. I have been absent from here a long time."

"Will you no longer be apprehensive?"

"When?"

"Soon?"

"No," he was forced to admit.

"Then you must go."

Collins thought about this. It was true that he would find no peace of mind until he was assured of Wakalyapi's well-being. There was no doubt he would have to make the journey to Standing Rock Agency before too much time had elapsed. It was requisite.

———⸙———

The End

David Rumsey Map Collection, David Rumsey Map Center, Stanford Libraries

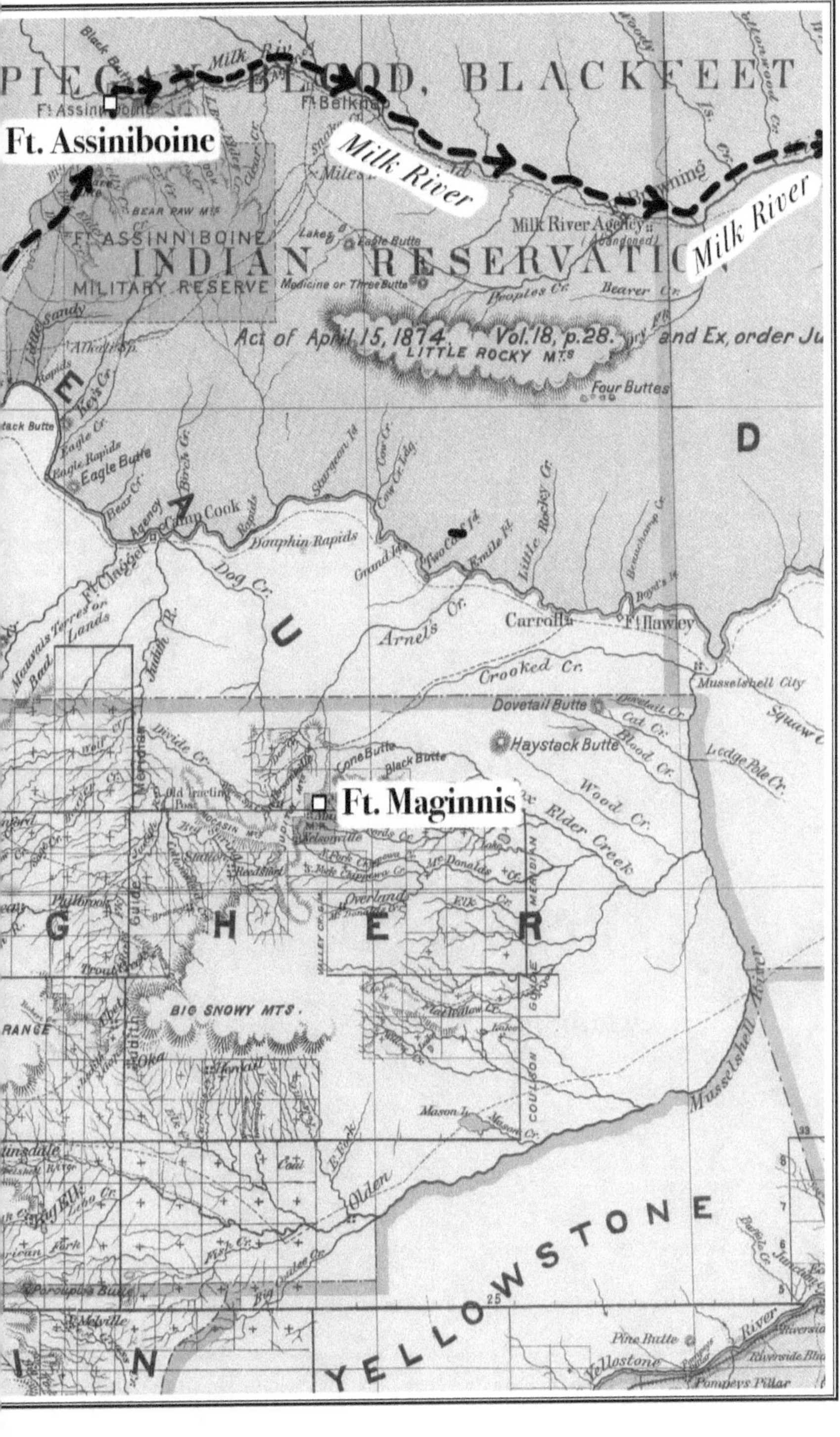

Ft. Maginnis

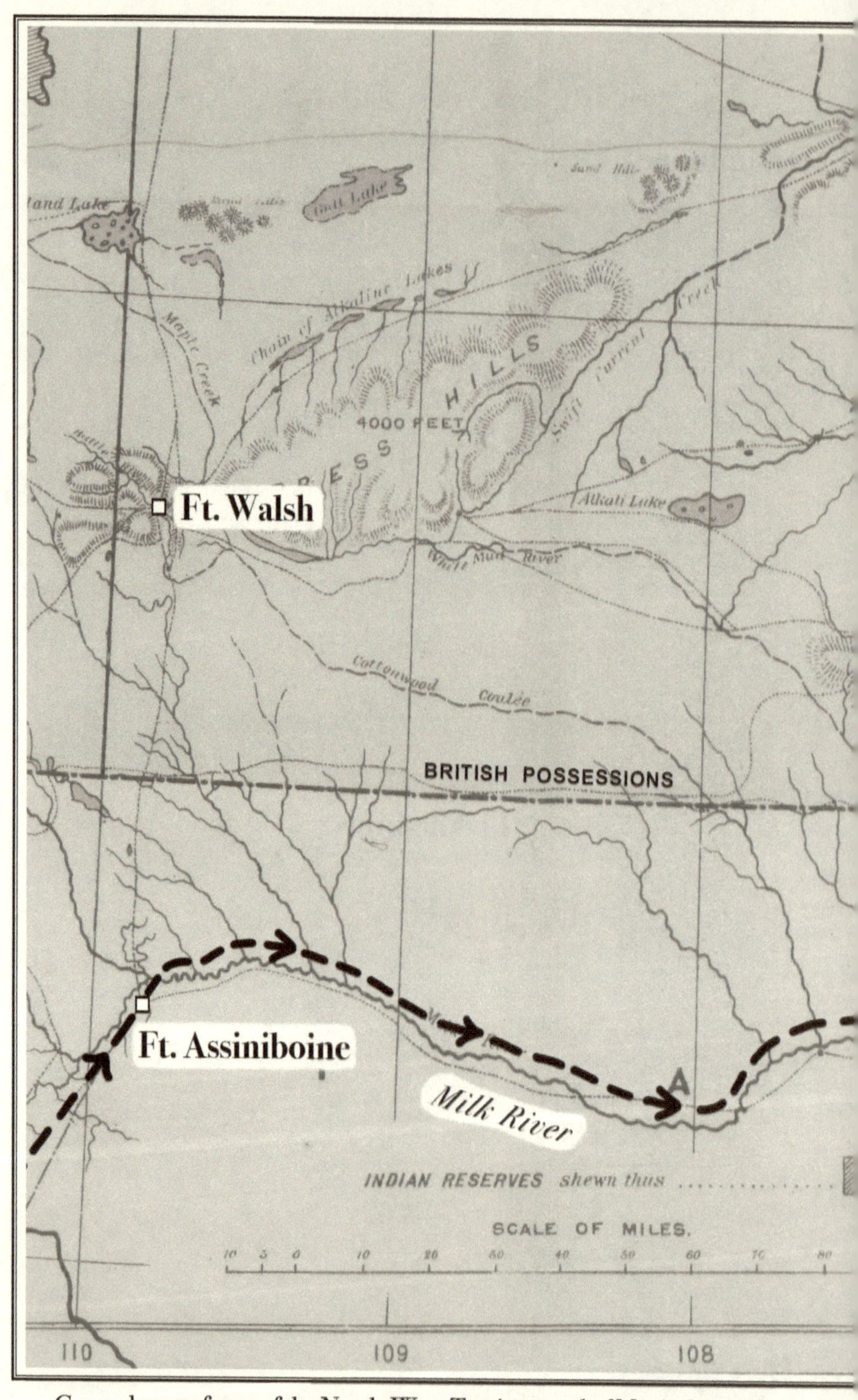

General map of part of the North-West Territory and of Manitoba, 1881, (CU14089245) by Canada. Dominion Lands Branch.

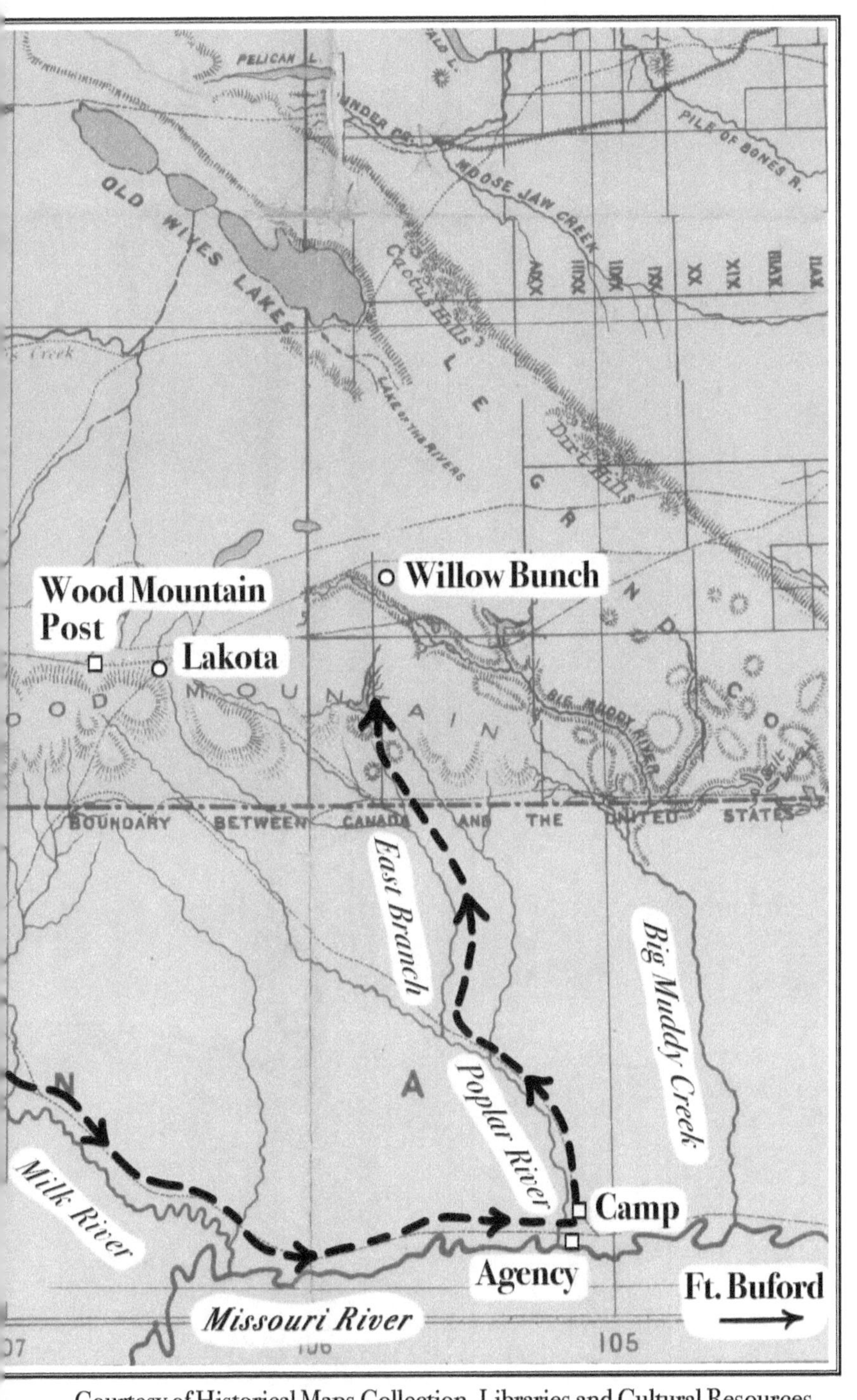

Courtesy of Historical Maps Collection, Libraries and Cultural Resources Digital Collections, University of Calgary.

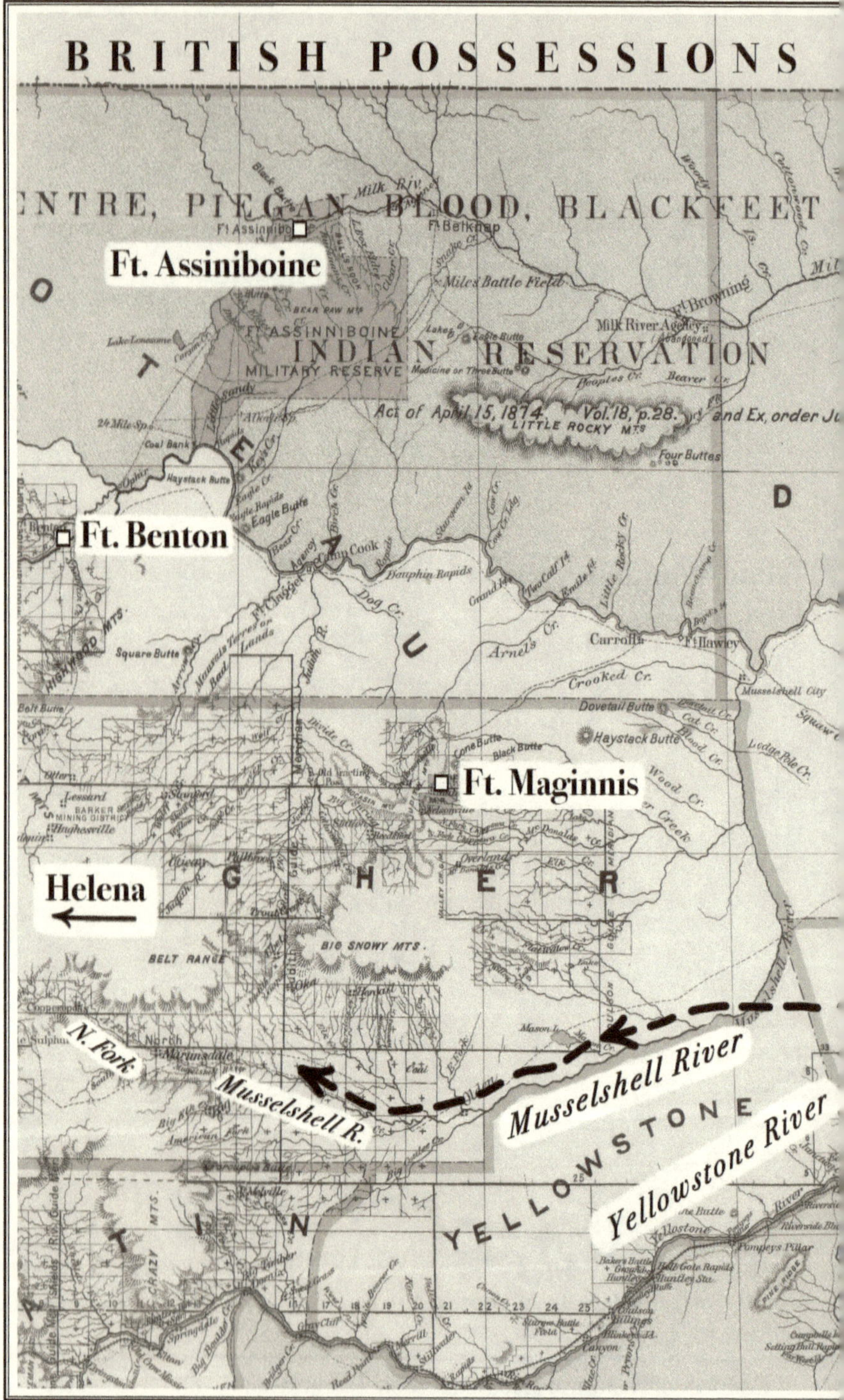

BRITISH POSSESSIONS
ENTRE, PIEGAN BLOOD, BLACKFEET
Ft. Assiniboine
Ft. Belknap
Miles Battle Field
Ft. Browning
Milk River Ag'cy
FT ASSINNIBOINE
INDIAN RESERVATION
MILITARY RESERVE
Medicine or Three Butte
Peoples Cr.
Beaver Cr.
Act of April 15, 1874.   Vol.18, p.28.
and Ex. order Ju
LITTLE ROCKY MTS
Four Buttes
D
Lake Lonesome
24 Mile Sp.
Coal Bank
Ophir
Haystack Butte
Eagle Rapids
Eagle Butte
Ft. Benton
Cook
Dauphin Rapids
Grand Id
Two Calf Id
Little Rocky Cr.
Carrolla
Ft. Hawley
Arnel's Cr.
Square Butte
HIGHWOOD MTS.
Crooked Cr.
Musselshell City
Belt Butte
Dovetail Butte
Haystack Butte
Lodge Pole Cr.
Squaw
Divide Cr.
Cone Butte
Black Butte
Wood Cr.
Ft. Maginnis
Lessard
BARKER
MINING DISTRICT
Hughesville
Stanford
Helena
BIG SNOWY MTS.
BELT RANGE
Coppertown
Mason Id
N. Fork
North
Martinsdale
Musselshell R.
Musselshell River
YELLOWSTONE
Yellowstone River
CRAZY MTS.
Springdale
Pompeys Pillar
Yellowstone
Huntley Sta.
GrayCliff
Stillwater
Canyon

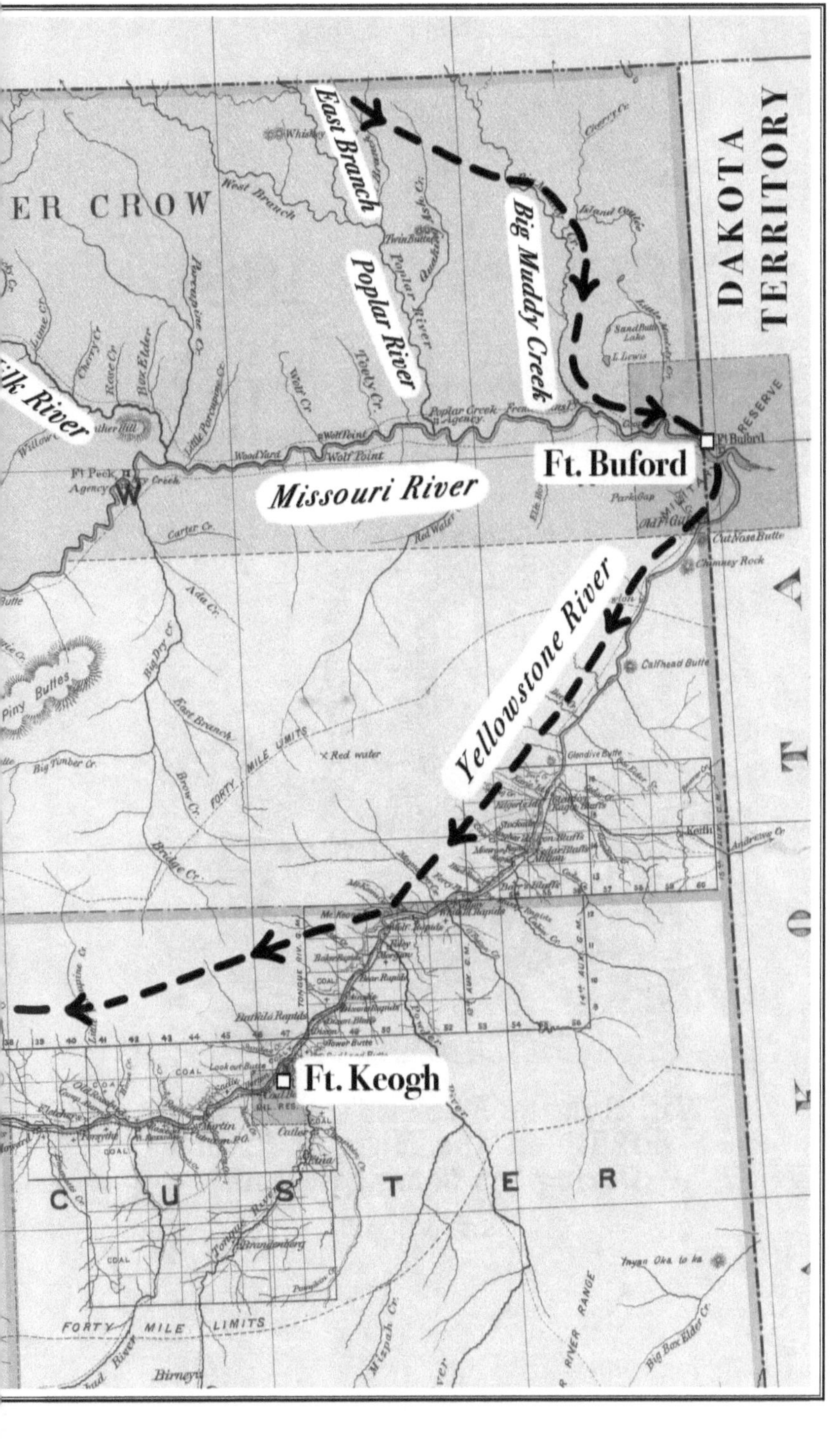

East Branch
Poplar River
Big Muddy Creek
DAKOTA TERRITORY
Ft. Buford
Missouri River
Yellowstone River
Ft. Keogh
ER CROW
lk River
Piny Buttes
CUSTER

1881.   1881.
Benton P Line
Will Run the FASTEST and BEST
BOATS on the Missouri River
During the Coming Season.

STEAMBOAT

Epilogue

On July 29, 1881, the steamboat General Sherman made its way down the Missouri River from Fort Buford toward Fort Yates with Sitting Bull, his family and around 180 of his people, including 44 warriors and head men Bone Club, Red Thunder, Four Horns and White Dog. When the steamer reached Bismarck, Dakota Territory, on the morning of July 31, a crowd of more than a hundred citizens were gathered to gawk at the notorious chief who had defeated Custer.

Sitting Bull was invited by a representative of the Northern Pacific Railroad and Captain Batchelor, one of the owners of the Yellowstone steamboat line, to visit the city. He was carried by an army ambulance into town along with the other principal men and Scout ("Fish") Allison, who had insinuated himself into the proceedings as interpreter. An informal reception was given at the Sheridan House, with spectators crowding into the spacious parlor, after which the Indians were taken for an extravagant meal at the Merchant Hotel and astonished those present, as well as the scores of people peering in the windows, with their refined use of cutlery.

Back at the levee, the area was thronged with hundreds of onlookers and Allison had been inexplicably replaced as interpreter by a Mrs. Harmon, the Métis wife of a post trader. Able to speak some English, Sitting Bull expressed his appreciation for the courtesies that had been proffered and signed his name several times for people who held out scraps of paper. After taking on freight, the steamboat departed downriver and arrived at Fort Yates and the Standing Rock Agency the next morning.

Originally created in 1873 as part of the Great Sioux Reservation, the agency was situated on the north side of the fort and both had been built upon the west bank of the Missouri River. Fort Yates had been constructed specifically to guard the agency and was named after a captain who was killed at the Little Big Horn. Friends and family members lined the riverbanks to greet the new arrivals, held back by a troop of soldiers with fixed bayonets. Sitting Bull, pleased to be reunited with his oldest daughter and former comrades, had been led to believe that he would be allowed to settle down among his people, but three weeks later the post commander informed him that he would be sent south to Fort Randall and detained as a prisoner of war.

In the middle of September, Sitting Bull and 172 of his immediate followers were transported to their new domicile, once again aboard the General Sherman, arriving on the 17th. The head man had resisted his removal from Standing Rock and soldiers prodded him onto the steamboat, with one trooper even striking the chief in the back with the butt of his rifle. It is unclear why Sitting Bull and his people were singled out for incarceration, when many of the other principal men at Standing Rock, including Gall and Rain in the Face, had been as antagonistic toward white incursions and had fought the soldiers at the Little Big Horn. Kept under constant guard, while surrounding settlements demanded increased military presence, the prisoners became exactly what they had feared; reservation Indians without dignity, liberty or purpose, with nothing to do but sit around and regret the loss of everything they held dear.

Almost two years later, on May 10, 1883, the steamer *Behan* finally delivered Sitting Bull and his people back to Standing Rock Agency. There, the chief began a portentous chapter of his life under the stewardship of Indian agent James McLaughlin, a vainglorious, domineering Catholic whose espousal of assimilation through the interdiction of plural marriage, sacred ceremonies and healing practices bordered on the fanatical. It was a relationship that would eventually lead to disastrous consequences.

It is estimated that a little over a hundred Lakota remained in Canada. Some of them stayed around Willow Bunch and Wood Mountain, but some migrated up north to the new settlement of Moose Jaw, designated as a water supply siding in the construction of the Canadian Pacific Railway. They established a permanent encampment and worked at various occupations or made items for sale, such as moccasins. Occasionally, friends and relatives would come north to visit. Later, some of the people returned to the U.S. to make land claims under the allotment system.

In October of 1910, after decades of the Lakota being intrinsically homeless, the Canadian government set up a tiny temporary reserve near Wood Mountain, where some of the people had settled. Only eighteen square miles in size, it was later abridged by half when the government awarded land to WWI veterans. Finally, in 1930, the reserve was made permanent. Its final extent had been reduced to a total of nine square miles, but those who had remained in Canada never ultimately subjected themselves to the authority of the United States government.

The Royal North-West Mounted Police were founded by an act of the Canadian parliament and organized under the direction of Prime Minister Sir John A. Macdonald in 1873. They were established as a federal law enforcement body, intended to administer treaties with indigenous populations, limit the illegal trade of whisky, especially from across the border with Montana Territory, maintain surveillance over the Métis settlements and hunting brigades, as well as promote western expansion. They constructed forts at pivotal locations throughout the North-West Territories and were granted legal and civil authority, including the power to dictate penalties and enforce them. When Sitting Bull and other principal men of the Lakota led their people across the boundary in 1877, the NWMP, particularly Superintendent James Morrow Walsh, built trust with the Indians and, for the most part, sustained friendly dealings with them until their final departure in 1881.

The first Métis people emerged in the 17th century from the progeny of European explorers and Indigenous women and giving rise to diverse ethnic identities. Becoming an integral part of the fur trade, Métis were employed by the Hudson Bay Company, Rocky Mountain Fur Company and American Fur Company and often worked as free trappers and boatmen (known as *voyageurs*) of transport canoes along Canadian waterways. They settled on both sides of the boundary between Canada and American territories and could be found in every trading post, including Fort Benton and Fort Union.

In the Red River region, the Métis developed a unique culture and language that blended Cree, Anishinaabe and French elements. They fought political and martial battles to win recognition from the Canadian government and obtained land and expanded rights in 1870, but were subsequently and brutally attacked by the Red River Expeditionary Force. Over half of the Métis people from the area fled west and, carrying on their traditions, formed hunting brigades that operated on the Great Plains extending from the North-West Territories south into Montana and Dakota territories.

Under strict laws for hunting, the Métis families traveled in distinctive carts, known as Red River carts, and subsisted on buffalo meat and the trading of robes and other pelts. With specially trained horses, one hunting brigade could bring down thousands of buffalo and support hundreds of families. As buffalo populations began to diminish, resentment arose between the Métis and Indian nations that relied on the animal for their survival. As a result, treaties were negotiated and occasional battles took place. When the North-West Mounted Police established forts, some of the Métis were employed as interpreters or scouts and settlements developed in the vicinity of the nascent posts.

Some families migrated south into Montana Territory on the Milk River, but were once more displaced by General Miles and the U.S. Army and several family groups relocated to the Judith Basin. By 1881, most of the buffalo had disappeared and the Red River Métis suffered starvation along with the Native populations. They sold buffalo bones, went to work on the construction of the Canadian Pacific Railroad, became farmers and ranchers or moved to towns to find employment. Some Métis helped build and expand Fort Assiniboine, but when the military post had been completed, the soldiers began deporting them to Canada. In 1896, soldiers rounded up over six hundred Cree and Métis people, destroyed their camps and belongings and, under the Cree Deportation Act, transported them across the boundary in train cars.

"APRIL 29, 1896. The Committee on Foreign Relations have considered the proposed amendment to the bill (H. R. 8293) 'making appropriations to supply deficiencies in the appropriations for the fiscal year ending June 30, 1896, and for prior years, and for other purposes,' appropriating $5,000, or so much thereof as may be necessary, to remove from the State of Montana, and to deliver to the Canadian authorities at the international boundary line, the refugee Canadian Cree Indians." *(Taken from Senate Report No. 821, 54th Congress, 1st Session)*

Michif is a Métis language that blends French and Plains Cree and Anishinaabe words. There are regional variations within the parlance. The language used in this book is considered Southern Michif. Northern Michif is influenced by northern Indigenous dialects.

Major David Brotherton spent most of his military career in the American southwest, beginning in 1851 and including the years of the War of the Rebellion. He was transferred to Fort Keogh in Montana Territory in 1877. In 1880, Brotherton took command of Fort Buford in Dakota Territory and was given almost sole credit for Sitting Bull's surrender. He requested to be relieved of duty in July of 1881. In August, the major was assigned to Fort Stevenson, but spent most of the next few years on sick leave and retired from active service in 1884.

Jean Louis Légaré received negligible recognition from the U.S. army and government for his assistance in bringing Sitting Bull back to America. Consequently, despite Major Brotherton's assurances prior to Sitting Bull's surrender, Légaré was not immediately reimbursed for the tremendous amount of money he had expended in feeding the Lakota and transporting large and small bands from the North-West Territories to Fort Buford in Dakota Territory. According to Légaré, having kept a meticulous account of his expenditures, he was owed approximately $46,000 and expected fair recompense from both the Canadian and U.S. governments.

In 1882, the Canadian Department of the Interior awarded him with a paltry $2,000. In the same year, he petitioned the U.S. Congress for $13,412, and provided supporting written testimony from General Alfred Terry and Major Brotherton. While Congress found in his favor, the settlement bogged down in the Court of Claims. Although Légaré made repeated efforts through the War Department, the Court of Claims, and Congress to be compensated for his services and expenses, he was consistently thwarted. The court determined that Major Brotherton had had no authority to commit the U.S. government to reimbursing Légaré for supplies purchased on behalf of the Indians upon their journey to Fort Buford. They also contended that he had been freighting in the employ of Leighton and Jordan, which was categorically false.

After years of petitioning, Légaré finally received a total of $5,000 from the U.S. government in 1905. In the 1880's he turned his hand to cattle and horse ranching, a cheese factory and the sale of buffalo bones. He also continued to maintain friendly relations with the Métis settlements at Willow Bunch and Wood Mountain.

Settlers in the West, especially miners, resented the Chinese due to their ability to take over abandoned mines and realize a profit. They were also vilified for their willingness to accept lower wages, such as during the construction of the transcontinental railroad.

Attacks on Chinese communities, beginning in the 1860's, resulted in destruction, massacres and removals. In 1882, Congress passed the Chinese Exclusion Act, signed into law by President Chester Arthur, having become president in 1881 upon the death of Garfield. The act denied immigration to the Chinese for a period of ten years and prohibited Chinese immigrants already in America from receiving citizenship.

Beginning in the 1850's, Chinese tongs imported Chinese women and girls from China to America for the sex trade. The Hip Yee Tong, in particular, was notorious for trafficking women to San Francisco and beyond. As mining communities in western territories thrived and multiplied, Chinese and white procurers transported Chinese girls to the region and forced them into a life of virtual slavery under the most appalling conditions. They were starved, beaten, raped, tortured and, when no longer able to fulfill their purpose due to disease or abuse, were either imprisoned without food or water until they starved to death, were killed outright or thrown onto the streets to die from exposure.

> "The Chinese girl reported kidnapped from a Chinese house of prostitution in Helena, really ran away from the house to escape the cruelty to which she was subjected. She was bought in China for $600. She told the authorities she would rather go to jail than return to the den." (Taken from *The Daily Enterprise*, Livingston, M.T. July 12, 1884)

Epilogue

WHAT WHITE PEOPLE BELIEVE

Author's Note

Native American, Chinese and Métis readers will hopefully understand that any denigrating or otherwise objectionable terminology in this text is used to illustrate prejudices and attitudes of the historical period within which this story occurs and were endemic to the writing of the time. The use of the insensitive word "half-breed" in reference to Métis people was the accepted term for descendants of fur trappers and traders and First Nations or American Indian women, despite their distinct cultures and languages. The term "Metis" is rarely found in archived newspapers or documents until 1885, following the North-West Rebellion in Canada under the Métis leader, Louis Riel. During this time period, the term was spelled without the accent aigu.

The names of various American Indian tribes mentioned in the book are given in the Lakota language and are not the names they use for themselves in their own language.

Hivernant (French for "winterer") was another name given to Métis people, especially those who were employed at fur trading forts.

Hopefully, all readers of this book will realize that any of the phrases and words in this book provided in non-English languages are easily understood in context or because the speakers later clarify the meaning in English.

Almost all the characters who inhabit this book actually existed, as reflected in the Dramatis Personae.

In case of confusion, the Royal North-West Mounted Police became the Royal Canadian Mounted Police.

There is a notable contrast between references to Sitting Bull found in NWMP documents and those in contemporary American newspapers, military documentation and the personal accounts still available. This is understandable, given the fact that only five years had passed since the Native American victory in the battle on the Little Big Horn River.

Some of Sitting Bull's dialogue in this book was taken from his speeches documented in the official reports of the Royal North-West Mounted Police from 1874 to 1881.

Most of Sitting Bull's surrender speech was gleaned from newspaper accounts penned by a correspondent who was present at the time.

Captain Walter Clifford did, indeed, document the translated words of the song a woman was singing in the Indian camp on the Little Muddy Creek, Montana Territory. It can be found in *The United States Army and Navy journal and gazette of the regular and volunteer forces v.19 1881/82* and various newspapers, originating from an interview he gave to the *Pioneer Press* of St. Paul, Minnesota shortly after Sitting Bull's surrender.

Although he was a man of his times and one who always followed orders from his superiors, Clifford wrote a letter to the *Charlevoix Sentinel,* in his home town of Charlevoix, Michigan, recounting the surrender of Sitting Bull and his indignation at the condition in which he had found the Lakota people.

Captain Ogden Read, commanding officer of Camp Poplar River, served as an officer in the 11th U.S. Infantry during the last decades of the 19th century. He collected over one hundred artifacts of American Indian provenance, including those taken from the Lakota camp attacked on the Poplar River in early 1881. He also acquired articles from traders and scouts, especially Joseph Culbertson, the mixed blood scout (whose father established Fort Benton for the American Fur Company and named it after the great American expansionist Thomas Hart Benton) and who seems to have bullied Indian people for his own edification at every opportunity. Captain Read fancied himself to be an amateur ethnographer, as did many military officers, and donated the collection to the University of Vermont. To date, none of the items have been repatriated to appropriate Indian agencies, a fairly simple task, given Read's scrupulous documentation.

Some of Charles Collins' dialogue with Lieutenant Kingsbury in the second to last chapter of the book was taken in part from a letter written to the editor of *Benton Weekly Record* by a rancher named James Fergus, published in January of 1882.

Some of Lieutenant Kingsbury's opinions were taken

from an editorial in the Butte Weekly, published in September of 1881.

—————⟨⟩⟨⟩—————

Charles Thompson should not be confused with James Harkin Thomson (sometimes spelled Thompson), a former corporal in the NWMP married to a Lakota woman. He ran the post office, school and telegraph office at Wood Mountain for many years. Charles Thompson, also a former NWMP policeman and also married to a Lakota woman, was reported by General Terry to have exerted undue influence over Sitting Bull, encouraging him to resist a surrender to the United States. In May of 1881, he was accused of forging a check and was jailed at Wood Mountain. There is reason to ponder whether this individual was falsely accused so as to remove him from Sitting Bull's camp.

A RENEGADE.

Capture of A Notorious Squaw Man.

News has been received from Fort Walsh, B. C., that the notorious Charlie Thompson, the ex-mounted policeman and the squaw man, who has been following Sitting Bull's band for some time, is now in jail at Wood Mountain. He forged a check upon another man named Thompson and had it cashed at Leighton and Jordan's trading post at Wood Mountain, where he was arrested by the Mounted Police. It will be remembered that General Terry recommended that the attention of the Canadian government should be called to the conduct of this man in influencing Sitting Bull against a surrender last winter. Thompson is a worthless fellow, who, by adopting the Indian mode of life even to the breech-clout, has attained certain mischievous influence over Sitting Bull. Fortunately he is now out of the way, we hope for a good long time.

Butte Weekly Miner, May 1881

Most of the contemporary newspaper and military personnel accounts of Sitting Bull's surrender at Fort Buford are denigrating and condescending. The so-called definitive history books written about Sitting Bull almost exclusively use these primary sources, perpetuating misconceptions about the chief, his appearance and deportment, and even his motivations. Some newspaper reports seem to have been made up of whole cloth or resulted from the creative imaginations of correspondents. Even General Phil Sheridan expressed suspicion regarding some of the newspaper versions of exclusive interviews with the chief:

> "I have seen in newspapers long accounts and narratives purporting to be related by Sitting Bull, which had, in my opinion, but little truth in them, and historians are cautioned against receiving them as correct." (Taken from Report of the Secretary of War, 1881)

Sadly, the tenor of Sitting Bull's surrender speech, if one reads between the lines of subjective accounts (the only ones available), illustrates that he actually believed he was negotiating as a respected leader. Certainly, the chief was initially unaware that every military and civilian version of his speech was derisively portrayed, but may have been made cognizant of this later on.

The United States Army and Navy journal and gazette of the regular and volunteer forces v.19 1881/82 offered this risible translation of Sitting Bull's justifiable demands (made in what he assumed was an honorable surrender council): "I want to be free and go about wherever I please and have a waiter."

It is the author's opinion that non-Indian historians have relied too heavily on the prejudicial leanings of primary sources *without* reading between the lines. Given the sum total of Sitting Bull's years of courage, leadership capabilities, membership in warrior and chief societies, ability to engender loyalty, as well as wide-spread recognition as an esteemed holy man, the clownish portrayals of him by military personnel and newspaper correspondents do not ring true. It is unfortunate that these false depictions of Thatháŋka Ìyotake (actually meaning Buffalo Bull Who Sits Down) have been maintained by historians for almost a hundred and fifty years.

One of the greatest perpetrators of misinformation about Sitting Bull is a writer known as Stanley Vestal, the pen name of Walter Campbell. According to Sitting Bull's own great-grandson, Vestal interviewed Lakota individuals who had in actuality betrayed the chief, including his nephew, One Bull, and Bull Head, one of the Indian policemen who willfully murdered Sitting Bull at the behest of Indian agent McLaughlin. Throughout the 1920's and 30's, Vestal relied upon a very finite number of informants, resulting in a limited and extremely biased historical perspective of Sitting Bull and surrounding events. Stanley Vestal's book, *Sitting Bull, Champion of the Sioux: a biography,* published in 1932, is still considered the definitive source of reliable historical information about Thatháŋka Ìyotake and is, along with Vestal's archived interviews (also suspect), the essential foundation for just about every non-Indian writer's book about Sitting Bull.

Regrettably, this reliance on limited sources is quite common, particularly regarding the history of Native Americans in the American West as written by non-Indians. If readers pay attention to bibliographies and referenced source material, the same names are present over and over. It is also not unusual to track back referenced primary source material, such as newspapers and military reports, and find that the writer has misquoted or blatantly altered the original material. This is especially true with history written before access to digital documentation.

Other degrading narratives about Sitting Bull in Canada can mostly be attributed to Edwin Henry "Fish" Allison, self-proclaimed scout, interpreter and Indian expert. He wrote the manuscript for a book entitled *The Surrender of Sitting Bull: Being a Full and Complete History of the Negotiations Conducted by Scout Allison, Which Resulted in the Surrender of Sitting Bull and His Entire Band of Hostile Sioux in 1881*, published in 1891.

Allison, in point of fact, had nothing to do with the surrender of Sitting Bull. Once again, probing between the lines, a reader finds a self-aggrandizing little man attempting to place himself in a position of importance and, because he never actually convinced Sitting Bull to surrender, Allison ensured that in posterity he would be remembered for this significant deed. His book is another of the resources predominantly referred to in historical research of Sitting Bull and accompanying events. In Allison's own autobiography, he wrote, "Sometimes it is best to fight, but often it is best to use strategy, and strategy, whether employed by the general or the scout, is falsehood. The lie, then, I say, is often a potential weapon."

By his own admission, Allison was driving a herd of cattle to Fort Buford, in the employ of a ranching firm on the Sun River, when he got the notion to put himself forward in the negotiations to bring Sitting Bull back under the authority of the U.S. government. After convincing the military of his unique abilities in negotiating with the Lakota, he was given tacit permission to proceed from General Terry and that of Major Brotherton. After several attempts, he failed and General Terry withdrew his support for Allison's activities in January of 1881. In his official report to the Secretary of War, Terry never gave Allison credit for Sitting Bull's surrender. General Terry gave exclusive credit to Major Brotherton and Major Ilges, the author of the improvident January attack upon Chief Gall's followers on Poplar River. This attack actually drove Sitting Bull and his people back across the border from their camp on Milk River, delaying the surrender for several months.

Many of the misconceptions regarding Native Americans in the western regions of the United States can be traced back to early explorers, trappers and traders. Whether through written material or word of mouth, the "expert" information provided by white men, who were first to have contact with Native groups around the Great Lakes and farther west of the Mississippi, was accepted as genuine and irrefutable. Men such as Father Jacques Marquette and Louis Joliet and the Verendrye brothers had come to either leverage the Indians' hunting abilities or immortal souls and could not be relied upon to offer any authoritative confirmation of the intelligence, societal equality, land management practices, medicines, dietary knowledge and cultural advancement of the tribes they encountered. Later, the Hudson Bay Company men ranged farther and farther in search of greater wealth in "soft gold," their name for beaver pelts, while the Spanish sent expeditions north, such as the Villasur Expedition of 1720, in an effort to defend their territory for the king.

Meriwether Lewis and William Clark were not the first, by any means, to have contact with American Indians on the west side of the Mississippi or Missouri rivers. According to some sources, trappers familiar with all the land from the Mississippi to the Pacific Ocean found it amusing that the explorers had not bothered to consult with one of them or simply hire a guide. Lewis and Clark, however, were responsible for rampant misinterpretations of their contact with Native people. And, more importantly, European contact prior to their observations had already begun to alter the fabric of Native societies and material culture. Later, traders and trappers with the American Fur Company, the Rocky Mountain Fur Company and the Missouri Fur Company, such as Lucien Fontanelle, Manuel Lisa, Alexander Culbertson, Kit Carson, Milton Sublette and Jim Bridger, perpetuated detrimental mythology regarding American Indians, all the while exploiting them for profit.

A self-proclaimed admirer of American Indians, the artist George Catlin kept painstaking records of his travels up the Missouri River during the 1830's. His artistic and written interpretations of everything he witnessed during his visits to Native villages and encampments were colored by colonial preconceptions of white ascendency, superior European civilization, acceptable behaviors and delusional denial of the brutality of white societies. Catlin believed himself to be the first to witness and document dwellings, dances, spiritual traditions, hair styles, weapons, hunting practices, customs and articles of clothing. This is paradoxical, considering he occasionally mentions that one or two white traders are residing in almost every community. He also seemed to be in complete ignorance concerning the extensive contact prior to the 1830's between European and American trappers and Indigenous societies and the resultant influences upon mores, gender roles, alterations in hunting practices, material and technological gains and losses. Catlin's writing and art seem to be resources for much of the accepted assumptions about early Native American history, cultural traditions and lifeways, including the asinine premise that Mandan people are descendants of Welsh explorers that navigated their way from Wales to the Gulf of Mexico and northward to the headwaters of the Mississippi River.

Beginning in 1837, not long after Catlin's travels up the Missouri River, a smallpox epidemic decimated American Indian populations along the Missouri by the thousands, thereby forever altering the balance of power between tribes and between Native nations and white invaders. The virus was knowingly carried to the upper Missouri by the American Fur Company steamboat, St. Peters in blatant disregard of anything but their own greed.

The complete misunderstanding of gender roles within American Indian societies in the western regions of the United States can be attributed to the fact that most of the early writers, artists and ethnographers were men and, as they did not value their own women, they could not countenance the equal status and prerogatives of Native women in every aspect of Indian customs, traditions, material culture and spirituality.

The winter of 1880 and '81 saw unprecedented amounts of snow. An early thaw gave rise to devastating flooding along the Missouri and other northern rivers in spring of 1881, causing destruction to towns and Indian encampments and halting steamboat traffic beyond Fort Buford for many weeks.

As is common in the 19th century American West, names of many waterways would alternately be called creeks or rivers, such as the case with Poplar River or Poplar Creek and Big Muddy River or Big Muddy Creek.

Frenchman Creek or Frenchman River was mostly known as White Mud Creek among the people of the North-West Territories.

Extemporalis: In Ireland, the native language was outlawed by the English beginning in 1367. Then in 1697, the Penal Laws were enacted to ban education, Catholicism and steal land from those who were not subservient.

The author extends heartfelt gratitude to the following:

Amanda Carlow, of the Lakȟóta Language Revitalization program in the Maȟpíya Lúta schools, for her guidance, translations and clarifications in the Lakȟóta language.

Robert Szucs, an incredibly talented artist who transports my words into compelling imagery.

Professor emeritus Jeff Sanders, whose his friendship, advocacy and mentorship over the years have been incredibly valuable and essential.

Dr. Richard Littlebear, Native language activist and writer, for his insights, support and humor.

Louisa Frank and Julie Schultz for their encouragement, kindness and unwavering validation.

The Historical Society of New Mexico and Montana Historical Society for their recognition of my research and authenticity.

Sheridan Stationary Books book club, in Sheridan Wyoming, for their enthusiasm and probing questions.

And all the other friends, two and four-leggeds, without whom I could not bear to navigate this world.

Additional Reading

The author encourages readers to peruse the books listed below that were written by Native Americans, paying particular attention to indications of the authors Josephine Waggoner and Susan Bordeaux Bettelyoun's assimilation into white society, all the while embracing their traditions, history and connections to progenitors. Readers should also pay special attention to contradictions in dates, locations etc., as well as subtle and not so subtle biases in non-Indian books about the period.

Witness: A Húŋkpapȟa Historian's Strong-Heart Song of the Lakotas by Josephine Waggoner

With My Own Eyes: A Lakota Woman Tells Her People's History by Susan Bordeaux Bettelyoun and Josephine Waggoner

Sitting Bull: His Life and Legacy by Ernie LaPointe, Great-Grandson of Sitting Bull

"Living descendant of Sitting Bull confirmed by analysis of DNA from the legendary leader's hair," by Jacqueline Garget: https://www.cam.ac.uk/stories/sitting-bull-descendant-confirmed

They Never Surrendered: The Lakota Sioux Band That Stayed in Canada by Ron Papandrea

I am Looking to the North for My Life: Sitting Bull 1876-1881 by Joseph Manzione

The Last Sovereigns: Sitting Bull and the Resistance of the Free Lakota by Robert M. Utley

Sitting Bull: The Years in Canada by Grant MacEwan

The New Peoples: Being and Becoming Métis in North America (Manitoba Studies in Native History) by Jennifer Brown

The Genealogy of the First Metis Nation: The Development and Dispersal of the Red River Settlement, 1820-1900. Compiled by D.N. Sprague and R.P. Frye

The Western Metis: Profile of a People, edited by Patrick C. Douaud

Becoming Little Shell: A Landless Indian's Journey Home by Chris LaTray

The Riders of the Plains: Adventures and Romance With the North-West Mounted Police, 1873-1910 by A.L. Haydon (Digital copy available at: https://archive.org/details/ridersoftheplain009801mbp)

Policing the Plains: Being the Real Life Record of the Famous Royal North-West Mounted Police by R. G. Macbeth, M.A. (Digital copy available at: https://www.gutenberg.org/files/22220/22220-h/22220-h.htm)

Official Reports, Royal North-West Mounted Police, Opening Up the West, 1874-1881, Introduction by Commissioner W. L. Higgitt, R.C.M.P.

"Montana and Métis" by Stephanie Hohn: https://stor-ymaps.arcgis.com/stories/81f70efbe59744428a187bb-c3b344ffb

BUREAU OF AMERICAN ETHNOLOGY CATALOGUE OF MANUSCRIPTS NO. 1755 SIOUX SURRENDER OF SITTING BULL E.H. ALLISON 1897. MANUSCRIPT AND NOTES: https://www.lib.montana.edu/digital/objects/coll2204/2204-B05-F34.pdf

"Lakota Place Names in Southwestern Saskatchewan," by Claire Thomson: https://www.skhistory.ca/blog/la-kota-place-names-in-southwestern-saskatchewan

AND "Digging Roots and Remembering Relatives: La-kota Kinship and Movement in the Northern Great Plains from the Wood Mountain Uplands across Lakóta Ťhamákȟočhe/Lakota Country, 1881-1940," by Claire Thomson: https://ualberta.scholaris.ca/items/0721e09a-8197-473a-8a38-f4299339d51d

About the Author

Juliana "Hoolihan" Clayton

J. Hoolihan Clayton is First Nations Plains Cree. Adopted by a white family and raised on a cattle ranch in Wyoming, she has lived a diverse and authentic life in the American West as a cowboy and wildland firefighter. With a degree from the University of Montana, she taught history and Native American studies for several years. Hoolihan now works full time as an author and research consultant.

PRINTING PRESS

List of Illustrations

PAGE 314: STEAMBOAT, *River Press* July 27, 1881
PAGE 324: WHAT WHITE PEOPLE BELIEVE, *Helena Weekly Herald* June 11, 1881

Illustrations from *Harpers Weekly* are used with explicit permission. Illustrations from *Frank Leslie's Illustrated Newspaper* are in public domain and were never copyrighted. All images are available through the Library of Congress Prints & Photographs Reading Room, Prints and Photographs Division, Prints & Photographs Online Catalogue. Newspaper articles courtesy of Montana Historical Society Library & Archives, Helena, MT.

www.ingramcontent.com/pod-product-compliance
Lightning Source LLC
Chambersburg PA
CBHW031114160726
47991CB00004B/1381